Scotch
at
The Rocks

Sara Powter

Bible Quotes from King James Version

ISBN: 9780645441550
Paperback

Pacific Wanderland Publications
ABN 99 768 734 831

Kincumber NSW 2251

saragpowter@gmail.com
www.sarapowter.com.au

1st edition 2023 printed by Kindle, an Amazon Company;
available on Kindle Unlimited & KDP

Cover Painting
Miller's point, ca. 1890s / Alfred Tischbauer
https://collection.sl.nsw.gov.au/record/9ALArLoY#viewer
In Public Domain

Cover inset
By Augustus Edwin Mulready
Wandering Minstrels 1876 (Flipped)
1876date QS:P571,+1876-00-00T00:00:00Z/9

Chapter Graphics all in Public Domain

Cover Design by
Beckon Creative
beck@beckoncreative.biz

Barrel sizes

Acknowledgement of Country:
In the spirit of reconciliation, I acknowledge the Traditional Custodians of country throughout Australia and their connections to land, sea and community. We pay our respect to their Elders, past and present and extend that respect to all Aboriginal and Torres Strait Islander peoples today.

Australian Historical Novels

Unlikely Convict Ladies Trilogy

Dancing to her Own Tune
(co-authored by Sheila Hunter & Sara Powter)
Amelia's Tears
A Lady in Irons

The Convict Stain Collection
(All stand-alone books)

No More, My Love
The Vine Weaver
Scotch at The Rocks {*Sequel to The Vine Weaver*}
Waiting at the Sliprails
(The following are coming soon)
Convict Shadows of the Past *(2024)*
In Defence of Her Honour *(2024)*
Gentle Annie Soames *(2024)*
I Can't Stop Tomorrow *(2024)*
Madeline's Boy *(2025)*

Early Colonial Days Trilogy

When Upon Life's Billows *(2025)*
Tuppence to Pass *(2025)*
Saddler's Song *(2025)*

The Lockleys of Parramatta

Hands Upon the Anvil
Out Where the Brolgas Dance
Diamonds in the Dirt
The Earl's Shadow
Once a Jolly Swagman
Jonty's Journey

Shelia Hunter's
Australian Colonial Trilogy

Mattie
Ricky {*Jonty's Journey is a sequel*}
The Heather to the Hawkesbury

Dedication and Thanks
**To the convicts of yesteryear, brought outbound in iron chains;
many were dragged from the loving arms of their family.**
Some were orphans, but most had grown up on the streets in poverty,
Like in 'Oliver Twist,' they became 'Artful Dodgers'
as they needed to steal to survive.
Even the nye-do-well rat-bag convicts married and had children,
many of whom became upstanding citizens in the community.

NOTE:-
My inspiration for this story was my husband's convict ancestor, John Turner.
He was sent to Sydney in 1838 on the *Lord Lyndoch* from Glasgow.
He had been convicted of buying whisky with a false cheque.
Smallpox and scurvy described from this voyage are accurate and come from
historical documents. Many died, and a third of those on board
were admitted to the hospital on arrival.

The *Whaler's Arms* and the Hero of Waterloo are authentic inns,
and the Hero of Waterloo is still in business at The Rocks in Sydney.
Both had underground passages to unload supplies.

My Thanks
To Stephen, my wonderful husband, who is always so supportive.
Thank you from the bottom of my heart.

And to Roby Aiken
who patiently corrects all my punctuation errors,
thank you, too.

To my Beta readers, Noreen Robertson and Linda Upcroft,
you are all wonderful!

Table of Contents

The grammar and language in this book are Australian English.

~   Time passing, same locality

        - different locality or country

Chapter 1   Turfed Out

$\mathcal{B}$rodie turned and looked back at the door of his home. He had lived in this hovel since the money ran out that his father had left them. His beloved mama, Mary Stewart, lay on the floor upstairs beside the body of her latest child. Both had not made it through the birth. He had done his best, but it was no job for a ten-year-old boy. The baby never breathed.

He didn't know what to do when his mother started bleeding so much. He had helped deliver the last three babies, and there was not this much blood. Sadly, all the children had died before they turned three.   H i s mama realised something was wrong, and as her life ebbed away. In a weakened voice, she drew Brodie to her, kissed him and said, "I love you, son; never forget that. Stay strong and safe. Now, son, grab the food and blankets and run. If McDuff finds you here alone, goodness knows what he'll do to you. Take what you can and leave." With her last breath, she murmured, "Tell Papa I loved him until the day I died."

A tearful Brodie would not leave her until she breathed her last. Her life just slipped away as he held her. He carefully covered her face with her nightgown. Then he did as she said; he wrapped all the food in their only blanket. He was too cold and numb for tears or to feel anything but sadness. His Mama was gone, as was his Papa. He knew he had to scarper before the landlord discovered his mother was dead.

When Papa's money ran out, Mama could not pay the rent on the bigger flat, and they moved to this tiny one-room attic at the top of their old place. When Mr McDuff visited to collect the rent, noises came from Mama's bed, like when Papa was home. His mama made him hide in the cupboard when the man came. Then, after many 'rent' visits from Mr McDuff, Mama said she was having another baby. Each visit left her with new bruises. He suspected that this mean man his mother protected him from was the father of this latest child, as Papa had been gone for nearly two years. At ten, he didn't understand how babies were made.

Brodie thought about his little brother Hamish. He had been two when they all came down sick with a red rash on their skin. Brodie heard later that it was called Measles. Hamish died that same week, and baby Twelve-month-old Caitlyn died only eight days later. Mama had been large with child at the time, and she was still sick when the baby was born. It would have been called Morag, meaning *star of the sea*, if she had lived, but she died at birth, just like this child had. He and Papa had delivered Morag together when he was last at home. That was in 1822, now over two years ago. Five children were alive when he arrived, but he had brought smallpox with him, and Brodie's oldest brother, Iain, then aged nine, caught the disease and died.

Brodie was proud that his brother had been the best dodger in the area. The family had survived on what Iain had been able to steal. The police could not catch him; Brodie was not nearly as good, so he had not helped. But being so skinny, Brodie had snuck off and found an apprenticeship as a chimney sweep's boy. His job had brought in the only regular money the family had.

Papa was only home for a week when he was called back to complete some repairs on his ship. He was gone for three weeks, and Iain was dead by the time he returned. Iain became ill the day Papa left. He first got a high fever, then a rash started. They were big red spots that made him feel sick, and these were the beginning of Smallpox. He complained that he ached all over. Then, the spots turned into huge blisters. When the vomiting and diarrhoea started, Mama was called from her dairy duty to nurse him. She had heard about Mister Jenner's cowpox treatment and knew she would be safe from catching smallpox as she had had cowpox the year before. Everyone else had been kept away from Iain. He didn't fight; he just gave up. His brother died in agony, and his groaning haunted Brodie for months.

Jane, another sister, had been alive back then. Papa had only been home for a month when she was run over by a speeding carriage and killed. She was only three. Brodie should have been used to death, but he hated it.

Now, he was utterly alone.

Brodie quickly gathered a bundle of warm things and the fresh food Mama had prepared so she could have some time off after she had the baby. He grabbed the knife and the sheath his father had given him and added them to the bundle. Brodie knew he needed to clear out and do it quickly. He kissed her cheek one last time. As they only possessed one blanket, he would need to take it. He had rolled it for her to use as a pillow.

Mama was now beyond care. He wanted to help; really, he did, but caring hurt too much. He laid the dead baby girl in Mama's arms and stood looking at them for some time before acknowledging he must leave her and flee. The pool of blood at her feet was beginning to discolour. He sniffed back his tears and walked away. He didn't look back; no one would be waving farewell this time. He knew he still had to front up for work or would be arrested for breaking his apprenticeship. Even his work would finish soon as he was beginning to get stuck in the chimneys. At ten, he was just too darned big. He was still as skinny as a little bairn but was getting too tall for the bends. He hated doing it, but it was a way of earning money for Mama.

He stopped walking when the realisation washed over him that Mama wouldn't need that money anymore. A drop of water fell onto his hand. He didn't have time for tears but couldn't stop them. He knew he needed to find somewhere to sleep, and soon. The night was not far away, and once the sun sank, it would get cold, very, very cold. With that thought, he sniffed again and moved along the squalid street. He was aware of a small nook he could curl up in safely. He just hoped that no one else had found it. He slept there a few times recently when the landlord visited Mama. He had been locked outside and told not to return until the morning.

The street grew narrow and ended up in a wall with a hole. Brodie crawled through it and saw someone else curled up in a ball in his secret hide-hole. It was a little girl, and even in the dim light, he could see she had been crying. She shrank back into the void.

"Are you alone?" he asked, hoping she would be.

The dark red-haired girl nodded, "Mama got tooked away to Heaven."

Brodie gave a small gasp. "Mine too," he said, sniffing back the last of his tears. "Can I stay here? I have some food and a blanket. We can share. I'm Brodie Stewart." He didn't want to, but she had less than he did, and he didn't want to be alone anyway.

Her head nodded, and she lisped, "I'se hungry."

Brodie carefully put his bundle down and sat down beside her. Without warning, she put her arms around him and hugged him. It was too much for them both, and they cried over their losses. For a few moments, they let their sadness out.

"What's your name? I'm Brodie." Brodie had bread, cheese, oatcakes, baps, black pudding, and two potato cakes.

"I'se Heavver," she said with her toothless lisp.

Brodie's heart both sank and soared all at once. He swallowed and said, "Well, Heather, we're going to have a bit of a feast tonight as the black pudding, tatie cakes, the pudding, and baps will go off, so we have to eat them now. The bread and cheese we can eat later. Mama only made these this morning. We were going to have a feast for supper; then the baby started coming, and then she died."

"Mine too, Brodie. Only mine died yesterday. The landlady throwded me out. I couldn't even get my dolly." Heather sobbed again. "I got nuffin' but my blanket and hairbrush, which I had wiv me."

"Well, looks like we've now gotta stick together." He smiled at his new companion. Goodness knows what life would bring for either of them, but for tonight, at least, they had food and lots of it. And at least it was spring, which would give them some time before the cold came, and they would be in real trouble then. That seemed a lifetime away. "Come on, Heather, sit up, and we'll eat."

The daylight was gone entirely by the time they had finished their repast. Knowing he had to be up before dawn to go to work, he packed away their food so the rats wouldn't find it and snuggled close to her.

Wrapped in each other's arms, they slept the dreamless sleep of innocence with the blankets wrapped around them. It was the first night of many, where they would seek the comfort and security of each other.

~

The rattling of a passing coal wagon woke Brodie. His regular alarm was the clip-clop of the horses' hoofs on the cobblestones. He had at least been warm with Heather in his arms. She was still asleep. He could see the first light of dawn easing its way through the gloom. He shook the sleeping girl's shoulder, "Heather, I must go to work. I'll be back this afternoon. Can you stay here all day? I'll be back for you tonight."

She sat up and rubbed her eyes. "Don't leave me, Brodie. I'se scared."

Brodie didn't blame her; he was too. "I have to go, Heather, or we don't eat. The food I have here will only last until I get paid. You can eat the rest of the baps and tatie cakes that we didn't finish last night and have the last of the black pudding, too. I have packed some for me to take to work. Tonight, we only have bread and cheese. We must make it last, as payday isn't for three days."

Heather was now fully awake. She knew what hunger was, and they were both still full after last night's feast. She had not eaten so well for a long time. "Brodie, I can work too. I need a bucket of some sort. Mama and I collected doggie poop for the leatherworker and tanner."

Brodie's jaw dropped open. "You're a *pure* collector?" Many times, he had stepped over the foul-smelling dog lumps.

Heather nodded. "Mama couldn't get any other work. It's better than *toshing*. We did that for a while too, and *bone grubbing* as well, but in the end, Mama sent me collecting the doggie poop 'cause I could do that by myself."

"Eewe, yuck!" Brodie said.

"I know, but we could eat with the money I made. At least it's not so dirty as sorting people's poop. Getting clean after *toshing* was both hard and cold." Heather said, "I used to go with Mama to the tanner, so I know where to go, and he knows me. I won't tell him Mama is dead."

"Okay, just be careful, Heather," Brodie said. "I have to go, or I'll get sacked." He tucked the blankets around her and crept out of their hole.

~

Brodie only lasted another few months as a chimneysweep before getting stuck. Unfortunately, that last time, the fire below had not been out for long; the heat of the scalding hot chimney flue burned him.

He didn't mind being sacked, but the burns he received on that last job would take time to heal. His feet and hands were badly blistered, and he had a big burn on his arm. They hurt. Mama used to put honey on them, but they didn't have any honey now; he didn't know what to do. He was waiting for Heather's return; he was miserable and wanted her comfort. She may only be six, but she had become vital to him over the last months. She had given him a reason to get up in the mornings and a purpose to try to survive.

Knowing Heather would not be at the hole, Brodie managed to wash himself in a horse trough that had just been scrubbed and refilled. It wasn't often he had the chance to have a bath, and as it was a warm day and no one was around, he stripped off his outer clothing and relished the cold water on his sore, blistered body. He stayed in the trough until the throbbing eased. He knew big boys were not supposed to cry, but he did. He hurt inside and out. He missed Mama, his brothers, and his sisters and wished Papa would return. He was still feeling miserable when the innkeeper came out and saw him.

"Hey lad, what are you doing?" The man asked without anger.

"Sorry, sir, I got burnt at work and needed to clean up. I'll go!" Brodie hopped out of the trough. He stood there in his dripping loincloth and moved to collect his clothing.

The man said, "Not so fast, laddie. Aren't you Ewen Stewart's boy?" The man spoke with a kind voice.

Brodie nodded. "Papa's not been home for a few years though, sir, and now Mama's gone too. She died in spring."

"Mary Macdougal is dead? Ahh that explains it then," the man said without explaining anything.

"Explains what, sir?" Brodie was still gathering his tattered clothing, but his teeth were chattering with both cold and shock.

"Lad, Mary and Ewen were friends of mine from childhood. I heard Ewen's ship went down, and news of his demise was only brought back last month. I went to find your mama, but she was gone." The man laid a hand on his shoulder. "Lad, your Papa is presumed dead."

Brodie sank to the ground in shock. It was all he needed. "Papa's dead, sir? He was my last hope." If he felt bad before, he felt worse now. He broke, and the tears refused to stop. No matter how hard he tried, he could not hold them back. Then the cold set in. His arms were wrapped around his knees, and he shivered as he sobbed.

The man looked at the trembling boy. "Come inside and dry off. I have a place you can sleep, it's not much, but it's safe and quite warm." Mr Findlay helped him up and saw he was burnt. He said, "I knew your mama since she was a girl. Mary was one amazing, feisty woman. Afraid of no man, including her beast of a father, Knox Macdougal, spelt one 'l'. She stood up to the villainous man to marry the love of her life. Ishbelle and I have her to thank for us being together, so giving you a safe place is the least I can do. I'd give you a room, but we don't have one you could use. We only are paid to work here, lad."

Although dressed, a shivering Brodie stood beside the trough, listening to the man. The man offered a warm fire, and for the moment, that was enough. He followed Papa's friend inside. He had no idea who Ishbelle was, but he knew his mother's name before marriage was Macdougal, and she had told him they spelt it with only one 'l'.

A roaring fire warmed him and soon dried his scant and sodden clothing. He was then handed a big bowl of steaming hot porridge with a dollop of cream on the top.

His burns were forgotten as he had his first hot food in months. "Thanks, mister, that was great," he said as he returned his empty bowl.

The big man squatted beside him. "It's Findlay, laddie; Calum Findlay. I may even have a job for you, Brodie, if interested. Like most inns, I have a rat problem. I have a little dog, but he can't cope alone. If you sleep in the coal cellar, you can stay as long as you wish and eat the inn leftovers. But you must catch and kill as many rats as possible."

Brodie's face lit up. "I'd love that, sir, but I'm not alone; I have a little girl I've been looking after. She's only six, and her mama died too; can she come?"

The innkeeper was astounded. "How do you cope, lad?"

Brodie's burns were once again throbbing with the heat of the fire. He moved away a bit. "We managed okay from the pennies I made chimney sweeping. But she is a *pure* collector, and it stinks. She brings in a few pennies each week doing that. Together, we manage to eat. We found a hole in a wall and have been living there. A dry coal cellar would be wonderful, especially with winter near."

The innkeeper tousled Brodie's now cleanish hair. "You astound me, young man. You are all but destitute yourself, and yet you take on another waif. Yes, you may bring her too. What's her name?"

Brodie nodded but brightened. "Heather, sir, she's a nice kid, and she works hard. I'll go and wait for her and bring her back if I may?" He left and went to pack up their scant belongings. He returned to their nook only a few hours after leaving for work.

An hour later, Heather silently snuck back and crept into their hole. She was carrying something. "Oh, Brodie, you're early. What's wrong?"

"I got stuck in a chimney flue, Heather; I got burned and sacked all at once. Mr Henderson was real mean to work for, so getting sacked isn't bad, but it means we got no regular money now. I don't know how we're going to eat without my pay." Brodie hurt all over now. The pain from the burns was pulsing through him. He felt ill and knew it would get worse if they infected.

"Well, look what I found, Brod." She produced a stone flagon of whisky from behind her back. "It was next to a dead man, so I tooked it 'cause he won't want it no more." Heather handed the bottle to Brodie. "Mama had some and used to put this on my cuts and things. Maybe it will work on burns, too."

Very gingerly, they set to work on the wounds. The whisky stung where the blisters had popped. The big blister on his arm had ruptured as he climbed into their hole. As she worked, a thought came to her. She remembered her last name. Heather's eyes flew open, saying, "Brodie, when you mentioned the name of Henderson, it made me think. I remember my last name; it's Anderson. Mama was Annella Anderson, but Papa called her Annie. His name was Angus. She teased him and called him Angry Gus when he lost his temper with me." The memory brought tears to her eyes.

"That's great news, Heather!" Once she had finished, Brodie thanked her for treating him. He told her about his encounter with the innkeeper. "Heather, I've found us somewhere safe to live. It will also keep us warm and dry for winter, and the man will even give us the inn's leftovers. We have to pack up and move in tonight."

Heather carefully hugged him. "If Mama were alive, she would say it was a God-send. I don't know about that, but I'm not going to turn down a safe, dry place to stay for winter, so let's go."

They were warm and dry, and Mrs Findlay had given them a meal of stew and dumplings. She also put a soothing salve on Brodie's burns and bound them up. It was the closest they had felt to having a home for months. That night, they slept the deep, dreamless sleep of innocent children. They had full tummies and a new blanket to share.

~

The pair lived in the cellar for five years while working at whatever job they could get in Glasgow.

By the time Brodie was fifteen and Heather eleven, they were doing everything they could to make ends meet as neither could find a permanent job. They managed to stay out of trouble, but their world fell apart one evening. All good things come to an end.

They were getting ready to settle for the night when Mr Findlay came to the cellar. He rarely called them up for a talk, and his voice sounded worried. "Brodie, Heather, I need to talk to you both. The owner has sold the inn, and the new man wants us all out." He saw the look the children gave him, and his heart hurt for them. He had never had a moment's trouble from either of them.

Brodie had worked hard, and most of the rats were gone. When his little dog died, he didn't replace it. The lad had shovelled all the coal whenever it was delivered. He had swept the courtyard and cleared away the snow. He even helped clean the rooms when required. He would work at any job he could get, from a Funeral Mute for the undertakers to working as the Link Boy for the drunk patrons from his inn, lighting their way as they walked home. He had become sick with cowpox when milking at The

Green, and his illness meant he could not work at all for a month. It had been a hard time for them both. During this time, Heather had tried leech collecting for doctors but had swollen so badly and then been itchy for ages. Brodie made her stop doing that after just one week. Instead, she got a job making matchsticks. That entailed outside work, and her clothing barely covered her. She now had a bad cough, and he was worried about her.

Callum Findlay was sad for them, but he had done his best. He heard rumours that Brodie's father might not be dead, but he stayed silent as Ewen knew where the inn was. Surely, he would have dropped in if he had returned. So, he doubted if the rumours had been true as Ewen didn't visit. Callum had ensured the children were fed hot porridge for breakfast every morning, but they refused to be helped much more other than accept the leftovers and food scraps from the evening meal. However, there were few of these.

Callum looked at them and said, "We're moving to Australia, lad. There's an inn in Sydney that is looking for a manager, and I'll do that for a while, but I'm hoping to purchase a lease there and have our own inn. The new job is at a place called *The Whaler's Arms*, which is on the waterfront in Sydney. I've been told they call the area The Rocks. If you ever decide to go out that way. Look me up."

Heather reached for Brodie's hand and grasped it hard. "We have to leave, sir? When?" Heather asked.

Mr Findlay said, "Yes, dear, we go in a month, so at least the worst of the cold will be gone. The missus and me, we've liked having you here, but it's time for us to move on. As I said, I don't own this inn; I only manage it, and it's been sold. Having you two here has been a bit like having our own bairns. The owner of this one has given me a reference that will open any door for me. I wish we could take you with us, but we can only afford a tiny area in steerage. Even that is costing us £20."

Brodie gave Heather's hand a comforting squeeze. "We appreciate you letting us stay, sir, but do you have any suggestions about where we can go?"

"No, lad, I don't. I asked, but the skilled Irish folk have taken all the jobs." Mr Findlay shook his head. He had tried to talk the new man into letting the children stay but refused. On hectic days, both children came to the kitchen and did the washing up. They had been paid with a hot meal, not because Callum wouldn't pay them but because that's all they would accept. They had asked for nothing more. Callum's heart sank; he had done what he could for Ewen's boy, but at fifteen, he now had to stand on his own two feet. Heather had stuck by him and been like a sister to him.

Brodie wasn't a child anymore. He stood eye-level with Callum and had begun to fill out. Heather, at eleven, had the makings of an attractive girl. Her mahogany curls were always clean and brushed. Initially, Ishbelle had helped her learn how to stay clean. Now Heather washed their clothes and kept them as clean as possible. Callum hoped Heather wouldn't have to go on the street as a prostitute to support herself. He could not imagine a worse job for a girl. He thought back to the week they had arrived. They had two old blankets, a half bottle of whisky, and Heather's hairbrush. They owned nothing else. Over the past five years, they had begged, borrowed, or earned a few warm clothes. Although he had given them a new blanket, their clothing was now virtually ragged. "Brodie, I will tell you that before we leave, we are giving you some of our clothing that we're not taking. Sydney is much hotter than here; we have far more than we can take. So, on Sunday, come upstairs, and we'll see what we can find for you both. If you can dress a little neater, you might even be able to get a job in a nice house."

"Gee, Mister Findlay, you don't need to do that," Heather said in appreciation.

Callum smiled. "No, I don't, but I'd rather see you two warmly clothed than let the rag man make a bob or two from them."

Sunday came, and the two orphans met the Findlays in the nice warm kitchen. They were each given a big bowl full of hot creamy porridge and sat down to enjoy their meal. Neither had noticed a pile of clothing sitting on the floor. What followed was a fantastic day for them both. Ishbelle Findlay suggested that they bathe before trying on clean clothes. Brodie went and dunked himself in the large stone horse trough. He had no soap but found that he could use his filthy shirt to rub off most of the grime. Heather had a proper hip bath in front of the kitchen fire. The first time Ishbelle had let her do this, she had wept when she saw how emaciated the poor child was. As an eleven-year-old, she should have started to develop breasts; however, the girl was still skin and bones, with no sign of any development at all. Both would soon have a supply of warm clothes.

Heather had been only nine when she had been permitted to bathe like this. Her feet had been swollen with leech bites, and she could hardly walk. Mrs Findlay knew hot water would help with the pain and let her soak her legs in the hot bath. Heather could not resist and stripped off and submerged herself in the warm, soapy water. The pain had eased in her legs, but the feeling of once again being clean was a delight. Ishbelle was surprised that orphans even knew about cleanliness, let alone strive to keep clean, but these two did.

Heather remembered that her mother had bathed her every Saturday night before they crept into church the following day. She didn't remember much about church but knew it made her happy.

With new clothing and looking clean and reasonably well-presented, Heather and Brodie door-knocked some of the bigger houses in the area. Brodie was told to scram, but Heather was employed as a laundry maid at one of Argyle Street's mill owners' houses near the inn. She was to start the next day and live in as the job provided bed and board.

Brodie had found nothing. Every door he knocked on he was turned away. Too big, too small, not experienced enough, too clean, not clean enough. Shortly before Heather started work at her new job, he managed to get some itinerant work milking the cows at The Green in the middle of town, but that only lasted until he became ill with cowpox. He hadn't been very sick, but enough to not turn up for work for over a week as he was considered contagious. They would not take him back, and he had been replaced in his absence. Heather and Mrs Findlay had nursed him and bathed the pustules in their whisky. Neither child had been tempted to drink the fiery liquid that Heather had found years before. He had ached all over, and the blisters on his face hurt, reminding him of when he had been burnt. Thankfully, he had no blisters in his eyes. What they would have done without the Findlays' kindness, they did not know.

As soon as he was on his feet, Heather had to leave. Frustration was embedded deep down in Brodie. He wanted to work; he didn't care what it was. He even started collecting the dog poop as Heather had done, but the tanners, leatherworkers, cordwainers and cobblers had an adequate supply of this foul-smelling substance. Now he knew what tanners used to make the leather so supple; he decided he no longer liked leather. He shuddered.

From tomorrow, Brodie would be all but alone. Heather slept cradled in his arms for the last time, and he kissed the top of her head as she slept. He caressed her downy cheek and then settled to sleep himself. With her curled up in his arms, he slept the deep sleep of innocence.

After Heather left, he still had a few weeks left in the cellar. He hated being alone and knew he needed to find somewhere to stay. Life on the streets wasn't looking too good. With so many new Irish immigrants in town, even their original little hole in the wall was now home to a family of four. He was pleased that Heather would be safe and secure in her new job. He hoped it would last.

Every day for the next two weeks, Brodie door knocked and hunted for work. Nothing! At fifteen, they expected him to have some skills, but no one would give him a job so he could get them. He even offered to work for bed and board, but no pay. Still, doors were shut in his face. Factories didn't want him as he was too old, nor did the mills. They could employ younger children for only a few pennies.

Then the Findlays left, and Brodie was homeless again.

For the first time since he was a boy, Brodie cried. He did what was required to survive. He started picking pockets as his older brother Iain had done. Since Heather relied on him, he had never before taken anything that he had not worked for, but with no roof over his head and no income, he couldn't rely on Heather to sneak him food. He remembered that he and his brother had attended a big riot on The Green ten years before, and a man had dropped his fat wallet. Brodie had seen it drop and handed it back. As a reward, he was given £5. He knew a new railway line was opening and figured there would be a crowd again. If he went, maybe something similar would happen.

What occurred was not what he had planned but somehow just happened. Brodie was standing near the tracks looking at the enormous belching engine coming toward him when the police superintendent started pushing everyone back from the railway lines.

Brodie and Superintendent Graham had had a few run-ins over the past year. It was not that Brodie had actually done anything, but the big, burly police superintendent was always suspicious of Brodie. He didn't believe that he was keeping out of trouble. Today, the man was just plain angry. There were too many people and not enough policemen to keep them safe.

With so many people pushing and shoving, Brodie saw a fat wallet lying on the ground. He bent to pick it up when another younger lad beat him to it. The boy opened it and grabbed a handful of money before shoving the nearly empty wallet into Brodie's hands. Not knowing what to do, Brodie stood holding the virtually empty wallet. He couldn't very well return it to the man now. He would be blamed for taking the money. Superintendent Graham turned at that moment and saw him holding the offending article. Brodie dropped it and took off. His long legs and youthful stamina easily beat the older, overweight policeman. But Brodie had just realised he could outrun any chaser. He had done nothing wrong other than be in the wrong place at the wrong time; now, this policeman was out for him.

He would often pick a pocket, then act as though he was picking it up for the victim while helping himself to a pound or two before handing it back. Rarely did he take more than he needed. He made sure that the money would be made to stretch for as long as possible. He saw Heather as often as he could, generally on Sunday afternoons, as that was her time off. As she got older, she became more and more precious to him. He loved walking and holding her hand.

~

A year passed, then two.

Brodie had managed to find scraps of work, but nothing permanent. He survived by eeking out the food Heather brought him and living on the few pennies he stole or even eating from the pig food bins placed out for collection.

Poor Irish families were flooding the city, and they had far more experience at doing all the paid jobs Brodie applied for.

Brodie was pleased that the Police Superintendent had changed.

Soon after Heather had started at the big house, Superintendent Graham and his police sergeants had it out for Brodie. He was tall for his age and stood out from the other street urchins as he was usually clean. This should have been good, but it set him apart from the others. Thankfully, that policeman superintendent retired.

Brodie soon made friends with one of the new constables. He had gone to this policeman's assistance a few times and helped him by being an extra pair of arms holding down a criminal while being arrested.

~

The children survived and grew into young adults.

Heather, at fourteen, had developed into a beautiful but somewhat quiet young lady. Working at the big house meant Heather ate more regularly, and this meant her curves began filling out.

Brodie found his feelings for her were changing. However, he did not let on that what he felt for her had changed dramatically from the sisterly affection he once had. That change started when he turned seventeen. He hid his feelings well. Brodie spent his nights dreaming of Heather, and a desire for a future with her as his wife now haunted his sleep. He ached to hold her in his arms as they had done for so many years.

Since the Findlays left, they were only able to see each other on Sunday afternoons after church. However, each Sunday afternoon, it became harder for Brodie to say goodbye to her. His hugs grew longer, and his reluctance to release her brought a lump to his throat.

~

Cold days blurred into weeks, then frigid weeks into months.

Winters came and went, and then they were children no more.

Brodie was not the only one who had noticed that Heather was no longer a little girl.

At sixteen, she was beautiful. Her figure was curvaceous and alluring, however, she was naturally quiet and modest.

Brodie's feelings towards her were vastly inappropriate for a big brother as she treated him as. When she threw herself into his arms, her soft bumps and curves made his lower body jump to life. However, he never missed meeting her on her day off.

Each Sunday afternoon, they met after she had been to church with the family, and they would spend their precious time together. She insisted that he keep up his reading skills by making him write words in the dirt on the Clyde Riverbank dust or mud.

He would do anything she asked him to do. But was aware that writing skills meant they could contact each other if needed.

Brodie's desire to kiss her was almost overwhelming him.

Chapter 2   Taking the Medicine

*F*or the five years Heather had been at the big house, she had gone to Sunday School at St George's Church, Trongate, with the other servants. It was just down the road from where she worked. She could now read and write well in both English and Gaelic, and she would teach Brodie on Sunday afternoons. Although her mornings were occupied with the service and Sunday School lessons, learning to read and write, Brodie would be patiently waiting for her as the class finished. If the weather were fine, they would go to The Green and sit talking or walking together if the ground was wet. He was thrilled that Heather had learnt to read. He tried to remember the lessons his mother had given him. The sessions Heather gave him refreshed his mother's teaching. He had not had the opportunity to write much since she died. Brodie now lived for these precious moments with Heather. Any contact with her was good, so he listened well. He would learn for her, even if she wanted him to learn how to do handstands while singing. He tried to picture his parents' faces and could not visualise them. He remembered his mother had dark hair, as he did, but her face had vanished from his minds-eye. All he could see was Heather. He was obsessed with his lovely dark red-headed girl. Her shining mahogany curls danced around her smiling, heart shaped face, and her skin was like ivory. Her hair often slipped out under her mob cap and shone like fire in the sunlight.

Over the years, Superintendent Graham was followed by Superintendent McKenzie, and recently, Superintendent George Lamb took over the role. Brodie liked him. McKenzie employed new policemen and one he came to know well. Although Brodie knew he had been named as a pick-pocket by a few of the gentlemen in the town, he had never been arrested for anything. However, he was finding survival harder by the day. He tried everything possible to get a real job, but none were available anywhere. Since having to fend for himself, Irish immigration had quadrupled the population in Glasgow in a matter of years. Many of them were now starving. Every nook and cranny was filled with poor, hungry families. Brodie had taken to sleeping in an alleyway behind a buttress. It offered little protection from the cold but was dry and usually out of the snow.

One of Superintendent Lamb's policemen, Kenneth Donald, had encountered the young man some years before. Brodie assisted him during a scuffle with a burglar. He had held the captive down while the policeman arrested him. With so few police, Brodie had come to Ken's aid several times over the past years. The policeman knew him to be one of the better street lads, and he never forgot that difficult arrest. He had been amazed that Brodie had vanished before the other police arrived. He asked for nothing for himself and had even reported a few crimes to him. Ken knew where he slept. Now and then, Brodie would find a bap or an oatcake or two stuffed in his hidden blanket. Sergeant Ken, as Brodie called him, knew the young man as a well-behaved local lad and not one of the new Irish immigrants. He felt sorry for him. On Ken's rounds one day, he found Brodie still tucked up and asleep under his blanket during the daylight hours. He wondered if he was dead and bent to feel his cheek. "Oh, laddie, you're burning up with fever. You'll have to go to the workhouse until you're better."

Brodie opened his eyes to the kindly face looking down at him. "No, please, Sergeant Ken, not there. I'll never make it out." Brodie had a fit of shivering, and then he coughed. "Anywhere but there, sir, please." Brodie looked up at the tall policeman now squatting beside him. "Please, sir, I'll be okay; just leave me here," Brodie managed to say after a fit of coughing.

Sergeant Ken flicked a lock of Brodie's damp hair from his eyes. He felt his forehead; it was dripping with perspiration. As it was a chilly day, he realised how sick the young man was. "Oh, laddie, my heart bleeds for you street urchins. I'll bring food and see if I can get you some medicine." Ken stood, looked down at the overgrown boy, and then walked off to sort out something for him. Ken was delayed in his return by an affray on the way to the shops. It was nearly dark when he had purchased the required items and made it back to Brodie. Brodie was so sick that he didn't respond to him when touched. Ken knew that he couldn't leave him there all night as he would be dead by morning. He only lived two streets away and decided to take him home until he was better. Ken hoisted the lad up, and Brodie partially roused. He leaned him against the buttress and gathered the rest of his possessions, wrapping them into his tattered blanket. They managed to make it the two streets to his home before Brodie collapsed, groaning, in a heap on his kitchen floor. Ken managed to get Brodie to drink some whisky before he passed out again. At least here, Brodie was warm and dry. Ken had some soup on the stove and a flagon of whisky on the table. He sat the sick lad up and made him drink some hot soup. Brodie almost greedily drank the hot broth before falling asleep again on the floor. Now, his visitor was warm and reasonably comfortable; Ken retired to his cot in the next room.

Brodie had slept for most of the first few days, only waking to drink or relieve himself in the chamber pot Ken left next to his blanket. On the fifth day, he was awake when Ken arrived home. He was feeling much better. "Hello, Sergeant; how did I get here?" Brodie asked in some confusion.

Ken felt Brodie's forehead, as he had done every time he passed his patient. "I brought you here nearly a week ago. I've managed to get you to eat and drink; then you'd sleep like the living dead. By the feel of you, the fever has broken. I gather you have been helping yourself liberally to the *peat reek*?"

Brodie nodded, smiling wanly. "Sorry, sir, it's a potent brew. I've never had a drink before, but it's nearly all gone."

Ken chuckled, "Not so, lad." Ken produced another small bottle of the illicit brew from his pocket. "This batch is so good that His Majesty asked for some himself. I rescued this confiscated booty from destruction, so there is an ample supply. Did you know illegal whisky is called *peat reek?* The barley is smoked over peat fires. But this is the Glenlivet stuff, and I've heard it called by various tags: Mountain Dew, Rotgut, Skullpop, Firewater and White Lightning. I think the last two are apt, as this burns all the way down. The King certainly liked it. It's why I thought it would work for you." Ken smiled, knowing he had a stack of small firkin-sized small kegs in the cellar. His superintendent had ordered that it be disposed of, and it was. With Dennis's assistance, they were making a big dent in the supply below them. The gallon bottle was nearly empty, so he poured the remainder into Brodie's mug. He would refill the flagon later. The brown medicine had done the trick.

It took another few days before Brodie was well enough to do much around the tiny flat. Ken had left the stone flagon of whisky with Brodie and told him to have some every hour or so to help kill the pain in his throat. By the end of the week, the gallon bottle was nearly empty again. Brodie found that the evil brew indeed killed the pain, but it also numbed him and the hurt of so much rejection for so long. A few times while he was sick, he had upended the bottle and drank deeply. He had slept for hours, a deep, dreamless rest. He was warm, dry, and comfortable. On waking, he would ache for the relief that the fiery brew brought.

Ten days after Brodie arrived, the police accommodation landlord heard noises in Ken's flat, and he knew his friend was at work, so went to investigate. Brodie was cleaning out the ash box on the stove when the man came and opened the door. "Hey you, what are you doing?" He was puzzled, as burglars don't usually do the housework when breaking in.

Brodie explained the situation. He was still as weak as a kitten and dizzy when he stood, but the fever had gone. The whisky was plentiful and helped dull the pain. Pain! The pain of being alone, the pain of being sick, the pain of having no home, and Heather was out of his reach. It was just pain, and it hurt. The whisky took it all away.

The landlord said to Brodie, "You must leave, lad. You can wait until Ken comes home, then you have to go. If others here think they can sneak in borders, I'll be overrun. What's more, this is police-only accommodation."

Brodie knew his respite was over. He would be back on the street tonight. He had missed seeing Heather on Sunday and knew she would be worried.

Ken returned, and they had a final meal together before Brodie returned to the darkness. Thankfully, the weather had warmed while he had been ill. Ken walked him to where he had found him and carried some of his possessions. Under the blanket, he also had a loaf of bread, a chunk of cheese and a flagon of the unbranded Glenlivet whisky for Brodie. He had gone way beyond his duty for the young man, but the lad had to stand on his own again. Ken thought back to when he first met him. Twenty was an awkward age at any time, but being homeless and in the cold made it more challenging. Ken had even suggested that Brodie apply to become a policeman next year when he was of age. He had even mentioned his name to Superintendent McKenzie before he left but had found that the boy was still too young. He needed to be at least twenty-one to apply. It would still be one more year before he could apply. How the boy was supposed to survive over that time, Ken just didn't know. He hated leaving Brodie on the street, but he had little choice. As Ken turned to leave, Brodie looked forlorn and waved a hand in thanks. When he was gone, Brodie sank to the ground in his hide-hole and wrapped himself in the worn blanket. He intended to sink into oblivion with a large mug of neat whisky.

~

Heather had indeed been worried when Brodie had not appeared for their Sunday *rendezvous*; he missed the next one as well. Heather had no idea where he was, but he had said he felt off when he had last seen her. There were only four days to wait, and she would hopefully see him again.

The following Sunday could not come fast enough for either of them. She had a special gift for him. After the washing day, she found a gold sovereign in the bottom of the copper only yesterday. She had taken it as the laundry staff often did. It was now almost burning a hole in her pocket. She had never had so much money before, but she knew Brodie needed it far more than she did. She was paid £6 a year, which was far more than she needed. She didn't need much more with uniform, board and lodgings provided. The coin was two months' wages. Heather left the church carrying a basket with a picnic luncheon, which she put down and waited for him to come to her side.

Brodie met her and greeted her with a big hug. "I've been sick, sis. Sergeant Ken took me in and looked after me."

Heather didn't wish to leave the comfort of his arms. "I've been worried sick, Brod. It's not like you to vanish." She stayed in his arms for a long hug. She was pressed closely as he almost crushed her to him. "I do miss being with you, Brod, but I have something for you." She pulled away, put her hand in her pocket, and drew out the shiny coin. "It was in the bottom of the copper, and no one saw it there. You need it." She squeezed the golden sovereign into his palm.

"Cor, Heather, you could get transported for taking this much," he whispered. He hadn't let go of her and slipped it into his pocket with one hand. He bit it and said, "It's real gold. I've often wondered." After pocketing it, he pulled her into another hug.

Heather nodded against his chest. "Shh, I know, but no one will even miss it." She was thrilled that she could contribute something to his well-being. He had looked after her long enough. The shilling or two she gave him was insufficient to keep body and soul together, and she dared not ask how he lived daily.

He finally released her, and they left the church grounds and walked to the river, where there was a secluded grove he had slept in a few times over the summer. She always brought her lunch with her, and today was no different. They sat on the riverbank eating baps, oat cakes with tatie cakes and black pudding.

She asked, "Do you remember our first meal together ten years ago?"

Brodie looked down at the beautiful girl beside him. In the two weeks he had not seen her, she had blossomed. He had missed her terribly. Her cheeks were rosy red, and her lips so kissable, and he so wished to do just that.

"Yes, Brodie, I was so scared that night, and you were like an angel that Mama sent to look after me. It's why I chose this food to bring today." Heather looked up at her protector, wondering how to tell him of her problem. She thought she would spit it out. "Brodie, I'm having a bit of trouble at work. I don't want you to do anything, as I'm pretty sure I'm safe enough, but I wanted you to know. As you can see, I'm growing up, and it's being noticed." She swallowed nervously before saying, "I know it was 1826 that Mama died, as we saw the new branch railway line open from Garnkirk. I only discovered what year that was as I overheard the cook discussing it this week. Papa died while he was building it, and Mama died only a little while later. I remember Mama's tears and when she told me Papa wasn't coming home ever again and why. I knew she was having another baby as her tummy was fat. She had lost the two after me." She paused. "So, Brodie, that means I'm now sixteen. I have bumps where I used to be flat like a little girl, and well, things have changed. I've grown up."

He watched her talk, and her moving lips drove him wild with desire. Mayhap his emotions were delicate after his sickness, but his feeling for the girl beside him was anything but sisterly. He had never kissed a girl, but he certainly wished to kiss Heather, and not in a sisterly way. He swallowed; he couldn't do that to her. He hoped she was leading up to something along those lines, though. "What sort of trouble, Heather? Boys?"

She nodded.

"Anyone in particular?" A wave of unfamiliar emotion swept over him like rushing water. He felt jealous. How could he think that? He had no reason to claim her.

Heather moved closer to him. She blushed and said, "It's my master's son; he tried to kiss me and… Oh, Brodie, I was so scared. I didn't know what he wanted to do, so I ran." He automatically put his arm around her and drew her close again. She looked up at him lovingly, "Brodie, you're not my real brother, and I was wondering if you would kiss me. You see, I've never been kissed properly, and I want to know what it should be like." She blushed before saying, "I've sort of dreamed you would be my first one."

His heart leapt. "You want me to kiss you? Like a brother?"

"Not exactly like a brother, more like this." She reached up and drew his head down to hers.

He had never kissed anyone before. He had never known another girl, and his emotions were raw after his illness. At first, his lips were gentle, almost like caressing a rosebud, but his grasp around her soon tightened, and the pressure increased. He felt her pull him closer. He lay down with her and rolled her on her back. He found that he was being pulled closer to her. Tempestuous surges pulsed through him. He wanted to tear off her clothes and make her his own, although he did not fully understand what that even was. All this was coursing through his mind until sanity prevailed. They were in public view on the river bank. He pulled away from her and lay on his back, breathing deeply, trying hard to regain control of his nether regions. Another minute… and well, he wouldn't think about that. "Heather, oh Heather, I think we're both grown up. I nearly lost my head then." He was slowly regaining control of the explosive feelings he had for her.

Heather was leaning on her elbows, looking down at him. "Brod, did you enjoy it as much as I did?"

He turned and met her smile with his own. "Oh, did I ever. But I don't want to take you to bed without marriage banns and a ring firmly placed on your finger. But Heather, we're too young for that yet. I have nowhere to live, no job, and no money for a ring, but I want you so much." It suddenly hit Brodie that if they married, she would be his forever. He rolled over. "Heather, we could become betrothed until you are eighteen."

The grin she gave him had him on his knee beside her before she realised he had moved. "Heather Anderson, will you be my wife?" Brodie's heart was in his mouth. He was twenty, and she was sixteen.

"Yes, Brodie, I certainly will. However, you're not quite right, you see, I also found out that we can marry here and even today. In England, it's older, but in Scotland, girls only have to be twelve and boys fourteen." She saw the amazement on his face.

"Seriously?" He said, with a slow smile, tilting up his lips.

She nodded. "We can marry by consent in Scotland, too, by saying that we are married in front of witnesses, and I think we need two of those." Heather again listened to the cook talking with the housekeeper over the copper as she washed. "Brodie, if we were married, you might be permitted to share my bed in my tiny room at the house."

Brodie had no idea if her words were true, but his heart sang. "You really want to marry me?"

Heather nodded. Her mahogany curls had escaped from under her mob cap with his ardent attention. One ringlet wobbled as she nodded. "And soon, Brodie, then we can be together in every way and sleep in each other's arms again."

Brodie wondered if Sergeant Ken would be a witness for them. He was the only one he could think of. But where could they even have a wedding night? The only money he had on him was the stolen coin she had given him. Life on the street stank; he hated it. And Mr Findlay's words often came back to him. He wondered if somehow they could get to Sydney, too. "Heather, have you ever thought about Mister Findlay and what he said about Sydney? There might be work for me there. Staying here, we would have nothing and no prospects."

Heather had few memories of her time in the cellar. "Brodie, I just know I want to be with you, wherever you are. I love you so much." She lay back on the grass again and tugged at Brodie's sleeve. "Brodie…" She didn't need to say more.

After their first kiss, his emotions had only quietened a little. He leaned over his new fiancé and gazed down into her beloved face. How had the little girl grown into such a lovely young woman? "I love you and am at your command, Heather. I've wished to do this for some time. I was too scared to acknowledge that my feelings for you were anything but sisterly." Brodie was once again pulled close to her. If their first kiss was an emotional session, their second one was beyond all expectations. He could feel her soft, rounded breasts pushing into his chest. Her soft, supple body fitted to his like a hand in a glove. "I will not take you until we are married, Heather, but I can't wait long."

"Then let's go and find your policeman friend," she said.

Brodie once again rolled over on the grass, waiting for his rapid breathing to quieten. "Give me a moment, Heather. I need to get my breath back." That wasn't really his problem, but hopefully, she would find out more about that soon.

On Sunday afternoons, Sergeant Ken was usually at home. Brodie had an hour until he had to get Heather back to the house. If worse came to worst, he could take her back to his sleeping hole and have their first time together there so they didn't dawdle. They had slept in each other's arms for years. However, to sleep with her as a wife would be vastly different. Brodie carried the basket that contained the remains of their picnic. He felt like running to Ken's place, but with so many out promenading on a sunny afternoon, he knew he must be circumspect.

Soon, they were turning into the street near Ken's flat. All Ken had to do was have a friend who could listen to them and hear them declare they were married. Brodie's heart was pounding with excitement, and he was nervous yet anticipating what would hopefully follow. Heather was also nervous, and she clung tightly to his hand. She had done that often enough over the years, but as a sister would to a brother, now it was different. She wanted him close, very, very close, and her fingers interlocked with his. They knocked on the door, and when Ken saw who stood there, he welcomed them inside. Sitting with him was the landlord, who had thrown him out. Brodie's heart sank. This man would not agree to his plea. He stood looking from one man to the other.

Heather, on the other hand, took charge. "Hello, Sergeant Donald, I know you from Mister Richardson's house." Heather smiled and gave the other man a curtsy. "I wish to say thank you for looking after Brodie while he was so ill. I was worried sick when he vanished."

He watched as Dennis bent to put more coal on the fire. The man at the table looked at the young girl. She was still clinging tightly to Brodie's hand. The policeman said, "I vaguely remember your face. But what's your name?"

This question was the opening Heather wanted. "It's Heather Anderson, sir, but Brodie and I want to be married."

Ken's attention was firmly caught. Dennis heard the words and stood up, and glanced at Ken. If Brodie agreed, they would be legally married right now. Ken asked, "Brodie, what do you say?"

"I want Heather as my wife, now, if possible." Brodie was grinning. "Heather, will you be my wife?"

Before either man could say a word, Heather added, "Yes, Brodie, I take you as my husband." They were married by all the laws in Scotland. As Sergeant Ken Donald was a policeman, he could vouch for their nuptials being legal.

Ken was stunned. "Do you two realise what you have just done? By declaring in front of witnesses that you are married, you realise it's now legal?" Ken asked.

Both nodded, grinning. Heather was now his wife. Brodie finally found some words; he spoke through his big grin. Brodie said, "Sir, you were the only person we could think of witnessing our troth for us. We've known each other for many years, and this way, I can continue to look after her. I'm not her brother nor related in any way, so I had no authority to protect her."

Ken was stunned. "Brodie, what happens if she has a bairn? You don't even have anywhere to call home."

Heather felt Brodie's hand tighten on hers. They had not thought about that, but they were now married, and that's what she wanted, and now she had a claim on him and vice versa.

"Have you even got somewhere to spend your wedding night?" Ken asked. Both shook their heads. They had lived in a hole in a wall; Brodie's current abode was a nook behind a buttress. So, any tiny cranny would do for this unusual couple. Ken looked over at his friend. "Brodie, Dennis and I were just leaving for the Police club. The fire is warm, and the floor is clean. Shut the door when you leave."

Brodie felt Heather's grip tighten again; Brodie looked at his friend, "Sergeant Ken, you don't need to do that. I can sneak into her room at the house, but I was wondering if you would stand witness for us if anyone asks."

Ken smiled and nodded. He was thinking back to his wedding night. He had had so little time with his wife, Shona, before she died of smallpox. "Yes, Brodie, of course I will, but laddie, stay here; I won't have you sneaking around to some dirty hovel. She deserves better than that. We'll be gone for about two hours. The candle burns for three hours." He drew a line on the candle. "About here is when we should be back. Come on, Dennis. We've had enough surprises for the day."

Dennis, the landlord, had remained silent since they arrived. "Sneaky brat, aren't you, Brodie? You could have told me that you were a close friend of Ken's. I hope you can get things worked out and somehow be together. However, if she gets 'up the duff' and has a bairn, she'll be sacked well before that. What will you do then?"

Brodie's head jerked up; their immediate decision had been made for her protection as well as to slake his lusts. "Quite honestly, sir, I have no idea, but she's being pestered at work already, and only by marrying her can I protect her," Brodie explained.

Dennis continued, "Living on the streets with a child and no job, no money, and no food is no way to start a marriage. Take it from me, laddie; I know from experience."

Ken stared at Dennis; he knew his background too. And of the injury to his hand that ended his career. The realisation of what could happen made Ken turn and say to Brodie. "I think I shall withdraw my offer, Brodie, because Dennis is correct." With hindsight, he was determined to make him understand his predicament. He gently took the young man by his shoulders and looked him directly in the eye.

Brodie tried to shake him off. He was getting angry.

"Brodie, hear me out. House staff are not supposed to be married at all. If you are discovered together, she will be dismissed on the spot. Even if they found out she was now married, she would be given notice. Brodie, please do not do this to her. Do not consummate this union if you love her, as I know you do. Be husband and wife in word, but not in action."

Heather was standing at his side. Her eyes welled with unshed tears. "Brodie, I want to be with you, but what if he's right? We need money from my work for us to live."

Brodie drew her to him. The young couple before him stood gazing at each other. They were miserable and lost for words. Brodie pulled her into his arms and held her close, but they stayed silent, thinking hard but unable to make any decisions.

Dennis was leaning on the doorpost, watching. His quiet voice broke through the standoff. "Brodie lad, nothing kills love faster than poverty; trust me, I know from experience. My missus left me and went back to her parents. She died in childbirth; I didn't even know she was in the family way. I joined the force soon after she left, but it was too late. Isla was dead. I worked with Ken for years, and then, after a brutal attack that left me injured, I now work in the Duke Street Prison as well as here as the caretaker. This is the only way I can make ends meet. Laddie, you canna even do that, as you're too young to join us. Kenny tells me you are only twenty. I could find you a room here then."

Brodie nodded; he pushed Heather slightly from him.

Dennis continued, "If what Ken says is true and you have no job or place to doss down, you will both end up in the workhouse. Is that what you want?" He stated nonchalantly, cleaning his fingernails as he spoke.

Heather grabbed Brodie's arm tightly. That threat had been hanging over them both since their mothers had died. Brodie gazed at his new wife, and yet, not a wife. He knew what they said was true. Brodie gently gathered her to him again and reluctantly said, "Heather, dear one, what they say is true. We are man and wife, so I can kiss you, but no more. Not until I have a job and somewhere for us to live." He brushed her lips with a quick kiss. "I will find some job and continue to look after you, this I promise. Next year, I'll join up and help Sergeant Ken on the beat. I can help there, sweetie; it will give us some money."

Ken stood listening. "Brodie, I'd love to have you work beside me. I look forward to that."

Brodie wasn't done. "However, I will say this, Heather: if things at work get bad, come here, and Sergeant Ken knows where to find me. We have nothing here in Glasgow anyway. If we have to leave town and go and work on a farm, so be it. We could even go to Sydney and join the Findlays."

She slid her arms around him, determined not to cry; she hid her head on his shoulder. Brodie felt much the same. He realised they had taken so long in discussions that it was time for her to return to work. As he could not be with her as a wife and didn't trust himself with her, he looked at Ken in mournful resignation. "Sir, will you walk back with us? We're now late, and with your presence beside us, she should remain safe." Both men agreed.

The four were headed down the street. Before they turned the corner, Ken stopped and said, "Say goodbye here, lad; if they see you kissing her, she will be dismissed." The two men walked ahead as Brodie bid his new sixteen-year-old wife farewell for the week.

Chapter 3   The Troubles Begin

ennis heard a ruckus and many loud voices in the mews. As they drew closer, they realised it was occurring at the back of the house where they were heading, towards the back of the Richardson's house, and he called Brodie to hurry up. He knew he might be needed, so he stayed with Ken and walked with the young couple.

Their arrival caused even more of a stir. Heather clutched Brodie's arm tightly; obviously, she was frightened to return to the situation she had left.

A raucous voice carried across the mews courtyard as they entered. "There she is, superintendent. There's your thief. She must have stolen it." It was Agnes's voice, Heather's immediate superior. They heard the shrill voice as it carried over the rabble.

Superintendent Lamb was in the back courtyard with Mr Richardson next to him. He saw his Sergeant accompanying the said thief, and she was clinging to a young man's arm. Superintendent Lamb wondered what the story was. "Thank you, everyone; I will take it from here. As you see, she is with a policeman already. Please leave it with me, and I'll get it sorted out. Go about your business now, and I'll get to the bottom of the story." He banished the rest of the crowd until just five of them were left in the yard. He waited until all the doors had shut before he spoke. However, he saw faces at various windows, and then he said, "Sergeant, this person has been accused of theft. But first, why are you with her?"

Ken was stunned. His mouth opened and snapped shut again.

All eyes, including Brodie's, turned to Heather. She was white and shaking but said, "I found a sovereign in the copper after we finished the washing. We had done many loads, and no one would have known where it came from. As many of the others have done before, I kept it." She turned to Brodie. "I'm so sorry, Brod, you said to return it."

While Brodie held his weeping wife in his arms, he dug into his pocket and pulled out the offending coin. Thankfully, they had not spent it. He held it out to the uniformed man in front of him.

The superintendent took the shiny disk from Brodie and groaned, knowing they were all watching from inside and had seen his action. He turned to his Sergeant. "Sergeant Donald, how are you involved?"

Ken stood to attention. "I've known Brodie Stewart for some years, sir. He has often helped me on the beat and keeps his nose out of trouble. On the whole, he's a good lad. He wishes to join the force next year."

Dennis raised his eyebrows at the comment. Until recently, he had no idea Ken had befriended the boy years earlier, but he knew he had had him stay in his flat. There had never been a peep of trouble from him. That much he knew.

The superintendent saw the small action and asked for his input. "You, sir, are you not the landlord for the constabulary residences?"

"Yes, sir, I was injured in the line of duty and now work at the gaol too," Dennis replied. "I barely know these young ones, having met them together today. They called into Ken's flat with a request." He saw Ken shake his head while the superintendent wasn't looking. Both knew that Ken would be in trouble if it got out that Brodie had recuperated in a police flat, let alone that they had married there so recently. Dennis didn't want that to be discovered, so he kept quiet.

The superintendent wasn't to be put off. "And the request was?" He looked at Brodie, but Ken answered.

Ken swallowed; he was about to bend the truth. It was more of a half-truth than a lie. "Sir, they asked if I would bear witness if they married. Both of us said we would. A person does not have to be known to another to bear witness to a Marriage by Declaration."

"I know how it works, sergeant," the superintendent said, somewhat exasperated.

Brodie was stupefied. Was Heather in trouble for stealing the coin? He had said that she could be transported for taking the money, but he didn't really mean it. He had willingly received the bounteous gift. She was still wrapped in his arms; he would protect her all he could. At least she was now his wife, so he had a claim on her. From that point of view, their timing was perfect. The superintendent met Brodie's petrified stare. He tried to remove Heather from Brodie's grasp, but she refused to release him. She cried out and clung tighter.

The superintendent said, "I'm sorry, miss, but you must accompany me. Stealing a sovereign can see you transported for seven years." He looked at Brodie's possessive hold on the young girl. "I gather you know her well?"

Brodie nodded. He turned to Ken but found he could not utter a sound. Ken came to his rescue. "They are local street bairns, sir. I know their story well. Young Brodie has taken care of her since she was six years old. She has been having trouble with the boys in the household and…" What he would have said, no one would ever know.

The superintendent cut him off. "Fine, bring him too. You can all come to my office to discuss this privately. Sergeant, get her possessions as she won't be coming back. They sacked her as soon as she was accused of theft. It seems you have no friends there, miss."

Heather tearfully shook her head. Brodie wasn't going to leave her alone for the sake of mere clothes. Possessions weren't necessary; she was. He was puzzled that neither Ken nor Dennis had let on about their marriage.

The superintendent pulled Heather from Brodie's grasp and took her arm. He led her out of the courtyard towards his office. Brodie grabbed her other hand and held it as if his life depended on it. Once out of the mews, the group slowed to wait for Ken. As they were now out of eyesight from the accusers, they were dawdling, so Ken caught up to them before they reached the end of the street.

Knowing the accusations against her, someone had already put her scant possessions in a blanket. Ken had grabbed the bundle from the narrow pallet bed that was pointed out as hers. The minute stark room was frigid room. Having glanced around and been disgusted at the poor servants' quarters of the wealthy man, he followed the small group as fast as he could. He would do what he could to help them. He still planned on keeping the marriage quiet for as long as possible. If she were known as married, she would be locked up with the matrons and drunkards in gaol rather than with the younger ones. Hopefully, his ploy would work. She would be kept safe if he could get her into Duke Street Prison and into a single Dandy Cell. Hopefully, Dennis could pull a few strings if required. If she could be put in isolation, she would be in solitary confinement, which would be safer, but she would need to spend the day working, probably weaving. Hopefully, they could even take Brodie in for visits.

Ken knew that if he waited outside, Brodie could even make it a conjugal visit if they wished. He now felt a bit guilty that he had not allowed them to be together as man and wife, as it could be their last time together for a long time. He saw the small group dawdling in front of him. He smiled as he realised that Dennis was still with them. Ken hoped the superintendent would be lenient with her. It was a first offence, and yes, the coin was worth a lot, but it's not as if she took it from anyone. He knew any coins he left in his pockets would be gone when his trousers were returned. The laundry staff took them as a gratuity. Everyone knew that. He would do the best he could for her.

The next hour saw the senior officer grilling each of them. Ultimately, the superintendent groaned and said to Heather, "Lassie, I have no trouble with you taking small pennies from the tub. My own laundry lady does this, but a sovereign is a different matter." He rubbed his nose and scratched his hair. "How much do you make a year?"

Brodie was still beside her, but he had been told to stay silent. She glanced at him, and he nodded. "Six pounds, sir."

The superintendent knew his salary was £200 a year and found it hard to live on that. "So, you saw a coin worth two months' salary and took it. Quite honestly, I don't blame you. How the heck do you live on that amount?"

Heather didn't realise the question didn't need an answer, so she said, "I got bed, board and a uniform, sir. I give most of the money to Brodie as he often cannot get work. We didn't need much, sir." She knew she had to protect Brodie, but she stepped closer to Brodie for her protection.

The superintendent felt himself softening over this case. "Miss Anderson, do you realise I would have had no proof if your man had not returned the coin?"

Heather felt the earth opening beneath her. "I didn't know taking it was stealing, sir. The other staff took the coins from the copper. I never have, but I saw it first this time as Agnes wasn't there. She usually pocketed all the money. Brodie told me I had to return it, and I was going to. I'm really sorry, sir."

The superintendent sounded angry, but it was not with either of these young people but with the system. According to his sergeant, these two had kept out of trouble up until now. He had spoken to Ken over the previous months since he took over the job and knew that a young street lad had assisted in various arrests; he now knew that boy to be Brodie. So he was angry, but not at Heather; his anger was directed at the rich mill manager who kept his staff on such a pittance and in frigid, unheated rooms. "Damn it, girl, I have a pocket full of sovereigns in my fob, and I would hardly miss one if I lost it. However, the stupid girl, Agnes, that you worked with reported the theft, and therefore, I must charge you." He noticed Ken almost hopping from one foot to the other. "Spit it out, sergeant."

Ken realised that the superintendent was on her side. "Sir, I told you the truth, but not all of it. Sir, I said that they came to ask if we would witness their pledge to each other. That was true; I told you that we agreed, and that was true, too. However, sir, they married by Declaration in front of us moments later. I hoped she would be released and the household would not have to discover their relationship. I knew she would be instantly dismissed if they were discovered. However, that has already occurred."

His boss sat upright in his chair and stared at the young couple beside Ken. "You married her? Are you serious?"

Brodie nodded. He tightened his grip on Heather's hand. It was the first question directed his way for some time. He said, "She was being accosted at work, sir. She is only sixteen, sir; it's the only way I could protect her; I have no rights over her otherwise. Don't get me wrong; I love her, I always have, but it's more than that. I care for her so much and want her kept safe. Sir, she didn't even know what she did was wrong."

The superintendent's hands were tied, and she had to go to prison. "Sergeant Donald, when you get to Duke Street, make sure she's in a Dandy Cell by herself and that she's, well…" He glanced at Brodie, "…kept safe and away from the rabble in the general population." He turned to Brodie, "I'll try to ensure she is looked after, but once she's in the system, let me just say, if you don't pray now, learn how to, for she will need it. She'll be taken before the magistrate tomorrow. Sergeant, I want you there to stand as a character witness for her, and you, lad, may accompany him."

Ken nodded, as did Brodie.

Heather then fainted. Brodie caught her before she hit the ground. He heard sounds around him, but he was concentrating on his beloved.

The superintendent's voice came from the doorway. "You have ten minutes to say farewell; however, I permit you to walk with them to Duke Street Prison. Sergeant, see to it. Deliver her yourself. Dennis, you work there, so go with them, please."

~

By the end of the week, Heather had been tried, found guilty of theft, and sentenced to seven years as it was over two shillings value. She was to be transported to Sydney. After the pronouncement of the sentence, Brodie had been dragged to Ken's flat by both police friends. He stumbled from shock most of the way back to their lodgings. Both men decided that he couldn't be left alone. Dennis had not realised that Ken had known the young man for so long nor that he had been the mystery assistant over the years. Brodie's mind reeled. She was gone, literally snatched from his arms on their wedding day.

After the trial and her sentence had been handed down, Dennis knew what would help and where to find it. On returning from the trial, they went to Ken's flat, where they poured Brodie a mug of neat whisky.

For the entire week after she was locked up, Brodie was rarely sober.

Ken fed him when he was home, but Dennis discovered Brodie had found Ken's whisky stash in their coal cellar. After Ken had gone to work, Brodie stumbled down the cellar stairs and passed out while hanging over a keg of the illicit brew that was stacked against the back wall. When he returned, Ken found Brodie still in the cellar. He was talking to himself with the small barrel wrapped in his arms. He was in a pitiful state and was unable to stand. The smell of ammonia from his urine and the stench of vomit hit him as he entered the enclosed room.

Brodie didn't care. He was sober enough to acknowledge Ken's presence. "I failed her, Sargn't Ken; I have let her down," he wailed, slurring his words. The policemen tried to talk some sense into him.

Dennis left them to chat and went to get a jug of water. He returned to the cellar and sloshed the pitcher of cold water over him. He said, "So what are you going to do about it? Drinking your life away, how will that help her? Brodie, you need to sober up before you see her. She still needs you." Dennis was gagging with the stench. Brodie had dried vomit down his front and had also fouled his trousers. "Brodie, in plain words, you stink, and you can't go and see her like this."

"See her? I can see her?" Brodie tried hard to focus on Dennis; he was seeing double. "I didn't know you had a twin, Dennis," Brodie slurred.

Half smiling, Dennis said, "I don't, Brodie, you're drunk. And you're not seeing her like this. Strip laddie, we'll get you cleaned up." It took an hour to get Brodie into a hip bath and cleaned up enough to make him eat something. Dennis had brought some of his own street clothes and made Brodie wash his. It was the first time the last of Mr Findlay's, either his clothes or himself, had seen soap for many a year.

His friends chatted while he bathed. Hopefully, Brodie would be sober enough to see her tomorrow. He would not be able to walk the distance to the prison today. The lad was so under the weather that he could barely stand unaided.

The following morning, with the assistance of his two older friends, Brodie managed to look presentable. His head felt like it was a foot above his shoulders and that it would explode. The light hit his eyes, and his bloodshot orbs felt like they had knives in them.

They arranged that Dennis would accompany him to the prison while Ken went to work. Before they left, Dennis had made Brodie assist him with his job cleaning the flats. Once done, the two walked to the prison on Duke Street. The work helped sober the young man.

It was a two-mile walk to their destination. The crisp, fresh air permeated into Brodie's whisky-soaked brain. His bender had left him with a stinking headache, and he felt ill, but he plastered a smile on his face. He looked forward to seeing Heather. Twice on the walk, he cast up his accounts. Dennis stood by, patiently waiting until he was able to keep walking. Their conversation was kept to a minimum as Brodie was in no mood to be chatty.

Their arrival at the four-story edifice made Brodie shiver. He had only seen this place in the dark when they brought Heather. He had not been permitted to enter, but he had kissed her goodbye. Ken and Dennis had taken her arms and escorted her inside. Ken assured Brodie that the superintendent's instructions had been obeyed, and she was safely ensconced in a solitary Dandy Cell. The view of Ken's white trousers and Heather's white Sunday-best dress entering through the main gate was seared into Brodie's mind. He had stood shaking back then and did so again as he approached the building today.

As Dennis worked here, he knew the place and staff. Before his injury to his hand and retirement, he had been the policeman who had shown Mister Joseph Gurney through the prison when it first opened, so he knew the layout well. He also knew where Heather had been placed; she would be in the solitary wing. Although he had not mentioned it to Brodie, he had checked on her several times since her incarceration. He had ensured she was well, safe, and being taught to weave on a Dandy Loom. He knew she would be permitted to do this in her cell rather than work with the lower-class women. He knew the women's cells were often crowded with thirty or more women, with beds for only twelve; the women sometimes had to triple up in a pallet bed. But other than overcrowding, they were all reasonably clean and well-fed.

Dennis was thrilled that Mrs Elizabeth Fry's brother, Joseph Gurney, had given the prison a top-rank rating. His role as police accommodation manager gave him time to oversee the good conditions at the gaol. Therefore, Dennis had access to come and go at will. This position also meant he could get Brodie in as a visitor to see Heather at any time. It would be up to them if they turned it into a conjugal visit, as they would be locked in the cell in private for the duration of his stay.

As they walked through the barred gates to the prison, the iron grill slammed shut behind them and echoed throughout the internal void. Brodie jumped.

Dennis didn't know if Brodie's head was pulsating because of the sound or fear. He led the way forward, and soon, they stood at Heather's cell door. He could hear the handle of the crank loom turning and knew that she was at work. He had to ensure she would not be penalised for lack of progress due to the visit. Dennis and the guard waited until they saw Brodie embrace her, and he ordered the door to be locked. He would not ask what they did behind closed doors. He would probably be able to tell from Brodie's demeanour when he left. Dennis sent up a double serving of gruel to Heather's cell as Brodie needed food, too. It wasn't much, but it was certainly better than he usually ate. He had discovered that the lad lived off scraps discarded by the big houses. He would often eat from the waste put out for collection by the pig farmers.

Ken was amazed when they heard how Brodie had managed for years to scrimp and save enough to feed two. For Heather, to be a *pure* collector was only one step away from being a *tosher*. Dennis knew that such people existed, but for two orphaned children to have lived this way and then have their lives come to this was just plain sad. Both men had decided to assist them where possible. Typically, *pure* collectors and *toshers* were filthy; selling dog filth and sorting through human body excrement for valuables was disgusting. These were two of the worst possible jobs that needed to be done. Most just wiped the excreta off on their clothing rather than wash their hands. These two had always managed to stay somehow reasonably clean. Even Brodie's clothing didn't smell too bad most of the time.

Heather had told him of Brodie's rat-catching work and milking at The Green in town until he caught cowpox. Brodie had also told them of Mr Findlay and how he had allowed them to live in his cellar for over five years. That alone was a dirty place to live, but again, they had stayed clean. Dennis' stomach had roiled when Brodie described what Heather looked like when she tried leech collecting as a child. Having never had one on her before, they had no idea she was allergic to them. Each of the blood-sucking bites made each bite on her tiny legs swell to as big as cups. The itch was so bad that he had had to bandage her hands to stop her scratching. Eventually, Mrs Findlay took pity on her and permitted her a very hot bath. She boasted that she didn't cry even then. Most other children were regular thieves, but not these two. Brodie admitted that he had occasionally stolen, but only if he had needed food for Heather. He would not let her go hungry if he could help it. He was determined that she would never end up on the streets as so many other young women had.

After having left them alone for some hours, mid-afternoon, Dennis returned to the cell. The loom was whirring away, and he looked in to see Brodie turning the crank handle for her so she could weave. Dennis met his huge grin; he knew all was well. Even with their visits, she would get her quota done. Again, Dennis smiled; no, they were not a usual street couple.

~

With Brodie sober again, he was permitted to visit Heather every second day over the next month. These were the days Dennis was at the prison; however, he was now spending more time there than usual as Brodie assisted daily with cleaning the flats. He could plough through the work with two good hands much quicker than Dennis could. Dennis was informed that a load of convicts would soon be transported to Liverpool. Heather was on the list, and she would be shipped out in early December. He wanted the young couple to spend as much time together as possible, for it could be the last time, if not forever.

Five months after Heather's imprisonment, Ken was summoned by the superintendent. He said, "Sergeant, that young couple you befriended. I gather you have kept in touch?"

Ken was surprised that his boss had even remembered the situation. "Yes, sir," he replied. He didn't want to give much away or tell him that Brodie was all but now living with him.

"I remember that the boy mentioned a man they lived with and something about living in a coal cellar, I believe? Their story has haunted me. Tell me, what more do you know?" Superintendent Lamb motioned for Ken to sit, then leaned back in his chair and waited for Ken's reply.

Ken filled him in about his protégé. "Yes, sir, the man's name was Callum Findlay, and he moved to Sydney. Brodie said he runs an inn near the docks. The inn is called *The Whaler's Arms*, on the foreshore at The Rocks in Sydney." Ken wondered why the query.

"I have had news that the girl is being shipped out. I feel for this couple, Sergeant, and it's been weighing on my mind. How the hell can we get these young people out of the poverty cycle when they are paid such a pittance? I believe you when you say the lad can't find work. No one can; it's tough with no home, education, money, or family." He looked up and saw people moving around the office outside. "Shut the door, Sergeant." He watched and waited as Ken did as he was told. The grey-headed superintendent continued, "I'm retiring, and I have an idea. The laddie was absolutely right; there is no work here for them, but there is in Sydney. I can get her pre-assigned to Findlay at his inn, and if you can arrest the lad for some petty crime, I will send him too at no expense. They could make a decent life together out there, Sergeant."

"Pardon, sir?" Ken was stunned; his superintendent was really telling him to arrest Brodie. Did he hear this correctly?

His boss said, "You heard me. I can pull some strings and write a request that they are assigned to this man, Findlay. At least I'll write a letter of recommendation for Brodie. They have a convict quota for each place, but if they are marked as a married couple, they should be able to be assigned together, if not nearby." Ken's jaw dropped. Ignoring him, the superintendent continued, "It must be a crime worth transportation, but nothing too bad. Poverty is not a crime here, but illicit brewing is. That should do it. Arrest him for selling sly whisky." He wrote something on a sheet of paper and handed it to Ken. "Take this to the tollhouse; there's an impounded supply stored there. A small firkin should do it."

Ken looked at the note he now held. It was permission to collect a small keg of confiscated whisky from the impound locker. "Why, sir?" Why are you doing this for Brodie and Heather?"

His boss looked up at him, and with a twinkle in his eye, he said, "Let's call me a romantic." He bit his bottom lip before adding. "In reality, I've been sacked, well forced into early retirement, Ken. Although I have only been here for two years, Superintendent Alexander Findlater is replacing me. I can only presume it is for a reward for something he's done. So, this will be my swan song to the force." He chuckled and leaned back in his chair. "I suppose all your reports will need to be in prose from now on. Robbie Burns was his protégé, you know." He sighed.

Ken's eyebrow lifted with interest.

His head lifted a little as he said, "At least I can keep one couple together. We arrested her on their wedding day, which never sat well with me. It's not what I'd like to call a nice honeymoon. Warn the boy that he may have a tough time in gaol, but they'll be together once they arrive. It's the best I can do. I thought about sending him as crew, but he would have to come back again, so that won't work. Getting them assigned together as convicts means they could have a life together. I may even retire there myself, away from the poverty here. All these hungry Irishmen tear at my heart." He smiled at the stunned look on the policeman's face. "Don't dare let on. I'm so soft, will you?" Superintendent Lamb winked at Ken.

Ken was stunned. No wonder his boss wanted the door closed. "I'll get on to it. May I say it's been a pleasure serving with you, and you will be sorely missed, sir?" He gave his boss a bow of thanks.

The seated man gave a half laugh that almost sounded like a choke. "You may miss me, Ken, but I drew the short straw and lost. I thought I could change a rotting system; however, I'm being replaced by one of the boys who will toe a different line. I tried to kick against the traces, but now I have my comeuppance. I am determined to resolve this situation before I leave, so you only have four days to act. Let them visit each other before his arrest, but make sure they know there's a light at the end of the tunnel." He flicked his fingers to his head in a mini salute. He put his head down and started writing again. Ken realised he was dismissed. He walked towards the door. Superintendent Lamb said, "Ken, it's been nice having a caring, honest man to work with. Thank you. I'll see you tomorrow with the young man. I'll do the paperwork and letters now."

Ken saluted and clicked his heels as he left the office. With his shift over, he hot-footed it home. Knowing that Heather was due to leave on the convict transport soon, he had to get cracking. Brodie had not fallen prey to the booze for some time, but Ken knew what temptations the drink was when one was lonely. He feared for him after she left. His steps picked up the pace. Brodie needed to be sober to cope with this news. The first ten days after Heather's sentencing, the boy had remained all but insensible. Now and then, he had smelled spirits on his breath, but he had not been drunk again. Now, he had to explain to Dennis and Brodie what the superintendent's plan was. His head was reeling. He had heard of people bribing police not to be arrested, but to have orders to do the exact opposite stunned him. He even carried permission to collect a firkin of illicit whisky from the impound locker to be collected for Brodie's faux arrest. This situation really would take some fancy explaining, but he thought it was almost laughable, considering what was in his cellar.

Both took the news surprisingly well. The plan was set in motion. Ken would get the small keg and hand it to Dennis. He would take it home while Ken did his shift. Dennis would take Brodie to see Heather and say their farewells. Towards the end of Ken's shift, they had made plans to find Brodie with his illicit booty and arrest him. He would march Brodie into the superintendent's office without making too much of a scene. The ball would then be set in motion. Heather and Brodie would probably not meet again until Sydney, which could be a year away; however, once there, they should be able to be together.

Chapter 4   The Long Farewell

$\mathcal{I}$n the months since Heather had been arrested, Brodie had obviously had at least one conjugal visit with his wife.

Dennis managed to sneak in regular visits after Brodie's arrest several months earlier. They were in the same prison but in different wings. Dennis had permission to use any prisoners to do work. Brodie was in with the main overcrowded population of male prisoners. Many were charged with theft, as was Brodie; however, many other convicts were filthy and unsavoury characters. Brodie tried as hard as possible to keep clear of them. In the two months since his false arrest, Dennis and Ken saw them both at least once a week.

The winter passed in relative comfort for both Brodie and Heather. For once, neither had to worry about where to sleep or what to eat. Everything was provided. Admittedly, for Brodie, the conditions were cramped, but he was warm and not hungry. He had to work from six in the morning to eight at night, but he loved being busy; for once, he felt useful. He had often helped Heather to reach the quota Dandy convicts had to produce.

After one of the visits to Heather, Brodie was deathly silent as Dennis walked him back to his cell. "What's wrong, laddie?"

Brodie looked dazed. He turned and stared at Dennis, "She thinks she's with child. Sir, she's expecting a baby, and I won't even be there for her. She's going to have to go through it all alone."

He spoke quietly, but Dennis could tell that his heart was breaking. Brodie was gutted. He said with a husky voice, "She wanted us to be together that way to make our marriage real. It's real, all right." Brodie groaned softly as they walked through the echoing passageway.

Just before Dennis opened the doorway into the next corridor, he heard Brodie punch at the solid stone wall and say, "Damn!"

"How far along is she, Brodie?" Dennis wondered if this would mess up the transportation schedule.

Brodie frowned. "She thinks about three months, maybe a bit more, but it's possible she could be up to five months as that was when we... you know. Our first time together was a few weeks after my first visit to her. As our parents died when we were little, we know nothing about how this works. Some years ago, she talked with the cook from her work when she became a woman. She thought she was bleeding to death. Besides that, neither of us knows anything about making babies. We've never had parents to ask about grown-up things. We just did what we felt was right. I'd slept with her in my arms for years for body warmth, but always fully clothed. We were never together that way, not until we married. Sir, I'd never even kissed her properly until the day we pledged our troth in front of you." Brodie fell silent.

Dennis noticed his glassy eyes and anxious face.

A pleading question soon followed the look of utter confusion on his face. "Sergeant Dennis, can you get someone to talk to her? Explain some things and what to expect. She said she had been sick a few times a few months ago, but she's fine now. She should have told me weeks ago but was scared to do so. She doesn't even know if this is normal; she did say her gown is getting tight."

Dennis nodded. If what he said was true, Heather was further along than three months. "I'll get Matron to have a chat with her, Brodie. I'll try to come again tomorrow, as she's supposed to be shipped to the departure point later this week. If she's ill, they may defer her transportation. They don't like them with tiny babes on a transport ship." He scratched his head with his good hand. "I'll chat with Ken and see if I can delay your transportation too. Leave it with me, Brodie, but stay silent about it all."

Brodie nodded, but Dennis could see he was very close to tears. These two were children in grown-up bodies. His heart had gone out to them soon after he had met them. Life was so unfair for these two orphans. They had been the topic of conversation between the two policemen more than once.

~

Heather and Brodie's departures had been deferred until after the baby came. Ken and Dennis manoeuvred his paperwork so he could be at the prison for the birth of the couple's child.

Kenneth Brodie Dennis Stewart arrived in March, only four months after Heather realised her condition. She had fallen with child the first week they had been together when she was just sixteen.

Matron and a midwife had sat with Heather and delivered the child while Brodie and the two men waited outside her cell.

When Brodie took little Kenny in his arms for the first time, an overwhelming sense of love flooded over him.

Brodie and Heather were permitted daily visits for the week before Brodie was shipped out to London.

Ken assured him that Heather would be on the next ship available. The two policemen promised they would look after her.

~

The *Lord Lyndoch* sailed from London in April 1838, and one of the three hundred and thirty convicts travelling at Her Majesty's pleasure was Brodie Stewart. On Kenny's one-month birthday, the convict ship weighed anchor and left London for its long journey halfway around the world.

Brodie passed this time in a daze. This time, he had no whisky to drown his sorrows. He felt down and confided his melancholy to some of his new cellmates.

One, a beefy murderer named Dick MacClaren, decided Brodie needed some life lessons to toughen him up. The evil-looking man-mountain with blackened teeth had everyone cringing if they even happened to even glance at him.

Brodie knew no such fear. He knew he should have shut his mouth, but he didn't. It was now too late to worry about that as he had, for some reason, poured out his woes to the murderer.

Dick had roared with laughter at Brodie's revelations. "Yer reckon yer had a bad life, kid. My ma was a whore, and she sold me when I was a little tacker to be a pretty boy for some rich gent. I knifed him after the first time he used me. I fled, of course, and spent the next fifteen years being paid to knock off more ne'er-do-well coves and tidy up the world a bit. I'm scared of nuffin' and no one. I got nabbed when I hesitated knifin' a kiddie. I saw mysel' in that kiddie; I did. He'd done nuffin' to deserve a knifin' but fight back from a bloke trying to do him over. So I did the rotten uncle instead 'n' I got nabbed. They should'a hung me they should, but they said I can lug barrels on the docks for the rest of me life. So twitch wrong, and I'll make a shiv and do ya, too. Get it?"

Brodie still didn't flinch. He had heard such stories but had never met a man who did murder for hire before. He swallowed and regretted his innocent trust in this criminal. Life on board this ship would be no pleasure cruise.

Less than a month into the trip, the first signs of illness appeared on board. Doctor Obediah Pineo soon realised he had a significant problem with his hands. Smallpox was one of the worst of all the horrible diseases to occur on a ship, Scurvy followed as the second worst.

The first patient had a sudden onset of fever and a general feeling of malaise, which could be any number of illnesses. After a few weeks at sea, it could still have been anything, even prison fever, but to be careful, he isolated the man. Even with so many on board, they had room for isolating the sick.

The doctor moved all the prisoners to one end of the deck and put the sick man on a bunk by himself at the other end. He still had no idea what the diagnosis was.

Then, a few days later, the tell-tale skin rash appeared. The flat spots soon became lumps, which then became pustules of infectious fluid-filled blisters. Smallpox!

By then, the first patient's bunkmate was also showing symptoms, as did others around him.

The second poor man didn't complain until he groaned in his bunk with headaches, backache, and crippling abdominal pain. He was vomiting and had diarrhoea. His vomitus and excrement infected all the others nearby.

By the time they reached the southern tip of the African Coast, ten convicts had already died, and more were ill.

Brodie was lucky. The cowpox he had caught as a lad had given him protection. He had no idea about the connection until Doctor Pineo asked if any convicts had contracted cowpox in the past.

Fifteen men and Brodie raised their hands.

It was then he remembered his mother nursing Iain. He knew that she had also once had a condition she had caught from milking cows. She had not been really sick, but she had a few blistered spots on her.

Brodie and these fifteen volunteers became the doctor's helpers in nursing the infected convicts.

The murderer, Dick, was one of the sickest. Brodie nursed him personally as no one else would go near him. Though the man was a bully, he was still in need. Brodie did not fear him as Dick was almost unresponsive. He was just as needy as the others.

Due to the sickness on board, the captain and doctor decided not to stop for fresh food supplies in Africa. Plenty of food was still on board, as little had been eaten, and the recovering prisoners were not showing any signs of scurvy. Their gums were not bleeding, and their condition was good; considering what they had already dealt with, the ship sailed on. It may not have been granted permission to dock anyway, so rather than risk spreading the disease, the *Lord Lyndoch* sailed on.

Brodie relished the time above decks. He sat watching the wind in the sails and the fluffy clouds pass overhead. He was given extra time out of the cells due to his hard work with the patients.

With the danger of the pox behind them, the unwilling passengers were allowed a little more freedom. Fresh air and sunshine aided their healing.

Brodie knew there were passengers on board, and he had been told that, thankfully, none had succumbed to the pox. He noticed one of the men on the top deck watching him while he nursed Dick. Being busy with his duties, Brodie paid little attention to the well-dressed gentleman, but he saw him often.

Having just recovered from the pox, the recuperating convicts were weak and in need of sunshine. Many of the sixteen nursing convicts were tired to the point of exhaustion. Brodie certainly was. He had tended Dick and a few others with twenty-four-hour care. He was exhausted, and he felt awful.

The patients were now irritable, and their joints were painful. Soon, sunburn became a threat, too. Often, they fell asleep while on deck, and then some got sunstroke. Those recovering from the pox still had spots on their skin, and their tender flesh sunburnt quickly. Because of their lethargy, the doctor missed the onset of the next dire wave of illness that tormented the unfortunate voyage.

Although the doctor kept his eyes on the recuperating patients, it wasn't until they were two weeks beyond the African port that he realised he had another problem on board.

Scurvy hit with a vengeance.

The symptoms he had put down to recovering from the pox were similar to the beginnings of the sailor's cursed affliction, scurvy.

This time, even Brodie did not escape the illness. He had neglected to eat while he was nursing Dick. After long hours of nursing the sick convicts, he had put his tiredness down to exhaustion. Now, he was paying the price of such dedicated care. Along with many others on board, he found that the slightest bump would easily cause his skin to bruise. The tell-tale black spots soon appeared, and his gums soon started bleeding in earnest.

Nine more convict bodies were consigned to the deep before the pickled cabbage, lime cordial, and stores of wilted citrus fruit did their trick. Unfortunately, the disease had already done much damage to the health of the convicts. Brodie's life hung in the balance for some time.

Dick, who was now reasonably well, took over nursing Brodie.

The roles were now entirely reversed.

Brodie received the twenty-four-hour care he had given Dick.

Sydney meant the end of their journey.

Once there, they could access the fresh fruit required to restore their health. There had been no sign of smallpox for two months.

Many prisoners were still very ill when the cursed ship finally arrived in port. A third of the convict cargo was taken directly to the hospital and took weeks to recover. Brodie and Dick were two of those. Dick was still weak from the pox, and with healing sores still on his body, he was kept at the hospital but insisted that he still cared for Brodie. He watched over Brodie as the lad healed. He shadowed him whenever he could, protecting him from unseen dangers. Not that there were any, but Dick protected him anyway. Brodie had no idea why.

It took eighteen days before Brodie was well enough to be assigned.

He was now fit enough to work and was to be sent to Mr Gates's wholesale bond store at the docks to work as a labourer. Knowing that his conviction came with a letter of introduction from the superintendent to the major in charge, he had been assured that his four-year term would be served somewhere near Heather. However, she was yet to arrive.

Unbeknownst to Brodie, Mr Gates had been on the ship as a passenger. He was the cabin passenger who had watched Brodie hard at work nursing the fearsome convict. He discovered that the young man had volunteered to assist the doctor and noted the malnourished lad working as hard as he could to help the various ill patients under his care. He also noted that Brodie was the only one to attend to the huge tattooed beast who lay slightly away from the other convicts.

Soon after he arrived in Sydney, Henry Gates decided he needed a store-man to clean and unpack the new goods. He went to Hyde Park Barrack seeking a worker, however, he had one in mind already. On making his request, Major Downes mentioned that Brodie Stewart was an interesting case who arrived with a letter of introduction from the Scottish police superintendent. Henry had already asked the boy's name on the voyage out, so he figured it was the same hard-working lad. Therefore, Henry had him assigned to him. The warehouse he would be working in was all but next door to Heather's placement at the inn where the Findlays were. Henry knew them well as it was the only inn with a decent tipple. Once the paperwork was completed, Major Downes handed Henry the letter from Superintendent Lamb; then, he bent his fair head over the book again while Henry opened the screed.

Henry sat reading the screed in front of him and chuckled. Henry's mean reputation had evaporated when he found his long-lost daughter nine years before. His only child, Franny, had also arrived as a convict, and he had known of her existence for some years before meeting her only when they met did they realise they were related. He instantly recognised who she was due to her similarity to his long-lost wife. It was a long and convoluted story, but it gave him a soft spot for a love story. The discovery of his relationship with Franny opened his eyes to the needs of the convict women and young ones. Brodie and Heather's case would play into his plan perfectly. Once Brodie was free, Heather could be assigned to him. If the boy were as reliable as he presumed, he would employ him when his term was up.

Major Humphrey Downes ensured Mr Gates understood this particular convict's conditions.

Henry smiled. "Oh, I do, sir, and I'm willing to agree to them both. Please let me know when her ship arrives, as I'm sure Brodie will wish to greet his wife and son. As they are married already, I will prepare their accommodation today so that it will be ready for them." Henry grinned as he was somewhat lighthearted over the assistance he could extend to the young couple. Henry knew what it was like to be separated from his beloved wife.

He had lost his own wife because of his sea travel, and on his return, he found that his expectant wife had vanished. It took twenty years to find his missing child. This couple and their story tickled his fancy. Yes, he would assist these star-crossed lovers. He even knew Callum and Ishbelle Findlay well. He returned to the warehouse to arrange for the young couple to live in the vacant loft apartment above his warehouse, which was all but next door to Findlay's inn. It was about time these young people were given a break. The loft accommodation already had a bed, table and hob brazier, and they could furnish it from the damaged stock in the basement. But he would make sure there was a bed, blankets and a cot for their baby. They could choose the rest themselves.

On the day of Brodie's release from the hospital, his new boss collected him for work. The man's brusque manner hid his compassion for the young man.

It was a tough facade that Brodie was to discover was for the benefit of the other staff and convicts. Ten days after he started work, Mr Gates called for Brodie to follow him.

Brodie did and walked half a pace behind Mr Gates. Once out of sight of the warehouse, he turned and said to the young man. "Heather's ship has arrived, laddie, and I've just had word she is about to disembark. Her assignment is through to the Findlays already, and so is her accommodation. Sadly, her assignment is not with me but with Callum Findlay."

"Seriously, sir? My family are here?" Heather was here, and so was Kenny. Absolute joy shone through Brodie's demeanour. Suddenly, he was standing upright, and he had cast off the remainder of his melancholy.

Henry looked forward to their reunion with delight.

The *John Renwick* had sailed less than a month after the *Lord Lyndoch*. It carried Heather, little Kenny, and one hundred and seventy-one other women. The surgeon, Andrew Smith, had examined her, found her healthy and permitted her and her baby to travel.

Heather was only seventeen and had no experience with a child, let alone a newborn, so she was floundering and had little idea what to do with a tiny infant in a confined space.

The ship's surgeon saw her predicament and chose three women to share her section of the cell. They were a widow and her two daughters. They seemed to be clean and better behaved than many of the others.

Tracy, Phoebe, and Josie Newshum were all from the Newcastle-upon-Tyne area and had been convicted together. The mother, Tracy, had been arrested for public order infractions. Her two daughters were about Heather's age. They did not elaborate on what their charges were, but Heather soon realised that this lady would be able to assist her.

Heather knew that sometimes saying *no* to a gentleman in public was enough to be arrested. Tracy may have even slapped him.

Kenny, thankfully, was a placid baby and was, more often than not, asleep. Tracy soon had Heather comfortable with what a mother should do.
The four women also learnt, a few weeks into their journey, why the doctor placed them in the furthest bunks on the deck.

The crew made night visits to the women closest to the hatches. Heather had seen streetwalkers in Glasgow and now knew what their action entailed. She had enjoyed similar activities with Brodie.

Ten days into the trip, the convict deck was visited at night. Heather was feeding and changing Kenny at about midnight, and noises were heard that she recognised. The whispers in the quietness were men's voices and soon muffled, and she could tell that the women were fighting to be released and were being gagged. Knowing they were being abused, she felt horrible about not being able to do anything to assist. All she could do was to let the doctor know when he came to check on Kenny the next morning.

Tracy heard her and gently told her to stay silent. While the noises of abuse continued, they tried to settle back to sleep. Kenny had already drifted off while feeding. Heather realised it was much easier with him tiny than as a running toddler, as some other children were. Thankfully, he would not be walking for the entire trip, as he would only be six months old by the time of their arrival in Sydney.

The following morning, Tracy went to investigate the area where they heard the noises. Three very young convict girls showed signs of an attack and violation. They each had bruises on their throats and mouths. Two had split lips, and all three were subdued. One by one, Tracy hugged them and sent them to join them in the rear bunks. The three girls gathered their meagre belongings and moved cells.

Doctor Smith appeared late morning. He had come to check on the babies below deck. Their mothers were the first to be permitted into the sunshine.

Tracy told him what had occurred as he went to the back section of the convict quarters. He had heard noises from his cabin and wondered who was walking around mid-watch. He had his suspicions but remained silent. "I'll keep watch, ladies. Mrs Newshum, can you please keep silent until I investigate it? However, do not hesitate to let me know if anything else occurs. If it becomes regular, I shall lie in wait and find out who it is."

The doctor didn't take long to find out who the three prowlers were. The ladies below remained ignorant of their identity, but the doctor had retired fully dressed and had risen when the noises outside his cabin disturbed him.

He had gone below and seen for himself what they did; he was sitting waiting as the culprits emerged. He had already had a run-in with this particular man and knew he would have difficulty keeping the convicts below safe for the five months ahead. There would be willing enough participants if asked, but using a woman when she was insensible or fighting was abhorrent to him. He challenged the main culprit as soon as he could get him alone. The man laughed in his face, saying he would take what he wished from the whores aboard.

More and more women found themselves the victims of vile abuse when asleep. Over the months, three girls had fallen with child, and one young woman had been beaten unconscious for resisting, and the doctor needed to move her to the sick bay for some weeks.

Some of the other women willingly cavorted with one of the ship's mates. One regularly had a visit from a crewman and boasted about her extra rations, so others soon followed, and the night abuses of the younger girls slowly eased.

Doctor Smith confided in the quiet group at the rear that he knew who it was, and although he mentioned no names, he confessed that he had challenged him. He said, "There is little I can do now, but I will report him when we reach Sydney." He asked if they could write, and all four replied in the affirmative. "Keep a record of when these assaults occur, and I will file that document with my Surgeon's Journal. Here's a notebook for you; please keep what records you can. Dates, times, etc." He handed over a pencil and a small journal to Tracy.

~

The five-month trip passed with only one death on board.
Although conditions below deck were certainly not sanitary for a small child, Kenny thrived. They had survived storms, hail, blizzards and inclement weather. They had been becalmed and had sweltered in unexpected heat.

One still night, when Kenny was miserable, he was disturbing the rest of the women, and many yelled at Heather to keep him quiet.

The doctor had heard and escorted Heather and the miserable child out on deck. The night was inky black, and she would have been fearful of the sailors around her if the doctor had not been beside her. He knew the fetid air below was part of the reason for Kenny's behaviour. It stank below decks. As clean as he tried to keep it, the women in the front cells objected. They would kick over the slops buckets and generally misbehave. The convicts at the rear were a better class of women, including the younger girls who were now with them.

On this particular night, the doctor wished to show Heather something. He had felt sorry for this girl. She had never complained once and had been helpful to all the other young ones. He escorted her to the railing and told her to watch the bow waves.

Walking the decks at night, he had seen a sight that could only be described as miraculous. The sea exploded into fireworks with each slosh of the bow waves. He wished he could show it to someone, but all the passengers were asleep; then he heard Kenny crying and smiled. He silently descended the hellhole below and went to Heather's cell. "Heather, bring him upstairs and see if you can get him to sleep in the fresh air."

For some time, they stood in the stillness of the warm evening, watching the bioluminescent effervescence of the splashes.

In the quietness of the evening, Heather sang a little Scottish lullaby to her child. Even the rough sailors nearby stopped their chatting to listen to her gentle, soothing voice. Some may have even recognised the beautiful lullaby from their mothers.

Kenny quietened. The adorable baby snuggled into his mother's arms and went to sleep.

The doctor quietly told her to look up.

Heather did, and above her, the heavens exploded in another display across the night sky; light trails shot across the sky as though being chased from their heavenly realm.

The doctor's quiet voice broke the silence of the night. "This heavenly display only occurs a few times a year, and to have both miraculous events occur at once is something I thought you would like to see. I heard the child was awake and knew he was unsettled. I'm guessing he's teething." It was so dark he could not see her face or gauge her reaction, but the gasp she had uttered when she first saw both displays was reward enough for the kind doctor.

After nearly an hour on deck in the peace of the evening, he escorted her back to the filthy bowels of the ship. All was quiet below deck, and she soon settled to sleep, dreaming of the magnificent sight.

Day by day, the ship drew closer to its ultimate destination and the new life ahead. Heather dreamed of reuniting with Brodie.

On arrival in Sydney Harbour, Doctor Smith did a final inspection of the convict women. Heather had not let on about her pre-assignment to any of the others, as she hoped that Mr Findlay would want her, but she could not be sure. She knew things could be very different if they would not take her. Mr Findlay had been so kind to them when they were young. But five years is a long time, and they may not even be at The Whaler's Arms at The Rocks anymore. She had no idea what was ahead of them, but worrying was useless. Tracy had patiently taught her about having faith, and she had explained that her belief in Christ was vastly different to religious zeal. Tracy revealed soon after she met Heather that she had a Bible concealed in her possession. Over the five months on board, word had spread that Tracy could read and had a book. When they were permitted to sit outdoors, Tracy would read to anyone interested. She started with the Gospel of Mark and explained how Jesus fitted into God's plan of redemption for them all.

Heather was spellbound. Things she had heard in the church in Glasgow over the years began falling into place. She had not done anything that she thought was really wrong, but Tracy told her about asking for forgiveness for the little things as well as the big things. Heather had never pushed herself forward; she had always sat and waited and tried very hard to be invisible. Her dark red hair means she had fair skin, which burned quickly, so she and Kenny would generally be sitting under the shade of the sails. This fact alone made her easily overlooked by the more raucous convict women. Sitting out in the fresh air with Tracy and her daughters was a delight.

The doctor only allowed mothers with children on the open deck when the weather was fine. Otherwise, a more secluded area with higher rope railings was safer for the children. Some children were very active and would run around.

The doctor had told them that they should arrive in mid-August. However, they met a headwind on the last leg, and they were delayed a little. They eventually dropped anchor in the still water of Port Jackson on 27th August. The night before they anchored, the doctor called Tracy to the sick bay for a while. She passed over a journal that documented the nocturnal visits. Being so dark, they could not identify the perpetrators unless they spoke, but the doctor knew who they were. Her work was a virtual duplicate of his diary of their activity. He, too, had noted the captain's vile activities, and it would be filed on arrival. Doctor Smith promised he would not let this abuse pass unreported.

Four days after they anchored, a grand lady descended into the hell hole. The convict women watched as the well-dressed lady wandered around the convict women. "Ladies, I am the Governor's wife, Lady Gipps. I have come to welcome you. Would Tracy Newshum and her daughters step forward as the doctor has asked to see you, as he has an assignment for all three of you." Tracy waited for her to move from the steps and slowly walked towards the great lady. She dropped into a full curtsy. Lady Gipps nodded and gently touched her arm but did not speak to her. Tracy went up to see the doctor. Although the stench below deck was overpowering, Lady Gipps circled the entire deck and met the women individually. She met and spoke to every one of the occupants. Heather had seen fancy people like this when she had been at work.

Lady Gipps reached the last group. Heather and the other girls curtseyed deeply. One by one, she greeted them until she reached Heather and Kenny. "What an adorable child, my dear!"

Heather dropped a deep curtsy. "Thank you, ma'am. He was born just before I boarded, ma'am. My husband was allowed to stay until I gave birth. He cuddled him a few times during that week, and then we were separated again." Heather tried to stop her inquisitive son from reaching out for the grand lady's cameo and pearl necklace.

However, Lady Gipps reached out and took Kenny into her arms. "Follow me, dear." Still holding Kenny, she turned and walked away.

Heather had no choice but to follow. Lady Gipps led the way back on deck, where she passed her husband, who was descending to inspect the condition of the convicts below. They passed with a smile and a nod. Lady Gipps let the way on deck and nodded for Tracy and her two girls to follow them as she walked by. She said loud enough for the captain to hear, "The doctor wishes to check out this little fellow before you disembark." Dropping her voice, she said to Tracy's girls, "He wishes to talk to you ladies as well."

Kenny played with the regal lady's necklace and tried to bite it. Lady Gipps laughed as she followed the doctor. Heather, Tracy, and her girls walked in her wake.

Once in the sick bay with the doctor, Lady Gipps turned and questioned the four of them more about their accusations.

Tracy asked the doctor if he had handed over her journal.

He nodded his reply. The grand Lady said, "Be assured that I shall get to the bottom of this issue. I am fully aware that many of you have been convicted of petty crimes. However, I also realise that some below decks deserve to be there. If the Captain and his friends are the culprits, it shall be fully investigated. Now we must reappear." She flicked the cheek of the adorable baby in her arms. "He really is sweet, my dear."

Heather reached for her son. She said, "Thank you, ma'am," and gave the lady another curtsy.

Lady Gipps said, "Well, dears, it's time for the next stage in your life. Let us return to the deck. I hope you don't mind, but you three Newshams will be a Government House with me. I have a project in mind for you." They had reached the deck. The warm winter sunshine was lovely. Lady Gipps looked at Heather and said, "But, you dear..." She smiled, pointed towards the shore, frowned, and stepped away from Heather. She recognised the man who stood beside the lad on the dock. Heather was about to return to the hold when Lady Gipps again appeared at her side. "Dear, I do believe someone is shouting your name. Look, mayhap that is your husband."

Heather saw a familiar figure on the dock who was shouting and waving. With the cacophony of noise around them, she had not heard him. Her heart skipped, and she returned his wave. She had learnt to pray and hoped that the good Lord was listening. Could they live together here? Were the Findlays still able to take her? She would find out sooner than she realised.

Lady Gipps waited patiently and softly spoke to Heather. "Dear, let me hold the little one again while you get your things. You four will come ashore with me, and Heather, you can greet him before the others disembark. You are already assigned and will be permitted to be taken there by your husband and his master." The Governor was already on his way back to shore.

The almost silent girl beside her teared up and could only nod in appreciation. "Oh, ma'am, thank you so much for this and for everything."

"Go, child. I'll take good care of your darling boy." Lady Gipps sent

Heather below deck with a wave of her hand. Knowing she had to descend the rope ladder herself, she handed the smock-clad child to the doctor and proceeded to disembark as elegantly as possible in a long gown. Kenny was carefully passed down to her, and they sat awaiting Heather in the long boat.

When Heather reappeared, Kenny had not long been settled in Lady Gipps's lap in the small rowboat tied alongside the convict ship. She hugged Tracy and her daughters before descending the rope ladder. They would follow in the next boat. Heather's descent was not elegant either, but climbing down a moving rope ladder never was. Soon, she would be in Brodie's arms; that was the only place she wanted to be.

Brodie watched Heather's descent with his heart in his mouth. He could tell it was her as her dark red curls shone brightly in the winter sunshine. He watched unwaveringly from the moment she had appeared on the deck the first time. He saw their long boat was cast off and knew that soon she would be beside him. The oarsmen dug smoothly into the water, drawing her ever closer with each stroke. The ladies had their backs to the shore; the First Lady was keeping Heather occupied in conversation.

Henry Gates, Major Tim Hinds, and the tall blond Major Ned Grace stood behind the governor's carriage with Brodie. Henry had met these men years earlier, along with Major Humphrey Downes, when getting his first allocation of convicts. Majors Hinds and Downes had taken over Brodie's unique situation. Humphrey remained in his office this morning, writing up the passenger list.

Major Grace was based in Parramatta; however, as a friend of both Sydney soldiers and Henry, he was interested in the unfolding situation. Not many convicts arrived with a letter of introduction from their arresting superintendent. He had only known of one other, and that was Bill Miller in Parramatta. Ned was here today as he was on the Governor's security detail for this trip. He had just seen the Governor into the coach.

Henry suspected there was a lot more to Brodie's story. He hoped that, over time, the lad would trust him enough to reveal everything. For now, he could see the excitement mounting in the young man. He had been about the same age when he had married. He would ensure he would get to the bottom of the couple's story.

The small craft arrived at the dock, and Lady Gipps was assisted from the moving vessel.

Henry grabbed Brodie's shoulder and held him tightly, saying, "If you run towards the Governor's wife, her security guards could shoot you." There were six armed, red-coated soldiers waiting to escort her off the dock; two more were in the boat with the two ladies.

They noticed that Lady Gipps did not hand the child to Heather but turned and beckoned Brodie.

Brodie broke free from Henry's grasp and sped towards Heather.

Heather was already in tears; they were in each other's embrace moments later. Their affection for each other was evident; they had even forgotten their son in the First Lady's arms.

A quiet chuckle broke them apart.

Heather introduced her husband to Lady Gipps. "Ma'am, may I present my husband, Brodie Stewart? He has not seen Kenny since the week he was born."

Brodie had never met anyone of such esteem and bowed so low she may as well have been the Queen.

Lady Gipps could not present her hand as she still held Kenny, "Rise lad, permit me to hand you this adorable child. I can see you in him. I've rarely met a child so well-behaved and quiet."

Brodie relieved her of her precious bundle. He was astounded that his son had grown so much. He accepted his child willingly, yet he feared he would break him.

Kenny saw his mother beside the strange man and reached for her hand. She took it, and the baby's fingers closed around hers. He shoved a dirty thumb in his mouth and rested his head on his father's convict shirt. As long as his mother was within sight, he was happy. He had been passed from person to person for over five months in the filthy dungeon. Phoebe and Josie adored playing with the happy baby, and he was never left alone for long. The noise below decks didn't even worry the placid child. He would fall asleep, be it in a storm or in the silence of a becalmed sea. Therefore, he was content with having a stranger cradle him, little knowing it was his father. He had been particularly crotchety on only one night, and the doctor had come to their rescue and taken them on deck.

Major Hinds and Henry Gates appeared a little behind Lady Gipps. They would wait and accompany Heather to her assignment. The Governor had caught the earlier longboat and was awaiting his wife in the carriage. Ned stood at the door of the carriage.

Lady Gipps stroked the small boy's cheek, then handed him over to Heather. She left Heather in Major Hinds' care. "Let me know how you settle, dear. Tell Majors Hinds, Grace, or Downes, and I shall soon know."

Heather and Brodie gratefully curtsied and bowed as she departed. The Majors saluted. Ned hopped up on the back of the departing carriage. Lady Gipps took her leave along with her bodyguards. Her carriage moved off, and soon she was gone.

After the official carriage had left, Heather retrieved her bundle from the longboat and the small group set off up the road.

While still holding his son, Brodie walked with his free arm around her, unwilling to let her go. Finally, they were together once more. A brand new life was now before them.

Chapter 5   Life on The Rocks

$\mathcal{T}$he Whaler's Arms Inn, where the Findlays worked, was all but next door to Henry Gates' Bond store. Both businesses were in the hub of commerce on the waterfront. Henry's importation and export business was mainly for wholesale purposes. He would ship out whatever cargoes he could source and bring in whatever he could make a good profit on. Since returning from England, where he had spent over a year with his family, he had much catching up to do. He had not yet had time to travel to Windsor to see his business, store, and house out that way, but he knew his manager there, Des Bolton, would have all that under control. Des had worked for him for nearly his entire fourteen-year conviction, during which time Des had married a widow. Only six months before his term expired, he had broken his leg. When Henry visited a recuperating Des, he discovered Frances, his long-lost daughter. Franny was the image of her mother, his beloved missing wife. Their daughter had inherited his bright blue cornflower-coloured eyes. The proof of who she was occurred when she produced the only link she had to her mother. It was a unique, handmade tiny golden key. This item unlocked Henry's fob-locket. He had worn it unopened for over twenty years. It contained twin porcelain portraits of his wife and himself. He had been unable to gaze upon his wife's face in all that time. It was all the proof he needed. Not only had he found his daughter, but he could once again see the image of his beloved wife. From his previous life of loneliness, he now had a family with four adorable grandchildren with the probability of more on the way.

In the short time Brodie had been with him, the young man, whom he had watched nursing patients so diligently on the ship from England, had wormed a way into his toughened heart. When he had read the letter of introduction from the Glasgow Superintendent, it brought back memories of his own separation from his beloved wife. The placement was perfect because his bond store was beside the Findlay's Inn. Henry discovered that he had become a romantic in his latter years. Since receiving the news that Brodie had been assigned to him, he had set about cleaning up the unused storeroom on the top floor of the warehouse. The couple needed a break in life and could make their home there. Heather could work at The Whaler's Arms, and if the Findlays didn't want the baby with Heather, Brodie could keep Kenny with him at work until they could sort out a way for the child to be cared for during work hours.

That small problem worked itself out quickly as Mrs Findlay took over the care of the adorable baby. Heather's job was to clean the guest rooms daily and ensure the hot water was delivered to the occupied rooms each morning. The young couple settled into their new life better than Henry had hoped.

Callum Findlay was one of the few innkeepers who purchased the bottled spirits that Henry imported. He was among the few places selling real Glenlivet and Heatherbrae Scotch Whisky. It was bottled in Scotland and not diluted with the tainted water in Sydney. The delicious peaty water from the creeks in Callum's native motherland flavoured the Scotch with an aroma and flavour that could not be replicated. Henry adored a *wee dram* of the good stuff himself. So, whenever he was in town, he would head to Callum's tap room for a *wee* drink and a conversation with his Scottish friend. Neither liked the more robust flavour of the equally potent Irish Whiskey.

On his return from England, Henry had been surprised to learn that Callum was not the owner or licensee of the inn, only the manager. The owner was a man by the name of Mr Farris. He had never asked before. Henry had never met this man but now heard Farris was negotiating to sell the inn's license to an acquaintance of his, George Clark. Due to his endorsement, the Findlays were assured of their continued employment at the inn. Callum managed the accommodation as well as the taproom.

George had ideas to upgrade the status of the inn. He installed a billiard room, and Heather's new work included brushing the billiard table and ensuring the room was ready for use again that afternoon. Henry knew George had a lovely sailboat and wanted to rent it to people for pleasure. This vessel would be a new venture for the town.

Within weeks of Heather's arrival, the inn was to undergo a makeover, so she was free to stay at the warehouse and settle into their new abode until the refurbishment was complete. The loft apartment was the first time the young couple had shared a bed for an entire night as a married couple, and also, it was the first time they had been together as man and wife for more than a quick coupling. Neither had ever slept in a proper bed with a mattress, pillows and blankets. Henry had supplied their bedding from the damaged goods in the store. Their mattress was a torn kapok one, and the woollen blankets were water-damaged and had shrunk, but the young couple were delighted. They could sleep in each other's arms and know they would not be attacked or robbed while they slept. The roof over their heads didn't leak, and they were together. The needed renovation would take six weeks, and Henry and Callum told them to have a delayed honeymoon. Brodie still had to work, but Heather was always close at hand and usually assisted in the warehouse while Kenny slept nearby. As she could read and write, she helped Brodie decant the products. His writing skills had improved, but she still wrote better than he did. After work, they would walk around to Mrs Macquarie's Point past the newly constructed Government House. The old official house was now dilapidated after being hit by another violent storm.

Heather was nearly bouncing as they strolled towards the eastern side of Sydney Cove. "Brod, can you believe the wonderful life we have here? I can keep working even with a child, and Missus Findlay adores Kenny. I don't even mind being a convict compared to life back home. We have three meals daily and a safe, warm place to live." She twirled around in her joy, and her laughter made Brodie gaze at his wife somewhat lustfully. He wished they were back in the loft and Kenny asleep. But that would come later tonight.

~

Three months after Heather's arrival, when Kenny was nearly one, he was toddling between them on their evening walk. As much as Brodie wished to hold Heather, their son needed both hands held to walk, which he insisted on often. Soon, he would be fully mobile. Living so close to the water, they knew they must watch him carefully. Brodie had wondered if he could make some sort of leather harness for him and planned to work out something on his return home. Brodie had something on his mind and said to Heather, "Sweetie, when Mister Findlay first mentioned he was moving here, I wondered why he wished to do that. I had heard nothing but bad things about this place; however, I think I will write to Sergeant Ken and let him know how wonderful it is and that we are both well and happy, not to mention together. At the very least, I want to write and thank both Sergeants Ken and Dennis for what they did for us. The climate is certainly much nicer. It was worth the separation to be able to live here, not to mention how wonderful Mister Gates is to us both." Brodie sounded somewhat serious.

Heather gazed at her husband. He was now quite tanned and was filling out now that he was getting regular food. He was no longer the skinny street boy but was a very handsome man. Her heart would skip a beat with just the thought of being with him. "Brod, can I say that I love it here? I know I'm a convict, and so many others are complaining, but Brodie, we have found a safe place to sleep, food aplenty and we're warm. We also have each other and Kenny; in reality, it's all because of our two sergeants and what they did for us."

Brodie grinned, his perfect white teeth shining in the sunlight. "I know, it's good, eh?"

She nodded; Heather was wondering how she should tell him of her suspicions. Now was as good a time as any, "Brod, I have more news to add to your letter to Sergeant Ken. You don't have to add the details, but I missed last month's flow, and I think we're having another child. I haven't been that regular with my monthlies, but my breasts are sore too, and they were with Kenny."

A very unsuspecting Kenny was hoisted up into Brodie's arms. "Are you kidding?" he said as he gathered her to him with his spare arm.

Heather's dark red curls bounced as she nodded. She said, "No, I'm not joking, and yes, I think I am. I've been feeling ill the last few mornings, so I must be about six weeks along, possibly a bit more. It's when I started being ill with this young man. My flow was not regular back then, either. It's why I didn't realise I was expecting," she said as she kissed her son as he snuggled into her husband's arms. She stroked his cheek. "You, my boy, will have a brother or sister next year."

As Kenny's eyes opened wide, he said, "Sis sis."

Brodie chuckled, "Or brother."

Kenny said, "Sis sis," again. He had a friend who had a sister, and it was a word he had recently learnt.

They walked for some distance, enjoying the long evenings and the warm afternoons. Neither liked the hot summer days they had experienced recently, but the evenings were a delight. They had also had a violent spring storm such as they had never heard before. The misty rains that permeated the soul in Glasgow were nothing like the explosive cloudbursts and lightning shows in Sydney. They had been so frightened in the loft that they had slept in the basement that evening. If Heather were expecting again, Kenny would be nearly eighteen months old when his sibling arrived. Both had learnt a lot in the intervening months. If Brodie were still in Glasgow, he would soon be old enough to join the constabulary. Here, he was a convict and had not even bothered to ask if his conviction would preclude him from applying. He didn't even know if they even had a police force here. The soldiers seemed to do everything that was required in Sydney. He was determined to find out about a possible paid job as he had less than three years to serve.

After an hour in the warm afternoon sunshine, they slowly strolled back to the warehouse. There were still numerous people meandering around as they were. More ships were arriving into the harbour daily, and Henry had told Brodie that he was expecting another shipment from Hobart. He knew they would be swamped for some time after its arrival as the dry goods stock could not be sold until it was de-cantered from the barrels they arrived in. Some time ago, Henry realised that he could source some consumable goods from a warehouse in Hobart rather than wait for supplies from London or other British ports, giving a faster merchandise turnover. Brodie could not wipe the smile from his face. Even Callum noticed it. They had been invited for dinner and went directly there after their walk. Neither had other clothes to change into, even for an invitation out. They were already wearing their Sunday best anyway, as their daily work clothes dried. Both were in convict garb, as were many others in town. However, few others had the freedom these two did. Both carried passes from their assigned bosses that permitted them to wander the town. They could not go further than a mile from the waterfront, but neither wished to anyway.

Henry was a purveyor of many spiritous liquors, including bottled wines, porter and spirits. The tariffs were steep, but he still made a good profit. This latest shipment from Hobart also contained sparkling wines, plus twenty-three cases of good wines and nineteen cases of top-grade champagnes for use on the best tables of the colony. It also included over thirty-two hogsheads of brandy and more of rum. There was one cask of soda water, forty cases of claret, eleven hogsheads of red wine, twenty-four cases of liqueurs, thirteen dozen bottles of cherry brandy and sixteen quarter casks of gin. The bottles could be sold immediately, but many other barrelled liquors needed bottling. The remaining space in the cellar at the warehouse was nearing capacity. The rest of that shipment was sitting on the main floor of the warehouse. There were also two hundred cones of sugar, ten cases of starch, eighty bags of coffee, seven bales of assorted empty bags; over one hundred crates of tanned hides, one cask of glue; five hundred and twenty-six-cheese wheels; two hundred and sixty-two rolls of tobacco, five cases of fully imported cigars and two bales of sacks. The sugar needed to be sewn in a calico bag to sell, and each needed to be weighed and priced. Much work was ahead for Brodie, and Heather would assist after Kenny was asleep. They could easily hear him if he cried with the loft door left open.

Henry was now sourcing new small barrels from Hetty and Des Bolton along the Hawkesbury River. And the farm, Franny's old abode where she had met Hector, could now supply most of the six and eight-inch barrels he required. He had placed an order with them shortly before his departure to England. The three-hundred-six and eight-inch barrels could be filled with decanted produce and sold. Some people would bring their barrels back for refilling. Other larger-sized casks would arrive from various other coopers in the colony.

Brodie's main job was to decant or repack the bulk items that had recently arrived. These dry goods needed to be transferred into commercially saleable containers. Henry had worked out long ago that the more expensive items were better imported individually. Especially the Scotch Whisky, but the other things he purchased in bulk and then repacked. Henry wished that the hogsheads of brandy were smaller, but as he owned some ships and chartered others, goods were constantly being unloaded. Many inns purchased them as is. Brodie was kept busy.

Henry had been delighted in the discovery that Brodie could read and write, albeit not well, but enough to keep a journal of his work. With practise, he will improve. Each bag or container had the contents written on it, and Henry had shown Brodie that he only had to copy the spelling and how to weigh or measure out the required amounts of each item.

Brodie now thanked Heather for the many Sunday afternoons she insisted they practice his letters and words in the dirt of the river bank in Glasgow. He was one of the few convicts who could both read and write.

Working in a warehouse with so much food available vastly differed from his previous life. He learnt what rice, sauerkraut, which he had detested eating on the ship out, flour, and vinegar were. He had never had any of these before leaving Glasgow. Oats and barley, he knew, but other grains were foreign to him. He knew the difference between Scotch Whisky and Irish Whiskey, and it was more than using an 'e' in the spelling. Henry had chastised him for leaving the 'e' out of the Irish whiskey and explaining that only the Scotch one had no 'e'. He did not make the error again. Henry had also taught him how to weigh up bags of dry goods. Henry had purchased five thousand small calico bags, and Brodie set up a table with a holder for the twine, scissors and scales to weigh the dry goods. Each filled bag was stored again in the emptied barrels so the rats could not eat the packets.

Once, he had had nearly a week between finishing the last load and when the next shipment arrived. He had spent that time sorting through some damaged items in the basement. Henry had thrown these to one end of the cellar and then all but forgotten the dead stock. He said it would all be burnt as it was unsaleable. Brodie asked if he could sort it out and see if anything was worthwhile.

Henry laughed; to him, it was rubbish. He said, "Laddie, if you find anything usable, keep it, or sell what you can, and keep the money."

Brodie was astonished. "Sir, you mean I can really keep the money from selling this stuff? I can fix much of it, but so many poor people here will love these goods. Some of it we might even keep for ourselves, if we may."

Henry was relieved that not only was he able to get rid of the things in his basement, but it was a way of giving Brodie and Heather some money. A commodity they had never had access to before. "Take it, lad, as I say, it would otherwise go on a bonfire. I won't sell second-grade goods to anyone, as it would ruin my reputation as a purveyor of top-grade produce." His eyes locked on Brodie's. "You, conversely, are a convict, and I shall give you a 'letter of consignment' to prove the items are yours to sell. Deal, lad! I hope you make a lot from it, but I want the cellar empty as I need the space, so get rid of everything you can."

Brodie found that all the items in the cellar had a red mark on them to be kept separate from the undamaged stock. Henry's only instruction was, "Make sure that red mark stays on there and explain that these items are seconds." Brodie set about sorting through the contents below. There was a coopered bucket with a stave slightly pushed in. He had seen some coopering tools in the workshop upstairs, and amongst them was a staving fork. He had the coopered bucket fixed with the tools from upstairs in less than half an hour. After checking that it was watertight, he removed the red mark, and it was put back into stock. Another one only needed the loops tightened as they had come loose. Next were a few bolts of fabric. One had obviously been wet, and the water had siphoned up the material and left a bad watermark. Heather could sew, so he carried that one upstairs for their room. It could be made into all sorts of things, including clothing. He discovered there was a leaking firkin of olive oil amongst the items. A puddle of the sticky substance had pooled on the floor. Brodie decanted that into various small stoneware bottles for sale in the warehouse and kept the last bit for their own use. Rather than throw away the leaking tub, he smashed in the top and turned it into a plant pot. This became the first of many casks that he recycled.

Ishbelle Findlay was teaching Heather to cook. She had quickly learnt how to cook rice. She found it was quite similar to oats. Heather also learnt how to grow vegetables. Brodie found a few large barrels that had been partially damaged *en route*, and although the contents were gone, Brodie sawed them in half, making great vegetable gardens. There was no open grassy area near them, but there was a small deck overlooking the harbour. With another child arriving, they would need more nourishment than the basic scant rations they were given from stores. Brodie had grown used to potatoes, and they were permitted to keep the cut or squashed ones. They still sprouted, and he discovered these grew well in the barrels, as did beets and turnips. Before long, about twelve of these broken half barrels produced a bountiful harvest that supplemented their rations. Much of the excess they shared with the Findlays.

Over a shared meal soon after Heather arrived in the Colony, Callum and Ishbelle Findlay invited them to attend church. They attended the Scots Kirk with Reverend Doctor John Dunmore Lang.

Heather jumped at the chance. "Please, Brodie, we have not even had Kenny Baptised. Reverend Lang could do it for us."

Brodie leaned back and folded his arms defensively. "Heather, I have no problems with that churchy stuff, but count me out. I live a good enough life, but I don't need that repentance thing you spoke about."

Heather's face sank.

He could see that he had hurt her. He sat up straight in his chair. "You mean you really believe those church stories?" Brodie was flabbergasted.

Heather's eyes never left his face as she spoke. She nodded. "On the way out here, one of the other convicts, Tracy, with her two daughters, Phoebe and Josie, explained it to me. I didn't think I'd done too much wrong, either. As you well know, even my conviction was trumped up."

He could tell she was in earnest.

She continued. "So yes, Brodie, I believe it all. On board, we would sit on the deck reading Tracy's Bible, and she explained about God's love and His forgiveness. We need to repent, even if we think we've done nothing wrong."

Callum and Ishbelle sat listening. Both fully understood what she was trying to explain to her husband. They would step in if required, but it was better coming from her. Heather continued while Ishbelle bounced Kenny on her lap. "Brod, you know we only stole when we had to. We didn't even sleep together until we were married. We didn't lie, cheat, or hurt anyone and worked hard to live honestly. But sin is more than that. If we don't bring glory to God, that is sin, too."

Brodie nodded. He didn't like where this was leading; he knew there was a 'but' coming. He thought he might as well ask it himself. "Yes, but what?"

Heather could see he was getting uncomfortable. "Oh, yes, Brodie, there's a 'but.' The 'but' is God's judgement. All of us have to be judged when God is ready. We have to answer for our every thought, word or deed. None of us shall escape, not one. The good people will stand next to the bad in the judgment line. The bad convict will stand next to the free man, the abusers next to the victims and so on. Tracy said that there is only one way to, in essence, get a free pardon from that Judgement of God. Tracy recited from the book of John in the New Testament. I know it was chapter three, but I can't remember the verses. But it said God sent his Son to die, so we didn't have to. Brodie, that's our free pass, believing in Him. That's all we need to do. That and try to live a good life." She pointed heavenward.

Callum chipped in, "Heather, the passage is John 3 verses 15 and 16, *'That whosoever believeth in Him should not perish, but have eternal life. For God so loved the world, that He gave His only begotten Son, that whosoever believeth in Him should not perish, but have everlasting life'."* Callum smiled as he finished and let Heather continue.

Heather's face lit up. "That's it, Mister Findlay, thank you. Brodie, you spent your childhood looking after me. Just like we do for Kenny." They all looked at the adorable munchkin who had now fallen asleep in Ishbelle's arms.

"We all adore him, don't we?" Heather saw Brodie nod. "Well, as we made Kenny, God made us. He wants the best for us, so He provided this pathway back to Him." She turned to her boss. "Mister Findlay, am I saying it right?"

Callum smiled so much that his eyes twinkled. "You're doing fine, lassie. Laddie, we learn about all this in church. Reverend Lang is a good preacher, sometimes a bit longwinded, but he's easy on the ears. Many of our countrymen worship there, so it is good fellowship, too. To hear our mother tongue again is a delight as he often gives a bit of his sermon in Gaelic; to hear Reverend Lang speaking the love and forgiveness of God gladdens the heart. I had not thought about Kenny's Baptism; however, he needs to be brought into the family of God."

Brodie didn't really understand what he was saying, but if Heather wanted Kenny Christened, he would go along with it. "Fine, get him dunked. I'll come, but I don't really want to know much more about it." Brodie heard Heather give a quick gasp. He got up and walked out into the darkness; he needed to think over her words. He had tried hard to be good; he hadn't done much wrong. Why should he need to ask for forgiveness? She was the one who took the money. He had accepted it from her and would not have given it back, but she was caught.

As he left, she turned her head so he would not see the tears welling in her eyes. In all their years together, this was the first time they had disagreed on something. Ishbelle saw and put her hand over Heather's but stayed silent. "Did I say it wrong, Missus Findlay? Did I mix it all up?" Heather pleaded to her friend.

Ishbelle patted the hand under hers. "No, dearie, you said it very well. Brodie has just never heard it before. Give him time."

Heather felt in her sleeve for a handkerchief. "But he didn't listen to what I said."

Ishbelle replied to her question with another one. "Did you understand the first time Tracy explained it?"

The dark red curls bounced as her head shook. "No, she had to answer lots of questions for me."

Ishbelle stroked the cheek of the sleeping child in her arms. "Exactly, dear! Brodie has cared for you nearly all of your life. For you to believe something he doesn't know about is hard. His understanding will take time, as Brodie has never needed to rely on anyone in his life except Sergeant Ken and Mister Findlay. I foresee more conversations, but let's not push him. He needs to want to change. You can't push it on to him."

Heather could see Brodie standing at the railing outside. He was almost rocking back and forth but thinking deeply. He spun around on the spot. Their eyes met through the glass. Her tears flowed freely, but she didn't brush them aside. Brodie burst in the door and soon had gathered her into his arms. He didn't kiss her; he knelt, holding her tightly. "Heather, do you really believe this stuff?" She nodded against his shoulder. Both were totally oblivious to the two other adults sitting at the table. Brodie's following words could be life-changing for them all. "Heather, you have been going to church for a long time; I haven't been since I was a bairn. If you think we should do this for Kenny, then we will. If you think I must do this repenting stuff, too, then you will have to teach me more about it." It was the beginning of a new way of life for them all.

Over the time they had been in the colony, they would head to the Scots Kirk for Divine Worship each Sunday morning. Initially, Brodie had gone as he loved hearing his mother tongue on the lips of so many others.

Now he went because he liked what the man said. He was determined to learn what he called "God, church and repentance stuff" if that was what Heather wanted him to do. He wanted to know why it was important to her, the Findlays, and Henry. Brodie found that the singing at church was good, and he liked that, but the sermons were a trial to sit through. After some time, he began really listening to what Reverend Doctor Lang was saying. However, there was one thing Brodie knew Callum was correct about speaking his mother tongue without trying to hide his accent, which was a delight. Brodie was also surprised that his boss, Henry Gates, was a church regular and believed in Jesus and in being forgiven. Why was everyone so sure he needed to be forgiven? What did he need to repent for?

The Findlays, Brodie, and Heather often spoke their native Gaelic when together, but all were fluent in English too. Brodie knew that Heather's church in Glasgow was a Gaelic congregation and all sermons there were in that tongue. He had listed from outside sometimes. Although Dr Lang came from near Glasgow, he mainly preached in English as not all who came to church were from Scotland. It took a while for Brodie to tune his ear into the language that boomed from the pulpit. After only a few weeks, it was Brodie who decided that he wanted Kenny Baptised. From that day onwards, he was happy for Heather to answer his question about the faith. Soon, he admitted to her that he, too, believed, but he still had many more questions. Some he plied to Henry, more to the Findlays, but frequently, it was to Heather that he asked to explain some intricacies of her faith. He wasn't too sure how accurate her answers were, but her explanations were easy to understand.

Their second child, Isabel Heather, born in November, was an adorable cherub. Issy's head had the soft down of babyhood but showed she would have the same mahogany locks as her mother. At three-and-a-half months old, she could sit up by herself. The first time she did this, her giggle had them all laughing so hard that she toppled over backwards. This fall made her laugh even harder. Brodie was a father to two at twenty-two, and Heather was still only eighteen. Life was good, and they were happy in their small loft apartment.

~

Three years passed quickly, and by 1841, Brodie's time had expired. He was now free. Heather could be transferred to his care. He wondered if they should move, as Mr Gates had said the accommodation was for convicts. He thought that maybe he should find somewhere to live. But they were happy in the loft, and his boss had said nothing about them leaving. Just the opposite, as Henry started paying him for his work, which Brodie did well. It was the very first time in his life that he had ever had a regular income.

Chapter 6   Shanghaied

Soon after Brodie's release from his convict term, Henry Gates came for a visit from his house in Windsor. His family had finally returned from England. Henry had introduced his daughter, Franny, and son-in-law, Hector, to the resident couple.

Hector and Brodie had eyed each other warily. A few times, Brodie had caught Hector watching him as he worked; this had happened too often to be a coincidence. He finally asked, "Hector, have I got a fly on my nose?" Brodie queried with a tilt of his head.

Hector was not at all embarrassed being caught inspecting his father-in-law's employee. They had met occasionally in the warehouse, but he had never had time to watch him work before. Hector had puzzled over his father-in-law's new assignee, wondering why he looked familiar. But it had only come to him when Brodie challenged him. Hector said, "No, you remind me of someone, and that is my great Uncle Knox." Hector saw Brodie stiffen.

Brodie's brow creased into a deep frown, and he paled, then almost staggered backwards. He asked, "Who did you say?" It was not a common name for a first name. Brodie's voice was low and had a jitter to it.

Hector wondered about the change of attitude in Brodie. "His name is Knox Macdougal, with only one 'l'. He is my grandfather's younger brother. You are so like him that you could be him."

Brodie had broken out in a sweat. He tried to speak, but no words came when he opened his mouth.

"Brodie, are you all right?" Hector was now a little concerned.

Brodie's face was white, and eventually, he shook his head, then nodded. "My mother's father was named Knox Macdougal, and they spelt their name with only one 'l'. Hector, my grandfather, disowned Mama when she married Papa. Papa was only a sailor, but he loved Mama dearly. I only met my grandfather once. She had written to him for assistance when Papa had not returned from sea. Months later, he came and found her with child; he quickly realised it was not Papa's child, and his ire was such that he slapped her. I hid. Then he struck her so violently she went flying across the room, and he called her vile names. I could still see him, and he hit her repeatedly and called her a whore, then stormed out. I didn't know what that meant back then. I never saw him again, but I'll never forget him or his name." Hector saw his Adam's apple bobble as he swallowed nervously. "So, he's still alive?"

Hector nodded, and bile from his stomach hit his tongue. "Sounds like the same deplorable man, Brodie." He had had run-ins with his great uncle many times over his early years. "I met him again when we were there recently, and he hasn't changed much. My grandfather was of the same ilk. I asked him about his daughter, my cousin, Mary, and he told us that she had died long ago."

Brodie nodded, then explained, "Mary was Mama's name. I was ten when she died in childbirth. That was about two years after Papa left on his last trip. That was only a few months after my grandfather's visit. We had no money, and Mama did what she could to keep a roof over our heads. Only the landlord ever visited that way, Hector." He needed to explain to Hector that his mother was no whore. "Hector, the landlord, used her poorly. In hindsight, I realise he took the rent differently, and she had little choice as he forced himself on her as she was often covered in bruises after his visits. I lay her tiny child in her arms when she died and fled. I knew I would not get any assistance from him. I just left her and the dead baby in our room." Brodie had sunk onto a barrel as they spoke. Was Hector related? That thought struck him. "You're my cousin then, Hector? I didn't know I even had one. Mama never mentioned any other family."

Hector's eyes glinted with joy. "And this means that you are related to Henry in a roundabout way, too."

Brodie's jaw dropped open. He gazed at his cousin, absolutely speechless.

"Do I hear my name being bandied around, son?" Henry had come in as Hector spoke.

Hector smiled at his father-in-law. "You do, Henry. You met my grandmother when we were in Scotland. Do you remember meeting her brother-in-law just before we departed?"

Henry shivered. "Do I ever! Never been so glad to leave a person in my life. I gather he was very similar to his older brother."

Hector nodded and continued his not-so-subtle questioning. "Do you remember me questioning him about his daughter, Mary?"

Henry nodded, "Yes, you could have cut the air with a knife when you asked about her. Why?"

Hector said, "My cousin Mary was Brodie's mother. The word Uncle Knox used for her was unpleasant, to say the least." Hector repeated Brodie's story. "Henry, Mary and I were of a similar age, and I remember she ran away to marry a sailor just before I left for Kent in about 1814." He paused before adding, "Henry, Brodie is the image of Uncle Knox."

Henry stood looking at his young employee. He had only met the unsavoury man during his three-day visit and stayed as clear of him as possible, but Hector knew his uncle well. A raft of emotions played across Henry's face until, finally, a smile settled on his thin lips. With a laugh, Henry said, "Then you're family, Brodie. This also makes it easier to let you live here permanently. I've been wondering how to word it. This accommodation has only been convict lodging previously, but I can see you are both happy here. However, it comes with a condition. You will then become the official caretaker of the building, and that means a pay rise. If you now called me Uncle Henry, others would realise that there is a relationship between us."

Brodie was both delighted and horrified. "Sir, you don't need to do this. I'm still just Brodie, an ex-convict." He would have said more, but Henry's hand was now raised, and he stopped speaking.

"When you arrived, your conviction placement came with a letter of commendation and a full explanation of how you came to be convicted. Brodie, I know that Superintendent Lamb manoeuvred your arrest so you could be with Heather. He explained it all in his letter."

Henry had long ago told Hector of the unique convict that inhabited the loft in the store, but he had never told Brodie what that letter had contained. Henry was pleased that the Major in charge had chosen him for Brodie, or vice-versa. "Brodie, in the time you have been here with me, have you begun to believe in God's incidents?"

Brodie chuckled and nodded. "I didn't, but over the last few years, they have occurred too often not to believe. Sir, for me to have been assigned to you of all people. I feel the good Lord is in His Holy Place having a good laugh at me." Brodie flushed with embarrassment.

Heather came in from the inn with the two children. She heard men's laughter coming from the store room and entered to join them. Kenny slipped his hand from hers and ran to his father.

Brodie scooped his son into his arms and gave him a big hug. "Heather, my sweet, come and let me introduce you."

Heather frowned; she knew these two men well. She bobbed a curtsy to Henry and repeated the action to Hector but remained silent.

Henry lifted Issy from her arms. "Tell her, Brodie, and no more curtsying from you, young lady. I'm now to be Uncle Henry to you both."

Heather listened to their revelations, absolutely stunned. Brodie had a family? Her heart sank. Would he now leave her? Her eyes were wide with apprehension as the information unfolded. Her eyes flooded with unshed tears.

Brodie saw her expression. "Heather, what's wrong? This is good news, sweetheart. I have a family. We are no longer alone."

"*You* have family, Brodie," was all she could utter.

Brodie realised what she was concerned about. "No, my darling girl, we are married, so *we* are family, my sweet. And to top it off, Mr Gates, sorry, Uncle Henry has offered that we can stay here permanently but as caretakers too."

A gamut of emotions crossed her mind. "We can stay? Won't you leave me? I thought you might wish to go to Windsor when they left, and I would have to stay." A single tear overflowed from her violet-coloured pools of sadness.

Brodie's heart sank; did she really think they were more important than she was? "Oh my sweet, I'll never leave you. I'm here, aren't I? I came as a convict so I could be with you. Why would I want to leave you? You are my life and the reason to rise every day, the reason I draw a breath each morning."

Henry rescued him. "Heather, you are as much family as Brodie. He is Hector's cousin, which means some permanence for you both. You can call this home for as long as you wish. If things change, or either of you needs anything, come to either of us."

Brodie now had his arm around Heather. "Sweetie, this is just wonderful. For once, we are not alone. Although the Findlays knew my parents, they are not family, but he can corroborate my background, Hector."

Heather wished she knew more about her own family history. At six, she remembered very little.

Brodie knew that. They had often talked about their families to keep the remembrances alive. Each tried hard to keep their memories of their parents fresh, but over the years, their parents' faces faded.

"Sweetheart, I could write to Sergeant Donald to see if he could learn more about your mother. Annella is not a common name. If Ken is still in town, he might be able to find out something about your family. With the information about your father's death on the railways, there should be some way to track them. I don't know why we never asked him before." Brodie saw a wave of mixed anxiety and excitement cross her face.

The upshot of this conversation saw various letters wending their way to Britain. Hector had questioned them about her parents' details. Brodie and Heather penned a letter to Ken Donald. They had kept him informed about their growing family and life in the colony. Henry wrote to Hector's father, his friend, Sidney Grey. He had much pull in England and could find out more than most others could.

A third letter was from Hector, who wrote to his manager in Edinburgh with a brief outline. Hector had pumped Brodie and Heather for every scrap of information they could remember. Then, shortly before Hector's return to his family in Windsor, he also wrote the entire story to his grandmother, Sìle, or Lady Sheila as she preferred, in Edinburgh, Scotland. Hector informed his grandmother that her great-nephew was here in Sydney, and he had been taken under Henry's wing. He also wrote of the loss of the other children and the name of Brodie's father. After writing about Brodie's background, he gave her a project. She had to work with her agent, Mr Featherstone, to find any trace of Heather's family in Glasgow. He filled in with the scant information he had and the year of her father, Angus Anderson's, demise in 1826 in Garnkirk on the railway. Unintentionally, none of the men mentioned to the others of their intentions. The four letters caught the same ship and journeyed to Britain.

~

Life at The Rocks in Sydney was becoming rougher by the month. Drinking houses, inns, and sly grog taverns with no license opened quicker than the Government could close them down.

Heather was thankfully not exposed to many of the worst patrons, but Brodie didn't like her working at the inn, although the Findlays were so good to them both.

After discovering Brodie's connection to Henry Gates, he found his status in the area was somewhat different. Henry used the young man for more and more trusted roles. Even when a convict, Brodie had proven he was honest. With more staff in the warehouse, even the senior stock manager, Thomas Tibbs, now found that some of the things Brodie was asked to do were previously his jobs. Unbeknownst to Henry, Tibbs had been skimming from the weekly cash deposits taken to the bank. Now Brodie had that job, and the stock manager was not pleased.

Brodie's new status also ruffled other feathers. Commercial trade between Campbell Stores, Mary Reibey's Shop, and the other Bond stores on the foreshore of the colonial town was brisk. However, selling sly grog was frowned upon, if not downright illegal. Years before, many people were distilling illicit rum, and the Government crackdown on the sale of the fiery brew had caused a coup over thirty years before. This coup was known as the Rum Rebellion. Governor Macquarie had set a tariff on all alcoholic imports and sales, and that was still the case. That duty paid for the new hospital in town, so much so that it became known as the Rum Hospital. Brodie had learnt all about this soon after his arrival. He knew he had been convicted of this exact crime, and thanks to his ill-advised words on the convict ship, word of his conviction had filtered into the criminal community.

Brodie shunned the approaches to pass off or sell any illegal brew. He let Henry know each time this occurred. Soon, the offers stopped coming. Since his Certificate of Freedom had been granted, Brodie found more and more walls were going up against him. Soon, wholesale purchases from

Henry's warehouse were being affected. The big bond stores were still regular customers, but the smaller orders of decanted spirits from ale houses had all but dried up.

Against Thomas Tibbs's advice, Brodie decided to visit some of the surrounding inns and let them know of the new shipment of spiritous liquors and wines that had arrived. The ship that had brought them was due to leave on its next trip to China later that week. The current shipment also included spices, fabrics, dry foods, the most exquisite floor rugs and numerous other products. Brodie had hand-written a promotional list of products and spent most of the week circulating his leaflets into each store. He would finish his work and then deliver more and more brochures.

He had visited all the shops, and sales had already picked up. He had completed all but the last licensed inn diagonally across the road from the warehouse. The Hero of Waterloo Inn was one of the larger and older public drinking houses in the area.

As he entered the pub's door, he was determined to talk to Mr Findlay on his return that night. Mr Findlay had told Brodie that the two inns were some of the oldest. Since that conversation, he had heard rumours of press gangs operating from some of the waterfront inns. That had included the one Heather worked in; however, that was only in past years. He wanted to get her out of working in such a place but didn't know how to disappoint the Findlays. He was deep in thought about his wife as he wished to get her transferred into his care. The pub door swung shut behind him, and Brodie was welcomed by name and invited to partake of a drink. A new man he had met in church the Sunday before offered him a *wee dram*. Reluctantly, he followed the man to a table near the back of the room.

Brodie accepted as he didn't want to offend the man. He knew he worked on a ship Henry had chartered but wasn't sure which one. He could see the manager was busy behind the counter, so he sat back to drink the free tipple. Brodie had hardly touched the strong spirits since his binge when Heather had been first arrested. He had no intention of knocking this drink back in a single swig. This liquid was quite bitter but drinkable. He sat conversing with the man about what it was like to travel. He continued sipping his whiskey. Soon, the room was swimming around him. He felt arms circle him, but he was powerless to resist. He was eased through a small door next to the table, and the arms supporting him carried him into darkness. Whatever was in the whisky hit him like a ton of bricks. Brodie had collapsed and was now insensible and unresponsive.

The voices around him echoed in the narrow passage. "Quick, light the lamps; he's out cold. Get him down the passageway and onto the ship. With what I put in his drink, he shouldn't wake until they are well at sea tomorrow, if not longer. He'll have to be put in the hold. Someone should find him there soon enough. I dare say Gates will miss him, but I'm over Brodie's fingers being in too many pies. I need him gone before our shipment arrives."

Brodie was in his best work clothing, and as it was a warm day, he hadn't worn his overcoat. He was unaware that his hat had fallen off as soon as he was hustled through the secret door. He was unceremoniously dumped at the bottom of a long underground passageway. He was taken for some distance, and he lay, unmoving, on the damp sandstone for some time. His bladder had opened, and now his trousers were wet. Just on dark, he was again unceremoniously hoisted up. This time, Brodie was dragged out of a tiny door that led directly to a jetty. Within minutes, he was all but thrown behind a stack of barrels in the hold of a ship.

~

A shaft of light hit Brodie's face, and it was like an axe hitting his head. He had not felt like this since that horrible night years ago. He now heard faint sounds of footsteps above his head. Confused, he knew they lived in a loft; how could footsteps be above him? Nearly awake, he moved slightly so the light wasn't in his eyes. Sleep then overwhelmed him again.

By the time he woke again, his bed was moving. He was cold, and he felt wet. Heather must be getting up to attend to the children. With his eyes tightly closed, he listened hard. The sounds were not of his children or the familiar sounds at home. He opened his eyes and saw nothing, not even his hand in front of his face. Darkness surrounded him. The shaft of light had gone. Encased by blackness, he tried to stand up. The floor was indeed moving. He suddenly realised why he was moving. Wave after wave of horror washed over him. The all too familiar sense of being locked below deck hit him; he was at sea. His surroundings were not of his room or even a prison cell, but they were ribs of a ship. Henry Gates had taken him below decks on one of his chartered ships not long after his assignment. It finally registered to Brodie that he had been press-ganged, shanghaied, kidnapped, call it what you will, and he had been sent to sea. His legs could no longer support him, and he collapsed where he stood. Aghast at the realisation, he uttered, "Heather, my darling Heather, I'm so sorry. Oh, my beloved sweet, you will worry so." Blackness overwhelmed him again.

The next time Brodie woke, the movement was far more violent. Some cargo was shifting with the crashing waves, and he knew he had to get out of the hold, or he could be squashed. He felt his way from where he had been placed and stood in the shaft of light that had reappeared overhead. His head was clearer, and his brain was now cognisant of his situation, but he was filthy and very thirsty. If the sea were not salt, he would drink it dry.

He listened and waited until he heard footsteps overhead, then yelled as loud as he could. "Help, help, hello. Get me out of here!" There was no response from above.

He hunted around for steps or a ladder, nothing. He felt his way along the cargo; thick rope nets held each pile in place. On each mound was a coil of rope with a loop at the end. He remembered seeing the load on the ship that Henry showed him. It was stored like this. He also recalled that there was a long pole, like a boat hook, near the hatch. He felt his way to where he remembered seeing it, hoping one would be on this vessel. His fingers closed around the long rod. The layout in this ship was exactly the same, so much so that Brodie was sure he was now in the hold of one of Henry Gates' chartered ships if not the very one he had been on before.

With the pole now firmly in his hand, he waited until he heard footsteps above him once again. While yelling, he banged the hatch above him. "Help, help, get me out of here."

There was the rattling of the bolts, and soon, the hatch was drawn back. Sunlight flooded in.

"Thank goodness," gasped Brodie. Although the light blinded him, a silhouette of a body appeared above him.

"Shiver my timbers, who are you, and what are you doing down there, laddie?" the surprised man said.

Within ten minutes, Brodie had been hoisted from the hold and stood on the ship's deck. No land was within sight, but Brodie knew precisely where he was. It was indeed Henry Gates's chartered merchant ship, and he knew it was heading to China. He knew Henry was hoping to purchase some tea and other produce. Henry had refused ever to buy or even handle any opium or medicinal laudanum, but it was a frequently requested commodity. Brodie remembered him saying, "Laddie if you think your head hurts after an overdose of whisky, then never try that evil substance. Laudanum and opium both overtake your soul and eat your life away. You get a craving for it that is virtually impossible to shake." Brodie had been offered it once or twice but had managed to steer clear of it. He held his hands over his eyes, protecting them from the dazzling sunlight then he was ushered to the captain's cabin. As a stowaway, Brodie was roughly dragged to meet the ship's master. The Captain had his back to Brodie as he entered. Brodie knew he stank. He had been out cold for goodness knows how long, his throat was parched, and he realised he had fouled his trousers. His best clothing was now disgusting.

The bearded captain slowly turned to eye the stowaway. However, his face blanched. He had been ready to explode before seeing who stood before him. "Brodie Ewen blooming Stewart, what the hell are you doing on board my ship?"

Brodie sighed with relief; although they had not met, he knew Captain Robertson was one of Henry's special friends. The man's Scottish accent gave his identity away. "Sir, I was shanghaied by being drugged at an inn in Sydney. How do I get home?"

Chapter 7   Heather's Angst

Brodie didn't appear for dinner. He still had not returned by the time the children were ready for bed. Heather prayed with the children, tucked them in, and assured them that Brodie was safe. As she pulled closed the curtain of their small alcove, she leaned back against the wall and prayed. "Dear God, please let him come home." She could hear a noisy rabble passing by on the street outside, and as much as she wanted to go and tell the Findlays, she wouldn't leave the children alone, even for a few minutes. She had promised Brodie long ago that she would never be on the streets after dark, not even to go next door to the Findlays, but Brodie had never stayed from home before. Where was he?

The tallow candle was nearly guttering. She realised that he was not going to appear that night. She reluctantly crept into their cold bed. She only removed her shoes in case Brodie needed her.

When she woke at dawn, the sheet covering her was twisted, and the blanket had fallen in a heap next to the bed. She didn't remember falling asleep, but she obviously had done so. Brodie was still not home. All was quiet outside, and the children were still, so she tugged on her boots and crept downstairs. Hopefully, he would have come in late and fallen asleep in the store. She checked in various places before deciding to go and tell the Findlays that Brodie had not come home last night. She knocked on the kitchen door at The Whaler's Arms.

Ishbelle Findlay was up and cooking breakfast for Henry and Callum. When Ishbelle saw who it was, she was surprised that Heather didn't have the children with her. Admittedly, it was just past dawn, but she never arrived without them in tow. Ishbelle then noticed her tear-stained face.

Heather blurted out, "He didn't come home last night, Missus

Findlay. he's not in the store, and I can't leave the children long, but I need to go and look for him." Heather's words ran over each other in her distress.

"Oh, my dear girl, I'm sure he'll be all right." Ishbelle had drawn the weeping Heather into her arms. Over the girl's head, she pleaded with the two men to say something.

Henry was first to grasp that she was talking about Brodie. "You say Brodie is missing? For how long?"

Heather pulled away from Ishbelle and quickly explained that Brodie wasn't at home when she returned from the inn the evening before, and she had not seen him since that morning. She said she needed to return to the children and hoped Brodie would be home when she returned. Having now reported Brodie's absence, she departed at a run.

Ishbelle served the fried eggs, bacon, and slabs of crispy toast. The three ate quickly, and Callum and Henry then headed to the store.

Heather was busy getting the children up and dressed when they arrived. She had cracked barley porridge on the hob and served two bowls for the children. She left the children eating as she spoke to Henry.   Brodie still had not returned.

Henry decided to delay his return to Windsor until he investigated this situation further. He had come in to ensure the critical consignment of naval supplies had left on its trip to China. The ship, *The Spicy Lass*, had left port in good time. There had been a morning breeze that had taken the vessel out to sea just before dawn. Henry wandered out onto the back decking; he gazed over the harbour. He knew of the rumours of press-ganging, but this ship had a good crew and didn't need more hands. However, the seed was sown, as this was the only ship that had left that morning. He was still looking seaward when Heather and Callum joined him. Henry asked, "Heather, do you know the meaning of being *shanghaied* or *press-ganged*?"

Callum Findlay swung around to meet Henry's face. A long, drawn-out "No, surely not" was wrung from him.

Heather was worried. "Surely not what, Mister Findlay? I have no idea what it means, Uncle Henry." Heather looked mystified.

Henry took her hands in his. "Heather dearest, we shall check out every possibility first, but I suspect he was somehow loaded onto a ship, my ship, and sent to sea. If that's what happened, Captain Robertson will take care of him, but if not, we shall find him; don't you worry about that, Heather."

Heather's gaze was fixed on his. The meaning of what he said sank in. "He's gone? He's on a ship, and he's really gone?" Her eyes filled with salty tears and overflowed silently down her rosy cheeks. Her eyes searched Henry's cornflower-blue orbs for an answer.

Henry didn't have one.

Callum shrugged. "We don't know for certain, lassie. But I know a certain inn still has a secret passage to the docks. Ours had one, too, but I keep the door locked."

It was Henry's turn to be shocked. "Passageway? You mean there's a tunnel under The Whaler's Arms too?" Henry was surprised. "I had heard of such things but did not realise it was so widespread."

Callum explained apologetically. "I'm not sure it's widespread, but it made unloading boxes and barrels into the cellar from the jetty much easier. However, it also made getting illicit merchandise out of the Inn easier too." Callum wondered if the inn he was running had been one of the culprits of such deception over the years. He knew of only one other nearby inn with such a tunnel. He also knew that Brodie had irritated the manager of that particular establishment.

Hopefully, Henry was wrong; hopefully, Brodie had been accidentally locked in a store room somewhere. Hopefully, he would turn up this morning unharmed and laughing at his misfortune.

~

Henry and Callum hunted high and low for over two hours. Eventually, they were resigned that they could not check everywhere themselves, and Henry decided to report Brodie missing. On arrival at the barracks, Henry saw a familiar figure as he entered the courtyard. However, his friend was not in uniform.

"Hello, Ned, this is a surprise. Where's the uniform?" Henry had never seen him in civilian clothing before, let alone dressed in the height of fashion.

Ned smiled at his greeting. "Ahh, yes, well, that may take a bit of explaining, Henry. You know I resigned a couple of years ago, don't you?"

Henry's head shook. "No, I haven't seen you since, let me see, about '38 when I returned."

Ned smiled. "Ahh, yes, you claimed the unusual convict with a letter of introduction from the arresting superintendent. I believe he turned out to be Hector's cousin?"

Henry nodded again, grinning; mischief twinkled in Ned's glance. "Well, Henry, I married the reason for my resignation, and we are returning home. She's at The King's Arms awaiting my return. We married on Christmas Day."

"Congratulations, Ned; who is she?" Henry didn't even know that Ned was courting anyone.

Ned didn't have time to reply before they were interrupted. Major Humphrey Downes walked up to them from his office. "Did he tell you? He's a sly one, our man here. Sorry, Your Grace, I shouldn't be so flippant to a blooming Duke, should I?"

Henry spun around to face Ned again. "What's this, Ned?"

Ned had the courtesy to look somewhat embarrassed. He shrugged, saying, "David died, Henry, so you know what that means."

Major Downes said, "You knew he had a title? Why didn't you say anything?"

Henry grinned with a nod. "Not my place, too, Humph. You're the third son in your family, and I bet a few others are hiding here as well, like Hinds. You have a title, too, so button it, dear friend! Ned never expected to inherit, so it's like flogging a dead horse by harping on about it. I know Tim Hinds is also The Honourable something as well. He comes across as being cut from the same cloth as you two. Your friend, Jack Barnes, out along the Bathurst Road, has a lesser title too and a walnut farm in Kent that doesn't produce anything." He chuckled.

Humphrey smiled in acknowledgment that confirmed Henry's comment. Tim had intended to catch this ship home, but his wife, Madeline, had just delivered their third child. He had also just discovered he had inherited his father's ducal estate. They had kept that silent so far.

Henry continued, "I have been to Ned's resplendent residence at home, and I was introduced to his family on my last trip. His father's portrait is in the main gallery, and our friend is his image, and I challenged him when I returned in '38."

Major Downes stood looking from one friend to the other. "Well, I never! You could have knocked me over with a feather when he told me. Being an Earl's third son meant I knew I would join the army. So Hector is your cousin, too?"

Ned nodded and shrugged, slightly embarrassed. "I never expected to inherit, Humph!" Ned had come to say his farewells to Humphrey before Christina was up. His friend, a doctor, Gerry Winslow-Smyth, dropped the information that Eddie's wife, Jenna, and Christina could both be carrying twins. Consequently, he had not slept well. He had risen at dawn and gone for a walk; the last two years had been a whirlwind of change. He had told his friends Jack and Bea Barnes the reason for his retirement but few others. Now he discovered other friends already knew his status. Bill and Molly Miller confessed they had always known who he was and had never said a word. He had resigned his commission to be near Christina and assist her where he could. Last November, his godson, Eddie Lockley, had been attacked by bushrangers and rescued by Gerry Winslow-Smyth, one of his best friends from school. Gerry had come to tell him that his father and older brother were dead and that he was now the Duke of Gracemere and had been since he retired. Ned proposed to Christina that day, and they married as soon as Banns were called. This morning, he had gone for a walk to clear his mind and found himself in his friend's office. He thought he would say farewell before they sailed. Ned asked, "What are you doing up here anyway, Henry? And how's your protégé?"

Henry frowned. "Yesterday, he was well, Ned; however, he didn't come home last night. It's why I'm here." Henry retold his suspicions about Brodie being kidnapped.

Humphrey Downes noticed the concern once again return to Henry's face. "Do you think that's what's happened, Henry?"

Henry gave his attention to the Major. "Brodie is missing Humph, and I think he may have been press-ganged. You know him, and it is the only reason he would not return to Heather. She came to the inn this morning at dawn and told us. Callum and I have scoured everywhere we could, but there is no trace of him. Brodie has been door-knocking with leaflets, telling shops about our new product lines. I know he completed the shops and only had a few inns to go. We discussed his progress during our luncheon yesterday. Now he's gone."

Henry looked from Ned's face to Humphrey's. "I was wondering if you could send some assistance. Callum and I have done as much as we can, but we have not got the authority to enter buildings and search for him." Henry also knew that his friend could also solve one more potential issue. "Humph, if Brodie has gone, I don't want Heather alone in the warehouse. Can she be transferred to either Hector or even to me? Callum told me this morning that he has purchased the inn at Richmond; they will move on soon anyway. He was going to tell them this week."

"Consider it done, Henry, and I'll set about hunting for the lad." Major Humphrey Downes turned and clicked his fingers, then made an action with his hands.

Henry and Ned watched as they heard activity increase behind him.

Ned smiled at the once familiar scene unfolding. "I'd love to stay and help gentlemen, but I've been away too long. My wife awaits," he said with a sly grin. "I no longer have any authority, so I can't even assist with a search. Humph, Henry, I bid you adieu. Come visit when you are in England next." He gave a slight bow, doffed his hat, then turned and left them to get on with their work.

By luncheon, the search teams had scoured every building in the dockland. While heading to The Whaler's Arms, a vagrant waved Henry over to him. "Eh, Mister Henry, you looking for someone?"

Henry came at the man's bidding. He knew old Frank as a local drunk, but he had sharp eyes when sober. "Yes, sir, a young relative of mine has gone missing."

"Young Brodie?" Frank asked. As the man spoke, he couldn't see any discernible change in Frank's appearance, but the whiskers moved.

Henry nodded.

Frank dropped his voice as he spoke. "He's been going around handing stuff out for your store. Towards closing yesterday, he went in over yonder and ne'er came out." Everyone knew him as 'eagle-eyed Frank', but he didn't wish to be known as a snitch. He didn't see giving a relative of the missing boy news as snitching.

Henry nodded his thanks and flicked the man a shilling. Frank's hand shot out and grabbed the shiny coin in mid-air. The hobo headed towards a grog shop that sold cheap home brew rum.

Once out of sight, Henry turned towards Callum's inn. With this information added to Callum's earlier story about tunnels, Henry asked Humphrey's men to scour the Hero of Waterloo Inn. Henry now had an eyewitness. How long Frank would stay sober no longer mattered. Brodie was seen going in but not out. He was either still in there or had been smuggled out somehow.

Ishbelle and Heather had prepared a stew and damper for the searchers, and once they had all eaten, they planned to storm the inn across the road. Rather than return to the loft for their afternoon nap, the children were asleep in the small room where the Findlays slept.

The searchers were about to leave when there was a knock on the back door. Callum answered the door.

Frank stood there swaying. "Got more news, sir." His speech was now slurred; he was obviously somewhat drunk.

Henry stood beside Callum and held up a shiny gold sovereign. "If it leads to finding the lad, you get this. If it's a wild goose chase, you won't." He did hand him another shilling.

Frank grinned, his teeth black, and his breath stank of grog. "The entrance to the passageway is at the back of the taproom on the left. There's a secret door in the panelling. Push it twice, and it will open. I've just seen it meself, so I knows it's there."

Henry turned to Humphrey Downes with a nod and a raised eyebrow; this was the information he needed. Even if they didn't find Brodie, they could see what was down this secret passageway and find out where it led.

Frank was told to sit outside and await their return. He slid to a slouch on the deck and promptly fell asleep.

Twenty soldiers, plus Callum and Henry, crossed the road and burst into the inn. The Major led the posse, and Henry was hard on his heels. Henry watched the man in the red uniform push and poke his way across the wall. He had not even noticed that two burly soldiers now restrained the Innkeeper.

No patrons were coming to assist him, so the manager had little choice but to watch the activities of the soldiers.

Humphrey tapped and knocked. Halfway along the back wall, just where Frank had said, the wall sounded different. The Major pushed twice on the panel, and a door popped open.

Henry heard a groan; the innkeeper knew he had been caught.

The first thing Humphrey Downes saw inside the opening was a hat on the floor of the hidden passage. He picked it up and passed it to Henry.

Henry turned it over and checked the name inside. Brodie had carefully added his moniker on the inside silk band. Henry confirmed, "It's his. Now, I know he's been here, but I need to know what's below. He could still be there."

Sadly, it was not to be.

Brodie was gone. They only found a pool of urine at the bottom of the steps.

Henry had to take the news back to Heather. He would not allow her to stay in the warehouse by herself. It was just too dangerous for the children and her to be there alone until Brodie returned.

As Callum and Henry had mentioned earlier, he had sown the seed of the idea of him being shanghaied. Callum's new inn on the Hawkesbury River at Richmond would be ready for him in a month. If Heather moved to Windsor with Henry's family, they would still be close if she wished to visit them. Henry had already run the idea by Humphrey, who agreed with him.

With their discovery that Brodie had probably been kidnapped, Henry had to let Heather know what would happen.

The soldiers returned to the barracks while Major Downes, Henry, and Callum returned to The Whaler's Arms.

Henry paused to chat with Frank and thank him, and he flicked him the coin.

Callum had not opened for trade that day. He had more important things to do. He had known Brodie most of his life; he felt the boy's loss like the loss of a son they had never been blessed with. He and Ishbelle considered Brodie and Heather's two adorable children as almost grandchildren. He was gutted. He entered the kitchen first, and Heather saw his face.

She knew from his compassionate look that Brodie had not been found.

Callum pushed her down into a kitchen chair in case she collapsed. "Heather, I need you to be strong. We discussed our suspicions over luncheon. They have been proven correct. We discovered his hat inside the secret door, just where Frank told us it would be. There was no blood nor any signs of a fight. We can only presume that he was drugged with the offer of a free drink and then carried out. There was no sign of a struggle or that he was injured. Do you understand?"

She nodded. The tears welled in her violet eyes again, but as usual, she remained silent.

Henry and the Major entered. He had waited for Humphrey to join him. Henry had heard Callum's words. "Heather, there's far more to just Brodie being shanghaied. The Major here has been looking for evidence of smuggling and wondered where they were doing it from. When Brodie returns, and yes, dear, I'm sure he will, we will have the evidence and proof of their guilt and exactly what is going on."

Over Heather's head, Henry's eyes met Callum's; he gave a nod. Henry continued, "Heather, there's more. The Findlays are moving to Richmond. Callum has purchased an inn out on the river not far from our house, so dear girl, as of today, Major Downes has arranged your transfer to me for your last two years. It should be Hector as Brodie's next of kin, but I'm here to sign the paperwork."

Heather was overwhelmed. Brodie was gone, her life turned upside-down in minutes, and she had to leave their happy home, the very first home they had made together. It was too much for her. She had held in her tears, hoping and praying that Brodie had fallen and hurt himself or been locked in somewhere. He was her life. She intended to let him know that she was with child again. She had suspected her condition over luncheon yesterday when she had felt ill. It happened again today. Now, she felt the room swirling.

Henry caught her before she hit the floor.

She could hear voices in the room but had no idea what was happening around her. She was being carried but was unaware of where to or by whom. She just knew it wasn't Brodie. She was placed on a bed, where she curled into a ball and wept. She clutched her stomach. Hopefully, Brodie would be able to get home before the baby was born.

Ishbelle saw her action. "Are you with child, Heather?"

Heather was too distraught to answer. Her nod spoke volumes.

Ishbelle continued, "Brodie doesn't know, does he?"

This time, the dark red curls shook. "I was going to tell him last night, but he never returned. Missus Findlay, I can't do this alone. I have two years to serve; I don't want to continue without him beside me." Her gasping breath softly murmured, "He's my life." With those words, her tears overwhelmed her. Her gasping sobs shook the bed.

Ishbelle climbed onto the bed beside her and pulled her into loving arms. "Dearest girl, you are like a daughter we never had. You are not alone; we are all here for you. And now we are sure that Brodie has been loaded onto Henry's ship; that means he'll be back in about five months, dear, and that should be in time for your child's birth."

The Whaler's Arms did not open that day or the next.

Heather packed all their worldly possessions, and within a day, everything was loaded onto Henry's private ketch. Henry's house was fully furnished; therefore, the furniture would stay in situ. To kill time, she had just remade the beds with clean sheets, washed the dishes and brought up a busked of coal. The two children were excited that they were finally going on Uncle Henry's boat. They would meet their cousins again and live at their house for a while.

The following morning, they set sail, and Henry met Ned on the docks. Their ship was loading up, and they would set sail later that afternoon.

Ned's vessel, the *Sarah Botsford* that they were booked on, sat alongside Henry's small ketch, *Franny's Joy*. Ned Grace, now Duke of Gracemere, took his leave from the colony where he had spent twenty-two happy years serving the Lord as a Major in the 48th regiment. He had risen early again to check that all was well for his group to board. Henry had filled him in on Brodie's status. Ned shared his commiserations, but there was little he could do. He knew that in England, press-ganging was a common way to obtain crew. He didn't like it or agree with it, but it was lawful. "Henry, if he is, as you think, on your ship, then I'm sure he will be quite safe. God will have a purpose in this, so trust Him. You say the ship is heading north?"

Henry looked around to see if there were any ears nearby. "Yes, Ned, the ship is full of supplies for the Navy at Canton Harbour. Captain Robertson will deliver the cargo to Captain Belcher on the *HMS Sulphur*. *The Spicy Lass* is one of two merchant ships carrying supplies. *The Island Gypsy* left a couple of months ago with the first consignment. I've been guaranteed access to the harbours after the war. If the gamble pays off, it will be very lucrative."

"Trust you, Henry!" Ned laughed. "I've never known anyone who can be in the right place at the right time so often."

Henry chuckled and pointed heavenward. "It doesn't happen without prayer, Ned. You know that. The Government knows I will do my darnedest to deliver what they need and keep quiet about it. A few of us have offered ships to restock their supplies for our Navy. Captain Robertson owns *The Spicy Lass*, but I have her under charter permanently, and she is one of the two ships doing this route. I have a third chartered ship in the old Spice Isles, and she is on her way to England with a load of sugar cones, peppercorns, cinnamon and nutmeg, amongst other things. It will load up with whatever it can get there and return to Sydney. There are other ships, too, but they do the local runs." They sat and discussed the potential cargoes from Canton and other Chinese ports. They were each given notice that their respective ships were preparing to depart. They took their farewells and went their separate ways with a promise to catch up again.

Henry left with a request to visit the next time he was in England. It was an invitation that he had every intention of following up. Ned returned to the hotel to start the round of farewells from his friends and godson, Eddie. Ned again had not slept well, and his stomach was still churning with concern about the possibility of Christina carrying twins.

Ned had spent twenty-two years incognito in a convict colony; now, he needed to return home and don the responsibilities of the Dukedom. He now had to return and arrange for his wife of only a few months to prepare for a massive upheaval in their lives. He was about to depart when he dropped a bombshell on Henry. "I didn't get a chance to tell you that Christina is Sidney Grey's first cousin; therefore, Hector's too. Their parents are siblings." Ned doffed his hat and walked off.

Henry was reeling. He returned to the inn to collect his luggage. His store cart was waiting, fully loaded with all of Heather and Brodie's possessions. He threw on his bag and sent the vehicle to the waiting ship. Ishbelle had taken him aside and shared Heather's delicate condition soon after breakfast. So much had occurred in such a short time. The poor girl would be emotionally fragile, even if Brodie had not been shanghaied. How would she cope? Well, only time and care would tell. Henry would do what he could for her. He knew his daughter would be who Heather needed. Franny had also grown up alone and had been horrifically abused in her youth. He had had no idea she was related until only ten years ago. Since then, she has continued working amongst the young convict girls.

Henry knew that Ned, in his role as a Major, had been in charge of the women in the Female Factory in Parramatta. He would sort out the young and innocent girls from the streetwise ones and often send the severely violated ones to Hetty Walker's farm on the Hawkesbury River or, more recently, Henry's place at Windsor. He also had other safe houses scattered around the colony that he had used over the past twenty years. However, Heather and the children would be taken into his home as part of his family. There, she would find support. Ned's retirement had coincided with the last significant arrival of female prisoners, so the number of convicts was dwindling with the cessation of transportation from England into Sydney. Other towns were still receiving convicts, but Ned's work here had finished. He could leave with a clear conscience. However, his retirement had also meant that he had been able to court Christina on the sly. Once at home, he was sure God would open up new ways for him to continue his philanthropic work. He was keen to meet up with Earl Sam Garney and also his friends Perry and Katy White, not to mention catching up with two of his best school friends, Robbie and his wife Amelia, and her brother Jimmy. All were now retraining injured soldiers and various other minority groups. He and Christina looked forward to seeing what doors God would open for them to assist the underprivileged. Ned knew he would return to visit his friend Charles Lockley. But for now, his time here was over.

As Henry returned to the King's Arms, he realised Heather had less than two years to serve, and they would now be years spent in the arms of Brodie's loving family. Brodie was only thirteen years younger than Franny and treated like the son Henry had never had and as a younger brother to Hector. Ned knew Henry had wished to do much more for this couple, but Brodie had refused more than the basics. A safe place to sleep and regular income was more than this couple had ever had in Scotland. Yes, Ned was content that Heather would be safe with Henry, Franny, and Hector, and they would spoil her and the children. He returned to his wife with a spring in his step.

Chapter 8   All at Sea

*B*rodie took some time to get his sea legs.

Amazingly, the captain moved the first mate out of his cabin next door to him and scrounged through some of the stock of clothing on board, where he found Brodie some black canvas shoes, a jacket, a hat and a few waterproof items. Captain Robertson had explained that getting his balance would take a few days, and then he should settle. Brodie would have to do without any other clothes until they reached the whaling island of Guam. They would have a few different ports of call *en route* to their destination as they were in a hurry.

Now reclothed, Brodie scrubbed his own clothing and hung it up in his cabin.

As they ventured further north, with only men on board, the weather would be too warm for much attire anyway. As they neared the equator, they often stripped off their shirts and sometimes just wore their drawers, if that.

Captain Robertson watched the young man settle in. He was impressed that after the first day, the lad was unprepared to sit back and do nothing. He wished to pull his weight. Unbeknownst to the lad, he had ended up as an unwilling passenger on the way to a war zone. The captain had yet to tell the crew about that. Their destination and more would soon have to be revealed to the lad. However, a captive audience would not be a bad idea for what he had to tell the boy.

As they sat at the mess table on the first day, Captain Robertson introduced Brodie to everyone as Henry Gates's protégé. He then explained how he had come on board, although most already realised he was the stowaway. Brodie was surprised at his welcome by the skipper.

With a sinking heart, Captain Robertson sat and watched the lack of interaction of the young man. Brodie was sad and demoralised. He was stuck on a ship heading far away from his home.

A few of the crew had initially been press-ganged onto other naval ships. Some had been given a free ale with a coin in the bottom. Not aware of the implications, they drank the ale and then hustled off to board the naval ship, having 'accepted the King's shilling'. They had been conscripted into the Royal British Navy after their time on board the naval ships had expired; these men signed on to the merchant ships after the cessation of hostilities, having decided they liked the life at sea.

After that first meal, the Captain took him aside. "Brodie, we can't turn around to take you home as we are under a time constraint. We can, however, send a letter if we see another ship. So write, and we'll send it over on a wire if they draw alongside. Sadly, we have not mastered transferring someone from ship to ship unless it's really calm. However, if we see one heading south, we will rig up a wire and send you over if the seas are calm enough. In the meantime, write her a letter."

Brodie's demeanour bucked up instantly. "Truly, sir, I'll do that! I just want my wife to know I'm safe." He sat thinking over the offer. "Is there really no way I could leave the ship?"

A flicker of concern crossed the Captain's face. He knew from personal experience that leaving home was hard enough, but to have been ripped from it would be crushing. He dared not reveal all yet. "No, lad, not unless it's calm enough to transfer you safely. I won't risk your life, Brodie. Few ships head north from Sydney; most come up via the South. Those that do come this way will take longer than our return trip as they call into other islands."

Brodie's face showed his disappointment.

The Captain asked, "Do you pray, lad?"

Brodie felt ill knowing he was stuck on board. "Yes, sir. I didn't, but my Heather showed me its worth. She believes wholeheartedly, and once she explained, well, I do now too."

He had started when he had first heard the young lad was married. "Then you're lucky." The Captain laid back in his seat. "At least that will give you some strength to sustain you. I imagine that it will be some five months before we return."

Brodie blanched. "Five months, sir? Five full months?" Both hands ploughed through his hair. "Five blooming, long months!" Brodie was shattered. "Ahhhh," he screamed with absolute frustration.

The Captain nodded, "Unless we get a tailwind and can find a return cargo, it could even be longer. This area is not on the normal trade routes, so we're unlikely to meet another vessel heading south. Your only hope is Henry Gates' other chartered ship, *The Island Gypsy*. She will be returning to Sydney after a resupply trip like us."

Brodie nodded but didn't ask more questions. He was aware of their destination but had not voiced that. That night, he set about writing a long letter to Heather.

Over the following weeks, Brodie settled into shipboard life. He asked the Captain for a role as a junior seaman and wanted to be taught the ropes.

Within a few days, he was almost one of the crew, only with a cabin to himself. He discovered that the majority of the sailors slept in hammocks below decks. Brodie's willingness to help where he could and to pull his weight soon negated any hard feelings the first mate had, as Adam Steers had given up his cabin for him.

Adam was stunned when Brodie made an offer. With a second bunk in the room, Brodie insisted that Adam move back into his own cabin.

The two became friends quickly. Brodie took pride in his work on deck and threw himself to any job that needed doing.

Adam discovered that Brodie was not good at heights when he made it up to the first spar on the main mast and showered those below with yesterday's dinner. Adam refused to let him up in the rigging again.

Brodie didn't mind this at all. Even standing and looking upwards turned his stomach, so he took his turn scrubbing the deck, a job most of the crew hated. He did it without complaint. He learnt to use a fid to splice ropes and how to make eyes into the thick ropes used on the deck. He even volunteered to sew the canvas sails when they tore. His neat sewing of the sale corners was an artwork in itself. He learnt to use a sailmaker's palm to push the thick needles through the canvas.

As the seas were relatively calm before they reached Guam, the Captain permitted Brodie to take a daylight shift at the helm.

Adam was on hand if required, but the seas were light for most of his watch. The timing for that venture had been good, as by the same time the following day, a local storm had blown up. A sail had been sighted in the middle of this squall, and hopefully, it would be their sister ship. However, it was too rough now to transfer Brodie, but his letter could still be sent home.

Brodie went below decks to retrieve his missive while Adam followed to collect the blue and white checked *rendezvous* flag. He would hoist it immediately, so if it were *The Island Gypsy* and came within sight, it would make way and join *The Spicy Lass* for a mail swap.

No one knew who owned the ship on the horizon as it was yet too far away; all they could see was a square-rigged ship sail, but it was the right size and shape. No flags were identifiable from such a distance.

From up on the poop deck, near the Captain, Brodie watched it draw closer. "Sir, is there no way I could transfer ships?" He descended to the quarterdeck and pleaded with the man.

The Captain shook his head and swallowed almost guiltily, then commiserated with the young man. "Laddie, your life is far more valuable to Heather in one piece. If I let you try, you will probably drown or get crushed. The risk is far too high. They are only about eight weeks ahead of us, but they can take your letter home to her. She will know you are safe."

From the lower deck, Brodie lost sight of the other sails.

Adam shinnied up to the spar on the main mast and clipped the checked flag onto the mast rope. He hoisted it up and tied it off when he yelled, "Brace, brace, brace." From his elevated height, he could see a set of rogue waves approaching.

On the quarterdeck, they saw a monster wave approaching.

The Captain yelled, "Cor blimey, grab something, Brodie! Wrap your arms in one of the ropes and hold tightly."

All the crew grabbed something to hold.

The Captain called a mate over. "Help me hold it, Sam." Sam and the Captain held the wheel tightly as the set of rogue waves approached.

The ship crashed through the mammoth rogue wave and shuddered down its back.

The deck was awash, and even the poop deck was drenched. The scuppers drained like horizontal waterfalls.

A second, larger wave approached and repeated its punishment to the wooden ship.

Then a third one, larger again, towered over them and crashed over the decks, hitting the vessel at the first crossbar on the main mast just below where Adam was still holding on for his life. Foam from the third wave enshrouded the entire ship in white water and threatened to send it to the deep.

Brodie thought that they would surely capsize. They didn't.

The vibrations shook everyone. Amazingly, those seconds of warning from Adam saved the lives of all on deck.

Brodie's need to send his letter had saved them all. Somehow, the ship made it through the triple danger safely.

Adam called again from the mast. "All clear."

The deck was still draining all along the scuppers. Sections of the gunnels had smashed. Anything that had not been tied down was either overboard or sloshing on the deck.

"Woah, they came out of nowhere," a drenched Brodie muttered as he unwrapped his arm from the halyard line. He knew holding this rope was safe as it was the one he had used to lift the sails, which he had learnt were called sheets. Other ropes dropped the sheets, and more still changed the angle of the spars. He had already pulled the wrong one more than once, so he was careful which rope he had grabbed.

The Captain released his white-knuckled grip on the wheel. Sam had already returned to his rostered duty; he had been passing at the right time. With his hands still holding tightly to the wheel, the Captain turned to him. "Brodie, are you all right?"

Brodie nodded; he would not admit that his trousers were not just wet with seawater. He presumed others were in a similar situation.

Captain Robertson turned to Brodie. "And that is exactly why we don't transfer passengers in seas like this. I may not be a landlubber, but I don't like the surprises of those waves."

The Captain actually hated rogue waves. He had seen them before in this area and had these at the back of his mind when he told Brodie of the dangers. He had often wondered if they were caused by earthquakes undersea. The seas seemed to settle as the other ship drew closer, but the Captain still refused a human transfer.

Adam sent one of the men up to the crow's nest at the top of the mast with a spyglass. He wanted to know if the ship was *The Island Gypsy*. Adam waited until the call of "Ship ahoy, it's her" came soon after.

Their sister ship had caught sight of them and changed tack. She, too, had been hit by the waves, but they were now heading directly for them.

Not long after, Brodie watched the practised crew prep the ship for coming alongside.

The Captain's call of "Tacking" saw the smooth transition of the ship's course change.

Brodie had discovered just how dangerous the tacking in a square-rigged tall ship could be. Brodie had learnt that "Tacking" went one way and "Wearing" turned the other. This tactic meant the ship followed a zig-zag course into the wind. Thankfully, the wind had dropped a little in the hours since the waves had hit.

The two vessels were now aiming for each other.

Brodie headed into the ship's mess and added a note to the back of his letter.

Heather, my darling one,

I am sending this with Henry's sister ship, The Island Gypsy. *Sadly, it's too rough to transfer me. Know I am well, and you are loved and missed. I will be home as soon as I can, but it will be some months yet. I love you so much, and I am so sorry that this has happened.*

Brodie.

Brodie kissed his message before he placed the letter into the waterproof oilskin satchel the captain had given him. He no longer needed persuasion not to attempt transfer in these seas; getting the letter across would be hard enough. He rolled up the pouch and buckled the straps closed.

Adam said that when they were close enough, he would send a rope over and transfer the letter.

Brodie stood at the rail on the poop deck at the vessel's stern and was well out of the way of the activity below. He was well above the waterline so that he could see everything. He watched the approach of the tri-mastered ship.

From the quarterdeck below him, Adam arranged a small harpoon gun with a large coil of thin rope.

Brodie watched, intrigued. "You're going to shoot it over?"

Adam chuckled. "Sort of, Brodie; I shoot over the rope right across the bow. They tie it off, and then we transfer the satchels. The long rope gives flexibility for manoeuvring. In seas like this, it is dangerous at best. I don't think the Captain would attempt this for anyone else, Brodie. You seem special to him, but don't even consider asking to go yourself. It's just too treacherous."

Brodie needed no second warning after the drenching from the rogue wave earlier. The ships adjusted their course to sail alongside each other in the still-rough seas. The manoeuvre took much skill from both skippers. Adam fired the harpoon and hit his target over *The Island Gypsy's* bow.

Brodie watched as the manoeuvre took place. The oilskin pouch was duly delivered, and another was sent back over. Brodie later found that it contained a letter for the Captain with changed delivery instructions for his cargo. The naval fleet had moved into a different harbour further north. With the transfer now complete, they pulled the rope back. A cheer was raised from both ships, and they resumed their courses.

With Brodie's missive now *en route*, he relaxed a little. There was nothing to do but stay out of the way.

For the next week, the wind was accompanied by scuds of rain. The deck was no longer a pleasant place to sit, so Brodie, Adam, or one of the other crew spent time playing chess in the mess room. Callum had taught him this game in the evenings when they had joined them for meals.

The trip to purchase stock at Canton in southern China would take another week. Brodie settled into the remainder of the voyage with the attitude that what lay ahead was an adventure. As he was here, he may as well enjoy it. The temperature was dropping as they headed north. Brodie had bought a few clothes in Guam, but it had been hot there, and while wandering around the clothing market, he had not thought of warm outfits. Thankfully, the Captain had come upon him near the ship's chandlery and outfitter and showed him what he would require.

Captain Robertson had sought him out to let him know about his passenger status. "I checked if any ships are heading south, and none are. So you're stuck with us until the journey's end. Sorry, laddie, but I'll keep you safe." He gave him money to purchase what was needed. Now outfitted in whalers clothing, Brodie felt that he now at least looked the part of a sailor. Back at The Rocks, he wore his best outfit promoting Henry's stock. Those items had nearly been consigned to the deep after he had fouled them, but he managed to douse them in seawater and clean them up the best he could, but they would never be worn to church again. At least they covered him. He now also had long boots and a full-length oilskin coat. There was a Russian astrakhan cap with ear muff flaps, and seal-skin flocked gloves. With a big smile, Brodie returned to the ship with both arms full of his new attire. A week out of Guam, the Captain requested Brodie's presence in his cabin-cum-office. "Brodie, you have never asked where we are heading and why. I'm unsure if you lack interest, but I will tell you anyway."

Brodie replied almost too quickly, "Oh, no, sir, I just felt that I'm such an encumbrance to you. Anyway, it was none of my business to enquire. I know that we are heading to China, but not why."

"Ahh, well, in that case, you may not like our destination. I presume you know of Henry Gates's ability to be in the right place at the right time?" The Captain knew Brodie was the store's caretaker, but he didn't know how much he knew of the Gates empire.

"I know what comes in and out and from where. I've not seen any come through from China for some time, so I thought the country stopped trade." Brodie had worked that out after he started working in the warehouse years before.

The Captain leaned back in his chair and looked at the young man standing to attention before him. "Relax, Brodie; I just thought you should be updated with our travels."

Brodie did relax. "Thank you, sir; I would like to know. Are we going to buy a cargo?"

A smile hovered at the corners of the captain's mouth. "Not yet. At least, I don't think so. You see, we have supplies on board destined for the resupply of the British Navy in Canton. However, the letter that came on board when your letter left told me the Navy had moved from Canton to Chapu near Shanghai. It is a few days' sail north of our original destination."

Brodie's eyebrows raised, but he remained silent. He was obviously listening. The Captain's bearded lips moved in an intrigued smile. They were vaguely familiar, but he could not place why.

The Captain continued. "We should arrive mid-May, which is about a week away. That will give us time to transfer the cargo and head south before it gets too cold." The Captain looked around to make sure the cabin door was shut. He chose his following words carefully. "Lad, we're heading into a war zone. A skirmish occurred in October last year, and the Chinese counterattacked the navy. My letter warned me that things were getting unstable again. March saw a skirmish, which the Chinese lost. Brodie, I plan to keep you close to me if it does. I want you to shadow me and my movements, as I may be unable to give instructions." He swallowed nervously. "Have you ever fired a musket?"

Brodie's mouth went dry. He shook his head in reply. "A war zone, sir? Really?" His thoughts went to Heather and their children. "Do you think it will get that dangerous?"

With his hands firmly placed on the desk, the Captain leaned forward and said, "Oh, I hope not, but stay vigilant. However, Brodie, if I say 'down,' I need you to drop flat onto the deck without questioning why. Understand? Seconds can save your life. Some of these Chinamen are pretty good shots. They did invent gunpowder, you know, so they know how to use the stuff."

Brodie was now nervous and shaking. "I will, sir, thank you, sir."

The Captain now stood. "Now, coffee? I have some on, and it's piping hot." The Captain walked to a small hob stove in the middle of the room and poured a strange-looking pot. The steaming hot black brew smelled delicious.

"Thank you, sir, hot and sweet, if I may." Brodie had access to this delicious brew at the warehouse.

The Captain was obviously going to say something else but had decided against it. With the news that had just been delivered to Brodie, he wished for his coffee to be laced with something more substantial and numbing. Yet the potent bitter-sweet brew hit the spot. As he sipped the scalding concoction, Brodie wondered how safe it was to have a coal stove on a wooden ship.

The Captain had said he would keep Brodie close to his side. He was determined to return him unharmed to his wife and children. He meant it.

Chapter 9   Hawkesbury River Bound

Callum and Ishbelle helped Henry in packing up the apartment in the loft. They had Heather and the children boarding *Franny's Joy* by luncheon the next day.

Heather was numb.

Overnight, her life had changed. Kenny and Issy were excited to be going on a sea trip. They were both on leather harnesses held tightly until the ketch arrived in Windsor on the Hawkesbury River. Of course, the much shorter trip could be traversed by road in less than a day, but with the luggage they carried, it was better to go by boat. At least on board the ketch, the children and Heather could walk around. Heather would have her hands full with two small children in a bouncing carriage.

Franny's Joy weighed anchor and set off out to sea. The trip would take a couple of days, but the cabins were comfortable, and the weather was good. Heather had made a tearful farewell to Callum and Ishbelle; however, they assured them they would visit from Richmond. Heather stood waving to Ishbelle until they passed the headland, which blocked the dockland from view.

As the sleek ketch had the wind behind her, she cruised along at about seven knots as her sails were full as the wind was brisk. From leaving Sydney Heads, it would take another hour or so before they turned westward into the Hawkesbury River at Barrenjoey Headland. The waves in this area could be unpredictable, so Henry ensured the children were safe indoors.

The first few hours of the trip were always the most trying.

Sometimes, they were downright uncomfortable with huge waves crashing over the bow. Today, they had only occasionally washed over the starboard side; hence, he needed to keep the children secured indoors.

Henry ushered her to the galley and sat the three Stewarts at the table. "Heather, children, we will be there later tomorrow. Until then, Heather, I want you to rest, relax and put your feet up. Children, you will come with me while your mama rests."

Henry sent Heather to her cabin while he placed a pile of books on the table and said he would read them stories. At the bottom of the pile, he had added *Jack and the Giant Killer* by Lee and Rusher. He asked, "Who's for a story?" The children whooped with joy.

He was planning to read Kenny the first story in the series as soon as Issy slept. If not, he decided to read that one to Kenny at home, as his younger grandchildren would love it.

Issy chose a thick book with a picture of a girl running on the cover. Henry smiled at her choice. "It looks like we are going to read *Cinderella*. Settle back, and I will tell you the story."

In unison, the children said, "Thank you, Uncle Henry." They settled down to while away the hours.

Henry had installed a comfortable armchair in the galley so he could lay back and read as the ketch sailed up the river. With a small child tucked under each arm, he started the story.

Heather was lying on the bunk in the cabin; she could hear Henry's voice reading to the children. Knowing they were safe, she closed her eyes to listen. The lapping of the waves on the hull soon lulled her to sleep. She fell into a deep slumber after staying awake for most of the past two days.

Henry read for a half-an-hour. Issy dozed off quickly, and he carefully lifted her onto one of the galley bench seats. With her now quiet, he put aside the book. He would finish that later for her.

Henry took *Jack and the Beanstalk* from the top of the pile. Kenny sat spellbound. He could hardly keep still as Henry read about the beans and the enormous plant that had grown from them. He found it hard to keep the child quiet as he kept asking questions.

When Henry reached the part where the giant was chasing Jack, Kenny was jiggling in his seat, squealing with glee. Henry was finding it hard to read as he was chuckling at the boy's antics.

"Does Jack get away?" Or "Go on, Uncle Henry, what happened to Jack? Read faster, please, go on." Kenny was now on his knees, pleading with the storyteller to hurry.

Henry was shushing the boy. "We'll have to wait and see, Ken. Shh, listen." He finished the story with sound effects and actions. He forgot about the sleeping angel near him, and the clomping of the giant's footsteps woke both girls.

Heather appeared in time to take Issy to use the chamber pot in her cabin. Henry wouldn't let the children use the head at the bow for ablutions, as the size of a small child and the larger head hole was a potential danger. Henry had built his ship after he had found his daughter; he hoped she would travel on it occasionally, which she did, so he made the toileting facilities in the bow into a small private area. As Franny and Hector had small children, he ensured he had facilities on board for them, too, hence the chamber pots.

Heather still had sleepy doe-eyes from her nap but was feeling much better. Henry greeted her with a smile as he finished up the story.

Kenny was bouncing with excitement about the demise of the great giant. He gave a full round-up of the story to his mother.

Issy sat cuddled in Heather's arms as Kenny related his version of the exciting episode. The young girl was still groggy from her nap and hid her head in her mother's neck.

The skipper negotiated the craft through the turbulent waters of the river mouth, and they rounded the headland and were now heading west up the mouth of the Hawkesbury River.

As they traversed the wide river mouth, the waves had calmed. The passage upriver would now be smooth sailing.

In some areas, the tidal current caused a bit of chop on the water, but the rugged hills passed by with amazing swiftness.

Henry pointed out the various bays and headlands as they cruised up the river with the incoming tide. The children stood on the seats in the main cabin and watched the sights as they passed. The two-day cruise had restored Heather somewhat. She still became weepy when she thought about Brodie, but Henry assured her frequently that she was no longer alone. That fact was evident when Windsor came into sight.

The ketch had twisted and turned along the river for two days. Henry smiled as he noticed Franny waiting at the jetty with Hector and their brood of six children. Joey was back from England for a year before starting at the University in Edinburgh. He had pre-enrolled for a double degree in Divinity and Classics but had taken a year off before starting. He could have started in September that year but wished to spend some time at home with his family.

Henry had previously been unable to spend much time getting to know Heather, so, with time now available, they sat chatting. He said, "Heather, you have not met all my family at once, but they look keen to have you stay with us. Look, they have turned out *en masse*. Hector, you know, of course, but Franny doesn't like the towns and rarely leaves home. All their children are currently at home, so you will get to meet them all."

Heather noticed the exuberant group sitting on the embankment.

Henry waved, and soon, many hands were fluttering in the breeze. The ship pulled into the private jetty and soon tied up.

Franny kissed her father and then turned to Heather. "Dear girl, welcome! I won't commiserate with you as Brodie will return, of that I'm sure." Franny was holding her little three-year-old girl, Etta.

Heather bobbed a curtsy, "Thank you, Mrs Grey, no sorry, my Lady."

Franny reached out and grabbed her hand. "We're cousins, Heather; first names, please. I'm just Franny or Fran if you like. Either will do."

Heather nodded, but her heart sank at the lady's kindness. "Thank you, Franny." She had already teared up. "Don't be too kind to me, or I'll go to pieces. I'm only just holding myself together as it is."

Franny smiled, then chuckled. "You're doing well, sweet girl. So, I won't tease; come on, cousin, let's settle these little ones."

Heather nodded. Thoughts flittered to what Brodie was up to, and she was worried that he didn't know she was with child. Her mind was only half on the children.

Henry's home, *Honeysuckle House,* was the most magnificent place she had seen. It sat high above the river and overlooked both directions from the verandah.

Over the weeks ahead, Franny would sit on the verandah with Heather, talking over their past. Both girls had arrived as convicts but with vastly different backgrounds. Franny had been brought up in an orphanage, as just after her birth, her mother had died from injuries sustained in an accident.

Franny detailed her history. "Heather, I was born with no knowledge of my heritage. The only identifying item my mother had on her was a small gold key around her neck. It was this unique item that Papa later identified as the handmade key that opened a fob locket containing miniatures of my mother and himself. The place and date I was born fitted my mother's disappearance." She went on to tell Heather about the abuse that had only threatened Heather. Franny added, "Heather, I carried those emotional scars for years, and it wasn't until Hector talked to me about God's love and forgiveness to those who abused me that I could move forward with my life." Franny paused, then continued, "We have six wonderful children. Joey sadly must return to England soon, but Alec will remain here and take over Papa's farm at Bathurst and the business. If this child I carry now is a boy, he'll get his share. The girls will have dowries from both grandpapas. When we married, Hector was serving a life sentence for murder, of which he was later cleared. We had nothing but each other."

Heather had wondered how Hector had met Franny; now she knew. Henry had already told her that Hector now had a title and was Lord Glenview, as he was a Scottish Baron. But she had no idea that he, too, had arrived as a convict. More than two decades later, his conviction was overturned when the real culprit of the so-called crime confessed that it had been an accident. In the meantime, Franny and Hector had met and married and had three children by the time she met Henry.

Heather had released a small gasp. "Franny, when Brodie and I married, we also had nothing. We still have very little, but having each other and that is enough. I was arrested the day we married by declaration. We had not even had time to be together as husband and wife. That came about two weeks later in gaol."

"Oh, Heather, that's simply awful!" Franny gasped.

Heather revealed the entire saga to her. "A nice retired policeman friend of ours would bring Brodie into prison and give us some private time together in my cell. We decided to risk it and be together that way. I must have fallen with Kenny the first time or two we were together. He was born less than ten months after we married. We named him after a friend of Brodie's, Kenneth Donald. He is also a policeman, and without his help, I don't know what would have happened to us. We married with them as witnesses." Heather gently dabbed at her tear-filled eyes. "Franny so much happened to us; we have Sergeants Ken and Dennis to thank. They arranged that Brodie could get arrested for a minor crime and sent out at no cost to us. They even allowed him to stay near me while Kenny was born. They also arranged the letter of introduction that was given to your papa."

Franny was stunned. "Brodie arrived with a letter of introduction? Truly?" She chuckled. "No wonder Papa has always treated him as special. He never said a word to me, although I bet Hector knows."

Heather waxed lyrical about Brodie. "Franny, Brodie looked after me when I was six; he was only ten. We lived on the streets in Glasgow. I slept in his arms and shared blankets in a secret hide-hole we had found in a back street. It was cold and tough, but it could have been much worse if it had not been for the Findlays. That's who I was assigned to at The Rocks. Anyway, a few months after we found ourselves alone, we were allowed to move into their coal cellar. We lived there for years. They gave us a bowl of hot porridge each morning, and if there was any stew left over from the inn meals, we were given that at night. I was a *pure* collector when I was little. Believe it or not."

Franny asked, "What's that?"

Heather said, "I collected doggie poop for the tannery, and Brodie worked as a chimney sweep until he grew too big and was burnt." She teared up thinking of him. "Franny, I owe my life to Brodie many times over. I would have died within that first week but for him. I love him so much! And not just because he kept me safe."

Heather sniffed in such a delicate way that Franny could have heard it in her grandmother-in-law's sitting room.

Heather continued with her story. "When I found out Brodie had been taken away, I couldn't breathe. Thankfully, Uncle Henry was there and caught me as I fell. Next thing I know, he has had my conviction transferred into his care for the last two years of my service, so I have moved here with you. Please don't consider me ungrateful, but I only want Brodie back, Franny. I need him; our children need him," While gazing at the peaceful river, she rubbed her stomach with sadness etched on her face.

Now that Franny had heard her story, many of the small snippets fell into place. "If Papa said he'll be back in five months, that is spring's beginning. I'm due in October; what about you?"

Heather answered politely, "About the same, maybe a bit earlier; I'm not quite sure as I'm not regular. Brodie doesn't even know."

Franny reached out and lovingly patted her hand. "Don't dwell on it, dear; it will only make it harder. Just be assured that he will come home to us all. Papa said that Captain Robertson is a wonderful man."

They had finished drinking their tea in silence.

Franny said, "Come, let us get to work. I have an order for something that might interest you. If you are like me, you won't like idle hands."

Heather nodded.

The girls set to work basket weaving for the shop in Windsor. Heather was a novice at this new skill but had five months to kill and thought she might as well put it to good use.

The maid, Lynne, was the wife of Victor Champion, the groom-cum-footman, and she was supposedly employed to teach the children to read. She had arrived free with her sister and been adopted by the family. The girls had married the two male staff and settled with the family. Lynne and Victor had one small child, a sweet little girl named Frances, whom everyone called Frankie. Lynne, too, was expecting another child in late July. Her sister, Maggie and her husband, George, were due to return from Bathurst next month. They, too, were having a child. Maggie had arrived in the colony in an interesting condition after her stepfather had abused her. He had violated her while their mother lay dying in the next room. Then, to salve his conscience, he had bought tickets for the sisters to Sydney and banished them both. Henry's coachman, yardman and groom, George Darcyville, had married her shortly before she gave birth. Maggie had presented her new husband with twin girls only days after their extraordinary marriage. He had given them his name and adored his girls. This child she carried would be his first. George and Maggie shared their time between Henry's farm in Bathurst and the house in Windsor. Their first child was due in August. So, the household would swell with four new babies in a matter of weeks.

Honeysuckle House was always a hive of activity. A couple of years before, Henry Gates had wished to have more help in the house without losing his guest rooms, so he built a new staff building; it was where Lynne and Victor lived. Maggie and George had a three-bedroom suite next to their apartment, and all the remaining ground-floor rooms were two-roomed units for men. The top floor was all single rooms for female staff. Henry had placed a lockable door at the top of the stairs to keep the girls safe. Victor and George's old rooms above the stables were now for single male staff, of which there was only one gardener. So he had the run of that floor to himself.

Henry had a beautiful, airy studio built for Franny adjoining the stables. Heather followed Franny inside. Franny was a vine weaver and basket maker. Her work made much mess and needed tubs to soak the rattan and vines to make them pliable for weaving. There were stockpiles of cane, other piles of cut branches for the sides, a box of assorted bases and many other stacks of tools, dried rushes, vines, etc. It was like a craft person's wonderland. Heather had never been in a position to have time to do anything for pleasure.

Ishbelle Findlay had taught Heather how to sew on a button and do darning, but Heather had never woven anything before. She saw the huge spools of twine lined up on a shelf on a wall. It was to one of these that Franny picked up and walked to the workbench.

Franny said, "Heather, I have been asked to weave or knot some decorative covers for some bottles. I wish to make a few designs and see if the customer would like them." Franny cut about a dozen lengths of twine, measuring each to ensure they were the same length. With a few deft movements of her fingers, she had a sample bottle sitting in a knotted cradle and knotted an open-weave pattern up the side of the bottle."

Heather sat spellbound, watching how easy Franny made her work look. Each row of knots was evenly spaced around the base of the bottle. In less than twenty minutes, the project was complete. For the neck of the bottle, Franny flattened out the remaining string and wound it flat around the neck. Then, she glued the ends into place and trimmed off the excess. "One completed. Would you like to have a try? There are different sorts of ways you can decorate bottles. These are good for candle holders. I want to show you how to weave a cane bottle holder next." Franny took a small circular base from the box Heather had seen on the floor. "Usually, I wouldn't say I like using these as I think it is cheating, but they can be useful. I normally weave my own bases; however, this is for an order."

Franny measured the required height, then doubled that and added more. She cut twelve ribs and put them in the water tub to soak; she added hot water from the hob in the middle of the room and checked the temperature. "If the cane is not wet, it won't be flexible and will crack rather than bend. Soaking the lengths in warm water helps." Franny was still measuring the cane, and Heather carefully added the lengths to the tub. "Heather, please grab that roll of thin cane and put the entire roll in the tub, too." Franny taught Heather how to weave the cane baskets. She then showed her how to attach a long handle. She then made Heather do the basket weaving and realised using the wet cane was relatively easy. By the end of the week, Heather could make three sorts of bottle baskets without assistance.

Franny watched her work and said, "These slim cane baskets are wonderful to carry a hot flask of fluid or a tall ginger beer bottle."

Heather and the children settled into their new life. Franny had made

Heather feel more at home than ever, except she felt empty without Brodie.

Neither girl had a sister, and this was how each felt about the other. Their husbands were cousins, so the bond between them grew. The seventeen-year age gap between them was nothing; both were expectant mothers with adorable children, and the conversation was often about the antics their little ones got up to.

At the end of April, when Heather had been at Honeysuckle House for six weeks, Henry called her into his office. "Heather, I was wondering if you know much about China. I have a globe in my office, and I thought you'd like to see where the ship is heading."

Heather, in her usual silent fashion, just shook her head.

Henry was unsure if that meant she wasn't interested or didn't know, so he showed her anyway. She absorbed every word he said. She had not even known there was a country called China.

Chapter 10 The Shanghaied in Shanghai

*T*he *Spicy Lass* called into Canton Harbour to see if they were required to leave any supplies, but they were waved on and sent further north to Shanghai. Captain Robertson's instructions were to meet with Captain Belcher on the *HMS Sulphur*. First, the Captain had to find the fleet, then hunt for the *Sulphur* from the myriad of foreign bays.

The view of the foreshore from the ship was rather depressing. The hills were brown and often denuded. The houses were vastly different, with pointed or peaked roofs, curled corners, and strange decorative features on the ridge line. Brodie had hoped that the land would look exotic, like Guam.

They passed various towns and ports as they sailed northward up the coast of China. After Canton, they passed Shantou, Xiamen, Fuzhou, and Wenzhou. Each foreign town was marked on the Naval map the captain was navigating from. Many had seen the Navy pass through.

The Captain knew the next town would signal their journey's end; only it would not be visible until they entered the bay from the north.

This area was riddled with islands, and Captain Robertson needed to figure out how accurate his maps were. He dropped the sails until they were under just one headsail. *The Spicy Lass* was all but coasting through the islands and slowly heading inland.

Even before they arrived at Hangzhou Harbour, they heard the sound of cannons. Their booms echoed across the water. They rounded a headland, and a shout from up high had everyone scurrying around. The lookout reported that a significant battle was underway on the other side of the bay. He shouted from the crows' nest on the very top of the main mast, "Hey, Capt'n, them guns barking are ours. There's some big battle on the far side of the bay."

"Damn!" The bearded captain said and swung into action. Within minutes, he had the ship tacking and doing a complete about-turn. The

Captain took Brodie by the shoulders and said, "Get below deck, lad and wait in your cabin. Please, son, I need you to go."

Brodie wanted to object. He opened his mouth to do so when the Captain said, "Brodie, for God's sake, just go! For Heather's sake and mine, leave now! You promised!"

Giving the Captain a filthy look, Brodie spun on his heel and headed below decks. He was frustrated as everyone else on deck had valuable jobs to do. In the time he had been on board, Brodie had tried his hand at nearly every role on board. Galley hand, sailor, sawbones assistant and any other position needed. He wanted to try them all except climbing the rigging again. As the sawbones assistant, he, at least, found himself helpful. He could roll bandages and mop up blood and scrub everything. He had already had to assist in amputating half of a man's hand. It had been caught in the rigging ropes and so badly mutilated that the ship's surgeon removed the pulverised fingers. Brodie had surprised himself that he had not passed out at so much blood. Maybe sitting in on the birth of his children had hardened him.

The onboard sawbones, Malcolm Sparks, did not like cleaning up after himself. So, rather than head to his cabin, Brodie went to the sick bay in the ship's forecastle. If they saw any action, their sickbay may be needed.

Brodie had learnt, years before, that strong spirits stopped wounds infecting. Heather had always liberally doused his cuts and wounds with neat whisky and then covered them with a clean cloth. The wounds had often scarred but healed well, with no infection. He remembered the pain of his burns when treated this way. Brodie decided to scrub the operating bench, such as it was. The large wooden table stood in the middle of the room. It had obviously seen recent action as it had stains soaked into the timber. It was also caked with detritus from previous procedures. Brodie thought that while it was unused, he might as well clean it up properly. His stomach had roiled as he saw the remains of the blood and gore on the floor; so much for cleaning it after a procedure. There was a barrel of seawater in the sickbay for this purpose; Brodie got to work with a cake of hard soap and a stiff-bristle deck-scrubbing brush. He scrubbed everything he could, and he noticed the sound of the cannons getting louder.

Trying hard not to think about what was occurring outside, he could not help but jump with each volley of cannon shot or musket fire. The sound of the large onshore cannons now rattled the instruments on the shelf. He wished he could see what was happening, but he had promised the Captain he would stay well below decks. He dared not look out of the forward hatches in case someone saw it move and aim for him.

Volley after volley of musket shots sounded out, and Brodie realised they were coming from onshore, not from his ships. He scrubbed on. The shooting eased by the time he was satisfied the room was clean. One shot had been louder than others, and he had flinched as he felt the ship shudder. He finished his work and was about to return to his room when the door burst open.

The Captain stood there white as a sheet.

Brodie expected a blast as he was not in his cabin where he should have been. Instead, he was roughly grasped and hugged by the big bearded man. "Thank God, son; you are all right. I do not know what I would have done if I'd lost you too."

At the Captain's words, Brodie stiffened. "Who died, sir? Do they need treatment?"

The Captain pulled back a little from his hug. "Brodie, you really have no idea who I am, do you? You were such a wee little laddie when I saw you last. Nearly eight, if I remember correctly. We lost so many of you that visit, Iain, to smallpox; then Jane was hit by that vehicle. Hamish and Caitlyn both died from measles. Four of our beloved children were gone in such a short space of time that I don't suppose you even remember me. You helped me with a birth even though I didn't know what to do. Sadly, Morag never breathed, but my Mary still had you. She needed you so much, Brod."

Brodie grabbed hold of the freshly scrubbed table. He was peering at the man intently as though seeing him for the first time. He'd never seen him with a beard before. "Father? But I was told you were dead."

The Captain pulled him to a bench seat near the forward hatches and sat with his arm around his shoulders. "Not so, son; lost at sea for some time, yes, then shipwrecked in a tiny isolated village in the Spice Islands. For years, everyone thought I was dead. I returned home to find your mother buried. I was told Callum had moved, and I didn't know where to go. I heard later that he was in Sydney somewhere, and I have yet to meet up with him. Well, that was about seven years after my last visit. The landlord told me that all my family had died. Brodie, I didn't know you were still alive, or I would have hunted for you."

Brodie was reeling. "Why didn't you tell me as soon as you realised who I was?"

His father said, "I could not tell you earlier as I was still stunned that you were alive, let alone on board my ship. I did not know how you would cope with the knowledge that I was not exploring the underworld in Neptune's ballroom." The Captain gazed at his son. "I couldn't risk it, Brodie,"

Brodie pulled away with a frown on his brow. "Why now?" He pushed his father away from him.

The Captain saw the hurt in his son's eyes. "I was scared of exactly this reaction. I thought making friends with you first would make the news easier. But I want to show you why now. Come!" He walked to the cabin door, expecting his son to follow him.

Brodie did.

The two moved towards the first mate's cabin and, when Brodie opened the door, saw that the room was not neat and tidy, as he and Adam had left it. There was a gaping cannonball hole near the porthole, and it had almost destroyed the cabin.

"Now, do you understand why? If you had done as I ordered, you could, and probably would, have been killed. I would have lost you before I had time even to acknowledge you. Son, will you please forgive me? But don't cut me out of your life."

Brodie saw tears well in the eyes of the big man.

Brodie fully understood. He smiled mischievously. "I need answers, Father. Like, why not use your, or I should say, our name?" Brodie frowned.

The Captain released a long sigh, then gave a small chortle. "I do, son. Being so young, you would not have known my full name. It's Ewen Robertson Stewart. Only your mother and Callum ever called me Ewen; I was, and am, Robertson to everyone else. Brodie, I am Captain E. Robertson Stewart, Master Mariner and, incidentally, owner of *The Spicy Lass*."

Brodie gasped, then smiled, but remained silent.

Robertson paused and looked at his son, waiting for a comment. He continued, "I was so surprised you did not enquire how I knew who you were, as we had supposedly never met. You, my boy, have actually changed little from when you were a child. You have filled out quite a bit and shot up, but otherwise, you are the same strong boy I knew and loved so well." Robertson waited for Brodie to say something, but his son remained silent. He continued, "However, I had no idea you were still alive, son, let alone living in Sydney. When Henry was talking about 'Brodie this' and 'Brodie that' and even 'I took Brodie over your ship,' it never occurred to me that it was you. For to me, you were dead. It's a common enough name in Scotland."

Brodie nodded; he was beginning to relax. He knew he had not met the captain when he had come aboard with Henry. He had not even wondered why the captain had been so kind and understanding. The realisation washed over him. Brodie finally said softly, "You knew my name, my full name. I have never even used it. I even forgot Ewen was my middle name until that moment. Mama used to yell at me using it all." The realisation of that had just then hit him. His head was reeling; his father was not dead; he was no longer an orphan.

Adam had said several times that he was special to the captain, and now things began to gel. Did his friend already suspect something? Brodie stood in the remains of their cabin; its total decimation represented the early shambles of his life. "Father, I will need time to adjust, but can I have a hug, please? It's eighteen years since the last time I hugged my father, and that was to say goodbye. Now, it's hello again." The sounds of the gunfire onshore had ceased.

The captain knew he had responsibilities on deck, but this could not wait. Captain Ewen Robertson Stewart opened his arms to his son. As he hugged him, he said softly, "You know, I never expected to be a grandfather.

You tell me you have children, and I've been itching to ask you about them. When we have time, you must tell me all about your family. Sadly, I must go and do my duty." He felt Brodie nod against his chest. He added, "Stay safe, my son. I can't lose you. Not now I have found you again."

~

The following hours saw a few soldiers with minor wounds get brought on board by the longboats for treatment. Brodie helped in the sick room.

These sailors later explained to Brodie what they had witnessed from on deck. There were neat rows of red-coated English soldiers and a mass of yellow-jacketed Chinese rebels.

The two groups were already in the midst of battle when their ship arrived.

The Naval ships were sitting offshore in readiness to take on the wounded. Longboats had taken the injured soldiers off the shore, and they were now waiting on the seaside of the anchored vessels to assist when required.

When the day was over, the skirmish at Chapu near Shanghai saw nine British soldiers and sailors killed and fifty-five more wounded.

The Chinese who lay dead or dying everywhere were quickly taken away by many of their peers. No one knew how many had been killed or injured, but there were many.

The wounded Englishmen were taken back to the various ships for immediate treatment. The better-trained ship surgeons took the most severely injured to the Naval vessels. It was from them that the crew heard the news that one of the dead was Lieutenant-Colonel Nicholas Tomlinson, commander of the 18th Royal Irish Regiment.

The Spicy Lass crew dealt with minor shrapnel wounds and non-life-threatening injuries. Brodie helped with bandaging and a liberal dousing of rum on and into his patients as a painkiller.

Having had their injuries dealt with, they were later transferred to the *HMS Sulphur*, which was eventually able to come alongside.

~

Because of the situation on shore, it took some days for Adam to realise that the relationship between Brodie and the captain had changed. The ship's carpenters attended their quarters and moved out their personal items until work was completed. However, Brodie had not appeared on the crew's sleeping deck.

Adam had wondered where Brodie had been placed. He thought it might be in the sickbay berths. He watched Brodie closely over the next two days.

The captain also stood watch over the lad. He also noticed that Adam had worked out that something strange was occurring. He knew that soon word would get out.

Adam watched, and a thought manifested; Brodie and the captain were seen laughing together. Adam noticed that they laughed the same way and had many similar mannerisms. As they left the mess one evening, Adam finally caught Brodie alone. "Brodie, what gives with the captain? And what's more, where are you sleeping?"

Unbeknownst to Adam, the Captain had arrived quietly behind him. "He is sharing his father's cabin, Adam. Keep it quiet if you can; we're still getting used to finding each other alive and well. Each of us thought the other had died nearly twenty years ago."

Adam was floored. "Captain, he's your son?"

Captain Robertson Stewart slid his arm along his son's shoulder. "He is! I thought he had died soon after his mother did, about eighteen years ago. He is the only one of our six bairns left alive. His mother was my Spicy Lass, Adam. Brodie had been told I had died in the typhoon that had shipwrecked me for those lost years. When I returned home, they were all gone. I presumed they were all dead." The captain looked lovingly at his son, "I thought I had given it away on the day you were brought to me."

Adam looked from one face to the other. He could see similarities now that he had overlooked before. "Truly? Neither of you had any idea when he came on board?"

Both Stewart men shook their heads.

Robertson said, "I never remarried either, as Mary was the love of my life. When she died, I lost the will to live for some time; then, I met Henry Gates. He gave me the kick up the rear end I needed. I built this ship with my payout from the typhoon shipwreck. Brodie, what you don't know about my ship is that she's named for your mama. My Mary was one heck of a spicy lady. She was my Spicy Lass." After that, the Captain gave a nod of dismissal to Adam. He escorted his son away from his first mate.

Adam was left speechless as the two men walked towards the captain's cabin; however, they did not enter, but Robertson led Brodie outside.

As they walked, Brodie asked, "Father, did you know Mama's father? Knox Macdougal?"

The strangled laugh forced from his father's lips inferred that he did. "I met the man often. I fought with him often, too and then snuck your mother out from under his very angry and rude nose. We first had an anvil marriage and consummated it so he could not claim it was invalid. Then later, after she was expecting Iain, we married properly in a church in Edinburgh, too, so we had a written record of it, but Iain was well on the way by then. Her father disowned her."

Brodie explained. "I only met him once. It was two years after you had vanished. We had run out of money. We didn't need much with just Mama and me, but she appealed to her papa for help."

As they were at anchor, they were alone on the deck. They had reached the rails of the poop deck. From there, in the fading light, the coastline of the foreign shore was like any other. It was hard to believe the fighting had occurred there only a short time before.

The hold was now nearly empty, and the Navy had been fully restocked. More food and ammunition would be needed, but Robertson had decided that his sailing days were over. He would spend his remaining years ashore with his re-found family. He would keep his ship. He might even allow another captain to skipper her, but *The Spicy Lass* would certainly remain in the family. He may even promote Adam to Captain. Henry would continue to charter her for his exclusive trade; however, he would also understand, having only recently found his lost daughter.

Over their talks, Brodie realised there was a conversation he needed to have with his father. He needed to tell his father of those years after he had gone. "Father, I need to tell you of those last two years in Scotland and about Mama." Brodie had no wish to say how his mother died, but his father needed to know. How else could he explain that she had died in childbirth? He had to know.

After an hour's conversation in the quiet of the evening, Robertson realised how tough life had been for his wife and son, having run out of money and thinking he was dead. He had no condemnation for his wife's actions, only for the landlord who had used his wife so badly and that the man had lied to him when he returned; the man had abused his trust and his wife. The scoundrel had known all along that Brodie was still alive and said nothing.

Robertson had left the town a broken man, never returning to Glasgow. He had sailed to the most distant place on the globe and traversed those seas. "Oh, my dear boy, if only I'd known." Robertson shook his head in the darkness. "No, no 'if only's' from now on! From today, we start afresh. Brodie, I have been thinking since you came on board. Wondering and praying, son, I have decided that this will be my last trip. I'm retiring and spending my life with the family I thought I'd lost. I've had twenty years wishing I had my time over again; well, now I do, and I won't waste it."

"Seriously, Father? You will do this?" Brodie's voice broke as he spoke.

Robertson said, "I will, son, but first, we must find cargo to return to Henry. Either that or some ballast like pig iron, as the ship will not be as stable with empty holds. If I can't purchase anything here, we may need to travel back through the old spice islands. I usually buy the best cargo I can for Henry, and then I get a percentage of it. However, before we leave here, I will try to buy some Chinese porcelain or some fabrics in Shanghai if I can get near the port. With closed Chinese ports, the prices for that stuff are better than gold. I've heard of others doing this and were successful if they arrived under a non-English flag. Those ships have returned with fabrics so sheer that it feeds through a lady's ring. I will hoist our Scottish flag instead of the English Ensign or Union Jack, and hopefully, they will let us trade."

Brodie had heard about some mighty fine pearls purchased in Shanghai years before the troubles started. Lady Gipps had been wearing them when Heather arrived, and Kenny had adored them. "Father, I have heard they also have pearls for sale. Could I try to get a necklace for Heather?"

Brodie could hear the happiness in his father's voice as he replied, "I don't see why not. I think we'll have a bit of fun shopping, won't we? I always used to bring you home something from my trips. I've not purchased any trinkets for nigh on twenty years."

"I still have the knife and sheath you brought me for my eighth birthday. It was the only other thing I took when I fled, along with a blanket and food. Heather didn't even manage to get that. She had to leave her home with only the clothing and blanket on her back and a hairbrush in her hand."

Robertson chuckled. "Then, son, I think she deserves a lot more fine clothing. I think we shall spoil her somewhat. What do you say?"

Brodie thought about Heather's reaction to her being given some exquisite silks. "I'm game; however, she won't be happy unless we get something for everyone."

"Hmmm," Robertson thought. "I wonder how much fabric I can buy. If she would like pearls, I'm sure other females will, too. Let's see what we can get, eh? We must be careful storing fabric as the hold can get damp. Pearls, however, I can keep in my cabin safe."

"I'd like to get her some dark green silk. It will go with her mahogany locks." Brodie fell silent. "I miss her so much. I now understand what you went through each time you had to leave."

Robertson nodded. "If I knew then what I know now, I never would have gone." He pulled his son into a bear hug.

Chapter 11 Unexpected Visitors

*J*t wasn't often that Henry Gates's house in Windsor on the Hawkesbury River received unexpected visitors. In fact, he actively discouraged any such persons from even being able to access his home. However, on a sunny day in May, two such men arrived without warning or invitation. Both gentlemen were in their fifties and exceptionally well-dressed.

Having just arrived through the back way, Hector watched them walking up the driveway from the town.

Neither man seemed to be in a hurry, but they were certainly walking towards the house. They were obviously not lost.

Hector had recently returned home from their shop in Windsor and had only time to remove his hat. He had left his horse in the backyard with Victor and arrived at the front door at the same time the visitors arrived at the front gate. He stood waiting as they drew close. "Good afternoon, gentlemen! To what do we owe this pleasure?" Hector enquired somewhat icily.

The taller of the two said with a very thick Glaswegian accent. "We are looking for Honeysuckle House and hoping we have reached our destination."

Hector was on edge, though he noted a Scottish accent; it didn't appease his anxiety. He liked unexpected visitors as much as his wife, which was absolutely nil. Quite coldly, he replied, "Ahh, sirs, that depends on whom you are looking for."

The second man, also Scottish, frowned a little. "Sir, we were hoping that we were somewhat expected."

Hector shook his head. He had no idea who they were.

A frown followed a glance between them.

The man continued. "We wrote but have received no reply to our missives. Our search has been fruitless until now. We have checked through the inns in Sydney Town and even with the kind Major in charge of convicts. He was non-committal about where she was but told us to enquire here. If we draw a blank here, the next stop will be an inn in a place called Richmond to see Callum Findlay."

The taller man spoke again, "Sir, we are searching for my niece. One I did not even know I had."

Both men dwarfed Hector; he wasn't short at six foot two inches in stockinged feet. Hector lightened a little. Although their Glaswegian Scottish accents had now eased his fears somewhat, the mention of Callum's name made him question them in a more welcoming tone. The man's mention of the Major comforted him, as only Major Downes would have given directions to Henry's house. He was aware of Franny's past and her abhorrence of meeting people. Putting on his best Baronial accent and manners, he said, "Well, I admit that this house seems to be a house of recently discovered family. May I enquire whom you seek?"

The forlorn uncle said, "Heather Stewart, née Anderson. I had no idea she was related when they all lived in Glasgow. Please tell me she is here."

The pleading note in his voice hit Hector hard. Hector did not need to reply. He heard footsteps behind him, and the screen door opened.

Heather appeared beside him. "Sergeant Donald, Sergeant Campbell, what on earth are you doing here?" Heather had heard Dennis's voice saying the last few words. Having grown fond of the men who had so ably assisted them, she pulled open the screen door and was in their arms. Her slightly rounded belly showed she was with child.

After the initial round of hugs, Heather introduced Hector to her protectors. "Hector, these are the two men responsible for Brodie and me being married. They protected us when I was arrested and then gave us time together. Then, to top it off, they somehow ensured that we were assigned near each other in Sydney. Our Kenny is named after Sergeant Kenneth Donald."

It was the most that Hector had ever heard Heather say. He also saw the smile she gave the men. It was the first time in weeks that she had been happy.

Turning back to her visitors, she added, "But why are you here?"

Now relaxed, Hector waved a hand gleefully, passing the question to Dennis for him to answer. She had obviously not heard their earlier conversation, "Over to you, gentlemen." Hector was going to enjoy watching the reaction of the quiet girl.

The taller man, Dennis Campbell, took Heather's hand in his.

"Heather, dearest, in all our conversations, you never mentioned your mother's name. When you were arrested, it also never came up. It was not until I received a visit from Kenneth here after he had read Brodie's letter that the jigsaw fitted together. Brodie wrote and told us that you were safe and settled, then asked to see if we could hunt for some family for you. A few weeks later, we had a visit from Mister Rory Featherstone from Edinburgh. He was looking for some family for you, too. He had managed to find a record of your parent's marriage."

Dennis turned to Hector. "The letter was from you, I gather, sir. I understand that you had written to him. I believe he is your agent in Scotland. That is if you are Lord Glenview and known locally as Hector Grey." He had picked up on Hector's slight accent.

Hector gave a single nod of acknowledgement; the small hint of a smile on his face showed he was guilty of the said instructions. He had actually written to his agent and his grandmother, and Henry had written to his father requesting the same thing. The letters suggested the same thing that Featherstone be set to do some research.

Heather discovered Hector had a title soon after he claimed a relationship with Brodie. She turned to Hector. "You did that for me, Hector, even back then? You knew I had no one. I was a six-year-old child and knew little about my family."

Hector put a caring hand on her shoulder. "I know, dear," Hector said lovingly. "I also had no one for so long. I know what it feels like to be so alone. I thought if Mister Featherstone could trace your father's accident, he might get somewhere, so I set my father to work. Henry also wrote to my father. Featherstone obviously found something."

A blast of cold air shot up the river; it made Heather shiver.

Hector turned to the two men. "Before we discuss this more, please come inside and warm up. I'm sorry for my hesitation; however, you are very welcome."

The chill wind blowing in from the river was frigid enough to slice right through them. Even in new overcoats, they were chilled.

Dennis and Ken sighed with relief; even though they had not yet told Heather why they had come, they were made welcome.

Hector ushered them indoors. After showing them into the sitting room, he called Franny and Henry to join them.

Heather was heard talking animatedly to both men, which surprised Franny. Henry went in directly, and Heather introduced him.

Franny paused outside and asked her husband, "Hector, who are they, and what do they want? Heather seems to know them."

Hector's grin gave Franny assurance that all would be revealed. He bent and gave his beloved wife a quick peck on her cupid lips. "Let's just say they have come in response to a letter I wrote a couple of years back. Heather knows them both and trusts them, too. It seems Mister

Featherstone has had some success on a quest I sent him on." He held the door open for their entry into the warm room.

Both visitors gasped as Franny entered the room. Neither man had expected to see such a fine-looking woman in the wilds of western Sydney. She was also expecting a child, as she had a gently rounded belly and positively radiated happiness. She could easily grace a palace ballroom and stand out in the crowd.

Franny glided across the floor as though she was floating. She took a seat next to Heather. Her glossy black curls rioted around her heart-shaped face. She was obviously the older man's daughter as they had identical periwinkle blue eyes.

Mrs Glassop, Henry's housekeeper, brought in a tea tray loaded with scones, mulberry jam and fresh clotted cream. She would have loved to stay and listen, but she politely gave a bob curtsy and departed.

Hector didn't even get a chance to introduce everyone before one of his visitors spoke.

As the door closed behind her, Dennis turned to Heather. "My dear, you heard some of what I said to Hector. I have come in answer to his letter from some time ago. However, before I say more, Heather, I need you to tell me your mother's name before I explain any further."

A micro frown crossed Heather's brow, and she looked puzzled, "My parents are both dead, sir. My Papa was Angus Anderson, and my Mama was named Annella, but I don't know her unmarried name. Mama never liked the name, so Papa called her Annie. I only remembered Mama's name as she hated it, so I was not named after her, but Heather after Papa's mother. Why, sir, what's all this about?"

Dennis sounded as sad as he looked. "Do you remember I told you I was married, and due to me being poor, my wife, Isla, could not stand having so little in the way of home comforts? She left me and went home."

Heather nodded. She remembered his words on their wedding day; however, they had never had anything much anyway. Being poor was all she knew, so she wasn't worried about that.

The clock in the hallway outside chimed as the chink of the teacups broke the silence in the sitting room.

Dennis drained his cup, and then he continued, "I told you my wife died in childbirth, along with our child? In my grief, I ignored my own family. At about the same time, my little sister married and left home. She married an engineer who worked on the railways. His name was Angus Anderson." Dennis paused. He thought back to his youth. Shaking his head to make the sad memories flee, he said, "Gus was my friend, but we grew apart when I married. I had nothing left, and I was jealous that Gus had been able to go to college and get a qualification. I ignored them out of spite, I suppose. I was not considered smart enough to train for anything. However, life doesn't always turn out how one plans. My wife left me, and then she died soon afterwards. I wallowed in self-pity, angry at their happiness. I heard Gus and Annie had a daughter and lashed out at them because they were so happy. Then I heard they had lost other babies, and I paid little heed to them or where they were living because of my own extended grief." He paused for a while again, obviously deep in thought.

Heather was still cold from being outside without a coat and moved to the fire to warm herself.

With another shake of his head, Dennis kept his story going. The retelling still hurt. "After some years, and not long after the incident which meant that I had to resign as a policeman, I had heard Gus had been killed. I cut myself off everyone but Ken because of this." He held up his mangled hand. "Anyway, I presumed Annella would go home to Mother. For some reason, she didn't."

Up until now, he had been addressing everyone. He now turned to Heather and spoke directly to her. "Heather, your mother, Annella, was my sister. This means that you are my niece. I had no idea, none at all, who you were. You reminded me of Gus, but the idea that you could have been related just never occurred to me."

Heather had blanched. "You are my uncle?" She had been standing near the fire, warming herself, but all but collapsed into the seat next to Franny again.

Dennis almost had to grab her to stop her from falling. "I am, Heather. Mister Featherstone double-checked everything and found that the details all matched. I wrote to His Lordship here last year but heard nothing back, so we came anyway. If I may, I've come to live here, to be near you."

Heather so wished that Brodie was here.

Ken added, "Me too, Heather. With Dennis leaving Scotland, I was going to be all but alone. I have now retired, and I thought Brodie's description of this warm climate sounded just too inviting not to come, so we have both decided to move here permanently. You two are as close as I have to any family, too. My wife died before we had bairns."

Heather looked from one to the other. These two men meant so much to both her and Brodie. For Dennis to be her uncle meant that she had a family to support her through Brodie's absence. He was someone she already knew and loved. Above all, he was someone she also trusted. He had already helped her through the most challenging time in her life. Big tears trickled slowly down her cheeks. "Thank you, thank you both so much. You have no idea just how much this means to me at the moment." Emotions threatened to overwhelm her. She choked back more tears of relief.

Ken wanted to give her a big hug. Being unrelated, he was going to stay within the bounds of propriety.

Dennis, having now a proven claim to her, knelt beside her and drew her into a big paternal hug.

This embrace was her undoing as she now wept freely into his shoulder. After a minute or so, her sobs subsided. "Thank you, Sergeant Campbell."

The man on his knees at her feet lifted her chin with a hooked finger and held her gaze with his own, "I think Uncle Dennis would sound wonderful, my dear. And I think Ken would appreciate the same moniker. What do you think, Mister Gates?"

Henry thought back to the day he had found Franny. He had watched and listened to the entire saga unfolding. "I think that as they named their son after Sergeant Donald, it would not be inappropriate to be known as an honorary uncle." He added, "All we need now is for Brodie to return, and we shall be a complete family again." He met his daughter's eye and realised she was thinking along the same lines.

Ken asked the all-important question as Dennis took a seat close to Heather and Franny. "Where is the laddie? I'm quite keen to see him again. Will he be home soon?"

His question was met with deadly silence by everyone. Both visitors saw the concern on all their faces.

Ken watched and frowned.

Heather almost whispered her reply to her uncle. "Uncle Dennis, he's on the way to China after being shanghaied."

Franny slipped an arm along her shoulder to show her support.

It was the first time Heather had been directly asked where her husband was.

Both visitors gasped with dismay and said in unison, "China?"

Henry nodded and took over the story on Heather's behalf and answered all their questions. He confidently announced that Brodie was on one of his chartered ships. He planned to fill them in later that it was only a supposition.

Dennis absorbed the information and asked, "So how long has he been gone, and when do you think he'll return?"

Henry again answered. "The entire trip will probably be about five months long, but it has been some months since they departed. It was a chartered trip by the government, and the Captain had a project to do. Then, it must find cargo and return. As they only left in March, I expect them back in September. Hopefully, before that, as any later, he will miss the birth of his third child."

Again, the visitor's eyes rested on Heather.

Dennis said, "Third?"

Ken grinned.

She blushed delightfully and smiled, nodding. "Other than Kenny, we have a daughter, Isabel. Issy and Kenny are outside with Lynne, Uncle Henry's maid, and Franny and Hector's children."

Dennis was fearful to ask but enquired tentatively, "Can I meet my great nephew and niece?"

Heather's face lit up like sunshine. She replied with a nod.

The question broke up the group.

There was much more to discuss, but for now, Heather led her guests to the workroom in the backyard.

The children were in there, supposedly doing some basic lessons with Lynne.

Issy was too young to do much, so she was drawing on her slate with chalk sticks; however, she kept using her left hand, and Skye was becoming quite frustrated in trying to stop her.

Heather had been going to join them in the warm workroom and weave some more bottle covers when she heard the familiar voices.

At only twenty-two, Heather felt like a child again. She skipped as she led everyone out through the kitchen door into the courtyard at the back. "I can't believe you are family, Uncle Dennis." She gave a gurgle of joy. "It's going to take some getting used to. I'm no longer so totally alone."

"For me too, lassie, me too!" Dennis replied quietly. He was immensely enjoying the novelty of the situation and their warm welcome.

Ken was hard on his heels. He had not seen his namesake for four years and presumed he would not recognise him. This child was the closest he would even have to a grandson.

The door to the workroom opened silently. Inside were various young people and children.

Hector and Franny's eldest child, eighteen-year-old Skye, sat with three small girls at her feet. Joey and Alec, aged sixteen and fourteen, were busy whittling some handles for baskets for their mother. Kenny was at their feet, playing with the shavings from the big boys' carving. Julia and Etta, at ten and three, were next to two-year-old Issy. All were drawing on slates with chalk. Skye had taken over the chore when Lynne, the heavily expectant maid, had fallen asleep in a cane chair on the far side of the room.

Their entry and the joyous noises woke her.

Lynne looked neither embarrassed nor contrite but waved to Hector and Franny and yawned.

Ken met Dennis's glance with a single raised eyebrow. He found that this household was very unusual and yet a delight. The maid was supposed to be watching the children, not vice versa.

Heather volunteered the information that Lynne was married to their coachman, Victor.

Issy saw her mother, and after numerous scolds from Skye for using her left hand, she threw her chalk down and ran to the sanctuary of safe arms.

Ken's eyes were on his namesake. He was easy to pick as he was the only burgundy-headed boy in the room. Both children had inherited their mother's startling light violet eyes. Issy's hair was a shade lighter, a lovely mahogany colour, similar to her mother's. Some other children had Hector's fiery red hair; the rest were dark and curly like Franny. All their children had varying shades of blue eyes, too. The older girl, Skye, was a stunning young version of her mother; she had also inherited her mother and Henry's periwinkle blue eyes and dark curls. Hector's boys were younger versions of their father; though the eldest had dark hair, the younger one, Alec, was a carrot top with a head full of unruly curls.

Heather beckoned Kenny to her side, and the little boy came at her bidding.

He stood obediently waiting for instruction.

Heather introduced their visitors.

Kenny looked at Sergeant Ken as though his eyes would pop. "I was named after you? But Papa said you live a long way away."

Ken smiled and knelt before the small boy. "Yes, you were, laddie, but I've come to live here and hopefully stay close to my adopted family. Do you think that would be all right?"

Kenny's head nearly nodded off. The smile he gave his namesake showed his baby teeth. Ken wished to enfold the child in a bear hug but resisted in case he scared him.

Dennis stood waiting patiently. His time would come, and he could claim a relationship with these adorable infants. He was shattered when he found out his child had died at birth. He never thought of having any family at all. Now, to find he had Heather, Kenny and Issy, with another child on the way, to say he was delighted was a vast understatement. So, Dennis stood near Henry, enjoying the interaction of his friend with the young lad.

Heather then introduced Dennis as their great-uncle.

Kenny had obviously heard all about him, too, as both knew his name. The small boy chuckled. "I can see that you are great, Uncle Dennis; you are so tall, so you must be extremely great."

Dennis smiled; for once, he did not mind the reference to his elevated height. "You might grow as tall, too, lad, for your Papa is not short."

Kenny was soon happy enough to hug his new great-uncle. Dennis had been privileged to give the child a few cuddles when he was born, but the little boy wrapped his arms around his neck and planted a wet, sloppy kiss on his be-whiskered cheek. When the lad was born, he was red and wrinkly, not the fresh-faced little lad Dennis now held so lovingly. His own flesh and blood, this time it was Dennis who smiled. For the first time in years, he was happy.

Henry watched as his own grandchildren were introduced to the tall strangers. Each politely bobbed a curtsy or gave a slight bow until they reached three-year-old Etta.

Henrietta Frances Macdougal Grey stood with her hands on her hips. "If you is their fambily, are you going to take them away? I don't wants them to go."

Hector looked at his youngest daughter and remembered back to her older sister, Julia, meeting her grandmother. She had precisely the same attitude.

Dennis knew that from his excessive six-foot-five-inch height, he was somewhat overpowering to a small child. He also knelt before the indignant child and took her hands. "Etta dear, I have just arrived. However, I promise that I shall do nothing of the sort. Any decision they make will be theirs alone. How about that?"

Etta frowned. "So you won't take them away?"

Dennis looked at Heather. "I promise I will not take them, but that doesn't mean they will stay. It is up to Heather and Brodie when he returns. I believe they have only been here for a few weeks, though."

Etta didn't like that answer. "Mama, make them stay; I don't want them to go. Not never, ever!"

Franny gathered her small daughter into her arms. "That's a long way off, poppet; in the meantime, let's get our visitors settled." Franny turned to the two men, "You will stay, won't you? As long as you don't mind the men's staff quarters, only one young man, the gardener, in there, or you can share a twin flat next to Lynne and Victor."

Henry and Hector always left the invitations to Franny as she was the most vulnerable person in the household. Having been violently abused from when she was young, it was an unspoken and unwritten household rule that all male visitors were left up to Franny to invite to stay; for her to issue an invitation without a qualm boded well for the future stay of the gentlemen.

Ken met Dennis's raised eyebrow enquiry. A slight nod met it. Ken smiled and said, "Ma'am, sirs, we are booked in at the inn in Windsor tonight. However, we would love to avail ourselves of your kind invitation from tomorrow. We would be interested in ideas of what sorts of occupations you may have for two unattached, retired policemen and how they could occupy themselves living in this colony. I'm sure the good Lord will open a door somewhere, but we know not where."

Their hesitation and a day's delay were more to give the family time to discuss the situation without the possibility of them overhearing their conversations. Having arrived unannounced, they had previously decided to spend the night in Windsor if an invitation ensued. They did, however, stay for the evening meal.

After dinner, Henry ordered the carriage to take them to Windsor. It would return and collect them at ten the following morning. Victor harnessed up the carriage and took them back to the inn.

After their departure, the various conversations at Honeysuckle House were all positive.

The hardest thing was for Heather to get to sleep.

Over dinner that night, all had commented on the smile she had been unable to wipe from her face. She was so excited that she now had a family of her own and that it was Dennis, of all people.

In the time, almost a year, that she had been incarcerated in gaol in Glasgow, Dennis had seen to her needs far more than any other prisoner. He had also permitted Brodie access to her cell, and these visits resulted in Kenny's birth.

Chapter 12 Homeward Bound

$\mathcal{R}$obertson and Brodie's shopping trip to Shanghai was very successful. Brodie still held an entire bolt of the most glorious sheer golden silk he had ever seen. "Father, I can't believe that fabric could be so sheer and yet so beautiful. Heather will love this."

Robertson had delighted in taking Brodie through the various stores in the enormous foreign city. They had sailed in under a Scottish flag instead of the British one, and the port manager gave them entry to the harbour and permission to trade. And trade they did. Robertson produced a stash of small gold ingots from somewhere in his cabin.

With Chinese ports being off limits for many years due to the opium wars, Robertson was welcomed, as he refused to carry the addictive substance, opium. He knew what opium did to people when they used it for a long time. Its only useful purpose was in the hospitals for operations. He had gold and silver ingots as currency as they were universal; he purchased everything he possibly thought would sell in Sydney. With his hold empty of the naval supplies, Robertson purchased most of what he was offered.

Chinese cargo was far more valuable than similar shipments had been some years before due to the opium trade embargo on English vessels. The hold of *The Spicy Lass* was now full of black gold, known in England as black tea. He had purchased substantial wooden crates of loose-packed black tea leaves in both black and green varieties. There were also various flavours, but predominantly the Oolong variety, which was the most popular. He had also bought fabrics of all sorts, including cotton, silks, a durable yellow cloth called nankeens, flat bolts of silks, including a dark green one for Heather and velvets in every colour they could imagine. Some were gossamer thin and sheer; others were polished damask silks with coloured embroidery woven into them.

Robertson also had a room on his gun deck for shrubs and trees. Amongst the decorative and edible plants were rhubarb crowns, cassia, and tubs of divine-smelling star jasmine. This last plant had the sweetest scent, and he knew this would sell well.

Other sellers were keen to push their floor matting, exquisite lacquerware, various fans and a range of fabrics, furniture in Western designs, as well as some smaller items in the Chinese style, and a vast array of exquisite eggshell thin porcelains. He purchased some of everything, and the porcelain and ceramics arrived in wooden crates packed in straw. There were entire dinner settings of the most beautiful willow pattern. Other settings were pretty pastel-coloured designs in delicate florals. Soon, they had filled the lower decks to capacity.

Robertson was unsure if they could return under a Scottish flag again, so he purchased every possible saleable item he could. Whoever was at the helm next time, he knew this would be his last trip and wished to make the most significant profit possible. He splurged and purchased a quantity of valuable jewellery for himself to sell. There were carnelian, jade and exquisite enamels set in silver and gold. He also acquired a special gift for Heather. This cargo was a bargain as no other British vessels bought such items. Brodie had asked him to keep his eyes open for a string of pearls for her. He did better than that.

He had sent Brodie and Adam off together while he went to see a pearl merchant he had heard was reasonably honest. The opera length of creamy pea-size pearls was far longer than what Brodie was after. Where Brodie had seen pearls, Robertson didn't know, but this strand was beautiful. It would coil around her neck in at least a triple loop and then some. Robertson also purchased more luxurious sea gems. Some were for Heather, and others he could sell at an immense profit. The long strands were available in various shades, and as he couldn't decide which she'd like, he bought them all. What he paid mere pounds for in Shanghai, he could sell for a hundred times that in Sydney. One small ingot purchased a sizeable bag of pearl necklaces. He saw a single tear-drop pearl that was half an inch long. It came on a golden chain, one so delicate that he feared to lift it by the web-like links. The shop owner assured him that it was strong and would not break. The next item he purchased was a graduated short single strand of pearls. It had a single three-quarter-inch golden pearl at the centre and varying shades of cream for the remainder of the strand, tapering to the pea size of pearls near the clasp at the back. It, too, was exquisite. Brodie had said that Heather had deep red hair. The creams and golds of this creation would look superb on her. There were exquisite blue butterfly wing brooches, matching earbobs, and pendants; the electric blues caught and reflected the light in a shimmering radiance. You could not help but be drawn to the natural magnificence of these items. Robertson purchased everything he could, including rings and earbobs that matched the necklaces, and the dealer added some single pendant drops for free. Each item was packed into a small silk pouch.

Brodie asked for nothing for himself but to return to Heather; however, Robertson saw and purchased an ivory-handled sword-stick, riding whip, and a matching walking stick, also with a concealed stiletto.

Robertson had told Adam to take Brodie to explore the city. He would never return to this port and wished his son to see everything he could. This was the only day they could go together. He paid an English-speaking guide to escort them for the tour. In Brodie's absence, he commissioned an entire wardrobe of clothing for his son. If his life had been as hard as the scant stories Brodie had told him about, then he and Heather still had very little. They lived in an attic above Henry's store and existed with the bare minimum of damaged furniture. He would fix that on his return to Sydney. He would buy a house large enough for them all to live in and still have room. Hopefully, more children would arrive, and the family would grow. In the years since he thought he had lost his family, money had come rolling in, but he had no one to spend it on. His finances were extremely healthy. Brodie didn't know that one day, he would be wealthy. Robertson hadn't bothered to mention it as he knew money mattered little to his son. He had realised that Brodie knew his true wealth was in Heather and their children.

~

After two weeks in Shanghai harbour, the now laden ship finally set sail homeward bound. Food and water had also been replenished.

In the weeks since Robertson had revealed his relationship to his son, they had spent many hours getting to know each other. Robertson often caught Adam watching him with a smile in his eyes.

As they were weighing anchor in Shanghai, his first mate said, "It does so warm my heart to see you, happy sir. I knew when I first brought Brodie to your cabin that he was more than just a stowaway, but you could have knocked me over with a feather when you told me he was your son. Too right, sir, 'tis true, but I'm right glad he is. Right glad, I am." Adam had also been impressed with how Brodie had coped with what had befallen him. Even after discovering the Captain was his father, he did not let the situation change his attitude. He still scrubbed the decks. Occasionally, he would share a meal alone in his father's cabin, but more often than not, they ate with the men in the ship's mess. Adam said to his captain, "Sir, I'd have his back any day I would. He's just a nice bloke."

Robertson smiled; he agreed wholeheartedly. Not only did he love his son, he liked him, too. He liked him a lot, and he was proud of him. Robertson truly liked the man his son had become. He had loved Iain, but as to approving what he got up to, he was not impressed. Brodie had pulled his weight from when he was little, but that was in the past. Now, the future was ahead of them both.

The Spicy Lass was now headed for home. They were southbound, and Brodie's spirits lifted. Rarely was the smile gone from his face. It was now early June, which was the summer height in this area. As they headed south, the weather would once again grow colder. Knowing it was typhoon season, the captain made haste to put to sea. The sooner they were out of the treacherous waters and south of the equator, the happier he would be. He had a new family to meet and a new life to start. He had always wished to retire and spend time with his family in Glasgow. He now had a second chance; he would not forego that opportunity again. He would buy a house in Sydney and settle down as a father and grandfather. He would not sit idle, though, and had already considered how to occupy his time. He was sure that some role would be found for him if he wished to volunteer his services in or around the harbour or docklands. He was sure God would open a door for his new life. He felt there might be an opening with orphans on the streets of Sydney. He had noticed a few waifs and stragglers hanging around the docks. He had another friend in town, Douglas Evans, also a retired sea captain, and he wondered what he did to keep busy. That was a conversation he looked forward to having.

Back in Windsor, Dennis and Ken had moved into the rooms above the stables at Henry's house the day after their unannounced arrival. They spent eight weeks with Heather, getting to know the children. However, their minds were thinking about their future. Both realised that their stay in Windsor would only be short-term, but they didn't know where to go from there. Discussions with Henry had been helpful, but no exact direction had still opened up to them, and they doubted it would in Windsor.

The three older men had bonded with the shared family connections. Henry could always use good help at his warehouse, and he realised that on Brodie's return, he would not feel safe alone on the docks. Henry permitted the Scotsmen to use Brodie and Heather's flat at the warehouse. It would mean they could look around the area until Brodie returned, which hopefully would only be another eight to ten weeks if the winds were right and if the Captain had been able to obtain good cargo.

Ken had quickly discovered that the boat was not the quickest way to Windsor, but it was the most comfortable for most of the trip. Although the sea between Sydney heads and the Hawkesbury River mouth was uncomfortable, to say the least.

They decided to venture out and see Sydney for themselves in late July. They decided to travel by Mail Coach for their journey back to Sydney. This trip would allow them to look around the countryside. They wished to have Heather settled in a new home by the time Brodie returned.

The two intrepid travellers set off on the Sydney-bound carriage. They had not been travelling for long when they saw their first kangaroo. The brown furry creature was bounding alongside the carriage and leapt to great height as it jumped.

Dennis first thought he was seeing things; he craned his neck to peer at the unusual sight bounding beside them, then said, "Ken, take a gander at this strange creature." Dennis was intrigued by what it could possibly be. He was sure his mind was playing tricks on him.

"Cor, Dennis, this must be what Kenny called a roo. He said they were bigger than him and bounded high. That fits the general description." Ken watched the fascinating sight. Both men were now straining to watch the unusual animal as it bounded into the bush.

The lady in the seat opposite them smiled. "Sirs, pardon for eavesdropping, but I hear from your accents that you are from Scotland. I gather this is your first trip by coach to Sydney?"

Both men nodded and replied in unison, "Yes, ma'am." Both reluctantly dragged their gaze from the animal.

The lady continued, "That creature is a small one, and it's called a wallaby. They are normally grey-brown in colour and usually very gentle. You can even hand rear the joeys, and they become tame like a pet. They are also soft and sweet-natured on the whole. If you travel further west, you will see the big red kangaroos. The big males stand higher than a tall man and are so muscly that they are somewhat frightening. They can rip out your stomach with their back claws if they so desire. Having said that, they are also normally quite timid and will flee rather than confront."

The two men sat spellbound at her descriptions. "Thank you, ma'am. Would you be able to inform us of other creatures we are likely to encounter? We've not yet had a chance to see anything of this amazing place. We came searching for my niece, and now, having found her, we are heading back to Sydney," Dennis asked aloud, quivering with anticipation at what other furry delights they should see. He adored small animals and had never been in a position to own one.

The lady nodded. "I'd be delighted, sirs. This is a country of strange animals. There are giant birds called emus, and they can outrun a man. They, too, can kick. I heard of a man who received such a blow from an emu foot and broke five ribs. Then there are the tree animals. They range from a tiny flying possum-like creature that fits in the palm of your hand. It's like a squirrel with flaps between its legs and is as cute as it can be. There are two other possums, a smaller one with a ringtail, and called that too, and a larger one with a brush tail. Both of these delightful animals love fruit and vegetables but are the bane of our fruit farmers. The most endearing of the tree creatures is one they call a koala. Some call it a bear, but I believe this is not so. Having said that, I don't know what it is if it isn't a bear of some sort. It's a full armload in size, and while not dangerous, it has sharp claws and can unintentionally scratch and cut deeply. I've only ever seen a few and only once up close. They are nocturnal, and you will rarely see them unless there is a fire or they need a drink. They live high in the gum trees. They are silent until the mating season, when they sound like a growling angry pig. When I first moved here, I thought it was an escaped convict outside, and I would stand at the back door with my gun and threaten to blow it up. Then my husband, Jack, told me it was animal noises. Now, I hardly notice them. The possum's call is similar to the koala mating sound, and the noise is fearsome unless you know what it is."

She smiled at the inquisitive nature of her co-passengers. "I'm Martha Turner, by the way. I normally come from Emu Plains by wagon, but I had to see a friend, Hetty, near Windsor, so I treated myself to a seat on the Mail Coach. My husband and I run an inn in Emu Plains."

Ken and Dennis introduced themselves and mentioned that Dennis was related to Henry Gates' new guest.

Martha knew all about Heather and Brodie from Franny and Hector. She admitted that she knew the family well and had delivered four of Franny's children. She was good friends with Des and Hetty Walker, whom Martha and Franny had initially been assigned. "I was Hetty Walker's first placement, but I only stayed for six months before heading down near Camden to Duffy's place."

The two Scotsmen initially had eyed her with suspicion. Was she an ex-convict? The word 'placement' had not escaped their notice. They had found that in the weeks they had already been in town, things were vastly different here to back in Scotland, where they would have been accused of fraternising with criminals. Class in the colony was 'Free and Felon'; however, the emancipated convicts were in a class of their own. Some had returned to the status they had prior to conviction; others bettered themselves. Disregarding her status, as she was so friendly, they decided to pump her for information about what else they would see.

Martha chuckled; seeing their indecision, she said, "Sirs, I remember when I first arrived, and yes, I was a convict; I was placed out on the Hawkesbury River for a time, recuperating at Hetty's farm. Franny replaced me when I left; it's how I came to know her. I still visit Hetty and Des. I presume you know them and know what they do on their farm? With transportation now stopped, the girls at Hetty's farm have a happy home forever. Most of them have served their time but have no wish to leave. I won't go into that, though; there was much trauma to be healed by Hetty and her care."

Martha paused momentarily and watched the passing bushland, recalling those happy days she spent getting well at Hetty's farm.

Franny had introduced the two men to Des Bolton and Hetty Walker the week they arrived. They knew Hetty to be the person to rescue Franny, and that was good enough for them. Hetty had never changed her name to Bolton when they married.

The two policemen thoroughly admired the couple's work to assist the underprivileged on their unique farm.

They saw a smile tip the edge of her lips, and then Martha continued the story. "For a London girl, I quickly learnt what beasties were nice and what was not. Some giant lizards and snakes swim and climb trees, too. The snakes here can also strike you nearly as far as their body is long; many of them can kill you with one bite. Yet the worst of the insidious creatures you will meet on land are the nasty, shiny black spiders. Those creatures can and do crawl into anything. I give you fair warning. Never ever leave any clothing of any sort on the ground. And check your shoes before putting them on. We place ours on a chair. One bite from the shiny black spiders, and you are dead."

Both thought ex-policemen gasped.

Martha leaned forward and looked at both men, "I am serious about these, sirs; take no risk with them; they do kill. To me, they are pure evil!" She leaned back in her seat and continued her vivid descriptions of the Australian wildlife. "The long-legged brown spiders that run across the walls only eat insects. I don't like them, but they don't hurt you normally." She saw the shudder of Ken's shoulders.

Ken was aghast at her descriptions. "Ma'am, your words make two big, brave Scotsmen quake in our oversized boots. What a fearful place you choose to live in."

Martha gave a small chuckle. "They aren't all bad, but I thought I should warn you of the deadly ones. There are two of my favourite animals that I doubt you will ever be blessed to see. One that looks like a cross between a duck and an otter is called a *platypus*. I was told they lay eggs, but I never see any signs of a nest. These strange creatures live in freshwater creeks and rivers and swim like a fish but breathe air. If you are up at dawn or dusk, you may be lucky enough to see one in a creek or river. The males, by the way, do have a poison spike, but as I say, I doubt you will ever see one. We occasionally see them in the Nepean River near our inn. The second amazing animal is called a spiny anteater. My youngest son tells me its real name is an *echidna*. These are lethal-looking but harmless as they only eat ants." She chuckled. "I wouldn't try to pat one, though. They waddle around like they don't have a care in the world. If you disturb them, they bury their heads in the leaf litter and think they are invisible. Having said that, if they are in the bush, and you look away, they can vanish under the leaves in seconds."

On that short trip, they learnt more about the colony's development over the last twenty years from Martha than they would have done at a library. She was a fount of interesting information. She talked about her daughter, Jenna, and son-in-law, Eddie, and in the next month or so, she was hoping to be a grandmother, probably to twins.

Sadly, Martha alighted in Parramatta to visit her family.

The two men were alone in the coach for some time; they had done little travelling and absorbed everything they could. They expected the trip to Sydney to be in reasonable condition; however, the road was abysmal. They were thrown from pillar to post and bounced up and down for various sections of the Eastbound journey.

By nightfall, they were arriving in Sydney. It had been a long and tiring day. They were keen to fall into bed, yet they still had to find the warehouse.

Dennis yawned. "Ken, I'm so dashed tired I feel like a little bit of luxury and spoiling ourselves on that top-quality hotel Henry mentioned. Two fancy harbour-side rooms sound nice. Why don't we stay at that King's Arms place tonight and seek our new abode tomorrow? I want a hot bath and a roast dinner if one is to be had. My mouth is watering for roast beef and Yorkshire pudding." Dennis was bone-jarringly tired. His tall body did not cope with sitting cramped in a bouncing coach for an entire day. He now understood why Henry travelled on his boat.

Ken stretched. "I'm with you, Dennis. The bath alone is enough to entice me to stay there. I'm beat!" Ken tapped on the carriage roof, and a communication slot opened above his head. "The King's Arms Hotel, please, sir, rather than our original destination."

"Right-oh, sirs," came back the cheerful reply from the driver.

He should, by rights, have dropped them at the post office, but it was only a bit further down the road, and it had been an awful trip. The rains had certainly cut the road up; they deserved a break. He had spent some time chatting with them at the halfway stop, where they changed horses. He felt sorry for the poor blighter who had just found out he had a niece and had come halfway around the world to find her. So he deserved a treat.

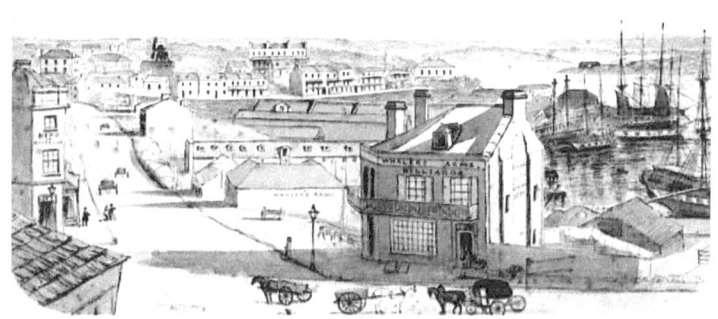

Chapter 13 House Hunting

*K*en and Dennis decided to stay for two days at the luxurious hotel. Both men had enough funds, considering they had planned to board somewhere for some months. To be given free accommodation for weeks was more than a luxury.

The day after arriving from Windsor, they had gone down to the Whaler's Arms to see where Heather had worked. The small inn stood by itself on the edge of the bay. The building looked partially built, as though half was missing. From there, they saw the small white store building for the inn. It was all but next to that was Gates Wholesale Emporium. They introduced themselves to the manager at the warehouse and presented him with Henry's letter.

Thomas Tibbs was not pleased to see these two overpowering men. He had a shipment of illicit goods due at any moment and wasn't pleased there would be strangers on site. He had managed to get rid of Brodie, Heather, and the screaming brats. Not that the children made much noise, but he was sure they sometimes did. As children went, they were little trouble; they were just nosey, far too nosey. Brodie had his fingers on everything, and he noticed things, especially when the books didn't tally. Mr Gates had given him access to everything.

Thomas grunted and showed the men where the stairs to the loft were. He quickly left them to settle in. Their hackney carriage was waiting on the street with some of their luggage. If required, it would return with the items they had placed in storage when they gave the word.

Although the place had not been cleaned since Heather left weeks earlier, it was immaculately tidy, but the upper room was tiny, cold and bleak. The sparce furnishings were all still there, and the beds had obviously been re-made with clean sheets, as there was a pile of dirty ones ready to wash. A large bucket of coal sat next to the hob fire in the middle of the room.

Assorted, clean dishes sat beside a basket that contained an assortment of odd cutlery. There were also containers of labelled dried products.

Dennis looked around the room in horror. "I say, Ken, I can't let her live like this. I want to buy a house and have them live with me. I know our flats in Glasgow were small, but this is minute and primitive. How did four of them survive in here?"

Ken walked over to his friend and placed a caring hand on his shoulder. "Dennis, for our bairns, this is the height of luxury. Think about the street waifs we would see in Scotland. Think back to the condition of their clothes at home. Look around you. It's clean, warm, and has everything they could want, including a stock of food. At home, they had to run about in the cold and snow barefoot with very little clothing. This place is absolute luxury compared to where I found Brodie living behind a buttress. He had found a small nook behind a pillar; he had been curled up in a tattered blanket. He had nothing else, yet his only concern was for Heather."

Dennis knew what Ken was describing, but it didn't make it any easier for them to realise they could have assisted them far more back then and hadn't. At least not until Brodie became ill and Ken took him home. Guilt freely flowed through both men, yet there was little either could have done. Both knew Brodie probably would have refused assistance anyway unless it was for Heather. It was this thought that kept Dennis from moving forward with his plans for the future. However, that would not stop them from looking around the harbour town. With the determination to find somewhere for them all, one of the first things Dennis wished to do was to buy a newspaper and look to see what houses were available to rent with the possibility of buying.

They decided not to move in that day but to stay another night at the hotel. If they could find a place to rent, then it may be available immediately. The loft room felt like they were encroaching on some private space belonging to the young couple. The men slowly closed the door and walked downstairs. Having been in the profession of policing for so long, they naturally moved quietly. Ken's clenched fist went up, and both stopped moving. Dennis knew the sign well from his foot patrol days. The conversation drifting up from below was enough to chill the souls of both Scotsmen.

The voice they had heard only a short time ago said, "I thought I'd got rid of the upstairs occupants by drugging Brodie and sending him to sea on Gates's ship. Now those damned Scotsmen want to move in just when the shipment of opium and grog is due to arrive. I managed to time the arrival when Gates was not around, but now we've got to dodge these two new chaps. They had better not interfere; that's all I can say. One word to the authorities, and I'm a goner." A voice came in reply, but it was softer, and neither man could hear what was said.

Dennis motioned for them to return upstairs and discuss what they had heard. They silently retraced their steps.

Once back in the loft room, they had a council of war behind the door. "Well, Ken, now we know for certain who's responsible for Brodie's disappearance and that he is still alive but just at sea. Henry admitted there was always an element of doubt about that. I must confess I'm relieved for Heather's sake."

Ken nodded. "And I'm relieved, for Brodie's sake. I, too, had wondered. Now, what are we to do? We're both retired and have no authority here. I think if we report our findings to the local constabulary, they will tell us to pull in our heads. Do you remember the name of the Major who helped organise the search for Brodie? Henry did mention it."

Dennis attempted to recall the conversation. "Dunn, Don, no, it was Downes. Hector said we could trust him. He's the one we met when we came looking for Heather. If we go and see him at the barracks, he'll know what to do. He can set a watch on the harbour, too."

With a plan now set, the two men noisily opened the door and let it bang. They then stomped loudly down the steep, narrow staircase, and while chatting about the room above, they nodded thanks to the manager and departed without further conversation. They had visited the Major at the barracks on their first sojourn in town and called in when on Heather's trail.

The two nonchalantly meandered up the hill towards the centre of town. They thought they were being followed, so Dennis stopped and purchased a newspaper, which they sat to read the advertising.

The Sydney Herald edition was the current one, so they hoped there might be something to rent short-term. As they looked to be reading the broadsheet, the man watching them got sick of waiting and soon vanished. Now clear of their trace, the two casually walked up George Street. From there, they would ensure they were no longer followed, cutting up King Street towards St James' church. They knew the Major's office was next to the barracks on Macquarie Street.

Dennis led the way to the guarded gates with the newspaper tucked under his arm. After naming the Major they wished to see, they were escorted to the office on the side of the courtyard. Again, a soldier escorted them past the three-story stone barracks building to the second building on the left. The delightful smell of freshly baked bread was wafting from the front building.

The bare-headed soldier was busy writing when they entered. He finished his words and, carefully replaced his ink pen into the holder, and said, "Good morning, gentlemen; how may I assist you this time?" The pleasant face that greeted them was comforting.

Dennis dived straight in. "Sir, I believe you know Brodie Stewart?"

The Major smiled and gave a single nod of assent, "I do."

Dennis sighed with relief. "As I said before, I'm Heather's uncle. We found her, thank you. We've been staying with Henry Gates for the past two months and have only yesterday returned from their place to see if I, or I should say we, can rent or purchase somewhere for the family to live with me. Sergeant Ken Donald is the person Brodie went to for assistance in Glasgow. It's a long story, and that is irrelevant for the moment. Sir, as I said before, we are retired Glaswegian policemen. As such, we move with stealth by nature. Henry has permitted us to stay in our bairn's loft until we find an abode for ourselves. Whilst departing, we overheard a conversation below as we exited silently, less than an hour since. Sir, are you aware of opium being smuggled into the town?"

The Major started at the word; he now gave his full attention to the two before him. "No, I don't want that evil substance to take hold here. However, what has that to do with Brodie? Take a seat and tell me all." The Major walked to the office door and closed it.

Now, they were able to talk without being seen or overheard. Dennis and Ken filled him in on the overheard conversation, kidnapping of Brodie, and expected shipment of illicit goods. "Major, the words opium and grog had been mentioned, but there may be more items in the shipment."

Major Downes digested the information, sat with his lips pursed and twiddled his fingers, with his thumbs tapping each other. He was obviously deep in thought. After some moments, he looked up, "Sirs, I'm going to ask a favour. You say Henry Gates has permitted you to stay in the loft?"

They nodded in the affirmative but stayed mute.

"Then, may I ask that you do just that? Your occupation there will waylay suspicion from me placing a man to watch the warehouse. I will, however, have them stationed around the building and out of sight. You will be unofficially undercover if you will. As ships are unable to contact shore, we may have to wait a while. Now that Mr Clark has taken over the Whaler's Arms Inn, he is on our side trying to clean up the area. I can also have men placed there, especially at night, as I presume that is when they will transfer the cargo. The loft has windows in the roofline, and you should be able to signal us at the inn from there if you see or hear something."

Soon, the plan was set, and reluctantly, the two had to leave the majority of the organisation to the Major. Both men were delighted that they would have a significant part in the entrapment of the consignment and arrest of the team involved. Thomas Tibbs was responsible for Brodie's absence, so he needed to be apprehended and charged. But he needed to be caught red-handed. They would be happy if they could keep Brodie and Heather's names out of the papers. The Major added that, for the moment, Henry would also be kept in the dark about the activity from his warehouse; they knew he would be horrified.

By the end of the day, Dennis and Ken had moved their bags into the loft. They had purchased some fresh vitals, and as the temperature dropped, they lit the hob fire. They settled in as best they could to the cramped loft. They had not shared a room before and discovered that while Ken was tidy,

Dennis didn't mind a bit of mess. Both realised that the accommodation was only short term so put up with the inconvenience of sharing. They kept the door open, and even though this brought a further chill to the room, it also allowed conversation from downstairs to be easily overheard.

Once settled in, Dennis once again perused the advertising in the newspapers. Two advertisements caught his eye. "Ken, there are two houses that are possible rentals, but prices are a little more expensive than I thought. However, I could rent it for a while and see if we like living there. It's still £260 for the year's rent. What do you think of this one?" He read the first advertisement aloud.

House For Sale, Freehold property. Well situated for business, containing thirteen rooms, now let for £260 per annum. The sale price is £1500. (Elizabeth Street, Sydney)

Ken said, "I think it is an awful lot of cold hard cash, Dennis. But thirteen rooms sounds like a good-sized establishment. I quickly looked, and all the other places were only a few rooms. I suggest we look at this place and see if it's suitable."

Dennis nodded in agreement. "This is the only other one, but it doesn't sound like it is in town."

To be Let or Sold.

A most desirable and commodious Established home suited for a family of the first respectability, within an agreeable distance of the town.

The house contains eleven handsomely furnished apartments, exclusive of cellarage, without Offices, and several acres of good pasturage attached. To be sold on very advantageous terms and a liberal credit or let to a respectable tenant at a moderate rent.

Apply to Messrs. Campbell and Scarr, Agents, Regent's Terrace, Hunter Street.

Ken said, "I think you're right about that, Dennis. It could be miles out of town, but we'll ask about it anyway."

Knowing that little would occur in daylight hours, without further ado, the two men decided to head to Hunter Street and see the agent for both houses. By the end of the afternoon, they had viewed the house on Elizabeth Street and decided it would be perfect. Dennis took a six-month lease on the premises with the option to either extend or purchase at the end of that time. Ken had stayed silent as the money was coming from Dennis. As they were heading back to the loft, Ken said, "That was a bit of fast-talking, Den. Six six-month lease for £100 is a good saving, and it's fully furnished with all the bedding and linens too."

"I know, eh," said Dennis with a cheesy grin. "We can move in when we wish, from August. However, we'll hang around the loft until the deal is done, then we'll settle in and get Heather to come back and get comfortable before the baby is due."

Dennis realised that with a baby and children in the house, Heather might need more help than they could supply. Neither particularly wished to cook or even clean such a large place; Heather would need some help with the children.

Ken took the words out of his mouth. "Dennis, how the heck are we going to manage in that huge place by ourselves? We'll need some staff. I wonder if the Major has any 'lifers' who need a placement. We would want ones with Tickets of Leave who can live in so they won't need payment. After meeting Franny, Mrs Turner, and some of the girls at Mrs Walker's place, I now realise not all convicts are bad."

Dennis's mischievous look answered Ken's words. "Heather and Brodie certainly are not. I wonder if the major might know of two attractive middle-aged ladies who might be interested in two retired Scottish policemen as husbands. I have a mind to take me another wife. What about you, Ken?"

Ken chuckled. "Let's try for a cook and housekeeper first and see what happens from there." The idea appealed to him, though; he had been alone for many years. With a new start in a new country, why not a wife? There was a small two-bedroom apartment at the back of this enormous house. If Dennis purchased it, he would ask about renting it from him. He had little ready cash on him as he had retired early. Dennis had been given a payout because he was injured on duty for a wealthy gentleman. As compensation, he was given £5000. Ken was not jealous, as Dennis was still in pain from having his left hand sliced open and all but cut in half through the fingers. Ken couldn't believe that Dennis didn't lose it. The wealthy patron paid for the best doctor he could and even sent him to Edinburgh for an operation. Dennis only had the use of two fingers and his thumb. He had to retire on the spot, no longer able to work on the beat. As he had been assigned this job, the Superintendent had put him in charge of the flats and permitted him to assist at the prison. He was also allocated a free room in the police flats as part of his redundancy.

Ken had befriended him when he found him soon after he started work there. His hand was still bandaged, and he was trying to use a broom. Ken had heard the item being thrown across the courtyard in frustration. They had been friends from that day. When Dennis said he was moving to Australia, it took little thinking for Ken to agree to come, too. They paid for their £10 tickets and packed up their few belongings, then left all they knew for a new life on the other side of the world.

Word soon spread that Dennis had taken the lease on the Elizabeth Street mansion. They had discovered that this was big news in such a small town. The two men again visited the following day to see what furnishings were required. This time, they walked through the rooms with a notebook in hand. Jotting down items that they thought Heather and the children would need.

The two-story house was immense.

The main bedrooms were upstairs and opened onto the covered area with dark green painted double French doors. Its mellow orangey-yellow sandstone was styled in the Georgian manner; however, some enterprising person had added a wide verandah all around it, top and bottom. The furniture was the envy of many. It was the most beautiful colonial-made red cedar furniture that was so well crafted that its finish was almost a mirror image. It was solid but lightweight. The dining room table had three optional panels that could be added or removed as required; all were in *situ*. Fully extended, it seated twenty, and there was a set of twenty matched cedar chairs. The seats of these were upholstered in a dark blue velvet corduroy. The curtains in that room matched the upholstery. Two matching sideboards and a dresser held the crockery, all made from the same red cedar.

"Oh, I say, Ken, this is a bit of all right, isn't it?" Dennis checked who the cabinet maker was. He had not seen furnishing like this in all his years of going in and out of the fancy houses in Glasgow. The name of Templeton's Cabinet Makers was chalked under the left-hand drawer and was only in Castlereagh Street. This business was almost next to him, as the mansion he had rented went through the entire block from Elizabeth to Castlereagh Streets. The rear access to his stables and backyard was from Castlereagh Street. "If I need more furniture, I won't have far to go. Look, they are all but next door."

Ken nodded but remained quiet. He was a little overwhelmed.

They left the dining room to peruse the other public areas and found themselves in a very commodious kitchen. It, too, was immaculate. The front of the range was freshly blackened, and all the copper bottoms of the pans that hung on the various hooks were shiny and clean. Whoever had lived here before had certainly loved the orderly cleanliness that went with many staff.

From the kitchen window, Ken looked outside. "Did you look at the stables before? I got sidetracked in the gardens and the established orchard."

They decided to investigate how many horses could be accommodated and discussed if they would require a vehicle of some sort. It couldn't be a gig as it wouldn't fit the family; a barouche or something larger was what they would need. They would have to see what was available.

On entering the extensive stables, they saw it could house up to ten horses, but only six stalls had recently been used. The other stalls were filled with feed drums and tack. The final stall had a vehicle of some sort covered with a substantial canvas sheet.

Ken lifted the corner of it and called out to Dennis. "Cor, now I understand why the price of this place was so high. Did you know it also includes a vehicle? There's a new three-bench-seat barouche, and it will fit us all. It's absolutely blooming-well magnificent, Dennis."

They folded back the cover and saw an immaculate-condition carriage waiting for some horses. It even had a fold-back hood for all-weather use.

Dennis stood with his hands on his hips, "Well, that does it; we're buying horses, Ken, and I'm going to purchase this house. I added up what I'd need to buy if I purchased the other place. With furniture, bedding, and all the rest of the paraphernalia required to fit out a house for the family, it would be over £600 at the prices out here. This vehicle alone would cost that, as it is fully imported."

The two walked around the French-polished carriage. There was not a scratch on it. Dennis said at the back of the carriage. He saw the gold leaf monogram on the rear luggage hatch.

Dennis gasped. "Ken, look; it's one of Lancelot Usher's coaches. I've seen these in Glasgow, but I had no idea someone would have wished to bring one here. This is a top-notch vehicle." They carefully re-covered the carriage before continuing their inspection of the area.

There was a loft above the stables; they found accommodation for six stable hands and a hob stove for their comfort at one end of the room. On the other side was a leather working area, a room full of excess tack and a feed loft and hoist from the rear gate.

Chapter 14 Concerns and Adventures

They meandered back, and Ken voiced his thoughts as they walked.

"Dennis, there is only one thing that worries me. This place is perfect, don't get me wrong. No, it's Brodie; we were not permitted to do much for him at home; I have a feeling he will knuckle down and object."

Dennis agreed. "It's why I didn't buy it outright. Even when I booted him out of your place the first time I met him, he didn't protest or complain. After that, well, I grew to admire and then like him. Heather, I adored her from when I first met her. I think even then, she reminded me a bit of my sister. They are very alike in mannerisms, but Heather is so quiet; Annie was never like that. She stood up for what she wanted and usually got it. Angus was a perfect match for her."

With the thoughts of the house no longer foremost, they returned to the dockland and into their small loft. As they entered, they shut the door at the top of the stairs with a bit of a bang and listened for the men downstairs to check it was closed. They heard footsteps approach and then recede.

Ken's senses were heightened. "I hope everything happens before we have to leave, as I think we would miss the excitement of an arrest." He then gingerly opened the door a few inches.

They set about preparing an evening meal of eggs and bacon, then decided to have a nap. They would take turns on watch tonight, listening to any happenings or sounds from downstairs that occurred during the night. The staircase funnelled up any sounds from the warehouse floor. Tibbs probably didn't realise how loud all their conversations were from above.

When night fell, Dennis said he would take the first watch. He would sit up listening to any sounds until midnight. He didn't think much would happen as had not seen any ships dock that day. The winds had been coming from the West, so entry into the harbour would require tugging a vessel into the jetty. The Major had said that Watsons Bay, just inside the harbour entrance, had a few ships awaiting a berth at the cargo wharves. Maybe theirs was one of them.

Their policeman days had seen them both do many a surveillance watch. Dennis had hoped that that was all behind him, but this one last foray would be for a personal purpose. None of their previous stakeouts had been as exciting as this one boded to be. Maybe it was because they had a family at risk. It had been a long day already. He had checked his fob timepiece a few times in the firelight and was surprised how slowly time had passed. He added some more coal to the fire and sat listening to Ken snore.

His rhythmical breathing made Dennis doze off.

Sometime later, something made him start awake. He didn't move, but he became aware that there were noises below. He rechecked his watch, eleven-fifty. He must have slept for an hour. He stood carefully and padded over to Ken.

With practised care, he placed a hand over his mouth and shook Ken. "They are here," he whispered.

Ken was out of bed like a shot. Neither had undressed, and both now donned their dark woollen overcoats, tugging them on over the thick grey pullovers they had each worn, then pulled on their boots.

Dennis lit a lamp from the fire and waved it at the window as was prearranged. A replying light flickered three times in the checkered glass window of The Whaler's Arms, then vanished. According to Major Downes, their job was supposedly over; however, neither Ken nor Dennis intended to miss out on the action.

They were both trained policemen; each had over thirty years of service under their belts. They quietly prepared for whatever endeavour or activity was required. Dennis's hand may not allow him to be on the beat, but he could still run. They were in the unique place of occupying the only other escape route from the warehouse building.

Major Downes would have made sure all the warehouse accesses downstairs were guarded; therefore, the hoist doors in the loft were the only other escape. However, they would have to pass Ken and Dennis to access it.

On their first visit to the loft, they noticed the door to the other side of the warehouse attic. It was bolted shut and padlocked. When they had returned to move in, the padlock had been removed, as had the bolt. They had said nothing to each other, but both had noticed the difference. Now they sat waiting.

Ken watched from the window and saw a movement of lamps from The Whaler's Arms. He couldn't see down to the docks, but as it was dark, the crooks would not want to give away their activities by using lanterns. He watched until the soldiers dimmed lights were just outside.

"Ready?" was all that Ken whispered to Dennis.

Leaving the lamp in the loft, the two crept out the door, closed it, and then tiptoed to the top of the stairs. Standing in the darkness, they stood and listened.

Ken counted to thirty under his breath. It was how long he would usually have given the soldiers before they broke in. Within moments of him completing his count, pandemonium broke out.

Major Downes's men charged in from all the lower doors.

Dennis could hear more shouting from the docks, so he presumed that more crooked opium importers were being arrested outside. As expected, they heard booted footsteps running their way. Standing in the shadows, they waited on each side of the landing. As their quarry approached, each reached out a foot; the man tripped, and he went head-first into the closed door of the flat.

The commotion and shouting below drowned out the noise of his fall. With one man already incapacitated, they stayed still, neither giving away their positions.

Sure enough, another person was heard running closer and then racing up the narrow staircase.

The two crafty policemen repeated their trick; however, the second man didn't knock himself out but was prostrated at their feet.

Ken soon jumped onto his back and had him immobilised by sitting on him. He was holding the man's arms twisted up behind his back.

Dennis retrieved their lamp and saw that they had captured Tibbs and his main offsider. When Ken saw whom he was sitting on, he sent Dennis to find a soldier or two to arrest them.

Minutes later, the Major himself appeared. "Good job, chaps! We saw these two heading your way, and I hoped you would deal with them. We nabbed them all. Plus, their booty has been confiscated, and the opium will be sent to the various hospitals in the colony. They also have a mountain of bottled whisky from Scotland. I have an idea of what to do with that, but for the moment, we will need to keep it for evidence. Come and see me tomorrow, and I will explain." He didn't wish Tibbs to know his plans involved the two visitors.

Neither policeman had said a word, yet he was sure Tibbs knew who they were as no one else would be upstairs.

The Major shackled, then hoisted Tibbs up and marched him downstairs. Tibbs was cursing all the way. The first man still lay insensible.

Ken and Dennis stood watch, ensuring the first man wasn't playing doggo. Their lamp made the staircase easily visible.

Two more soldiers appeared and carried the unconscious man away.

Dennis checked his fob, "It's one o'clock, Ken." The entire campaign had taken just over an hour.

With Tibbs gone and his cronies arrested, Dennis and Ken returned to their room. They moved two chests in front of the loft doors, just in case they had missed someone. They shrugged off their coats and shoes, stretched out the blankets, and climbed into the beds to sleep. It had been many years since they had had such excitement.

Ken mumbled. "We did well for a couple of old bobbies, Dennis. Those wives you are keen to find for us may yet find a spark in us."

Dennis grunted an unintelligible reply that sounded like, "I'm not old." He was already nearly asleep.

Soon, both were snoring regularly.

~

The following morning, it was well past dawn when they awoke. When they did rise, Ken put on some porridge to heat as they washed, shaved and changed for their interview with Major Downes.

Neither man was in a hurry as they realised the criminals would all have to be processed, and the confiscated ill-gotten gains had to be catalogued and put under lock and key. Both wondered what idea the Major had in store for them.

Once dressed, they meandered up to the barracks to see the Major. Out of habit, they checked that they were not being followed. They were pleased to find that no spectres or sneak thieves were shadowing them.

They were again escorted from the main gates to the Major's office on arrival, only this time; they had no need to ask to see him.

They were offered mugs of hot sweet tea as before in the warm room and shown a seat. This sweet substance was a brew they had become used to at Henry's house. It was always served in large mugs, not dainty cups and saucers.

The Major was tired but obviously very happy with the evening's outcome. "Ahh, the heroes of the hour! You two were far more than just in on the kill; you took down the two principal characters. We've been trying to catch them in the act for years. To find the entire gang in one night and not miss a single man is wonderful. The ship's crew have also been arrested. That occurred while the main action was taking place inside. The ship was a privateer, and as it had already unloaded, it was already being silently rowed out to sea. They were caught in the lighthouse's beam off Watson's Bay and were taken into custody as well. The ship has also been confiscated, and as the Captain is the vessel's owner, it is now forfeited. I may award it to Henry as compensation."

Dennis gave a small gasp. "You caught the ship too? So, Heather and Brodie will be safe now?"

Major Downes nodded. "We didn't miss one of them, thanks to you two. Their cargo on board was not just opium but bottled whisky, rum, and numerous other products that should have had duty paid on it. We know the whisky was stolen from another ship, as I'm sure most of the cargo had been. The crew on this vessel were escapees from various prisons and settlements throughout the colony and Britain. Gentlemen, we will not destroy the produce, but we must dispose of it legally and return some of the proceeds to the Colonial Secretary for use in the colony. With two of Scotland's finest policemen overseeing the sale, I'm sure the Government will make a nice profit from the disposal. You, of course, would get the other half of the profits. I know little about the taste of whisky, let alone the good bottled stuff, as I'm assured this is. I'm a rum man if I drink at all, but I'd prefer a hot sweet tea any day."

"Excuse me, sir," Ken said, somewhat confused. "Do you wish for us to really sell the confiscated booty?"

The grin that appeared on Humphrey's face transformed his face like an overgrown youth. The Major grinned so broadly that it reached his eyes. They twinkled with mischief. "Yes, I know you are new here, and I thought it would give you a good cash base. From what you told me the other day, your two charges could certainly use the funds. You see, I must confess that I actually know your protégés well. Henry Gates is a friend; it is how I knew where Heather was. What do you say?"

Somewhat stunned at the suggestion, Dennis said, "Thank you, sir, but we know little about sales of any sort."

The Major smiled at Dennis knowingly, "Are you willing to learn? I shall add some enticement, Sergeant Campbell; I can transfer Heather Stewart to your keeping for her final year and a bit of her sentence. Henry Gates is not really family, and Hector is only related to her husband. Henry happened to be here to sign the paperwork. Nevertheless, you are her blood uncle, and I must consider that there is a slight chance Brodie may not return. I believe you have also taken a lease on the house in Elizabeth Street, possibly with an option to purchase it."

Dennis was flabbergasted. He nodded.

The Major bit his lips to stop himself from smiling, "I confess, I lived there until my recent marriage. It's a lovely house." He then continued, "Notwithstanding, I foresee a bit of trouble trying to persuade Brodie to move in with you; however, that is your problem." He chuckled. "He's a determined lad, that one. He has a good reputation and stays away from trouble. Mind you, his ugly guardian angel makes sure he stays safe." He smiled to himself. The Major was thinking of a very rough earthly angel named Dead-eye Dick. It was a wonder he had not questioned about not seeing Brodie around.

"He always has, sir." They presumed that the Major meant God.

Humphrey smiled knowingly.

Ken turned to Dennis, then back to the Major, "Can we have a moment to discuss this?"

"Sure thing, sirs," The Major glanced from one face to the other. "Oh, and I should say that this whisky is a potent brew. It is bottled by Glenlivet and Heatherbrae Whisky distilleries in Scotland. The shipment was *en route* from Scotland to London when the ship was boarded. The pirates stole the entire cargo. I received word to watch and see if some bottled products appeared on our shore. Admittedly, I did not expect some six hundred crates of bottled branded Scotch whisky to be on board this vessel. The insurance had already been paid out on this, so the Government confiscated the shipment. There are also some hogsheads of other spirituous liquors, sixteen crates of the best bottled French cognac, plus French Champagne and wines by the dozen, and goodness knows what else as we have not finished sorting the consignment."

Dennis bit his lip, trying hard not to laugh. He knew that at one stage, Ken had some twenty firkin barrels of illicit Glenlivet in his coal cellar. Brodie had drunk his fair share of the potent evil liquid, downing the remains of a nine-gallon firkin of the Scottish elixir in a week. How he had not died from the binge, they didn't know. Both doubted if the lad would ever touch the potent brew again.

The two men stood and walked to the far side of the small room. Dennis said, "I don't really wish to become a storekeeper, Ken, but if this stuff really is the good stuff, it could set our young ones up for life. I think we should take it on."

Ken looked at his friend. "When I left Scotland, I never wished to see whisky ever again. We drank that last small keg way too quickly, Den, and now to be paid to sell the stuff is a bit of a bad joke. As you say, the money we make would set them up for life. So, I agree, we do it."

"Agreed then. We dispose of Scotch whisky, legally this time." Dennis winked, then returned to the Major. "We'll do it, sir; I noticed there was a shop front for rent just down from the rear of the house in Castlereagh Street. You'll have to help set it up for us as we're not shopkeepers and we'll need staff too. We joined the police soon after John Stenhouse started the force in Glasgow. We know little else but protecting the people from drunks and the like. Now, you wish us to sell this potent brew to them?"

The Major released a long sigh of relief. "I am relieved as I would not make this offer to anyone else. I would not trust them. I'll fix all that and the shop front too. That's the Government part; I also know the Castlereagh Street premises, but I was thinking of somewhere nearer the docks. Did Gates say when he's expecting his ship back?"

Both Scotsmen shook their heads.

Ken said, "Not exactly, but he hoped they would meet up with the sister ship and pass on some mail if not Brodie himself. That first vessel should be due in soon."

The two visitors watched the Major, who sat writing notes. He also had an official-looking document in front of him, which he had just signed and then added a note to a fat ledger.

After a few moments, the Major said, "I suggest that tomorrow, or as soon as you can, move into the new house and get settled."

Ken saw Dennis give an imperceptible nod. "We'd like to, sir; however, it's so large that we were hoping to obtain some staff. You wouldn't have any willing ladies who could cook and do housekeeping for us? Heather will not be able to cope with a new babe on the way, and she's never lived in a place that big. It would overwhelm her."

Dennis chipped in, "Talking of Heather, can her remaining time be transferred to me immediately? You mentioned something earlier, but I'd like to get her settled before Brodie returns because I have a feeling if she is settled and happy, he may not wish to uproot her back to their loft."

Major Downes picked up the document he had just autographed and said, "I had a feeling you would ask that. Here's the official transfer. She is now off stores and fully under your care. I'm sure Henry won't mind."
Dennis's arm snaked over the desk and slowly took the transfer certificate. "Sir, you already had this arranged. I do thank you." Dennis's eyes drank in the information he read and smiled. He was delighted.

The Major closed the large ledger and tidied his desk. "Follow me, gentlemen; I may have just the two ladies for you; however, you will also need a groom, a footman of sorts, and possibly a nursemaid too, sooner rather than later, as Heather is due in a few weeks, isn't she? You may find you require other staff once you are settled. Let me know, as I have many lifers yet to place again. They are often returned to the barracks at the end of a placement." The man shook his head and sighed. There were so many convicts and so many lives to care for. He hoped to have as many placed before he left for England in a few months.

The three men exited the warm office into the chilly day.

A breeze was wafting the delectable smells across the quadrangle from the nearby bakehouse. They walked towards it, and the Major entered the stone building and beckoned the men to follow. The room was full of people, most of whom were bedecked in flour, and that substance hung in the air as a mist.

The Major called four names, and the four persons walked towards them from various areas of the large room.

Dennis and Ken saw two men and two middle-aged women approaching. One lady met Ken's eye and smiled shyly, then dropped her gaze back to the ground in abject humility.

Ken's heart did a little jump. The woman was about his age and so beautiful. She had white blonde hair, and he had caught a quick glimpse of the palest honey-brown eyes that he had ever seen. They were the colour of a dram of neat whisky. He didn't even notice the other three persons called forward. They were Dennis's problem.

Dennis, however, noticed one of the ladies who had not been called forward. His eyes met hers across the bowl of flour. She flashed him an angry glance and turned her back to him. He chuckled at her feistiness.

~

As the meeting occurred in the major's office, the *Island Gypsy* was sailing in through Sydney's heads. It had safely carried Brodie's letter across the miles and would soon reach Heather. By that evening, it had pulled into the private wharf below Henry's warehouse, where only hours earlier, all the action had occurred.

They set about unloading and sorting out the consignment of goods collected in Guam. They intended to sail eastward to purchase cargo when an American trading ship arrived in port. The quick-thinking Captains negotiated a bargain deal and quite literally purchased his entire load, lock, stock and barrel. Amongst the things on board were crates of guns, lead shot and gunpowder. There were also tools and barrels of grain. Even if only those items were saleable, the entire cargo would profit handsomely. However, there was so much more, including delicious spices and exotic foreign goods. The trader had come for copra and was delighted to take more than two months off his trip.

With Tibbs and his minions gone from the warehouse, the Captain was unsure what to do about unloading his cargo into Henry's locked warehouse. He wondered where Tibbs was and discovered he had been arrested when he went to seek a tot or two of rum at Mr Clark's establishment, where the story unfolded.

~

The four new staff were hand-chosen by Major Downes. They were all long-term convicts. The Major had assured the men they were all friendly people and had been caught stealing to feed their families or similar. Knowing poverty was illegal in England, the two Scotsmen had compassion for the four. Heather and Brodie had been in similar circumstances. The two women, Katie and Polly, were in their late forties. Both ladies were attractive enough to cause the men to each draw in a breath.

The Major introduced them and then took the men back to the office, where he explained who they were. "Catherine or Katie Sorrenssen is the fair-haired one. She's a widow and an excellent cook but known to be a little vocal and occasionally boisterous."

Katie was the one who had taken Ken's eye. He smiled knowingly at Dennis's glance, then winked.

The Major pretended not to notice. "Polly Johnson was caught stealing food from the kitchen where she had worked in London. She is nearing fifty and has been a servant all her life. She had never married. Her elderly parents were starving, and both were ill; she was the only one earning anything. I asked, and apparently, they died soon after her arrest. Sadly, it was probably from starvation. Life is so damned cruel sometimes."

Both men inhaled in horror, knowing life could be harsh.

The Major took a deep breath and continued, "Wilfred Jones, known as Wilf, is a returned soldier with only one eye. He had been unable to find work in England after the war and was also caught thieving food. Due to the value of what he stole, he was sentenced to life. Now, the final new staff member of yours is Zane Arnold. He is a mere lad of twenty-six. The poor boy was born with his face covered in a huge red birthmark and would have had a horrific time trying to get work anywhere. Zane is a trained groom, having been born into a big household where his father worked. Sadly, he was mercilessly bullied until he stole a horse and fled. That brought an instant life term. He was lucky he wasn't hung, but the judge took pity on him."

Regardless of what they did in the past, Ken and Dennis agreed to take all four.

Zane found that in the colony, other people's wounds were also visible. Here, he discovered that few teased him, as many knew the burden of wounds of various sorts. Some were self-inflicted, and others were from scourges. The injuries of others made him realise he was no different to any of them. Zane realised that here in this town, he would fit in well. His scant beard now covered much of the disfiguring red mark.

Dennis noticed Zane had flinched when they spoke to him. The reason was immediately evident. Dennis put a caring hand on the young man's shoulder. "Zane, I need your healthy body, as mine is…um, somewhat stunted." Dennis showed the lad his distorted and disfigured half-useless hand. "Will you come and help me?"

Zane's eyes dropped to the remains of the man's mangled hand. Their eyes met, and he nodded, and for once, a smile slipped across his lips. "Yes, please, sir, I'd like that." Zane's head lifted a little with new confidence.

"Good lad!" Dennis replied with a grin and a pat on his back.

The four needed to finish their day's work and then be allocated their last supplies from Government Stores, including new outfits. They would be brought to their new place of work when word came from Dennis that they were moving in.

With the crooks' capture now completed, the two men took their leave and went to pack their bags. The rest of their possessions were still in storage and would eventually be sent directly to the new house when the time was right. They arranged delivery of their possessions to the Elizabeth Street home *en route* to the warehouse. They called the agent to see if they could get the house a few days early. It was empty, so we were granted permission.

Ken sent word back to the barracks and said they would be at the house by mid-morning the following day. They decided not to send word to Henry and Heather until they were settled. Hopefully, that would only be a week or so.

~

The move went well, and by the end of the week, Ken had written to Henry and told him of Dennis's new address. He sent the letter by coach rather than sea, as the ship only went weekly. It was up to Henry now. None knew if Heather should come to stay or not. Being so close to the hospital, the baby's birth would not be a problem if she wished to have it there.

Dennis delayed his letter to Heather, and it was just as well he did.

~

A few days after the arrests, the Major told the retired policemen that Tibbs had received a twenty-year sentence and was being shipped to Moreton Bay to serve his time. It was not likely he would see the light of day again.

The *Island Gypsy* had taken a week to unload. However, the Captain still had his precious letter to deliver and found that Heather was no longer at Henry's warehouse. With the Findlay's gone to Richmond, he was at odds about where to send his precious missive.

Ken and Dennis had been keeping daily checks on the warehouse since Thomas Tibbs's arrest, but on each visit, they had missed the Captain.

Until Henry had been told what had occurred and appointed a new manager, the two Scotsmen picked up the reins for him.

Thus, eventually, Captain Muller, the skipper of the *Island Gypsy*, found Dennis in the warehouse. After a short discussion, he discovered Dennis was Heather's uncle, and he passed over the letter to her.

Dennis decided to take both letters to Windsor instead of sending them, as Brodie's letter was too valuable to hand over to the postman.

Ken reluctantly offered to mind the warehouse while Dennis journeyed westward. Hopefully, Heather would return with the family. There would be room for them all in the new house.

The Captain and crew unloaded the remainder of the cargo and then went to enjoy their shore leave.

Chapter 15 The Scotch Shop

By the time Dennis returned with Heather, Henry, and the children, three weeks had passed. Major Downes had arranged more staff for their new venture, although the new shop was not in Castlereagh Street as he expected. The Major had decided to move it closer to Henry's warehouse on Lower Fort Street at Dawes Point.

There was a small, empty, two-storied shop at the north end of The Rocks, and all agreed this would be a perfect spot for their project. The vacant shop was on the far side of Henry's warehouse and just along from The Whaler's Arms. The name they all had agreed upon was *Scotch at The Rocks*. However, it would not just be Scotch Whisky that they would be selling, but all the other illicit and bootleg grog that was currently under lock and key, plus the confiscated very expensive bottled wines, brandies and other tipples.

Major Downes and his men oversaw the fit-out of the building and the stocking of the basement with stock. The contents of the Government impound were transferred to the storeroom under the shop. There was a bounteous supply of confiscated demijohns of home-brewed hooch, rum, and assorted other spiritous liquids, including the French wines and Champagnes from the latest haul. Some demijohns were labelled, but many were not.

The expensive Glenlivet Whisky, however, was individually bottled in glass. The haul also included some of the Heatherbrae Whisky and Ledaig variety from Tobermory in Mull. Both were single malt whiskies but were vastly different flavours. There were various other brands, too. There were also small firkin casks of the Glenlivet brew that Ken and Dennis had consumed over the past ten years. This was the pre-bottled, almost neat spirit. Since the confiscation of that original batch, this particular single malt whisky was now legally made. This Glenlivet-branded spirit had become popular in London when the King conscripted the entire consignment in the early 1820s. Since then, the Scottish Speyside distiller, George Smith, had been issued a legal warrant to make the potent single malt brew. It was known as a top-quality drink, but neat, it was almost lethal in strength. Even Henry could not afford many of the Scottish bottled delicacies. He would purchase the concentrated barrels and bottle them in Sydney with boiled rainwater to dilute the mixture to the correct percentage of alcohol. This local mix lacked the flavour of the peaty water used in Scotland and, therefore, tasted vastly different.

Dennis managed to persuade Henry that Heather should return to the new house with him.

Henry agreed, realising that if she was settled, Brodie was unlikely to move the family back into their small loft room. He, too, had been concerned for their welfare; however, with no authority over Brodie, he could not force them to move to better quarters. Henry was also aware that Dennis had her assignment transferred to him. And as such, her uncle now stood in *loco parentis* in Brodie's absence. In essence, she had no choice but to go with him. However, Dennis still left the decision to her.

Heather didn't complain, as she wanted to be nearby when Brodie returned.

Having related the conversation he overheard and the entire saga that followed, Dennis assured her that Brodie was no longer in danger in Sydney.

The voyage back from Windsor was again made by sea.

For Heather's seven-month expectant state, travelling on the very bumpy roads was not an option. The sea voyage meant the children didn't have to sit still as they were under supervision in the cabin again, and Heather could use the chamber pot as often as required.

Parting from Franny and the rest of the family was hard. Etta threw a tantrum until they promised she could visit.

Heather always knew she would have to leave when Brodie returned.

Etta was not impressed at all, and no amount of hugs could console her.

Henry and Dennis arranged everything and presented her with a *fait accompli*. All she had to do now was follow their instructions. Henry was itching to visit the house and see if it was as vast as Dennis described. He was not disappointed.

The open-topped carriage that collected them from the dockland stopped in front of a double-storey Georgian house. The glowing sandstone shone in the afternoon sunlight.

As they drew up outside the house, Dennis watched Heather's face as she realised this was her new home.

Heather murmured, "We're going to live in there?" The house was larger than the one she had worked at in Glasgow.

Dennis was relieved that she had not rejected the idea outright. "Yes, love, it is big enough for the entire extended family to have rooms here. After what you two have been through, it's about time you had someone spoil you." Dennis watched his niece's face.

Heather was unaware of the two big tears that slid down her cheeks. She turned to meet his loving look. "Thank you, Uncle Dennis. Thank you so very much. We thought we had everything when Uncle Henry let us stay in the loft. It was the first time we could sleep without fear and know we would have food, warmth, and security. Here…" she paused as if thinking, "…Oh, Uncle Dennis, I don't know how to live in a proper house. It will keep me busy cleaning it anyway." Heather had made no complaints nor any presumptions either. She presumed she would be the housekeeper. She had never been given anything and also expected nothing for free.

His heart went out to his niece, and he loved her even more because of her attitude. Dennis had yet to tell her she had four staff members and possibly more later. Now seemed like a good time as she was just about to meet them. "Ahh, yes, well, about that. My dear girl, you won't have to worry about that. You see, we have four staff members, two ladies and two gentlemen, all long-term convicts who need us. So we are helping them as much as they will help us. Zane, our coachman, you have already met. Here's Wilfred now, so let's venture in and see your new home." The man had scrubbed up beautifully, and in a new uniform, he had taken on the role of a quasi butler-cum-footman, as well as helping Zane in other household work.

Heather was astonished, but she was given no time to reply.

The children were out of the barouche and through the front door before Heather had alighted.

Polly grabbed them before they could get into mischief. She had prepared the children's room and took them to see where they would sleep. They were so excited that no sooner had they seen their new room than they were again downstairs telling their mother about it.

Ken was nowhere in sight, and Dennis figured he would still be at the warehouse. They had come via Castlereagh Street, and Dennis had seen the shop front there was still empty. He wasn't that concerned as he wasn't in a hurry to start selling the stolen grog. His main concern was for Heather and the children.

Robertson, Brodie, and the crew were on the way home on *The Spicy Lass*.

There had been no more rogue waves on the trip, but the seas were the uncomfortable sideways beam seas for much of the journey south from China to the first port of call.

Their stay in Guam would be because Robertson had given his crew some well-earned shore leave. The seas were still treacherous after a passing hurricane, so they waited a week in Guam before setting sail again.

While there, they stocked up on fresh foods and tropical fruits. By the time they left port, they were all relaxed and refreshed for the return voyage. On the trip north, Brodie discovered that the bitter-sweet taste of pineapples had multiple beneficial side effects. They assisted with an upset stomach, and when eaten regularly, they stopped the itch of midge bites. He had received a good dose of those on his last visit to the island. Regardless of the benefits, he also found that they tasted delicious, and their consumption didn't give him the trots as coconut did.

Robertson decided to fill the few gaps in his hold with tropical fruit and was assured that green coconuts and pineapples travelled very well. They were also shown how to grow a new plant from the top. So, along with the thirty large boxes of coconuts, pineapples, papaya, and whatever else they could buy, there was an entire barrel of soil and some empty troughs to plant the tops in as they ate the fruit. Much of the fresh fruit was for the crew's consumption.

Robertson had purchased the pawpaws, sometimes known as papaya fruit, in various stages of ripeness. He also added a box of large golden yellow passionfruit, boxes of green mangoes packed in straw, and assorted other fruit, including star-shaped ones that Brodie had never tried before. They were crunchy and tasted like an apple. Robertson also made Brodie taste various stages of coconut. The green nuts had a delicious sweetish taste but had somewhat bland water inside them, and the flesh was soft like jelly. The ripe nuts had hard, white, nutty meat that was delicious to crunch on, but Brodie discovered that overeating this treat flowed through his anatomy very fast. He learnt quickly to limit consumption of this delectable treat. Another delicacy that Robertson handed to his son to try was a fish dish. Brodie had eaten freshly boiled lobster last visit and couldn't get enough of it. Robertson gave him a small serving of diced white meat and said, "Son, this dish was rich man's lobster."

Brodie eyed his father somewhat sceptically and took a small square of the white meat. Popping it in his mouth, he was prepared to spit it out when the mix of flavours hit his palate. "Oh, Papa, that is delicious." He took the banana leaf dish from his father's hand and scooped up more of the exquisite food. "What is it?" he asked as he indelicately licked off the last of the creamy, tangy sauce from the leaf.

After Brodie had finished the cup-size serving, Robertson answered him. "That, son, is raw fish marinated in lime juice and then soaked in coconut cream. I swear I would prefer to eat this to lobster any day. It's good, isn't it?"

Brodie baulked for a moment. "Seriously? That was raw fish? I would not have known." He asked if he could have more or if it would upset his stomach.

Robertson chuckled. "Go for it, son; the cook made a bowl full, and the crew won't touch it as they know it is uncooked. Having said that, the lime juice chemically cooks the fish, and the meat goes white, just like when you cook it with heat. Throughout the islands, they serve everything in banana leaf plates, so I thought you would like to have it as they eat it here."

Robertson had told no one but Brodie that this would be his last voyage; he decided to tell the crew the night before they arrived in Sydney. That would give the cook time to prepare a special farewell meal and for the crew to say farewell shipboard style. Unless he could escape from the ship with Brodie, he fully expected to be thrown in the harbour on arrival, as was the tradition. This was his crew's way of saying a fond farewell. As he had previously thought, he would not sell the vessel, but he would put Adam in as Captain to sail her so the crew would still have a living. He would leave his ship in God's hands but under Adam's capable care. He would tell him when they arrived in Sydney, but for most of the journey south, Adam was in command under Robertson's watch.

The ship sailed on.

~

In a matter of weeks, *The Spicy Lass* reached the calmer waters of the inner passage through the reefs of Australia. As they were not in the open seas, they anchored overnight rather than risk running onto a coral reef.

The surroundings were beautiful and worth the detour. It wasn't really a detour as the route was much shorter, but this passage was wrought with danger. Robertson was usually wary about sailing this route down the coast, as great dangers were associated with running aground on unseen coral heads, known as bommies. He would never go this way in summer or late autumn as the storms came in quickly and could easily run them ashore on an isolated reef. With no help in sight, they would certainly perish. However, the southbound passage was hastened on this trip by unseasonal northerly winds. They typically met the sea breezes from the south or similar in the Whitsunday Passage. But he wished to show Brodie the stunning Whitsunday Islands, the fringing coral reefs, and the beauty of the vibrant corals and plentiful multicoloured fish.

There would be time for crabbing at the overnight anchorages *en route,* as sailing this area at night was almost a forgone shipwreck. The fishing was also fabulous, and most crew would undoubtedly partake in this addictive sport. In this area, it was not hard to catch some of the prettiest fish they had ever seen. No sooner was a line dropped overboard than a fish was attached and pulled on deck. Only the big ones were kept.

They launched a long boat at low tides and hammered oysters off the exposed rocks. These were so large that it didn't take long to fill large containers of them. Although most of the crew liked them raw, the cook deep-fried some in a light, crisp batter and served them with a bit of salt, pepper and a twist of lime juice.

What time they would save by taking the shorter route would be lost by anchoring overnight. However, it was like being on holiday and a treat for the crew.

Robertson knew about some excellent bays with fabulous fishing. If the northerly winds held up, they would only stay one night; if not, they may spend a day or two fishing and relaxing.

The last time Robertson came through the Whitsunday Passage, he had stopped in the protected Cid Harbour, where he had caught a yard-long, pinkish-orange fish with blue spots called a coral trout; the entire crew had feasted off the delicate soft flesh of the large fish. There were many other fish, and some had blue bones, making eating them easy. The crew also caught tuna, mackerel and assorted other fish with troll lines from the back of the ship. These large fighting fish caused great excitement; as the fish took the hooks, the wooden spools of the line started rattling across the deck. Whoever was closest would grab it and haul it in. They had often trolled in the open seas but rarely had success. However, sailing through the Whitsunday Passage, they often caught a bounteous feed. So much so that the excess would be salted down or pickled in brine and stored for later consumption; another incredible sight in this area was the whales.

As Robertson took Brodie ashore in one of the ship's longboats, the crew rowed towards a sandy beach on South Molle Island when the Captain urgently told the crew to ship the oars. The rowers immediately hauled in their oars and stood them to attention.

The whale approached them and silently rose beside them. Its huge eye taking in the sight of the occupants on the craft. It sank with hardly a ripple and slowly moved under the longboat, rising silently on the other side. Again, the enormous mammal partially rolled on its side; the other eye looked at the crew.

Brodie was stunned. It was so close he could have reached out and touched it. Robertson gripped his hand as it moved towards the giant animal.

The majestic beast was easily four times longer than their boat. It could crush it with the flip of its tail. Everyone sat silently; all were scared out of their wits. The three-inch wide eye that gazed upon them was immense. As quietly as the enormous whale had appeared, it sank into the depths and vanished for some minutes. Fearing what the giant beast would do next, the long boat crew sat in petrified silence with the oars still standing erect.

Robertson gave the order to hold still.

The crew sat watching and waiting.

The whale reappeared about three hundred yards away and leapt fully out of the water in a complete breach. With the majestic beast now safely in the distance, Robertson ordered to make for the shore on the double. They aimed for the gently curving Southern Molle Island beach that faced north-north-east.

The longboat glided through the shallow water and crunched onto the sandy coral grit. The ship was still anchored in Cid Harbour; therefore, it was well out of sight on the other side of the wide Whitsunday Passage.

The wind sprung up as the tide changed. The crew realised the trip back across the passage would be bumpy. They walked the length of the coral sand beach and enjoyed the winter sunshine.

Brodie and Robertson discovered the lone coconut tree on the beach's southern end. It was laden, so they planned to collect the coconuts from the angled tree that overhung the shore. This tree must have floated in long ago in a storm. Years later, it had survived another cyclone, and even though it had nearly a forty-five-degree angle, it had kept growing. Six feet from the end, the trunk turned skyward. The tilt of this tree made it easy to get to the nuts. One of the sailors shinnied up its trunk and lopped off as many green coconuts as he could reach. They loaded their booty into the long boat and left the bay.

As expected, the return trip was more challenging than their outward journey. The breeze had stiffened substantially with the tide change, and the waves were now coming at them sideways and growing by the minute. Some of the beam sea swells were even threatening to inundate the now-laden longboat.

As the rolling waves approached and towered over the timber longboat, Robertson watched his son's anxious white face. The fear etched on it was reciprocated in his stomach. Even as a captain, Robertson hated small boats. He was cursing himself for putting them all in danger. Each of the waves towered over the longboat. The sailors worked hard to row as fast as possible; their rigorous efforts to move the craft back to the ship took a lot out of them.

They eventually reached the calm waters of Cid Harbour and climbed back on deck. Brodie made them laugh when he kissed the deck as soon as he stepped from the rope ladder; however, many felt the same. The longboat, complete with coconut cargo, was once more hoisted on deck with the block and tackle mounted aft.

With the winds up from the wrong direction, the crew were happy to spend the remainder of the day fishing. A few even took a dive from the stern for a quick swim. Sharks had been seen in the area, so dips were quick.

With the Captain at the helm through the southern section of the passage, the ship set sail soon after dawn the following morning. The breeze was gentle, but all knew it would pick up at tide change, and they wished to be well clear of the reefs.

Adam took over his watch once clear of the coral reefs and islands. But he had learnt much about the Whitsunday Passage.

By tide change, the wind turned off-shore, and they could catch it without tacking. They had cleared the most dangerous part of the coral islands. All the sails were now billowing in the stiff breeze. The sleek ship ploughed on towards home with the sails filled and angled to catch every breath of wind.

~

A week out from Sydney, Brodie was lying on his back on the uppermost poop and watching the action on the sails above him. He was fascinated by the mechanics of sailing against the wind. "Papa, how can the sails billow with the wind from one direction, and the ship still head south?" He was intrigued that the wind was coming from the west-south-west, but the ship travelled south.

Robertson had brought a mug of tea for them each, and he made himself comfortable beside his son. He chuckled. "I've told you they are called sheets, Brodie, not sails. It's all to do with the action of a small thing called the rudder. You can't change the direction of the wind, but we can adjust the sheets to catch it. The wind blows and tries to take us where it wishes, but with a rudder, we steer the ship in the direction we wish it to head. We can use the wind rather than the other way around. Such are our Christian beliefs, son. Please think of your life before Heather told you about her new faith. You were blown hither, thither and yon with little direction. You behaved as that is what Mama taught you, but you had no grounding for your actions."

Brodie sat up and drank his tea. "True, Father, it took time, but I could see that Heather really believed in what she told me. I didn't think I'd done anything so bad that I needed forgiveness. I had tried to live a good life. We didn't even sleep together that way, you know, as man and wife until we were married. I did get seriously drunk on Sergeant Donald's illicit whisky the week after Heather had been arrested, but even then, I didn't hurt anyone, and I didn't steal it either, as he had told me to tuck into it. I had tried to keep my nose clean, unlike Iain, because I knew that's what Mama and you would have wanted. She hated that Iain stole things, but we had so many mouths to feed and so little money that we had little option. My chimney sweep work paid little enough, but at least it was regular honest income. After Mama died, I wasn't sorry to lose that job. It was soon after that that I first met Sergeant Donald. I knew there were few policemen and a lot of crime. Father, I tried to work with the law, rather than against it. So when Heather said I needed to repent, I lost my temper. I stormed out of the Findlay's kitchen and was ready to yell at the world." His hand swept across his eyes; they had misted at the memory of his anger. "Papa, I was so angry at her, and I should not have been, and she was my entire life, but it was like she was saying I wasn't good enough for her." His head hung in shame at the memory. "My temper only lasted seconds before I realised that if I trusted her, which I do, I figured she must know something I didn't. She didn't get angry with me or at my fury but patiently explained everything. She put it in terms of a really bad convict I had told her about."

Robertson looked puzzled. "How so, son?"

Brodie explained. "There were some really bad eggs in the convicts on board my ship. We all were so sick on the way out, first with smallpox and then with scurvy. The doctor needed helpers, so as I'd had cowpox when I was a teenager, I knew I was protected. I helped nurse the murderers, thieves, and other convicts. One big bad man in particular. Some died, but we got most of them through. Then, after skipping Africa to restock, I was run down, and I got sick with scurvy. That same tough criminal who was on the mend now nursed me. This particular man, I thought, was pure evil. He boasted that he had been caught only after killing nearly a dozen people. He took delight in telling me all the gory details, which I shall never repeat as they gave me nightmares for weeks. Yet, he sat nursing me when I was sick. He sat beside my bed in tears. It took ages to find out why. Remember, I didn't believe in Jesus or know anything about forgiveness at this stage. I did what I did because I already knew I was safe. This brute of a man, Dick, saw it differently. He saw me as a petty thief, whom he had bullied me somewhat mercilessly for the first weeks until he became ill. I sat beside him, sponged his forehead, and fed him; I changed his bedding, wiped his bottom and generally nursed him. You know what I mean? I did the same for all the others. Apparently, no one else had ever shown him any care ever before. His remorse was greater because he had given me such a bad time. He was officially recovering but still too sick to work, so he was sent to the hospital in Sydney with me. He pandered to my every whim, bringing food and drink and bathing me as I had done to him. He changed because I didn't treat him any differently. I cared for him as I did for the others. But in doing so, he changed. He saw me as a, um, well, a goodie-two-shoes and told me so. Remember I told you I had been arrested to get free passage to be with Heather? Stupidly, I had mentioned this to Dick soon after leaving England. After I nursed him, he saw me as an innocent giving my life for an evil, no-good person. He could not do enough for me. He still watches over me. I know he's kept a lot of bullies away from me."

Robertson saw Brodie's Adam's apple bobble as he swallowed, trying not to tear up.

Brodie remembered how sick he had become with scurvy and nearly died. That would have left Heather and Kenny alone. "Dick thought he would be put on a road gang or smashing rocks, but he was assigned as a labourer on the docks. As I worked at Henry Gates' warehouse, I see him regularly around The Rocks. When I arrived, he stood up for me against a gang of drunken sailors who were harassing me. I know Dick still looked tough, but he had changed. Major Downes thought so, too, or he would have put him on a chain gang in a quarry to the coal mine in Newcastle. Instead, he was unshackled and carrying cargo for the harbour master. Papa, Dick can hoist a full Gorda-size barrel up on his shoulder and carry it with ease. I can't even roll those big ones by myself. He was given the nickname of Dead-Eye Dick as smallpox had scarred his face, but one eye copped it badly. He has tattoos all over his arms, bits missing from him everywhere, and only half an ear. He is one scary man, yet I'm greeted with a bear hug and a laugh at every meeting." Brodie glanced at his father. "Sir, I understand what you mean about the small rudder moving the ship. It's sort of the same as my one small act of kindness to a beast of a man who turned his life around. I have since spoken to him about our faith, and he is also a believer now. He has made his confession, and he is really a different man. When Heather said, 'If a man condemned to death took your punishment for you, you would thank him. But if a good man offered to take your punishment, you would be more than surprised. Well, Jesus did just that for me. He died in place of us; only he was without sin. He had no reason to do what he did; Jesus did it anyway.' Papa, I suddenly understood what she meant. More than that, though, I understood that I needed to ask for forgiveness and, yes, trust Him."

Brodie pointed heavenward. "I'd always been self-sufficient, admittedly not very successful; then suddenly she's telling me I wasn't good enough. That hurt so bad, but I listened to her and the Findlays, and what they told me made sense. I had been protected all my life; somehow, I knew that. Things happened too often for me to have been without someone watching over me; even finding Heather that first night on the street gave me a reason to fight on. Then, the policeman found me when I was so sick and took me home; I'm sure I would have died if he had left me on the street that night. He was friends with Sergeant Dennis, who worked at the prison; everything just fitted together. I've already filled you in on all that. But this faith bit, it was as though suddenly my life found direction. Not only that, it made sense." Brodie sat gazing up at the sails above him again. "It took just one tiny change in my life, and things fell into place. Even to me, being shanghaied and put on this ship of all the ships that had come into Sydney harbour. Because of that, we found each other. Father, I believe because I know it's true. Jesus is our rudder; He shows me direction, and I know that nothing happens by chance. I suppose it's why I wasn't furious when I found myself here."

Robertson's heart was singing. He had been around so rarely in his son's life that he had had very little influence on him. The last time he had been with him, so many disasters had occurred that he wasn't sure if his son would remember him kindly. With four children dying in a few months, and he had been responsible for some of that, he wondered if Brodie would hold it against him.

Robertson said, "Son, I'm proud to be your father, and I always have been. Even as a child, you were the responsible one. Iain was a naughty scallywag. He would not listen to anything I said and even less to your mother. Don't get me wrong, I loved him dearly, as I did with Jane, Hamish, and Caitlyn, but you were the emotionally strong one for some reason. Brodie, you had a good head and a great heart, even back then. Yes, you were a skinny little imp, but you used for good even that. You took yourself off and found an apprenticeship to a chimneysweep of all things. I would never have permitted you to do that had I known. I chose your name for various reasons, a brodie can mean a steep cliff, but it also means a chieftain and also a second son. You are aptly named, my son, for you are strong like a chieftain. Iain didn't have that get-up-and-go that you have. When he got sick, he gave up without a fight. Your mama told me all about it."

Brodie nodded, remembering the loss of his big brother. When Iain became ill, he curled into a ball and gave up in a matter of days.

The two sat in silence for a time, and then they recalled and discussed the days when the family was complete. Now, there were just the two of them.

The memories ate at Brodie's tough resolve to hold his tears back. After a while, the fading faces of his lost family caused him to brush away tears. Brodie said, "Damn rudders!" He sniffed back his emotions. "Here I sit amazed at the sails, sorry Papa, sheets, and we end up getting all sentimental and maudlin over our past. I am determined to be the best father I can be for my children, but honestly, I don't know how. I love them, and I'm there for them as much as possible, but…"

Robertson interrupted him. "No 'buts', son. Those two things alone are what I should have done for you all. But I was, and am, a sailor. Twenty-five years ago, I was young and stupid, thinking I could have both. I was wrong, completely, totally and absolutely wrong, and it cost me nearly everything. Had I given up the sea back then, all our family may well have been with us now. I should have given up the sea, but I was young and selfish and wanted it all. Your mother was certainly worth that sacrifice, but by the time I realised it was too late, my spicy lass was gone. I had a lot of time to think when shipwrecked with only natives as companions. It was only then that I saw her true worth. I intended never to leave her again. She had the most amazing zest for life. When I came home, you were all gone. So, be there for your family; let your children see your love for their mother; be a good example for them, and love them. Kiss Heather in front of them and cherish her son. Always put her first. Showing and telling your love is a strength, not a weakness. Never be ashamed of that emotion. I learnt it is character building, not soul destroying."

Brodie saw through the strong captain facade the lonely, hurting widower he really was. His father was flesh and blood and felt the pain of losing most of his family, as Brodie did. He reached out and touched his father's scarred and gnarled hand. "Papa-bear, I want you in my life, any way you can be. You will always have a place in my heart and home." It was the first time Brodie had reverted to his childhood name for his father.

Robertson didn't want him to see his face as he spoke. He feared rejection, so he looked out to sea. "Brod, I was thinking of buying a house in Sydney. Would you live with me? All of you, of course."

Brodie sat up and pulled his father around to see his joy-filled face. "Papa, are you serious? We'd love to! We would be a real family then."

Robertson turned back to Brodie, delight etched on his face. "You mean it? You will come?"

The big lump in Brodie's throat meant he could only nod his acceptance.

Relief settled deep into both men. With the confidence of being forgiven, wanted, and loved, they sat talking about the options of houses available. In less than a week, they would be arriving in Sydney.

A new life awaited them both.

As the weeks passed, Heather and the children loved living in the big house on Elizabeth Street. Katie and Polly spoiled her with all sorts of treats.

Henry was content that she was happy and set about finding a new manager for his warehouse.

Ken and Dennis had both refused the position he offered; however, Ken had an idea.

Henry was about to head down to look over his staff when Ken quietly took him aside. "Henry, you have the perfect candidate for the job, only he's missing at the moment. You tell me he knows the work and loves the responsibility. Wait until Brodie returns, then offer him the job. I'm sure he'll jump at the chance. We can watch over it for another couple of weeks; then, we'll willingly hand it over to him. What do you think?"

Henry looked deeply into Ken's gaze with a slow groan. He said, "You would think I should have thought about that. He's been all but doing the work for years. Of course, he would be perfect, and what's more, I trust him." Henry put his hand out to Ken. "Deal, Ken, now to get the boy home. Captain Robertson should be back in a matter of weeks. I do hope he found some good cargo. If I know him, he has sailed into some Chinese harbour under a Scottish flag and done a corker of a deal. I can't wait to see what he's brought. If you think Brodie is special, wait until you meet this man. He can turn his hand to absolutely anything. He had to learn as he was shipwrecked on a tropical island for years. The stories he tells will turn your toes. He never mentions his family, but I know he was married at some time as he named his ship *The Spicy Lass* after his late wife."

Chapter 16 Celebrations

*A*t the end of August, a sail was sighted at Sydney Heads, and the flag went up the pole to notify the harbour master of the imminent arrival of another ship. Minutes later, a messenger from the warehouse arrived at the house, breathless. "Mister Gates, sir, it's them; they are back." The lad didn't need to say whom; there was only one person they were all missing. Dennis had also received word, and as he was leaving their shop, he joined the others to welcome Brodie home.

Wilf and Zane had practised harnessing the brougham up in record time. They realised that Heather would wish to be at the dock when Brodie arrived. Within minutes of the word arriving, the plan was set in action. The family piled into the vehicle while still in the stables. The new mare, whom Issy named Whinny, was backed into the shafts as Henry hopped in. By the time the mare was harnessed, the family and Henry were waiting. Wilf led the horse onto the back road, and Zane quickly jumped into the driver's seat and headed to the wharf. Driving a lady ready to drop a baby was disconcerting at best; having her say, "Hurry, Zane, hurry," all the way down didn't help. He decided it was better to get her there in one piece than to appease her, so he drove carefully but didn't dawdle.

The ship was drawing alongside Henry's private wharf when the carriage arrived. The first rope was thrown and tied to a large steel bollard by a deckhand; other ropes followed and were secured to various horn-shaped bollards along the jetty. Before the gangplank was even lowered, Brodie had slid down the first tied line and was running along the dock to the approaching family group. Brodie had eyes for only one person. His beloved Heather was almost unrecognisable in a voluminous gown and overcoat. She wore a new gown and had her gorgeous dark red hair tied in a neat bun at the back of her head. He didn't even acknowledge his children before wrapping his arms around his beloved. He stood as if frozen for a moment, just drinking her into his memory. Brodie then lowered his head and received the welcome home only his wife could give him. Not a word had been spoken; they were not needed. He was home, and that was all that mattered. As he drew her closer, he felt the movement in his stomach. Only then did he draw back from her. "Oh Heather, my darling one, I had no idea we were having another child." He had been gone for five months, and she was obviously heavily expectant.

Heather lifted her hand and cupped his beloved cheek. "I came home and was going to tell you the day you left. I'm due next month." She pulled his head down for another passionate embrace. He still had not noticed anyone else nearby.

A cough was heard that sounded vaguely familiar, but he hardly acknowledged it. What finally drew his attention was that both sides of his coat were being tugged. It made him lift his head from Heather's lips and look down. Keeping Heather close, he lifted one child, then the other, into his arms. He gave each a welcome home kiss.

Kenny said, "Papa, look, all our old uncles are here too, see."

Henry's smile met his eyes, "Not so much of the 'old uncles,' young man," he said as he relieved Brodie of his son.

Heather took Issy in her arms. Brodie was about to get a big shock and would need his arms free. Brodie finally looked around him and saw two familiar figures totally out of place. Shocked but absolutely delighted, he said, "Well, the day couldn't get much better than this. Sergeants, what are you both doing halfway around the world?"

Dennis and Ken shook his hand in turn, and Dennis answered this query. "Well, that, young sir, will take some explaining. Suffice to say, your letter made the weather here enticing." As he spoke, another person ambled towards the group.

Brodie had seen his father approaching as he spoke to his unexpected friends. "Everyone, Heather, I wish to introduce you to someone even more unexpected than these two wonderful men."

Henry saw Captain Robertson walking towards the group and lifted a hand in welcome. Brodie had beckoned him to come. With a slight nod and a smile, he watched not Brodie's face but Henry's. Brodie was almost bouncing with happiness. "Heather, sweetheart, I want you to meet a man whom I thought was dead. Captain Ewen Robertson Stewart. Papa, this is my beloved Heather, and these two imps are Kenny and Issy, your grandchildren. Apparently, we are also having another one soonish." Brodie's grin was as broad as Robertson's; however, everyone else, including Henry, stood speechless.

Henry was the first to recover. He said, "Your father, Brodie? Robertson, how? No, what? No, forget that. He's your son, Robbie?"

Brodie had his entire family with him, and he was ecstatic. "Sweetie, we have so much to tell you, but Papa wishes us to move in with him and…" He saw her blanch. "Sweetheart, what's wrong?"

Heather didn't answer him but turned beseeching eyes to her uncle. "Could you explain, please, Uncle Dennis?"

Dennis nodded and smiled at Brodie's stunned face. "Brodie, in a nutshell, I'm Heather's uncle; I'll fill you in on the details later, and I've taken an option on a house that will fit us all. We've already moved in. I suggest we return there and discuss it in private. What do you say? Sir?" He looked at Robertson with an eyebrow raised.

Robertson squeezed his son's shoulder. "I think that's a good idea, Brodie. It will take an hour to sort things here, and then I can meet you where you please. Henry, are you happy if Adam takes over for the moment?"

Henry nodded; he was determined to be part of the discussions as he had the manager's job to offer Brodie. "Sure, Robbie! It's your ship, but we need to sort things out. I certainly want to hear this story, so I'm in. But it's your crew, and we can do business later."

Heather and Brodie meandered back to the ship. Dennis had taken Issy from her, and Henry still held Kenny. Henry whispered to Kenny that the new man was his grandfather. Kenny shook his head violently. "No, he's dead; Papa said so."

Robertson had heard the interchange and said, "I thought I was too, young man, but instead, I ended up living on an isolated tropical island in a small native village. I was there for some years before a ship eventually passed by and rescued me. So, I'm not dead. Lad, I thought your father had died, so I didn't look for him."

Kenny eyed him suspiciously; eventually, he reached out a hand and poked him. "You feel real." The four-and-a-half-year-old twisted in Henry's arms and turned to Robertson. "Do grandfather hugs feel different?"

Henry saw Robertson's twinkling glance. "I don't know because I've never given one. Would you like to try?"

Kenny nodded, "I think I'd like to." He stretched out his arms, and Robertson took him gingerly. After so many years, he was once again cradling his own flesh and blood, albeit a generation removed from the last time he held a child, but this little boy was his family. The emotions were almost overwhelming to the bearded, toughened sea captain as he cuddled the young boy.

Henry watched them, knowing the exact feeling. Ten years earlier, he had had a similar meeting with his grandchildren, Skye, Joey, and Alec.

As they had left to meet Brodie, Ken and Dennis had said to their shop staff that they would not be back that afternoon. It was the first time Madge would be given the full responsibility of locking up for the day. The middle-aged woman whom the Major assigned to the store knew her work well. However, Kitty, the giggling girl who helped her, was a trial and drove Dennis crazy. Both men knew there would be adjustments to be made once Brodie returned; they didn't expect that they, too, would be required to make some. Dennis was somewhat disappointed that Brodie's father had even more right to assist them than he did as a mere uncle. Time would tell as to what was decided.

Two hours later, Robertson joined the family at the new house. He had been delayed by the harbour master getting details of his Chinese shipment.

Now, outside the house, he stood admiring the attractive building. Henry walked up behind him. "How did I never realise, Robbie? I always presumed Robertson was your surname. It's Stewart?"

His friend nodded. "Robertson is an unusual Christian name, but it was my mother's maiden name. Ewen is so ho-hum in Scotland, so I rarely used it. Mary, my spicy lass, and Callum Findlay were the only ones who called me by my first name. I never bothered correcting anyone else, as it never bothered me. All my paperwork is under E. Robertson Stewart, though."

Henry also knew the hurt of losing a beloved wife. "Robbie, we'll work it out, you know, the house and all. You may even wish to go halves with Dennis. The children would benefit from you both at hand."

Robertson had a lump in his throat. Unable to answer, he again nodded. He should have housed Mary and his six children in a grand house like this. It was magnificent. Now, there was only Brodie left. He would do what he could to ease their path in life.

Henry watched his friend's face. He stood waiting, then said, "Let's go in." The two long-term friends walked through the front gate and up to the door of the beautiful mansion. Henry didn't knock but opened the door and walked inside. Robertson followed, looking around at the splendour as he walked. They followed the sound of the voices and found them all in the large sitting room. On entry, Ken and Dennis rose and bowed a welcome.

Brodie would not release his hold on Heather, and they sat cuddling on a double settee. The children were on the floor, playing quietly. The words that sprung to Robertson's mind were 'happy families' and, more importantly, they were his own family. He was no longer on the outer but closely bonded with his son and his family. The five months in close confinement with Brodie had bonded them in a way he had never expected.

After a round of handshakes, Polly collected the children when she brought in the tea tray. With just the six adults left in the room, the discussion soon turned to houses and accommodation. Polly gave the bearded man a shy smile.

As they finished their tea, Dennis thought he would get in first. He addressed Robertson. "Sir, I have the option to purchase this magnificent building, but I postponed as I wished for Brodie's input. With your arrival, I would be honoured if we could come to some joint agreement. Mind you, I've not yet spoken to Brodie about this, so we will all start on an equal footing of knowing nothing."

Henry watched his friend's face as he could not ascertain his feelings from behind his black beard.

Robertson didn't really know where to start. He'd had little time to ponder over Henry's quick words outside but thought it might well be the answer. "Sir, like you, I'm somewhat thrown in the deep end. I told Brodie that I would love us to share premises, but this seems admirable. I gather you have no other children or family?"

Dennis shook his head and said, "No, only Heather."

Robertson's eyes flicked to his son. "And I only have Brodie. Whatever we purchase will go to them anyway. Henry suggested the way in that we could go halves in this abode." He raised an eyebrow enquiringly to Dennis.

Dennis didn't need a second to think it over. "You'd do that, sir? There are thirteen bedrooms here and certainly room enough for us all. The cost is rather on the steep side, but I feel it is a good use of my money as it will give them security. As I said, I have not discussed this with Brodie yet."

Heather said nothing. She would benefit no matter what decision was made. As long as Brodie was with her, she didn't care either way. Brodie had looked from one man to the other. He, too, had been listening but not contributing to the conversation. His face was not unreadable, though; he was almost bubbling with joy. "Let me get this right; you both wish us to live with you?" He looked down at Heather under his arm, "Sweetheart, I feel our lives will never be lonely again. What would you like to do, my love?"

All eyes were now on her. "Can we stay here, Brod?" she whispered. "If your Papa and Uncle Dennis can go halves, then I think everyone would be happy."

Brodie hoped they had all heard. He added, "I really don't care where we live as long as you are all close to us. We've been alone for so long, and I think, no… that's wrong; I *know* that we no longer wish to be so alone. We have a family; I want you all close, but would you be happy with that arrangement?"

"Fine by me," said Dennis.

Ken added, "I'm in, too, if there's room."

Brodie looked at his father. "Papa? What about it?"

Robertson chuckled. "I think I'll go and get my things and choose a room. Henry, what about you and your family? Brodie told me that Hector is my Mary's cousin. Knox is really his uncle?" Robertson looked over to his friend. Henry nodded; he heard Robertson whisper, "Poor sod!"

Henry sighed in relief. "We already have our rooms, Robbie; I think that only leaves two rooms for you to choose from." Henry chuckled. "Mind you, my family have not seen the house yet; we can shuffle their rooms around. Alec will need a room with good light as he'll be at university from next year. Joey returned to England for this year's start in September. He should be arriving there soon. The three girls can share. And the baby can go in the nursery with Heather's new one. I'm sure we can manage." He turned to Dennis. "Mayhap you should have chosen the house with the acreage after all." Henry's blue eyes twinkled.

Robertson met his son's gaze across the room. "So you're happy with that, son? The final decision is yours. Mister Campbell and I can work out the finances later."

Dennis frowned and turned to Robertson. "Just one thing, sir, we're now all family. They interlinked in some way, except Ken and I also have an idea about that. So, I think it's first names only from now on." All agreed. Before Dennis and Robertson went and discussed the finer points of ownership, he said, "Have the children been Baptised, Heather? If not, Ken can be Godfather to them all; if they have been, there is always the next one. What do you think? That would make him quasi-family."

Brodie and Heather had their heads together, whispering their love. Heather replied, "We had Kenny Baptised, but not Issy. She can be done when this one arrives," Heather said as she rubbed her stomach.

Henry had one more topic to discuss. He waited until they had sorted out a few more details, then turned to Brodie. "In your absence, we had a bit of an incident. We discovered who it was who arranged your, um, shall I say, trip. Thomas Tibbs, my Sydney store manager, has been bringing illicit consignments and using my warehouse as a distribution centre. He needed to get rid of you as a big one was coming through, but he didn't know when, so he wanted you out of the way."

Brodie felt Heather's grip tighten as she rested her hand on his leg. He was going to get around to asking about his kidnapping, but the conversation had been sidetracked.

Henry continued, "Dennis and Ken came looking for you both and found Heather at Windsor with me. After a few months with us, they decided to return last month and look for somewhere to live. Before they found this palace, they stayed in your loft. Unfortunately for Tibbs, it was the week his last illicit consignment arrived. Dennis and Ken overheard the plans. Rather than challenge him, they sought out Major Humphrey Downes. Now, I knew nothing about what was happening, but Humph later told me about the stakeout he arranged down at The Rocks. The Whaler's Arms was filled to the brim with soldiers, and secret signals were arranged. Brodie, they caught every one of them red-handed, and then when Tibbs and his off-sider tried to escape via that door in the loft, these two heroes tripped them up and sent them head first into the closed door. Both are now in chain gangs for life."

Brodie exclaimed, "Cor, Uncle Henry. I knew nothing about this. I knew he hated me, but I had no idea he was a crook. So, he's the one who drugged me? I wondered as I didn't think I made any enemies."

Ken answered. "Laddie, I heard him say so with his own lips. He waited in the tunnel and ensured you were aptly disposed of without actually hurting you. He paid the man to buy you a drink and helped shift you onto Henry's ship. Thankfully, he did no more than drug you."

Almost under his breath, Robertson muttered, "You should have smelt him when he was found."

Ken heard and smiled. "I had him living at my flat when he went on the bender after Heather was arrested. I know what you mean."

Brodie had flushed beetroot red. "Thanks, you two, I heard that! And I know I stank both times." Both men chuckled in reply.

Henry watched the repartee between the men, then added, "Well, this leaves me a manager down, Brodie. I need someone who knows my business and someone whom I can trust. Someone who won't diddle my books or bring in sly grog. Would you know anyone who could suit?"

In all innocence, Brodie responded, "No sir, but I'll keep my eyes open for you if you'd like."

Henry threw back his head and roared with laughter; the loud sound made Heather jump. Henry said, "Oh, Brodie, I'm offering you the job, lad. A permanent position running the entire warehouse and working with Dennis and Ken in their new venture. As a matter of fact, they will tie in well. Previously, you have taken all the seconds and sold them; well, you'll be too busy to hawk them around the town now, and I'm sure their Scotch Shop could fit a corner of miscellaneous items."

Brodie's brow furrowed. He said, "Scotch shop?" but he turned to the two sergeants with his eyes wide in anticipation of the answer.

Ken filled him in. "Major Downes feels he can trust us and has set us up in business near the Lower Fort Street warehouse. We now run a shop front that legally sells confiscated items taken by the Government and those caught with illicit grog. We call it *Scotch at The Rocks*. The shipment Tibbs brought in contained many cases of..." he paused, expecting Brodie's reaction to his reply, "...of Scottish bottled Glenlivet Whisky, amongst others."

Brodie groaned as Ken expected. "Glenlivet," he muttered, "I never wish to taste that stuff again, ever." Brodie looked greenish as he even said the name. He looked across at his father. "I told you I went on a bender; I didn't know the stuff Sergeant Ken had in his cellar was the undiluted Glenlivet whisky. It's got a kick like you wouldn't believe. I didn't drink much from the cask, but I had no idea you were supposed to mix it before drinking."

Robertson actually knew exactly how potent the stuff was. Admittedly, not the particular Glenlivet, but he too had gone on a bender, as Brodie called it, when he found Mary was dead. He couldn't face the world; it had too many memories with him. He had just fled to Edinburgh and got drunk, so he didn't reply. He might tell his son one day. Brodie chuckled; he spoke with the mirth audible in his voice. "So, two of Scotland's finest sergeants are now selling sly grog at a Government-sponsored Scotch

Shop?" This time, Brodie was unable to contain his laughter. He certainly knew of the stash in Ken's cellar that was, as Ken explained, "legally disposed of," which they were aiming to do without wasting it. "Hot whisky really chases you two, doesn't it?" he added with another chuckle. Henry had no idea what he meant.

However, Robertson had been told about the illicit contents of Ken's cellar. He met his son's glance again, and he, too, was biting his lips, trying hard to hold in his merriment. For two upstanding policemen, these two fellows looked like they would be good housemates: five Scots and an Englishman in cahoots. "You know, I think I'm going to like being a landlubber with you *gadgies*." Ken smiled; by the frown on Henry's brow, he obviously had no idea what a *gadgie* was. "Henry, it's a local Glaswegian word for a man or a fellow, Henry. And with Robertson, there are six of us. Young Kenny was born there, too. Issy is an Australian."

Heather felt the child within her kick. "As this one will be, too." She had been sitting for so long that her feet were pins and needles. "Will you all please excuse me for a few minutes? I will be back in a minute, gentlemen."

Brodie assisted her up and had a hand on the small of her back as long as possible. He had hardly had time to see her alone, but after five months of separation, he could wait until tonight before they made their private hellos. His face showed the starvation each of the others felt, too. He watched her leave, not realising others were watching him.

When the door closed behind her, he met his father's smile with a strange comment. "Papa, we're all here because of a sovereign, you know. She found one at the bottom of a copper and gave it to me." He shook his head in disbelief, shaking away the horrors of the six-month separation. "Dennis, how did you find out about the connection? You certainly didn't know when we were there."

Dennis laid back in his seat; the worst of the revelations had been made, and now he was just filling in the blanks. Dennis took in the peace that had swept over Brodie's persona. He was relaxed. "No, Brodie, I had no idea. Remember, Heather was married when arrested, so she was sent under Stewart, not Anderson. I knew my sister had married my good friend Angus, but your letter started the ball rolling in joining the dots. Then Hector wrote to his agent, who dug deeper, and after some time, he found me. I wrote to you here last year, but as I received no reply, I decided just to come anyway. Well, we had already finished our supply in the cellar. Superintendents had come and gone faster than you can cross your legs, and eventually, we got tired of the many changes. Knowing that Heather was family made me decide to move here. Then Ken decided to retire, and we came together. We cashed up and left." He released a long but contented sigh. "We managed to finish the stuff in his cellar; now we find we have to sell more of the stuff legally." Ken was chuckling to himself.

Chapter 17 Scotch at The Rocks

*A*fter purchasing the home, they named the large house *Heatherbrae House*. Not that there was a steep hillside covered in heather in sight, but it was a lovely name and had ties to all the main occupants. Henry claimed a connection through Hector and his Scottish heritage. As he now had a permanent bedroom, he came and went more frequently. Prior to this, he had stayed at the *Whaler's Arms*.

A now clean-shaven Robertson had handed his ship over to Adam for future trips. He had to learn to be a land-lubber.

Brodie had slipped into the managerial role at the warehouse with little fuss. Henry hovered for the first weeks but more to see what Robertson had brought for him to buy. When *The Spicy Lass's* hold was finally unpacked, the bolts of fabric caused oohs and ahhs of delight.

The plants had survived the trip, and Henry claimed two of the star jasmine pots as two of his Japanese honeysuckles on his verandah had died; the Chinese vine would smell as delightful. The fresh fruit Robertson had brought had long since been consumed, but the pineapple tops had been kept and seemed to be happily growing in the long tubs. Other fruit seeds had also been planted, and the tiny papaya plants were already six inches high. No one knew if they would live or bear fruit, but it was worth a try as they cost nothing.

Brodie had forgotten about the pearls for Heather; they were still in his father's safe. He had been astounded when his father had shown the yard-long strand of knotted creamy pea-size pearls. They had a lovely smooth feel and a lustre that shone. They flowed through his fingers like silk.

His father also admitted purchasing more for her and hoped he would not mind spoiling his daughter-in-law. Hopefully, they would have more children, and Heather could share them.

Brodie collected his gift for her and waited until they were alone. She was changing for bed when he gave them to her. The night he had returned, all thoughts of pearls had fled as he was content to hold her close.

However, that was not good enough for Heather. She had peeled off her clothing and awaited him in their bed in her natural state. Her welcome home was all he had dreamt about for the last months. She did not let him down, and she never would. They had been through too much together. Her enlarged stomach was a delight to Brodie. To see her so happy and well and carrying his child was a comfort and a joy.

~

Soon after Dennis and Ken had moved in, they realised they would need to set up a nursery or two for the new baby and the children of the extended family. They had discovered a room previously used for such, but it had been stripped completely. Next door was a bedroom, but it had no furniture; it needed to be set up for children. This was strange, considering everything else in the house had been left *in situ*. As they were unlikely to get any answers to their questions, they decided to refurnish the room with new items.

Remembering his original thought of purchasing more furniture from Templeton's Cabinet Makers, the people who had made the majority of the exquisite furnishings, Dennis ventured into Castlereagh Street to visit the furniture shop. The cabinet maker sign was still there, but he discovered the Templeton's had been bought out the previous year. Andrew Lenehan was a bright-eyed Irishman and was the principal owner; his brother Michael worked there when not employed elsewhere. If the inlay boxes and small furniture items in the shop were an example of the quality, then this man's skill was even better than Templeton's work.

Dennis ordered a turned spindle framed cot and a nursing chair, upholstered in the palest green velvet fabric. He also ordered a six-drawer tallboy for the child's clothing and nursery needs. Should Heather need to sleep in the room, there was a single bed and also a small change table. He also added a rocking chair to the order and two high chairs for the dining room as he realised Franny's children also needed equipment when they visited. Once he set up Heather's nursery, he would duplicate some of the items for Franny. Dennis also designed the children's room next door. It needed new and more appropriate furniture, so a pair of cedar beds were added along with another tallboy, a set of drawers and a large wardrobe. The furniture included a combination of drawers, shelves, and hanging space.

As Andrew had little storage, the items were delivered as they were completed.

Dennis paid for each piece on arrival and added a small down payment for the material of the following item on the list. The now beautifully appointed nursery sat in readiness for its occupant.

Two weeks after his arrival, Robertson had emptied his safe. The flurry of activity meant it had taken that long to unpack and price everything that Robertson had in his hold. Henry had been overjoyed with the cargo.

Brodie waited until Heather stood before him au natural. He slipped off her dressing gown, and one by one, he pulled the pins from her glorious hair. She shook her head gently, and the mahogany mane unfurled and covered her shoulders, reaching well below her breasts to her waist. She had no idea how glorious she looked. He reached into his pocket, pulled the long strand of creamy pearls out, and slipped them over her neck; the lower edge of the strand nestled around her stomach. "You know, every time I see these on you, no matter where we are, I will remember you like this, my darling love. Naked as the day you were born, and carrying my child. You are so absolutely beautiful; you take my breath away."

"Oh, Brod, they are lovely," she said as she fingered the beads. Her long dark red hair fell in soft curls. The colour of her ivory skin and the cream of the pearls reminded Brodie of a painting he had seen in a book. It was called *Birth of Venus;* only Heather's hair was much deeper in colour, and she did not need to cover herself in front of him. He could not imagine a more beautiful sight.

Henry had purchased all the cargo except the pearls and some unique fabrics the two had purchased for family use. Robertson had decided to keep those for a while. If he had more granddaughters, they would each receive some jewellery.

Brodie had finally brought the fabric he had purchased up from the warehouse. When he had presented Heather with the bolt of gold silk he had chosen for her, her reception of it had not entirely gone to plan. The bolt of gossamer thin golden silk soon lay discarded on the sitting room floor.

As Heather had reached out to stroke the material, the first of her significant contractions occurred. She had had a sore back for most of the day and had soldiered on through the occasional pains. The first real contraction hit as Brodie passed her his gift.

She had doubled up in agony. Through the pain, she said, "Brodie, it's time. This little one is coming."

He had been with her through Issy's birth and now knew the procedure. He hated seeing her so racked with crippling pain. Thankfully, their newest staff member, an Irish girl named Ciara, had taken the children. She had been on the very last convict ship to arrive and had five of her seven years still to serve, and Major Downes had sent her along as a nurserymaid. He figured that as they were doing something for him in selling the whisky, sending a nursemaid was the least he could do. The children adored her on sight.

Although Heather had a slight frame, she seemed to carry the babes to term well and had only had a few hours of labour for the other two confinements. Hopefully, this birth would be similar.

Polly heard the cries and realised what had occurred. The staff knew Brodie well enough to know he would not leave Heather.

Dinner was put on hold as Polly told Katie to prepare for the birth. Katie had a loaf of bread cut and some cold meat sliced for anyone hungry. The roast could finish cooking later.

Zane was despatched to tell the men from the warehouse and shop, and Wilf was to fetch and carry hot water and whatever else was required.

An hour passed, then two.

Heather was writhing in agony. The baby seemed to be stuck.

Brodie stuck his head out the door and asked the four waiting men to pray and pray hard.

Contractions were only five minutes apart, and then they stalled.

Robertson managed to grab his son's arm before he retreated into the room. "Son, is she up on her feet or lying down?"

Brodie was so tired, but it was nothing to what Heather felt. With his exhaustion audible, he replied, "Lying down, Papa, why?"

His father drew his exhausted son into his arms for a compassionate hug. "Son, in the islands where I lived for some years, the women gave birth squatting after walking around a lot; it might be worth a try. They had a special hut where the midwife and a few helpers would assist the travailing mother to move around while in labour. When Iain was born, I had to do this with your mama. Do you remember helping me with Caitlyn's birth, or was it Hamish's?"

Brodie gave a single nod. "Iain had cleared out, so it was just you and I, but it was Morag's birth that I remember most, and she died, as did Mama when she birthed the last baby. It is that birth that scares me the most, as there was so much blood. Will you help me? I can't do this alone, Papa; I can't lose Heather too."

Brodie's tear-filled eyes and pleading words tore at Robertson's heart. He nodded nervously. The last thing he wanted was to interfere in the intimacy of the birth. However, they both remembered losing that perfect little baby. Brodie knocked gently on the door.

One of the occupants called for them to enter.

Robertson followed his son into their spacious bedroom. Katie and Polly were beside Heather and assisting her back into bed.

Heather had just used the chamber pot, which was why Brodie had left.

Brodie returned to Heather's side. "My sweet girl, Papa said that in the islands, the women walk a lot and then give birth squatting; I was wondering if you would be prepared to try?"

Her trusting but pained eyes met his. She gave him a brief nod. "I'll try anything, Brodie. It's not moving, and I'm so tired. I'll need you both to support me if this child is to come today. I don't think I can even stand alone anymore."

They soon had her up and walking around the room. Both men supported her; she would turn into Brodie's arms for each contraction.

Brodie knew she was strong, but her grip on his shoulders and arms was excruciatingly painful. He could not imagine what she was actually feeling.

Robertson watched their adoration for each other and remembered his feelings for his wife. His eyes met Polly's gaze across the bed, smiling at her. After so many years, he was beginning to feel his heart again, and this young woman was the cause. She was everything Mary was not. Polly was sweet and demure and from a poverty-stricken background. Mary was vivacious and from a luxurious home, which she sacrificed to be with him. Polly's parents had died from starvation when she was arrested. Mary's mother, Iona, was long since dead, and her father was an obnoxious, overbearing, dictatorial, autocratic monster, as Brodie had discovered.

Polly had spent much time sorting out the library with him, and they discovered that the attraction was mutual. For Robertson, life on land seemed to have turned in a different direction than he had planned. He knew that for a relationship to progress, he had to have a discussion with Brodie; however, now was certainly not the time.

For half an hour, little changed, then Heather bent over with her hands on her knees. She was almost doubled over and having a breather from the walking. Soon after she stood up, she felt the child had turned.

The pains then came hard and fast. Two minutes apart, then one minute, they were almost continuous.

Brodie knew he would have bruises on his arms from her clenching grasp, but he didn't care. He wished he could take the pains from her.

Finally, Heather needed to use a basin.

Knowing this meant that birth was imminent, Robertson reluctantly left them to the delivery. He had stayed for Mary's deliveries, only missing one or two, but Heather was not his wife. After showing Brodie how to sit in a chair and wrap his arms around her, he left them to the delivery.

With her sitting this way, he could support her weight, she could brace on his legs, and with two huge pushes, the child finally arrived screaming.

The sound of the new cry was heard from outside the shut door. The four anxious, waiting men each released a long sigh of relief. All had spent time praying for the occupants, and considering three of their wives had died in childbirth; all were desperately worried.

The relief of the entire household was profound. The child was alive and a big, healthy baby. No wonder Heather had trouble; he was a smidgeon under nine pounds. Even better, Heather was well and surprisingly; she had not torn during the protracted labour.

No one had noticed the passing of time, but a check of the mantelpiece clock showed it was five minutes to two in the morning.

Once the afterbirth had arrived, Brodie carried Heather back to bed, and she fed the child. Although tired, she wished to show her baby to all the uncles and her father-in-law. She was assured they were all still outside praying and waiting for the arrival of the newest member of the household.

She and Brodie had refused to let them know the names chosen for the child. Now was the time for the big reveal.

With Heather sitting in bed, Katie opened the door to the four waiting men. Robertson was first to enter. As he did so, Brodie handed him his second grandson. When all four visitors stood around the bed, Brodie introduced him. "Please meet Ewen Dennis Henry Stewart."

They each had a cuddle of the swaddled child; all were careful not to touch his face. None had washed properly after work and knew babies were especially susceptible to illnesses. After greeting the newest family member, they all retired to their rooms to get what sleep they could.

Brodie saw a small incident that made him catch his breath. As his father left, he bent and gave Polly a quick peck on the cheek. He had caught them chatting a few times, but this was far more intimate than a passing word. It was eighteen years since his mother died and twenty since his father last had seen her. His father deserved some happiness, and he thought he would chat with him later and give his blessing if that was what he wanted. That was a discussion for the morning. Brodie placed his sleeping son in the cane crib next to their bed. He crept in beside the already sleeping Heather and gently drew her into his arms. Soon, the household fell quiet as everyone got some much-needed sleep.

Unseen by anyone else, Ken walked a weary Katie back to the kitchen. Weeping softly from exhaustion, she ended up in his arms and lifted her face to him to thank him. The peck on the lips he planned to give her deepened into a long and satisfying kiss for them both. The fair-haired, beautiful widow had won his heart at first sight. She had shown that his interest in her was reciprocated. She, too, had never intended to remarry after her husband died, but life had not turned out as she had planned. Ken had laughed when Dennis said they might find wives amongst the new staff. Ken had caught Polly and Robertson together many times. He even interrupted a passionate kiss and quickly reversed silently from the room. They usually worked in the library, where they were found sorting something, but usually together. It had encouraged him to ask Katie if she would court him.

Ken then wondered if Madge Jamieson had caught Dennis's eye at the store. He had seen her gazing at Dennis as if moonstruck. Ken had spent more time assisting Brodie in the warehouse with Henry than in the shop with Dennis. Kitty, the girl who worked there, was a giggling nightmare and had only lasted a month before Dennis asked the Major that she be assigned elsewhere. Madge was now alone at the shop at night, and Dennis didn't like that situation. He had first seen her at the bakery when seeking servants. She glared at him and turned her back on him. He had asked if she could be reassigned to the shop, and the Major willingly agreed. He discovered that she had been accosted by an ogling customer and was convicted for defending herself. She had pushed him over, and he injured himself as he fell. He pressed charges, and she was convicted and transported. Madge had read Dennis's admiration as the lust she had seen in the other man's face. They had soon sorted out the error, and as Madge was alone at the shop now, it gave him an excuse to be first up and out each morning before the others questioned him too hard.

Until the week of the birth, Heather and Dennis had worked there together. Much to the surprise of the senior men, Heather joined the family breakfast two days after the birth. She asked Brodie, "How soon can I return to the shop, sweetie?" She had bounced back and was her usual self.

Dennis almost choked on his toast and fine-shred lemon marmalade. "You've just had a baby, Heather. Give yourself time to heal."

"I'm fine, Uncle Dennis. I can take Ewen with me, and it's only for an hour or so. With everyone doing everything here, quite honestly, I'm bored." She huffed in frustration. "Even the children don't need me around all of the time. Ciara is a delight, and she's content to take them for a few hours each day. Not that I can stop them, for she takes them outside, and they are always off on some adventure."

Brodie suggested she give it two more weeks, and then Zane could take her down for an hour or so over luncheon each day.

All had expected Henry to head back to Windsor soon after the birth. For him to be still in Sydney was a surprise to them all. He seemed much happier of late and even appeared to have a spring in his step.

By the time little Ewen was a month old, the reason for Henry's continued presence soon became apparent. His excuse was a widow named Sylvia Flukes. She was a seamstress working from her tiny cottage up in Millers Point. Henry had met her at church, and as she lived alone, he could only publicly see her and escort her home from church. However, that seemed to take longer each week.

The change in him one morning was evident to all at the breakfast table. Henry extracted a copy of the local newspaper from his back pocket and laid it on the table. "I thought you may like to see this notice in today's paper." He took a bite of his toast and passed the paper to his friend Robbie. He didn't explain, but Robertson picked up the news sheet and read about the engagement of Sylvia Flukes to Henry Gates. "Henry, this is wonderful news; I did wonder why you had stayed in town. With Franny expecting her child soon, I thought you would return home quickly after Ewen arrived."

Henry's grin spoke volumes. "We are travelling back by carriage tomorrow. I would have preferred to go on my ketch as it's far more comfortable, but as we are as yet unwed, an overnight trip is not possible."

Brodie had taken his father aside the morning after Ewen's birth and questioned him about Polly. He had given his approval should it be required. With Henry's news, he watched as Polly met his father's shy glance, and she gave him an imperceptible nod.

Robertson said, "It seems love is in the air, folks. For Polly has agreed to be my wife." He put out his hand for her to stand with him and receive the family's congratulations. "Humphrey did all the approvals, and they have just come through."

Brodie, holding Heather's hand under the table, had not realised that the relationship had progressed to that stage. He felt her give his hand a gentle squeeze.

Robertson looked at Brodie and said, "Son, when you reach my advanced age, life flies by all too fast."

Brodie exclaimed, "Fifty is not old, Father, but I understand and trust me, I'm delighted. Congratulations to you both; no to you all!"

Ken coughed as though embarrassed, "All is actually correct, people, for Katie has agreed to court me."

Dennis roared with laughter, "Well, that's no surprise. You should have seen him the day he met her. I don't think he even noticed there were any of the other of the thirty or so people in the bakehouse."

Ken's face coloured with embarrassment. "Well, you did sow the seed that we should look for wives."

Another round of congratulations ensued. Then, all eyes turned to Dennis. All knew of an attraction between him and their competent store clerk. Madge was a vivacious brunette with a knack for merrymaking. This made work in the shop harder to leave at the end of the day. He had called her feisty even before they met. She was all that and more. Madge and the new young girl, Naomi, lived in a tiny room above the store.

Dennis blushed with the perusal of everyone. "Oh, all right, Madge and I are courting too. Now leave off."

Ken chuckled, "Seems your wish has come true, Dennis."

Chapter 18 Changes

*H*enry and Sylvia left on the coach for Windsor, and life settled down at Heatherbrae House.

A week after they left, news arrived from Windsor that Henry Sidney Macdougal Grey, to be known as Harry, had arrived safely. He was a healthy eight-pound baby, and Franny was fine.

Lynne and Maggie had already had their babies, so with three small crying children in the house, Henry and Sylvia only stayed a week. They made their excuses and returned to Sydney. Franny, Hector and the children would come as soon as Franny felt up to travelling.

Henry returned to his room at *Heatherbrae House* and started planning his own wedding. It will be held in Sydney in early December. On his return, he noticed a change in the sleeping arrangements. Robertson and Polly had secretly married in his absence.

Major Downes had assisted Robertson in obtaining accelerated permission to marry from the Colonial Secretary, a requirement for convicts; they only needed a special license to marry. As soon as Heather was officially back up on her feet, the four of them slipped away, and the wedding was done secretly by the Reverend Doctor Lang.

Brodie was ecstatic and jokingly called Polly "Mother," to which Polly poked her tongue out at him.

The extended family celebrated Henry and Sylvia's wedding in the first week of December. It was also a low-key affair in their Scots Kirk at The Rocks, with the Windsor and Sydney families joining for the happy event. For once, *Heatherbrae House* was packed to the rafters.

The day after the wedding, the Reverend Doctor John Dunmore Lang conducted a triple Baptism. Issy was Baptised first with Franny, Dennis, and Sylvia as her godparents. Ewen was next, with Ken, Polly, and Robertson as his godparents. Harry, as the youngest of Franny and Hector's brood, was last. His godparents were his older brother Alec, his big sister Skye and Brodie.

When Hector first asked him, Brodie refused. "Hector, I have no idea what a godparent does, so I do not think I will do the role justice."

Hector had wondered, too. "I had to ask too, Brodie, and this is a brief outline I wrote for you after my various enquiries."

Brodie took the small sheet of paper from Hector and read the information. *"Godparents make the same promises on behalf of the child being Baptised as parents do."* He glanced at Hector and nodded, saying, "I can do that." He kept reading.

"Godparents promise to pray and support the child and help the parents bring up the child in the Christian faith. It is an important and responsible role. Godparents can be family members or friends. However, you must choose people who will be interested in your child's spiritual welfare and who will pray for you and your child. Being asked to be a godparent is a good opportunity to think about your own faith. Baptism can help you with your questions about the Christian faith. It will also help you to support your godchild in developing their faith."

When he finished, he said, "So, it's sort of stand-in as a parent in case something happens to you both. A spiritual parent."

Hector nodded and placed a caring hand on Brodie's shoulder. "Brodie, you are my only cousin here in Sydney, and I'd be honoured if you would stand as his Godfather. My other cousin, Callum Fraser, has moved to Bathurst with his wife, Clara. So they are not around."

Brodie had finished reading the screed. "I'd be honoured to do this, Hector," Brodie said with relief. "I should have asked about it when Kenny was done, but I confess, faith was so new to me back then that it never occurred to me. The Findlays are his Godparents."

With the children Baptised, the extended family returned to Heatherbrae House to celebrate.

The week before the wedding, while the entire extended family sat around the fully extended table, Henry dropped a bombshell that he was moving out of both houses. Everyone had just presumed he would keep his room at Heatherbrae House and live with Sylvia in Windsor at Honeysuckle House.

Henry stood in his place at the table and gazed around at the family. "I have a tidbit of information that will affect you all a little. Franny, Hector, with my marriage next week, I will still be keeping my room at the house in Windsor; however, it will no longer be my principal place of residence. Ken, Dennis, Robbie, I will be relinquishing my room here as Sylvia and I have decided that it would be best if we had some time alone for a while." He passed a newspaper to Hector. There was an advertisement circled. Henry tapped the advert as he passed the paper over. "I've taken it for a year, and then we'll see what happens."

Hector read the advert in the Sydney Morning Herald aloud.

"Nov 19th 1842,

To Let, that splendid marine villa known as "The Hermitage," Vaucluse. The house contains six apartments, besides a detached kitchen, with servant's room over stores, pantries, &c.; with a large two stalled stable, coach-house, and hay loft, with gardener's home attached, a large fowl-house fitted up into different compartments, a yard and duck pond, and a never-failing supply of the best spring water. The whole comprises about six acres and is all fenced in and subdivided into different paddocks; the whole is laid out in walks; there are between three and four hundred fruit trees, some of them in full bearing; it commands a water frontage to Rose Bay, has a boat wharf, and a fine sandy beach, where bathing may be enjoyed all hours of the day; the situation is first-rate, and only requires to be seen to be appreciated; it commands a beautiful view of Sydney and the whole of the Harbour, and no ship can pass or repass without being seen from the house. All applications for any of the above apply to Alexander Dick, Jeweller, opposite the Barrack Gate, Sydney."

Hector looked up. "You've taken a lease on *The Hermitage*. Isn't the W.C. Wentworth's house down on Rose Bay?"

Henry grinned from ear to ear and nodded. "Nice, eh? I believe he's moving to his father's estate at Homebush. I try to stay out of politics and the legal hot potatoes that he and the various governors throw at each other, but I'm not averse to renting the best house in the colony. I believe it was the sight of where the immense party was held after Governor Darling departed many years ago." Henry grinned at the astonished faces of those sitting around him. "I've been staffing the property for the last week, and Sylvia and I will be moving in straight after the wedding. Wilf is taking my things along this afternoon, so I thought I had better tell you."

~

As planned, Henry and Sylvia had their wedding night in their new house. They had appeared at church the following morning, smelling of April and May and moonstruck. They were totally besotted with each other.

Polly and Sylvia had met a few times and became friends.

The two new brides stood together and had a few words. Marrying for the first time so late in life had come as a shock to Polly. The intimacies of marriage were a delight; however, the itch that accompanied them was not. Sylvia had noticed her discomfort and whispered something to her just before the Baptism service.

Polly started in surprise, followed by a nod.

Franny heard her whisper, "So it's not my fault? Soap eh? I'll have to have a chat with Robbie."

Franny wondered if she would be game or brave enough to broach the delicate topic of a man using soap to excess on certain private parts of his anatomy. She caught Hector's eye, and when he came to her side, she did some whispering herself.

Robertson watched the two conclaves off to the side and meandered over to see if there was an issue.

"Hi, Hector; what's going on?" Robertson hoped it wasn't serious.

Hector subtly walked Robertson slightly away from the waiting group and said in hushed tones, "Nothing wrong *per se*, Robertson, other than your excess usage of soap. Sylvia picked up on Polly's discomfort, and I bet she will suffer in silence rather than say anything to you: married man to married man, no soap below the waist. The benefits pay off. Trust me."

Robertson groaned softly, half with relief that nothing was wrong and half with excruciating embarrassment. "Got it, no soap. Lye stings the eyes; I should have remembered that. Been a long time since I was married, Hector."

Hector escorted Robertson back to the family group. He talked as they walked. "I'm sure Henry will have had the same information from Sylvia. She seems to have him well in hand. He's like a lapping puppy when she's near. You should have seen him when I first met him. Everyone in the colony stood in fear of the man. Now he's like a kitten in her lap. Moving to the Vaucluse House is a wonderful decision on his part." Hector saw Robertson nod. He added, "On the other hand, Polly would be horrified, so don't think of copying him and moving out. She obviously misses being part of a large family. For her to belong to you all, well, she's like a flower opening from a tight bud."

Robertson had held out his hand to his new wife. "She's my bud, Hector. And I love her dearly." He lifted her hand to kiss before whispering something to her. She blushed beetroot red and then nodded.

Hector heard him reply, "Sorry, sweet cakes, no more soap." He watched Polly lovingly place her cheek against Robertson's arm and gazed up at her tall husband with adoration.

Hector heard her whisper, "Thank you." Hector chuckled to himself as he followed them into the church.

Henry had just handed his grandson back to Fran.

Hector stood waiting for his wife to join him; she had Harry in her arms again. A smile of utter contentment settled on her exquisite face.

~

A month after Christmas, Ken and Dennis made a dual announcement about their engagements. Both had needed to obtain permission from the Colonial Secretary, and with Humphrey having returned to England, it had taken time, and their wait seemed endless. They knew that poor Edward Deas Thompson was tied up in the political turmoil with both Executive and Legislative Councils, and he was a go-between for Governor Gipps and WC Wentworth. Still, surely he could sign two permission slips.

Now Dennis and Ken were eagerly awaiting the joys of matrimony. They now had to wait a month for Banns to be called.

Easter 1843 saw the double wedding of Ken and Katie and Dennis and Madge. They witnessed each other's vows. Dennis and Madge married first, then Madge signed as Margaret Campbell for the first time as she witnessed Ken and Katie's marriage.

They had discussed the housing arrangements, but both ladies were delighted to be included in the growing family house. Neither wished for their own establishment and were content to keep things as they were. They rearranged the bedrooms to add a new wardrobe to each large room. Madge moved up from the store, as did the latest assistant, into the ground floor servants' room. Their shop bedrooms were turned into expansions of the shop.

Both were spirited ladies who brought much laughter into an already joyous household. The three older couples, having no children of their own, doted on the little Stewarts.

Madge, Heather, and Dennis were happily running the store on their own. The shop was becoming known for supplying only top-notch spirituous liquids, and all walks of society patronised it. The home-brew hooch was the tipple of the lowly. The well-to-do purchased the French wines, Champagnes and Glenlivet whisky, plus the very expensive Heatherbrae Scotch flagons. The poorer patrons bought the cheap grog and locally bottled spirits. The sales were split with the Government.

Heather and Madge rearranged the stock and decided to have a tasting night monthly. They had a special deal, of buying three, get one free. These evenings became a great draw card for the bottom line. Considering they had not had to buy any of the merchandise, all sales were pure profit. The building had been a government-owned but unused residence, so there was no rent. With the money coming in thick and fast, the business was a great boon to the Government coffers.

The funds were allocated to refurbishing the Rum Hospital as the dispensary was moving from the South wing into the central building of the Hospital. The North wing was already used as Parliament House. The original stone hospital had been constructed from the initial income from rum tariffs in Governor Macquarie's day.

Brodie had set up a room of damaged, repaired, or second-hand goods in a small room beside the main shop floor. This also became a source of interest in the community. The old flat above had become a second-hand items sales room for pre-owned items. People could leave things for sale on consignment, and the shop took a percentage. Soon, this was a reason for many to visit the shop; few left without purchasing alcohol.

Ken had been at a loose end and had become involved with a boys' orphanage run by a lad who was an orphan himself. Ricky English and his two adopted brothers were assisting other street children. Ken felt this was an excellent way to occupy himself. He had never wished to sell whisky, and when this opportunity came about, he grabbed it.

Through this venture, he met many other men his own age. This brought the entire household into fellowship with others from St. James

Church up near Hyde Park Barracks. One of the men at the church was retired Captain Douglas Evans; he became a particular friend of the group.

This ferocious-looking but kind-hearted man was one of Robertson's friends, fellow captains, and a retired sea captain. He and Robbie had much in common, even shipwreck stories.

Unlike Robertson, Douglas had returned to his family and given up the sea, realising how blessed he was to have survived.

Robertson had never had that chance with Mary and the children, but he was content with Polly as his wife and Brodie and Heather to share his life. Friends like Douglas brought enough sea stories into his life to keep him satisfied. Both had maritime skills they were willing to teach, and the orphan boys loved learning these necessary skills. Splicing ropes and making and sourcing ships' chandlery soon became a new hobby for Ken.

Soon, the Scotch shop also became a custom-made marine ropes order centre. Henry's warehouse had generic ropes, but they could adjust them for specific purposes. They had turned another of the unused upstairs bedrooms into a small chandlery for ropes and other nautical paraphernalia. There were turned wooden pulley wheel replacements, cleats, toggles, twine, and other ephemera. They would obtain broken items, repair them and then resell them. They carried not just all varieties of ropes but many other spare parts that could be handmade by the boys.

The most unusual objects they had in stock were artificial limbs that could be fitted and made to order. The boys at the orphanage had been taught whittling, and the red cedar limbs were made for sailors who had been injured. Two other Scotsmen, Hamish and Fergus Macdonald, brought whittling skills and wood carving to the orphan boys. Hamish had lost his leg to a sabre cut, and Andrew Lenehan had gifted him a new leg. This spawned the idea for this unusual sideline. More than one sailor had lost a limb while at sea, and these cedar limbs could be made to measure with a padded cup for the stump. Some limbs, like Hamish's, even had hinged knees and ankles.

Ken loved learning what was required and how to make all the unusual items. The roles in which they now all found themselves differed significantly from the position of their previous lives. The three men were often accompanied by an ill assortment of mismatched youth who followed their senior tutors like pied pipers.

Life was good.

Chapter 19 More Scotch

By the spring of 1843, Heather realised she was expecting a child again. This baby was due at Easter the following year. Her days in the shop were once again shortened, but this time, it was due to extreme tiredness.

One afternoon, Heather said, "Brodie, I was nowhere near as tired last time. I can hardly pull myself around this time."

As the months passed, it became apparent that this confinement would not be like the last ones. Heather was already larger than she had been for the previous three.

Brodie was almost panicking. "Papa, what if this child is bigger than Ewen? She won't be able to pass it. It will be just too big."

That evening, when Robertson retired to their room, he said the same to Polly. He drew his wife into his arms and said, "Brodie is concerned about Heather's size and that this child will be too large for her to deliver. She's so big she could be carrying twins."

The two froze and looked at each other aghast. "We'll have to get her to see a doctor. He should be able to tell if there are two babies," Polly said in amazement.

They slept on the idea, and realising that there was a possibility that Heather was carrying twins, Robertson took Brodie aside before breakfast and suggested a doctor should visit her and why. On rising, they arranged an appointment for mid-morning.

Only Brodie was permitted to be with her for the examination. His exit from the room confirmed his father's suspicion. As Brodie left the room, he almost stumbled and fell into his father's arms. "Twins, Papa! We're having twins. No wonder my poor girl is so big. And he says they come early. She said she was due about April; he suggested we plan for March, if not earlier." Brodie was reeling with the news.

Before the doctor left the house, he scrutinised the nursery and approved the facilities.

When Robertson suggested they purchase a second cot, the doctor said, "No, try the two babies in the one cot. Twins often prefer keeping their siblings near because they are so close in the womb. They settle better and seem to thrive if kept together." As there was already a second nursery for Franny's visits, everything was on hand, should it be required.

~

The twins arrived in March 1844. After spending hours walking around the room, She delivered Annella Mary Polly after only five hours of labour. Annie, as she was to be known, was a lusty babe who was born clenched fist first. She was followed by her slightly larger brother, Robertson Angus Callum, to be known as Bobbie. He had to be smacked to draw his first breath. He proceeded to drench Katie and the doctor with a golden stream as he was held aloft. They were six-pound babies, but Heather found delivering them was easier than Ewen. Delivering the two afterbirths was the painful part.

Again, Heather was back on her feet only days after her confinement, though feeding two meant that she was constantly tired.

After one feeding session, Robertson arrived with a massive glass of thick black stout and handed it to her. "Get this into you, my dear. It will help with both the tiredness and the recovery. I want you to have a glass each day. My mother swore by it, and she had twins. I should have told you before, but they both died when they were little. We didn't have much money back then."

There was no reoccurrence of the request for Heather to go to the shop too soon, as looking after the twins kept her busy. Ciara had the other three children, and Kenny, now six, was learning to read and write. Robertson took over the education of his grandson.

Polly and Issy sat in on the lessons while Ewen played nearby.

~

When the twins were nearly eight months old, Robertson was hard at work teaching when an unexpected knock was heard on the front door.

Polly ran to answer it and found a legal-looking gentleman on their doorstep.

"Good Morning, madam! I'm seeking a Mr Stewart, Mister Brodie Stewart, and I have been directed to this abode."

Polly assured him that he had come to the correct house and that they would send for him. She invited him in and ushered him into the sitting room. Polly returned to the library and sent Robertson to talk to the man. She took the children to the kitchen and left them with Katie, then told Zane to get Brodie as soon as possible. She prepared a tea tray and took it to the gentlemen.

Polly and Katie requested that they stay in their positions after marriage, as neither wished to join society. Katie loved cooking, and although they now had a cleaning maid come in daily, Polly and Katie still did all the other household duties. When Polly placed the tray down, she joined her husband on the settee.

Robertson filled her in a little. "Polly love, this is Mr Featherstone, Hector's man of business from Edinburgh. It was this gentleman who found the link between Heather and Dennis." Polly nodded and smiled a welcome. He then said, "Mr Featherstone, this is my new wife, Polly."

Polly thought quickly, knowing that both Heather and Dennis would wish to have long talks with him; she said, "Sir, please know you are welcome to stay here. I know others will wish to catch up with you. I gather you will be heading to Windsor to see Hector?"

The November heat was sapping. Even in the coolness of this room, the perspiration beaded on his brow. The man said, "I would appreciate a bed for a night or two, Missus Stewart. I have much to discuss with Mister Brodie and wondered if Lord Glenview could be called to visit us, as some of it also involves him. I feel Mister Brodie will need more than a bit of encouragement to take up his inheritance if my reading of Mister Knox's letter accompanying his will was anything to go by. I presume he met the lad once."

Robertson gasped; however, he walked to the writing desk and quickly wrote a note for Hector to come on business as soon as possible. "I'll send this immediately to Hector; however, it will take two or three days for him to receive it and return here. You may as well make yourself comfortable, sir." The letter would be despatched to Hector as soon as Zane returned with Brodie.

After that one comment to Robertson, Mr Featherstone remained silent about his journey's purpose. After their tea, he was shown into the guest room and settled in to await his quarry's arrival.

It was not until after luncheon that Brodie came. Only then was the man's purpose fully revealed.

Robertson was invited to sit in on the meeting. The three men were cloistered in the sitting room for over an hour. After that time, Robertson stuck out his head, hoping to find either Polly or Wilf nearby.

Polly was sitting on the staircase, patiently waiting. He called her over, kissed her reassuringly and asked her to bring Heather.

Heather's entry brought the three men to their feet.

Brodie introduced her and slid his arm around her. "You're not going to believe the news, my adorable blossom. I'm not quite sure if I'm happy or angry." He gave her a quick kiss on the cheek. He turned to the stranger and said, "Please, Mister Featherstone, can you tell her because I can't."

The visitor nodded. "Missus Stewart, I believe your husband met his grandfather but once. I understand the meeting was somewhat volatile; however, Mister Brodie apparently came over in good light."

Heather knew about that explosive interview shortly before his mother's demise. She simply replied, "Yes, sir."

Mr Featherstone continued after acknowledging her comment with a single nod. "Suffice to say, Knox Macdougal is now dead. He lived until his late nineties and ruled his business with an iron fist. He only had two children: a son who died childless when very young and Mary Isla Macdougal Stewart. As you know, she is deceased."

All three nodded.

The man continued, "In Scotland, daughters have the right of inheritance, unlike in England. Therefore, all his estate passes from Mary to Brodie. It was at Knox Macdougal's wishes that I personally come to deliver the news to his grandson." He turned to Robertson. "He had no idea you were still alive, sir, or he may have changed his will. However, that is neither here nor there, as he is now dead and gone. Lady Silé, his sister-in-law and Mister Hector's grandmother, summed up his existence in a few words. She said, '*The world will be a happier place with him out of it.*' As to that, sirs, ma'am, I can't say, but his volatile temper was well known. It was through her that he knew where the lad lived."

Brodie was fidgeting and ready to spring from his seat. "Please, sir, tell her."

Mr Featherstone again replied with a single nod. "Ma'am, Brodie's grandfather, Knox Macdougal, has left him his house, land and distillery in the Speyside area of northern Scotland. Macdougal's Heatherbrae Whisky is a hand-made, single malt whisky made with the lovely peaty water of the heather-lined peat valleys of the area. It's a top-quality tipple, if I dare to say so. It is my wee dram of choice when I can afford it, ma'am."

Robertson was lying back in his chair, smiling at his son. "Get on with it; tell her the rest, Featherstone," he said with relaxed ease. The smile on his lips belied the abruptness of his words.

The man of business quietly said, "Ma'am, the estate's net worth is now some £60,000 plus £5,000 a year at least. Brodie Ewen Macdougal Stewart, Esquire, inherits everything Mister Knox possessed as the last surviving descendant. All of this goes to the sole surviving child of Knox Macdougal's daughter Mary."

Rather than being happy, Heather dissolved into tears in her husband's arms.

Brodie did not expect this reaction. He looked to his father, who shrugged, then softly said, "Sweetheart, darling one. Why are you weeping?"

The tears flowed for a little longer; then Heather raised her reddened, tear-filled eyes to him. "All those years we starved on the street, he wouldn't lift a finger to help you. You were just a child and innocent of anything he accused your mother of. All those years, we were so alone, and we had no one to turn to and no way to keep warm. He didn't have to take you in to live with him but could have given you an allowance, but he chose not to. Now, my wonderful Brodie, our children, all six of them, will benefit from this."

"Six? Seriously?" Brodie was stunned, firstly that she'd decided to drop the news that she was expecting again at this moment and also that she wanted him to take the money. "I'll have to think long and deep about this. I will not make my decision until I talk to Hector." Brodie got up and walked away from the conversation towards the window. He stood clenching and unclenching his fists. His greatest wish was to storm out and tell his grandfather what he could do with his money, but the man was dead. He totally agreed with his wife.

The initial meeting wound up with Brodie refusing further discussion. Until he spoke to Hector, Brodie declined to discuss this topic more.

With time on his hands, Mr Featherstone spent days looking at the sparse community. On arrival, he wondered why these now wealthy landowners would stay in such a desolate place; however, the week he had already spent in town, he found the climate growing on him. Considering it was mid-November, and this was supposed to be spring, the balmy sea air and lack of smoke and fog were a delight. True, some mornings were a little brisk, but overall, the area had an agreeable climate.

~

It took a week before Hector and his entire family, less Joey, came to stay. Henry and Sylvia came for afternoon tea, and the story was repeated to the Greys and Henry. At the end of this meeting, Brodie requested more time. He still had not given his answer to the Scotsman.

Only Polly, Dennis, Ken and their wives were absent.

Two days after their arrival, Robertson, Brodie, Heather, Hector, Franny, and Henry met with him in the sitting room.

Mr Featherstone had a private message for Hector from his grandmother. He had little chance of seeing him alone for some time and eventually gave up. This time, the agent stood clasping and unclasping his hands, wondering how he would broach the delicate subject of his request. In the end, he came straight out with it. Rory Featherstone turned and addressed Hector, "Sir, Lady Silé was hoping to see you. She is ageing and would like to hug you again before she passes. For the moment, she is well enough but ageing. Master Joey and your father, Mister Grey, were up with her when I departed. Since the passing of Mr Sidney's brother, they come from Kent each holiday and spend the entire summer with her. Would you consider returning with me, sir?"

Hector and Franny had already discussed his ageing grandmothers. They delayed arriving this week to arrange the household so they did not need to return to Windsor before travelling to Britain. It was a good time to sail with Harry, as he was now old enough to travel but not yet walking. Hector had a glint of delight in his eye when he met his agent's gaze. "Sir, we are already booked on the barque, *The Hind,* for London and plan to set sail on December 16th. I'm sure there will be an extra cabin, and we can travel together."

"Seriously, sir? Oh, this is a delight." Mr Featherstone was pleased that he did not need to plead or cajole His Lordship into returning. He hoped they could travel together as the time had passed slowly on the long voyage out.

In the days she had been in town, Franny had enquired if a companion would be available for the voyage, as she found that Mr and Mrs Bean and their two young children would also be on the ship. Therefore, she engaged the services of both a nursemaid and a nanny for the journey. There was only one other female cabin passenger, all the rest of the travellers being men. Skye was now nineteen, and Hector had insisted that she return to London for her Drawing Room presentation to Queen Victoria at Easter the following year.

Now, Hector stood at the fireplace, deep in thought. In the space of about ten days, he had much to arrange. Gone were the insecure days of being a life convict. When his cousin had confessed to the attack and the consequences of his friend's untimely death, his conviction had been overturned. Now, he was a confident businessman. He turned and said, "Featherstone, I will make some requests for this trip. Firstly, as you know, I refuse to use my title so that I will be known simply as Hector Grey, Esquire, and this is how we have booked. And secondly, you will be Rory and I, Hector, from now on. We are friends and, yes, business partners, too. If word spreads on board that Franny and I are titled, then we shall stick to our cabins, and this is not a pleasant way to travel."

Rory Featherstone swallowed. "But, sir, I'm your agent."

Hector saw the almost dread on Rory's face. "Yes, and I arrived here as a convict. Admittedly, that was overturned, but we are all equal in God's eyes. It's first names or nothing. You are a good and trusted friend as well as my Agent. Grandmother would have disposed of your services long ago if you were not. Considering his bad start, my cousin, Callum Fraser, has things in hand with Des Bolton out west. Now, you will have Brodie's estate to manage, too. Though somehow, I do not think they will return to claim it." Hector caught Brodie's almost angry glare.

Brodie's interjection of, "I don't want it though, Hector," made Hector smile.

His comment made Hector say, "Don't nix Knox's money, Brodie." He heard Brodie gulp in astonishment. "If you refuse it, Brodie, you will only harm your children and Heather. You have Dennis and your father in your life now, but the distillery and Uncle Knox's money will bring you wealth and security, such as you have never had or known. It will also enable you to assist others, like Ricky English's boys' home. An influx of funds from an anonymous donor would help many. Rory Featherstone and his firm will be capable of overseeing the Scottish side of things for you, and Henry's bankers here will sort this end. Remember, your three sons will need something to live on, and Kenny may even wish to claim the house when he inherits. And then there are your daughters, who will all need dowries."

Hector continued, "Brodie, you are only, what, twenty-eight?" With five children, more may follow. Hector saw the surprise on his cousin's brow; the last two children were barely crawling.

"One already is, Hector!" Brodie muttered but grinned.

Hector smiled as he glanced at Heather. Her face suffused in a delightful blush.

Robertson nodded his agreement. "Son, I agree with Hector."

Hector continued, "Do you think I did not have to get over my own grandfather's treatment of me? Trust me when I say Riordan Macdougal made his brother look like a saint. Knox was a pale shadow compared to the hate I encountered when living with him. I can assure you that it took some swallowing of my pride and, yes, much anger. Father had it all tied up for me before I even knew about it. My dear friend Rory here saw to that." He turned to his agent and winked. He turned back to face Brodie. "Those two mean Macdougal brothers were two peas in a pod. You only met Uncle Knox once, but he came to stay with us often. I learnt to hide once in the priest's hole, but once I got stuck in there." He chuckled at that memory. "I, too, carried the well-aimed bruises that they both willingly delivered. I was a half-breed, but you, at least, were pure Scot. To have carried their name would have been a trial; thankfully, neither of us does. Stewart and Grey are delightful names and ones to be proud of."

Robertson and Brodie both agreed with that statement.

Hector saw their nods and said, "Nonetheless, about the inheritance, the money is not illegally obtained, and it is making more each year if I know Uncle Knox's business." He saw his agent nod. "Brodie, I say take it and use it as you wish. Give the stuff away or throw it around. Be extravagant or hoard it for the children, but take it."

Brodie and his father shared a questioning look. Brodie then said, "Are you sure, Hector?"

Hector gave a bow-cum-nod. He placed a reassuring hand on the young man's shoulder. "I am, cousin, very sure."

Brodie's heart pounded. "Then, reluctantly, I will accept it." He took a deep breath as though having shaken a weight from his shoulders. He looked toward Heather to ensure he had made the correct decision.

She nodded her agreement.

He turned to Hector. "Will you arrange things for me while you are there? I won't ever go back, but Kenny might one day. It will all be his."

Rory added, "I will draw up the paperwork for you. Hector's father,

Sidney, and then later Joey can act as your Power of Attorney."

His father said, "Hector will, son. Brodie, tell that delightful wife of yours that she can make a list of whatever she pleases, as with your inheritance, she can have whatever she wants."

A feminine voice chuckled from the settee and said, "I have everything I want, Papa Robbie; I have your son and your grandchildren and good health. I have you, Uncle Dennis, all the other family and Ken. That is all the wealth I need." Heather was serious. She had spent most of her life in Brodie's care with little more than the clothes on their backs. They only needed what they had.

Robertson knew that with this money, many other street orphans in Glasgow and Sydney would soon find an anonymous benefactor. Rory Featherstone would have an interesting role in front of him.

Brodie stretched out his hand for her to join him. She stood, and he enfolded his beloved Heather in his arms for a reassuring embrace.

After a few minutes, Heather drew back but stayed in the loosened circle of his arms. "Brod, it's your decision, and my love for you will not change whatever you choose."

Brodie held her at arm's length, gazing into her face. He did not even release her when his stepmother entered with the tea tray. "My darling love, one word from you and the money will be refused, but…"

She placed one finger on his lips to silence him. "Uncle Dennis and Ken will be able to have their *wee dram* each night for the rest of their lives." Heather then cupped his beloved face and said, "I have everything I need right here. But the children will need it, Brod, and so will all the orphans in both our countries." She gave him a brief but passionate kiss.

Reluctantly, he nodded. "Fine! Then I will take the dratted stuff." While drawing her into his arms, he muttered in a not-so-quiet voice, "But they will have more than a wee dram. Our uncles will have enough blooming Scotch whisky to quench the thirst of the entire darned colony!" Then he saw the funny side of the entire fiasco. He chuckled. "Wait until Ken and Dennis hear about the details of this. They will be busy selling the stuff until they drop. They won't drink the bottom out of this stock."

Robertson gave a half-laugh. "A wee dram my foot. It's scotch on the rocks daily for us all." He smiled. His spicy lass, Mary, had unknowingly provided a safe future for her family after all.

Reluctantly releasing Heather, Brodie sipped the hot, sweet tea Polly had just handed him. He stood staring into the dark liquid and said, "Uncle Dennis aptly named the shop 'Scotch at The Rocks!' Who would have believed it?"

Chapter 20 Epilogue

$\mathcal{B}$rodie and Heather waited until the household was quiet, and they tiptoed down the stairs and out into the starlit evening on the green grassy lawn. Brodie drew his beloved Heather into his arms as they had done since childhood. He rested his head on her mahogany locks and breathed in her clean scent. "Do you ever think back to those days in Glasgow when we lived on the street? We had each other and nothing else, yet it was enough."

He felt her head nod against his chest.

Brodie was glad she could not see the tears welling in his eyes at the memory of those traumatic days. "When I arrived at my little hole to find you in there, my heart sank, then you told me your story, and all I wanted to do was to hold you and take away your hurts. I missed my Mama, Papa, and my siblings and well, all of them, but I now had you. I wanted to hold you and keep you safe because I had lost all of them."

He heard a small sob escape from her, so he drew her closer. "I would have given up, you know, but you were such a game little bairn, and I needed to look after you. You did everything possible to ease my lot, *pure* collecting and then even finding that first damned bottle of whisky. Do you know, I've just realised that it was a bottle of Grandfather's Heatherbrae stuff. I've seen the label often enough now to realise what it was. It's so funny that it's now come full circle."

Heather moved in his embrace and slid her arms around him. "Brodie, I was only a little tacker, but I do remember how scared I was. I could not believe it when you came with food and a big warm blanket. I thought you were an angel or something. Mama always talked about guardian angels, but I didn't believe in them until you came that night." Her shoulders shook at the memories. Her face was pressed into his chest.

Brodie could feel her tears soak into his shirt. With his voice kept low so only she could hear, he said, "Sweet Heather, for Ken and Papa to now be working with Ricky's orphans here is wonderful. We both know how alone we felt, and when both the Findlays and then later all of our police friends came to assist us, I willingly admit now that I wept when Mama died and often afterwards."

The two fell silent for some time. The young couple were deep in thought about the past.

Heather was stirred from her reverie when she heard Brodie gasp. "Look up, Heather!"

She lifted her head from his chest to look where he pointed.

Above them, the sky exploded into trails of vibrant beams of light. They had often seen similar displays when children. Tonight, the dark evening sky had come alive. Memories of a quiet night on the voyage out flooded over her. Heather moved to beside him rather than stay in his arms, gazing heavenward.

Brodie was surprised to hear her chuckle.

Her tears now forgotten, she said, "Brodie, this proves to me that God is everywhere. We used to see these in Scotland, but we're far from there." She snuggled closer to him again in the cool evening air, and they stood watching the amazing display above them. "I saw them on the ship out too, but I said nothing to Doctor Smith."

After more shooting stars darted across the darkened sky, Brodie spoke again. "Do you remember that night when Mr Findlay came and dragged us out of the cellar to watch the rainbow dance across the night sky?"

Brodie heard her soft reply of "Yes."

They stood gazing at the magnificent performance occurring above them.

There was a pause in the display, and he bent down and lifted her chin to kiss her lips. Not pleased with the peck, she deepened his action to the point that Brodie had forgotten what was occurring above him. After being occupied delightfully for some time, Brodie suggested they retire to their luxurious abode upstairs.

With the chill air permeating their attire, they quietly re-entered the house and returned to their enormous room. Space-wise, the room was about the same size as the coal cellar in Glasgow police accommodation; however, this room had every luxury that money could buy.

The two policemen had not spared a penny when they refurbished their room, but not to be outdone, Robertson had supplied silk sheets and a luxurious down quilt and pillows for their bed.

With the conversation still fresh in their minds, a chuckle escaped them both when they opened the door to their lamp-lit room. From having absolutely nothing, they now had so much that they knew they had to find a way to share their bountiful blessings.

The Heatherbrae Scotch Whisky factory in Scotland would now mean that they could be very generous to the orphans in Sydney and help similar children in Glasgow and Edinburgh. Rory would have his hands full.

Brodie knew that locally, The Benevolent Society assisted the poor but always needed funds. They helped the distressed, the aged, and the infirm. Ken and Robbie would also ensure Ricky's orphans would not miss out on anything. Brodie knew Ricky would refuse an outright donation from him, but an anonymous donation and then a regular supply of ongoing funds for food could not be refused. He would also sponsor some of the brighter students to be fully educated properly.

Brodie knew there were plenty of lonely children in Sydney. He also knew it would make his grandfather angry that he was giving away perfectly good money to some of the children who had been born to streetwalkers and prostitutes, as well as convicts. With the thought of his grandfather's hard-earned money providing for the needs of the poor and dispossessed, Brodie smiled as they prepared for bed.

He watched as Heather disrobed, and his eyebrows arched as she placed her night rail on the end of the bed instead of drawing it on. With a grin, he blew out the lamps and crawled into bed beside his beautiful but naked wife.

Heather, as usual, had needed no words to explain her needs. Her waiting arms received Brodie. That she was already carrying their sixth child was a delight.

Outside, the astronomical display continued unnoticed by the young couple. The first cicadas of the season sang their mating chorus as silence finally fell over Heatherbrae House. Tomorrow, the sale of scotch at The Rocks will once again continue.

*Honest **Reviews** of my books help bring them to the attention of other readers who are more likely to read something from a new-to-them author if it has more reviews (even if they are not five-star). You can quickly and easily leave a quick rating or a short review on **Amazon**.*

Scotch at The Rocks

If you loved this book, these are similar.

Unlikely Convict Ladies - Trilogy

Dancing to her Own Tune

Co-authored by Sheila Hunter and Sara Powter

Sydney 1790s to England 1830s

Annie White is released after serving seven years as a convict in Sydney. She gets a visitor who, with his help, she can start a baking business. She is then asked to assist another sick man, **Sam** Corbett. Annie nurses him back to health, and a relationship develops. They settle into a life together, barely making ends meet; she realises she's expecting a child. Sam has his past laid bare and must adjust to the revelations. They both must face their accusers and find that the answers to their questions are not what they thought. Their life experiences seem to cling to them, and unable to shake them off, they end up back in England. They must face their ghosts and discover they are not who they think they are. How can they turn their anger and spite into love and forgiveness? The Dance of Life goes on.

ISBN 9780645110715   ISBN9780645110722

Long-listed in the Historical Fiction Company Competition 2022

October 2021

https://amazon.com/dp/064511071X   https://amazon.com/dp/B09JC378YV

Amelia's Tears

Parramatta 1828 – England 1840s

In the Parramatta Female Prison, **Amelia** awaits her assignment. Forced to leave the relative safety of gaol, she is assigned and now faces her worst nightmare. A foul man claims her and makes her life a living hell. Then, her world goes black. A glimmer of hope arises when she hears from her brother, Jim, who has enlisted a friend to help her. She writes to Jim, pouring out her heart and telling him of the horrors of her new life. He encourages her to stay firm in her faith. All she can do is pray. When Major **Ned** Grace, her brother's friend, enters her life in Parramatta, he starts to ease her path. Things have changed, as now she has a child in tow. How can Amelia forge a new life for herself? What man could want her with her background and a child at her side? Who is the gentleman who turns her tears of sadness into tears of great joy?

ISBN: 9780645110739   eISBN: 978-0-6451107-4-6 Hard Cover ISBN 979-842061-7953

April 2022

https://amazon.com/dp/0645110736   https://amazon.com/dp/B09SS855BR

A Lady in Irons

England 1800s - Parramatta 1808+

Katy is mourning the death of her husband after he died in a shooting accident. Barely coping, she awaits the birth of their child. If it's a girl, she must hand the family home to her husband's brother. The day after giving birth to a daughter, she and her daughter are left on the side of a road. She collapses and is found by someone she thought had died in a fire ten years before. **Perry**, badly scarred himself, nurses her back to health. They marry and move in with her widowed friend, Mary.

After some years, she discovers her husband and friend in each other's arms. Now living in a love triangle, she flees. Grasping the only straw available, she intentionally gets arrested and is sent to a colony far away. By doing this, her marriage can be annulled.

What happens in the Colony is different from what she expects. Governor Macquarie comes to her rescue.

But what of Perry and her children?

ISBN: 9780645110784   eISBN:9780645441505

November 2022

https://amazon.com/dp/0645110787   https://amazon.com/dp/B0BCWSXB9Z

180

The Convict Stain Collection
(Stand-alone stories)

NO MORE, MY *Love*

Hunter Valley, NSW 1820s

Jess Elkin is distraught when tragedy ravages her family. She becomes the victim of a carriage accident and is nursed back to health by the driver, **Marcus Ryan**. Marcus was not expecting to fall in love. Yet, when Jess's fortunes suddenly turn for the worse, Marcus must decide how far he will go to pursue her. As time passes in Newcastle, Australia, Marcus must take a business trip and is taken by pirates. Jess is left wondering if her will keep his promise to return to her… Will she ever see him alive again?

ISBN: 9780645441536   eISBN 9780645441581
April 2023
https://amazon.com/dp/0645441538   https://amazon.com/dp/B0BSBH143Q

The Vine Weaver

Hawkesbury River area 1820s+
New Beginnings and Old Threats

In the 1820s, Australia, **Joel and Hetty Walker** live on a secluded farm on the Hawkesbury River, which becomes a healing haven for the protection of young convict women. A series of events brings **Fran Rea** to the attention of Hetty, and she is taken to the farm. Fran and Hetty develop a cottage industry under the compassionate eye of farmhand **Hector Macdougal;** Hector's loving words change lives. It is to him that Fran turns when threatened.

The vines now must draw them close to survive the future revelations, and of those, there are many. **The story continues in Scotch at The Rocks…**

ISBN: 9780645441512   eISBN: 9780645441529
June 2023
https://amazon.com/dp/0645441511   https://amazon.com/dp/B0C6Z552Y2

SCOTCH AT THE ROCKS

Glasgow, Scotland, early 1800s to The Rocks, Sydney 1830s

Orphaned children Brodie Stewart and Heather Anderson live on Glasgow's streets. Although hungry, somehow they survive and keep out of trouble. Heather finds a job and looks to be settled; things go pear-shaped for them both. Eventually, they marry by declaration, yet even that gets messed up, and they are both arrested soon after they make their vow. In 1838, they were transported to Sydney as convicts. Heather arrives within weeks of Brodie, and they are assigned close to each other. They are now living on the docklands in Sydney, called The Rocks. They now have to forge a new life halfway across the world from their homeland.

Adventures abound, and Brodie gets press-ganged. While he's away, Heather's life changes and soon, she's officially selling Scotch Whisky at a shop in The Rocks.

You can take a Scot out of Scotland, but where did the Scotch come from?

ISBN 9780645441550   ISBN ebook 9781923097001
November 2023

Waiting at the Sliprails

The Bathurst Road 1830s
A Convict's Tale

Bea Dawes's term of conviction nears an end, and she has few options other than marriage to a stranger or going on the street.

Jack Barnes, the hired drover, wants a wife. Bea accepts his offer; then, she discovers that he could be gone for months, leaving her alone with **Billy and Netty**, part of the tribe of Aborigines who live on his secluded farm. Bea learns to love her husband and also this wonderful aboriginal couple.

Drought ravages the farm, and Jack must hit the long paddock with the flock. In his absence, a visitor arrives, threatening to destroy everything she has worked so hard for. Can Bea touch her heart? Can she cope? Will the drought ever end? And when will Jack return?

ISBN: 9780645441543   eISBN: 9781923097032
August 2023

Convict Shadows of the Past

Two Jennifers, two hundred years apart

When aged eight, **Jenny Kellow** learns of her convict family history and discovers that she was named after a convict from nearly two hundred years ago. Her grandfather's stories inspire her to dig deeper into her ancestors' convict past. From her grandfather, she hears stories of bushrangers, convicts, and life in the infant colony of Parramatta. She sets about retracing the footsteps of her convict great-great-great-grandmother to honour her. Jenny's search starts with microfiche back in the 60s, and she learns about the small tin mining town in Cornwall and the production of a cheese that sets London afire. Then she discovers her ancestor, **Jennifer Kellow,** has brought these cheese-making skills to Parramatta, where she taught others her craft. Echoes of the past can still be heard if you know where to listen. But who was the first Jennifer? Why is she so elusive?

ISBN: 9780645783315   ISBN ebook 9780645783322
A NaNoWriMo 2022 book winner

January 2024

In Defence of Her Honour

London 1800s to Parramatta 1819

Bill Miller had been raised and educated with the sons of the family. The youngest, Bert, had been his best friend. However, jealousy intervenes when Bill's excellent schoolwork curtails their friendship. He wins a scholarship and enters Oxford University. When Bill's father, the old butler, dies unexpectedly, Bert insists that Bill take over the position, but it's more to oppress him. Bert's jealousy grows and festers. Now looking for a way to rid themselves of their new butler, a ruckus ensues, and Bill is arrested for assaulting Bert. The housekeeper and her daughter, **Molly Ross,** vouch for him, but it's too late; Bill has been arrested and sentenced to be transported. With Bill gone, Molly now needs to defend herself from Bert. After hitting him with a pan, she is arrested and sent to Sydney. Bill and Molly arrive with letters of introduction and compensation from Bert's father. Soon, they are running the best Inn in Parramatta with an endorsement from the Governor.

ISBN 9780645441567 ISBN ebook 9781923097049
April 2024

Gentle Annie Soames
A 1788 First Fleet Convict Story
Her dreams lead to unexpected outcomes. An Australian First Fleet story.

Annie Soames is shattered by the cancellation of her debut into society, so when she hears of a position as a carer for the nearby Marchioness, she grabs it.

Oliver Quilpie, the recently married Marquess, discovers his arranged union is not to his taste; he is drawn to his wife's companion. Unfortunately, he is unable to keep his hands off her. For revenge, Annie mimics his every move while riding but is dressed as a highwayman. However, she had now fallen in love with him. This action finally leads to her arrest and transportation to a faraway land.

After some years, Oliver's wife dies, and his thoughts turn to Annie. He seeks to find her, but she has vanished. He is horrified to discover she was transported to New South Wales as a convict on the Lady Penrhyn. He follows with a shipload of supplies.

Will Annie want to see him?

ISBN 9780645441574 ISBN ebook 9781923097063

July 2024

I can't stop Tomorrow
Irish Famine 1840s to Avoca Beach, Australia

Escaping bigotry and prejudice in Ireland, the **O'Shane** family lives on a secluded farm on the west coast of Ireland. The potato blight soon decimates their farm. It's always darkest before dawn, and the two remaining girls cling to the hope of a new life. With the kindness of strangers, the oldest girls, **Clare** and **Kerry O'Shane**, head to their cousin, Sal Lockley, in Parramatta, Australia. A new, wonderful life awaits them both. **Shéamus Connor** is the annoying teenage boy who reluctantly draws Clare's affection. However, living in a convict town means ruffians abound.

John Moore is an angry and troubled Irishman, content to live alone on another secluded farm until he discovers Clare and two other lads need rescuing.

Can John protect her from the pain inflicted by an evil world?

Can Shéamus find his lost love who had fled?

ISBN: 9780645441598   ISBN ebook 9781923097056

October 2024

Madeline's Boy
England 1830s to New South Wales 1840
All is not straightforward when money and a title are involved.

Madeline is asked to care for her best friend's son when his life is in danger.

Christopher is the pawn between a greedy, unscrupulous uncle and his inheritance. Maddie must do everything she can to keep him safe, including moving halfway around the globe to take Chip to his guardian, Major Humphrey Downes, in the Australian Corps in Sydney. Humphrey's best friend, another soldier, Major Tim Hinds, meets Maddie, and with the support of these two men, a chase around the colony ensues.

Will Maddie and Tim be able to find happiness together?

Can the three adults keep Chip safe until he's old enough to claim his inheritance?

ISBN: 9780645783308   ISBN ebook 9781923097094

January 2025

Early Colonial Days Trilogy
WHEN UPON LIFE'S BILLOWS

Sydney 1795-1800 - Governor John Hunter

Captain John Hunter is born to a life at sea. The wind blows where no man knows, and John is caught up in the gale. From the wrecking of his ship, the HMS Sirius, in 1790 to becoming the second Governor of the colony of NSW, John seems to always be in the wrong place at the wrong time.

Helena Rosedale is not a typical female convict. She fights tooth and nail to stop The men from abusing her. She gains the name of Helena Hellcat.

Crispin Milroy is one of the Governor's security detail. Can he win the fair lady's heart? Life in 1795 in Sydney Cove is raw at best. Food is scarce, and disease often raves the settlement. Life throws them everything possible except death. Somehow, they survive. What trials will the young couple face to make a new life in this raw town? How can John ease their path?

ISBN: 9780645783339   ebook ISBN: 9780645783346
Coming 2025

Tuppence to Pass

London 1800s to Parramatta 1820s - Governor Lachlan Macquarie

Josh Callan is a London lad who makes the best of the life that has been dealt to him. Stealing from the man who killed his father gives the family a change of direction. Josh is arrested, but the judge belittles him, saying he's not worth tuppence. He is sent to the penal colony of Sydney as **Governor Macquarie's** term starts. He proves his worth and falls on his feet, becoming the Governor's groom.

Life in the Colonial town opens opportunities they could never have dreamed about in England, but can Josh find his niche in life?

Where will this new life take Josh and his family?
ISBN : 9781923097070 eISBN: 9781923097087
Coming 2025

Saddler's Song

London 1790s to Parramatta 1840

George Ellis is a tanner's son living on the outskirts of London. When disease takes his family, he seeks to find a new life for himself. Hearing from a friend about the possibility of setting up a business in New South Wales, he sells up and leaves all he knows. His beloved violin is the most valuable item he has, and his talent for making beautiful music is hidden from all but a few.

Ben Parker is a saddler and, like George, is now alone in the world as his father is dead; Ben also sells up to move to the new colony. Having booked passage on the same ship, the two meet up and combine their skills to start afresh in a new world. During the journey out, George's skill as a violinist is revealed.

On arrival, the two find accommodation with a family who have many lovely daughters. Two lovely ladies steal the hearts of the lonely lads, but how will the business survive in an animal-started land? Access to their primary material is limited. Where will this lead them, and what is the song?

ISBN : 9780645783353   eISBN: 9780645783360
Coming 2025

A 100-year, six-part Australian Colonial series

The Lockleys of Parramatta

Hands upon the Anvil

A blacksmith's life and love are more than work

Parramatta 1830s

Eddie Lockley's parents were transported for their crimes. Can a steadfast lad rise above his origins and guide others to succeed in a land of opportunity?

Ten-year-old Eddie longs to help his mum and dad. Living in a convict town with his family, the keen youngster has been working with the local blacksmith since his sixth birthday. But when a lieutenant doesn't stop abusing his older brother, the young boy yearns for the day when he can stand up and end the torment. Though he's thrilled when his mentor offers to send him off to learn his letters, Eddie fears he won't be around to watch his sibling's back. But as he takes on the biggest adventure of his life, the brave believer soon discovers God is looking out for everyone he loves. Does this young man in the making have what it takes to change everything for the better?

ISBN 9780994578235   Ebook ISBN 978-0-9945782-5-9   Hardcover 9798496177368
Released 2021
https://amazon.com/dp/0994578237   https://amazon.com/dp/B08TB51L19

Out Where The Brolgas Dance

Gold is found, and so is love

Parramatta 1840s

How can a question change so many people?

It's the 1840s, and discoveries across the Blue Mountains continue. Major Mitchell's new road is complete, and towns are planned and being built. Abundant land is available for those who want it.

William "Wills" Lockley, 18, has laid a solid foundation for a respectable career as a blacksmith, but the Lockley lust for adventure flows deeply within his veins. He dreads the monotony of work at the blacksmith's forge and yearns for adventure in a new frontier. Wills meets six Englishmen who have the means to make his dreams come true. What they discover changes the Colony and their lives forever. Gold fever ensues. In the West, Wills has to deal with an uncertain romance. Does she even want him?

ISBN 9780994578242 Ebook ISBN 978-0-9945782-6-6 Hardcover ISBN 9798755445504
Released 2021
https://amazon.com/dp/0994578245   https://amazon.com/dp/B08T6NS3XX

Diamonds in the Dirt

Diamonds, love and money… but there is much more to life.

Parramatta 1850s

Luke Lockley, the youngest Lockley son, has completed University, and his life has no direction. No job, no money, and no love. Desperately alone, he prays for guidance. How can Luke trust that God has a plan for him if he can't even find a job? He does the only thing he can … he prays. Within a week, life has changed … oh, how it has changed as his brother Wills turns up with a suggestion. Would Luke be interested in joining the expedition with John Evans? **Reverend William Clarke** needs assistance on a Government Mineral Survey. The challenge, adventure and finds are life-changing for many. However, it gives Luke meaning, purpose and direction. The condition of his heart problems also takes a turn. Can he walk away?

ISBN:9780994578273 Ebook ISBN: 978-0-9945782-8-0 Hard cover ISBN 979-8788011141
Released 2022
https://amazon.com/dp/099457827X   https://amazon.com/dp/B09NH1MLXZ

The Earl's Shadow
Who or what is the 'shadow'? How does it affect so many?

Parramatta 1860s

Charles Lockley is the Earl of Coxheath and spends his youth as a convict in Parramatta; he had no idea he was an Earl. He had minimal education and few social skills. His eldest son, **Charlie,** is no different.

Now faced with his own mortality, Charles has to work out how to live the remainder of his life after a near-death experience. He is called to step way out of his comfort zone in London. His action will change the world for many. The echoes from the past still haunt Charlie. London is calling the family, and they can't postpone the trip. How does **Jim Leslie**, the Cobb and Co. coach driver, fit in? And precisely what is *'The Earl's Shadow'* that he speaks about? What happens if the 'Shadow' is gone?

ISBN: 9780645110708 Ebook ISBN 978-0-9945782-9-7

Released June 2022

https://amazon.com/dp/0645110701 https://amazon.com/dp/B0B158SKSK

Once a Jolly Swagman
An old black Billy Can contain the secrets of an incredible life

An Australian Historical Novel

Set in 1870s Parramatta and Kent, UK

Rick Lockley, battling his family's expectations, runs away to find himself. **Jack,** a jolly swagman, takes him under his care. Even after years together, Rick knows little about the old man.

On his death, Jack leaves Rick his precious billy can; the contents reveal Jack's identity. Stunned, Rick must travel to England to finalise Jack's wishes. There, he uncovers Jack's life of love, betrayal and a link to his own family. Rick also discovers there is much more to learn about this enigmatic man.

ISBN 9780645110753   Ebook ISBN 978-0-6451107-6-0

Released Sept 2022

https://amazon.com/dp/0645110752   https://amazon.com/dp/B0B5JN1WCV

Jonty's Journey
Gems, Love, Artists and a Golden Lion

Australia and South Africa 1880-1902

Sydney Jeweller, **Jonty** Evans' passion for gems takes him to Africa at a volatile time. He finds the diamonds he wants and gets given a lion cub. Jonty gets all but kidnapped. His experiences in the Transvaal plunge him into questioning everything he knows of life. Soon, nightmares haunt him.

On return home, he nearly messes up his love life with **Lottie** before it even starts, and he struggles to settle. Lottie's father, **Luke** Lockley from Parramatta, takes him in hand and points him to someone who can help.

Jonty is then recalled to Africa as a liaison and reconnects with his lion, Chimbu when he saves the life of his security detail. His life journey introduces him to the most amazing Heidelberg artists, politicians, poets, rebels, and the scapegoat soldier Harry Breaker Morant. Can Jonty bury the past and regain the peace he's lost?

ISBN 9780645110777   HC ISBN 9781923097124   Ebook ISBN: 978-0-6451107-9-1

Released Feb 2023

https://amazon.com/dp/0645110779   https://amazon.com/dp/B0BLJ7ND1Q

Australian Colonial Trilogy
By Sheila Hunter
Co-Winner of 1999 NSW Senior Citizen of the Year, In the Year of the Senior Citizen

Mattie
Coming of Age in Convict Australia

Twelve-year-old London street urchin **Mattie Paul** is convicted of petty theft and sentenced to seven years of transportation to the penal colony of Port Jackson, NSW. Peg, another female convict, takes Mattie under her wing and gives her a chance to make something of her life by teaching her to read. Mattie seizes every opportunity that comes her way. Though life is not particularly kind to her, she battles through earning her freedom, marrying and becoming a mother in her homeland. On this journey, she encounters bushrangers, is widowed, and becomes an entrepreneur in the Bathurst goldfields. She mixes with escaped convicts, but her spirit is indomitable, and she becomes a pillar and much-loved treasure of her adopted community. Mattie may be a fictional character, but her experiences are only too real and invest us in immersing ourselves in the lives of those remarkable women who helped to make Australia what it is today. *(Mattie's story continues in The Lockleys of Parramatta - bk 2+)*
ISBN 9781503252370 & ebook AISN BOOTTEDBTO
(The Story continues in The Earl's Shadow)
Released 2015
https://amazon.com/dp/150325237X   https://amazon.com/dp/B00TTEDBT0

Ricky
A boy in Colonial Australia

Ricky English and his mother immigrated from England to join his father in the new Colony of Sydney. On arrival, there is no sign of his father. Ricky's mum uses the tiny amount of money they brought to get lodgings in a run-down building. Things go from bad to worse when his mother dies; he is thrown out of the rooms, and the caretakers confiscate all their possessions.
Ricky lives on the streets of Sydney Town as a street waif. Ricky finds safe places to sleep and befriends freed convicts who can help him survive. One day, he encounters a lost child and helps reunite her with her family. These people try to help him, but because of his stubbornness, he insists on doing things his way, but he has found a mentor and confidante. The story follows him through his life. He survives and turns his life around, helping others along the way.   **(The Story continues in Jonty's Journey)**
Paperback ISBN 9780994578211   Kindle ASIN: B00MLYN6IG
Released 2014
https://amazon.com/dp/1500770574   https://amazon.com/dp/B00MLYN6IG

The Heather to The Hawkesbury
Four Scottish families brave a new life in a strange land.

Mary Macdonald and husband **Murd** and family; her brother **Fergus** MacKenzie; sister-in-law **Caro** MacLeod; cousin **Alex** Fraser and all their families who have had to emigrate from the Isle of Skye during the "Clearances."
The story follows the four families from Scotland on the ship out to the NSW colony in the 1850s. Mary does not cope with the changes and losses that occur in the first months in the colony. The other women in the family rely on her, and she nearly crumbles. The families struggle together through accidents, losses, trials, floods, and hard work and forge a strong bond with their new country. Trials, tribulations and triumphs see the four families make a firm mark in their new homeland. The immigrants from Scotland helped make Australia what it is today.
ISBN 978994578228   ebook AISN B01A21JYWQ   Large Print ISBN1533473641
Available on Amazon/Kindle & Large Print
Released 2016
https://amazon.com/dp/1503251438   https://amazon.com/dp/B01A21JYWQ

Author Bio

Sheila Hunter and Sara Powter were a passionate mother-and-daughter team of amateur genealogists. While working together on their family tree, Sheila and Sara made many captivating discoveries. The greatest of these was finding four convicts, and these four had very different perspectives. They were sent to Australia from 1792 to 1814 during the height of Convict transportation. Before her *passing* in 2002, Sheila adapted some of these histories into enchanting stories, her Australian Colonial Trilogy. Sara later had these published. A fourth she left unfinished, and this inspired her to finish it. However, before she did, **The Lockleys of Parramatta** were created. The first two in the series were completed before she completed 'Dancing to Her Own Tune' for her mother.

Vividly living through the Colonial Era, these books delve further into the theme of overcoming adversity in Colonial Australia and how it developed, the demise of the Convict system and the discovery of mineral wealth.

Sara intricately weaves accurate archival data and a charming narrative to create a series of tales of faith, love, loss, and redemption.

And so, two hundred years after her family arrived in Australia, Sara continues the Australian Colonial stories started in *Lockleys of Parramatta,* followed by the **Unlikely Convict Ladies** Trilogy.

No More, My Love, The Vine Weaver and **Waiting at the Sliprails** are stand-alone novels, and all are part of my *"Convict Stain Collection."*

More Historical Fiction books are to follow... as eight more are already in the editors' queue.

See her web page to keep up to date with more stories.
With an online store available for a signed copy of Sara's books.
www.sarapowter.com.au
(Australian Postage only)

Feel free to email me at
saragpowter@gmail.com

Amazon Aus QR

BOOK BUB https://partners.bookbub.com/authors/6273615/edit

FACEBOOK https://www.facebook.com/profile.php?id=100063887262514

FREE Newsletter signup
https://preview.mailerlite.io/preview/41388/
sites/77987646202184961/wCAAcK

Bibliography

Scottish Female Convicts/Gaols
https://www.femaleconvicts.org.au/pre-transportation/the-prisons/scottish-prisons

Scots Kirk in Sydney - descent
https://trove.nla.gov.au/newspaper/article/2197810?
searchTerm=scots%20kirk%2C%20sydney

End of transportation off. 1840, but last in 1850
https://dictionaryofsydney.org/entry/the_end_of_transportation

Press Gangs at Walsh Bay
https://walshbayhistory.net/timeline/1826-1850-landscape
https://trove.nla.gov.au/newspaper/article/71621194?searchTerm=press-gang

Chinese Opium Wars 1842
https://www.nam.ac.uk/explore/opium-war-1839-1842

Vaucluse House
https://sydneylivingmuseums.com.au/stories/vaucluse-house-brief-history

Demijohn photo
https://centreforstories.com/story/terry-hawser/

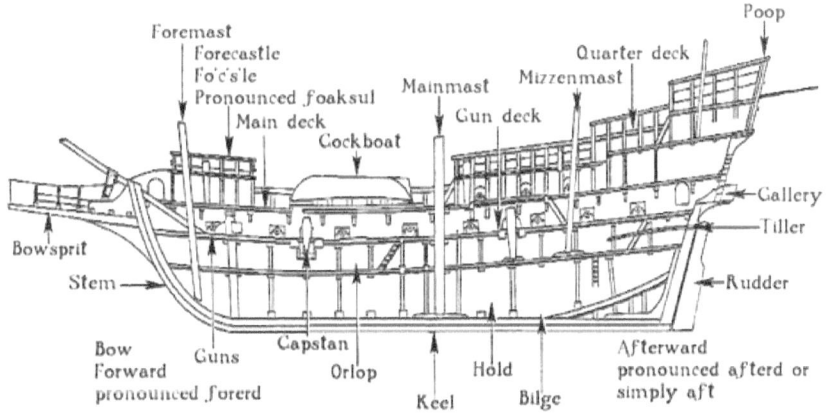

Characters

Ewen Robertson (Robbie) Stewart b 1792 - sailor - supposedly died at sea (Captain E Robertson Stewart)

m1 1813 **Mary** Stewart nee **Macdougal** b 1793- died in childbirth d 1826

  (Mary, *daug. of Knox Macdougal m Iona Bray, Sile's, brother-in-law, -from The Vine Weaver*)

> 1 Iain b 1814 died of smallpox aged 9 (nearly ten), 1822
>
> 2 **Brodie Stewart** b 1816 convicted & transported 1838 (*on Lord Lyndoch*)
>
> m 1836 **Heather Anderson** b 1820 Convicted and transported 1836-7
>
> (*parents - Angus Anderson & Annella Campbell - Dennis's sister*)
>
> > #1 Kenneth (**Kenny**) Brodie Dennis Stewart March 1838
> >
> > #2 Isabel (**Issy**) Heather Stewart November 1840
> >
> > #3 **Ewen** Dennis Henry Stewart b October 1842
> >
> > #4 Annella (**Annie**) Mary Polly Stewart b March 1844
> >
> > #5 Robertson (**Bobbie**) Angus Callum Stewart March 1844
> >
> > #6 Hector **Hamish** June 1846
>
> 3 Jane b 1818 - run over aged 3 in 1822
>
> 4 Hamish b 1820 died of measles 1822 aged 2
>
> 5 Caitlyn b 1821 died of measles 1822 aged 1
>
> 6 Morag - still birth b & d end 1822
>
> 7 Landlords baby, stillborn girl. 1826

m2 **Polly** Johnston *(Dennis' housekeeper)* m in Sydney 1842

Mr **Callum Findlay,** *Glasgow Inn keeper* & *The Whaler's Arms at The Rocks in Sydney*
Ishbelle Findlay *No children*
Sergeant **Ken** Donald, a Police sergeant in Glasgow m in Sydney, 1842
m1 Shona - died of smallpox
m2 Catherine (**Katie**) Sorrensen m in Sydney 1842
Dennis Campbell - *caretaker at Ken's flat, works at Duke St Prison (Heather's uncle)*
M1 Isla d in childbirth
M2 **Madge** Jamieson m in Sydney 1842

Mr Rory **Featherstone** - Hector's Edinburgh Agent
Thomas Tibbs - Henry's Sydney Stock Manager. Gets sacked
Adam Steers - 1st mate on *The Spicy Lass - new Captain*
Major **Humphrey** Downes - Major in Sydney left April 1854
Major **Tim** Hinds - Major in Sydney m Madeline 6 children + Humphrey's nephew Chip
Major **Ned** Grace - a Major in Parramatta in 48th Batt. Aka Duke of Gracemere
m **Christina** Meadows (widow) returned to the UK on *Sarah Botsford March 1842*
Henry Gates, b 1782
 m Jan 1803 **Julia** Penwick (owns ships *The Spicy Lass, Franny's Joy +)*
 #1 **Franny** Rea b Sept 1803
 m **Hector** Macdougal Grey (*son of Sidney Grey m 1792 Sarah Macdougal*)
> children 5+
>
> 1 **Skye** Sarah b 1823
>
> 2 Joel (**Joey**) b Easter 1826
>
> 3 Alistair (**Alec**)Hector Desmond b June 1828
>
> 4 **Julia** Susanna Macdougal Grey Dec 1833
>
> (lost a pregnancy on board from England, early miscarriage)
>
> 5 Henrietta (**Etta**)Frances b 1839
>
> 6 Henry (**Harry**) Sidney b October 1842

m2 **Sylvia** Flukes - seamstress in Dec 1842

Henry's Windsor staff
Margaret *(Maggie)* **and Lynne** Woods - *sister maids from on board The Ferguson*
George Darcyville, Henry's yardman/groom m **Maggie** Woods 1838
     Twin girls mid 1839
Victor Champion - Henry's coachman m **Lynne** Woods 1840
     #1 - due July 1842
Mrs Glassop - Henry's housekeeper

Dennis' staff
Catherine (**Katie**) Sorrensen - married **Ken**
Polly Johnston married **Robertson**
Wilfred (**Wilf**) Jones
Zane Arnold - young man
Madge Jamieson - store clerk at the shop - m **Dennis**
Ciara -Convict nursemaid - five yrs left to serve.
Rory Featherstone - Hector's man of business in Edinburgh.

Real People
First Police Superintendents in Glasgow
Superintendent **Graham** 1829-31
Superintendent David **MacKenzie** 32-35
Superintendent George **Lamb** 1836-37
Superintendent Alexander **Findlater** 1837-1840
Governor & Elizabeth Macquarie